ARMY OF THE UNSETTLED

ACADEMY OF THE APOCALYPSE, BOOK 3

K. A. RILEY

D1521490

NOTE FROM THE AUTHOR

The Academy of the Apocalypse Series:

Dearest Reader:

The events of the *Academy of the Apocalypse* series take place immediately following the conclusion of the *Conspiracy Chronicles*, a nine-book series make up of three interconnected trilogies.

Although the *Academy of the Apocalypse* draws upon characters and references some events from the *Conspiracy Chronicles*, it does not require intimate familiarity with what's come before.

But it couldn't hurt, right?

Either way, it's an honor to write for you, and I hope you enjoy getting to know these characters and exploring their world, which, let's face it, could just as easily be ours.

KARiley

SUMMARY

In the days before Epic—the mysterious albino techno-geneticist—is expected to light the fuse for an all-out war, Branwynne and her Asylum have been given their first major assignment: track and report back to their teachers about the moving caravan of the Army of the Unsettled. What could be simpler?

When the violence of a broken world hits close to home, Branwynne and her friends find themselves pulled into the bizarre and unexpected world of the Army of the Unsettled.

In way over their heads, weaponless, and with no backup on the horizon, Branwynne and her friends are about to discover there's a big difference between *learning* about the end of the world and *surviving* it.

DEDICATION

To Dmitri Shostakovich.

To my mom, my cat, and to the rest of you unsettled folks and felines out there who just can't sit still. Bless you all, keep moving, and don't let anyone tell you when it's time to stop!

EPIGRAPH

"I never come back home with the same moral character I went out with; something or other becomes unsettled where I had achieved internal peace; some one or other of the things I had put to flight reappears on the scene."

— Lucius Annaeus Seneca (1st century Roman philosopher)

"People wish to be settled. It is only as far as they are *unsettled* that there is any hope for them."

— Ralph Waldo Emerson

IV. In Memory of the Dead
V. The Eternal Question: Why and for What?

— Dmitri Shostakovich (Movement titles for Quartet 3 in F major, opus 73)

PROLOGUE

Our mission was simple:

Track and report on the movements of the Army of the Unsettled.

Easy-peasy.

There are seven of us in this particular reconnaissance crew: Me, the five members of my Asylum, and Matholook. (He *might* be my boyfriend. The jury's still out on that one.) With Haida Gwaii—my white raven and telempathic companion—that makes eight.

According to the instructions we were given, all we had to do was spy on a few outlying settlements, gather some intel from the Outposters, and catch up with the Army of the Unsettled, the slow-moving city of campers, tractor-trailers, monster cranes, RVs, and assorted construction vehicles roaming around in the deserts, ravines, plains, and prairies of Arizona, New Mexico, Colorado, Utah, and Wyoming.

While we were doing that, Kress and her Conspiracy would be gallivanting off somewhere west of the Rockies on a rescue mission of their own at one of those creepy, techno-genetic

Processor-prisons, this one in Nevada's Great Basin National Park.

(I recently discovered Kress and her friends have been on maybe a dozen or so, life-or-death search, rescue, and reconnaissance missions I was totally unaware of. Who knew teachers had lives outside of class?)

So...they're off being heroes, while my team and I are here, picking our way through a wasteland of steppes, sand dunes, scrub brush, scorched fields, crevices, and canyons—much of it littered with abandoned military jeeps, deserted tent camps, a network of broken fences and half-built walls of concrete and synth-steel, and countless drifts of sun-bleached human and animal bones pushed by the wind over time into long, sand-blasted knolls along the curved, cratered highways of melted asphalt and buckled blacktop.

It's broiling hot out here, and we have to keep taking these little potassium iodide tablets to help ward off the threat of radiation poisoning from the Atomic Wars that made so much of this country uninhabitable. We've been lucky so far. The thumb-sized Radiation Isotope Identifier clipped to the clutch lever of my Grip-bike has remained thankfully silent, so we're pretty sure we're safe.

True to our intel, the settlements we've come across so far have been abandoned. It's been the same each time: No Outposters. No Scroungers. No Survivalists. No Unsettled. No action.

No fun.

Despite the heat, the depressing desolation of this abandoned wasteland, the grainy particles of desert sand that keep finding their way into my underwear, and the apparent pointlessness of our mission, at least we get to cruise around at breakneck speed on our mag-powered Grip-bikes. *That* part's been pretty fun.

So far, we've explored four of the abandoned settlements we were told about.

Made up of ripped tents and crushed aluminum sheds, they were small, temporary colonies—not much bigger than a city block—walled-in but with the security doors open, completely stripped of supplies, and without a soul in sight. Which is to say that we haven't come across a single piece of useable information to bring back to the Academy.

When the fourth and final site turned up empty, I called it a "Ghost Town."

Arlo, looking like the Grim Reaper with his hood draped over his head and his long-handled scythe gripped in one hand as a walking stick, squinted out over the bleak terrain surrounding the abandoned settlement and said, "More like a Ghost *World*."

What if he's right? What if the war we've been training to survive has already happened?

Granden—our history, government, and political science teacher at the Academy—taught us about an article someone once wrote called, "Suppose They Gave a War and Nobody Came?"

"The idea," he explained, "is that wars don't happen because of chance, mistakes, or misunderstandings. War is a *choice*. And the trick despots and dictators use in waging war is to make the people who are going to die in them forget that fact. War is never inevitable."

I guess that makes sense. Only, now I'm looking around and thinking, "What if they gave a war and *everybody* came?" What if that's what happened here? What if there really is no one left?

Half afraid of what we still might find but even more afraid we might not find anything at all, we resume our mission.

Other than investigate the few scattered settlements, the only other thing we had to do was get close enough to one of the small, roving detachments of the Army of the Unsettled to gather intel about their movements but not close enough to get caught.

How hard could that be, right?

Just once, I'd like something that starts out simple to stay that way.

Now, in the blazing hot desert of the deadly, war-torn American West, and only a few boring and completely unproductive hours into our "simple" mission, we've run into a potentially serious snag.

Faced with our first challenge, I'm already wondering how many more surprises might be in store for us before this is all over.

One thing is for sure: This particular "snag" is going to end in somebody's death.

Whether it's our death or the death of the snarling, wild-eyed, knife-wielding girl who just sprang out of nowhere and attacked us, well...that remains to be seen.

1

JUMPED

THE WILD-EYED GIRL totally caught us off-guard.

How the frack did she manage that?

With stealth rivaling mine when I'm patched into Haida Gwaii and when I'm focused and at my best, this feral teenager —her hair a dreadlocked mess of thick, sun-bleached tangles and craggy crusts of dirt—seemed to come out of nowhere. It's like she'd been buried in the red sand out here in the fields of jagged rocks and thorny scrub brush, just waiting for someone, anyone, to pass by so she could pounce.

I think I read somewhere there are spiders that do that.

It's no wonder she got the drop on us. This girl has some seriously deadly, desert-animal camouflage. She's one hundred percent, blend-into-the-background all natural. Everything about her—the weather-beaten pants, the dusty jacket, the beige scarf, her hair, the ruddy skin, and even her slate-gray teeth—it's the exact color palette of the blazing, blistered desert.

The girl can't be more than seventeen-years old—same as me—but the exposed skin along her upper chest, on her wrists below the cuffs of her wrinkled jacket, and above the tops of her unlaced, mismatched brown boots is creased, ashy, and brittle, like someone planted the head of a teenage girl onto the body of her own slowly-decomposing great-grandmother.

I have to give her credit for this little ambush. Sure. There are places to hide out here. There are endless dunes, a few clusters of smooth rocks, low fields of scattered foxtail agave and Mexican feather grass, the occasional shallow crevice or canyon, and a debris-covered highway not too far from where we are now with a few dozen civilian and military vehicles, stripped bare and sizzling in the sun and all lying on pretty much every angle imaginable (except for standing with their four wheels on the ground as I'm pretty sure the manufacturers intended).

But my Asylum and I are supposed to be alert. We're supposed to know better than to walk into an ambush. We're *supposed* to be trained for combat, and prepared for all the obstacles we're likely to face in our mission to restore peace and order to a suffering world of deeply entrenched corruption, sadistic divisions, and the most barbaric acts of violence.

The fact that this girl appeared out of nowhere is bad enough. On top of everything else, she's inhumanly strong and unhesitatingly fast.

With the vortex of dust flying from her ratty clothes and clumpy, dirt-caked hair, she might as well be a human sandstorm.

In less time than it takes for me to register her existence, she's got me sprawling to the ground, Libra and Ignacio slamming into each other, Matholook on his knees with a pink-rimmed, baseball-sized lump already forming on his forehead, Sara laid out on her back and wide-eyed in shock, and the scuffed blade of a black-coated, twelve-inch Bowie knife pressed hard enough to Mattea's throat to leave a thin red mark I can see from here.

Arlo is the only one of us left standing, unharmed, and apparently *not* wetting his pants.

With his face shaded by the deep hood draped over his head, he's got one arm bent around behind him, his hand on the long wooden handle of his scythe. But he doesn't draw the weapon from the quick-release straps that keep it secured to his back. Instead, he raises his other hand and asks the girl to stop. It's a simple request, almost like he's asking for a small favor from an old friend. From under his hood, his voice is echo-y, eerily polite, and unnaturally calm.

For someone who looks like the Grim Reaper, he's got an easy, pleasant way about him.

"We're just passing through," he assures the girl. The ridges of scar tissue on his face glisten purple and crimson under the shadow of his hood. He digs his boot heel into the ground. The motion is almost imperceptible, but I know he's bracing himself to launch an attack if things go too far. "We're no threat to you or to anyone else," he promises the girl.

Which isn't exactly true. If this girl is from the Army of the Unsettled—which I'm sure she must be—we are *definitely* a threat.

But Arlo does what we've been trained to do: de-escalate, deflect, deflate. "Only when you've exhausted all options," Brohn taught us at the Academy, "only *then* do you engage."

"There are enough enemies out there as it is," Kress always adds. "Don't go around making more when you don't have to."

Good advice. And what happens when some wonky-brained stranger decides to make an enemy of us?

This particular enemy, stone-faced and with frothy bubbles of saliva forming at the corners of her blistered lips, answers by pressing the long blade—serrated on one edge and razor-sharp on the other—a little more firmly to Mattea's neck just under her chin.

Mattea swallows hard and winces as the girl, her feet planted in a wide stance amid the rocks and wisps of dry vegetation curling around her ragged boots, gives Mattea's wrist a little twist behind her back. Mattea is smart enough not to make any sudden moves since even the slightest flinch could startle this barking nutter and send the slicing edge of that knife...well, that's something I'd rather not consider.

After all we've been through together—the adventures and the endless and painful combat sessions in the Academy—I've never seen Mattea so much as shriek or complain. So to see her bottom lip quiver like this, to see a single tear pool in the corner of her eye and then go trickling down her cheek...It's like Death, itself, has a blade to her throat and is about to claim one more soul to take back with him to the Underworld.

Not on my watch.

Arlo, his hands still raised, turns his palms out to make sure the girl's attention is firmly focused on him. At the same time, he gives me a quick glance and the tiniest nod of his head.

Got it!

Springing to my feet, I whip out my Serpent Blades. Brandishing one of the S-shaped weapons in each hand, I snap out the curved, retractable knives at each end. My eyes narrow into a squint as I prepare to launch a full-on attack against the leather-skinned girl with the menacing weapon pressed to my friend's throat. The Unsettled girl has her dirty fingers clamped to the nylon-covered handle of her knife and a wild, "I don't give a frack" look in her eyes.

Those ice-cold eyes lock onto mine and freeze me in place for a second.

There are seven of us in front of her, plus a telempathic white raven, who's circling around overhead. So why is this girl smiling?

"It's okay," Mattea says, her voice a trembling gurgle of fear and tears.

I don't know if she's talking to me and our Asylum or to the girl.

Swallowing hard enough to nudge the knife, which is still pressed firmly to her throat, Mattea's eyes flick back toward the girl. "We're just out here looking for information. That's all."

"*Estás mintiendo.* Even got not true for war," the knife-wielding girl says through a broken-toothed smile.

Damn!

From what we've seen in our limited experience, the Unsettled seem to have two types of people in their army: ones who speak English and ones who speak this sort of distorted slang version of English laced with what I think is Spanish.

Just our luck we get jumped by one of the slang-speakers.

Mattea risks reaching up to curl her fingers in a gentle arc around the girl's dry, scaly forearm. When Mattea speaks, I don't know if it's from blind terror, the knife pressed to her throat, or her Emergent ability doing something dodgy to my ears. Either way, her voice sounds fuzzy, almost artificial, and not like her own. "Harm come when harm do. *Guerra próxima* in the us ain't the harming."

Fortunately, we have an expert translator with us.

The Unsettled girl's eyes get wide, and the knife moves ever so slightly away from Mattea's neck. I don't know how Mattea does what she does, but from what I've heard and seen for myself around the Academy, she can pick up pretty much any language—its diction, syntax, pronunciation, colloquialisms, and everything—almost immediately. I've seen her talent in action, but I'm still amazed by it.

Someday, I'll have to press her into telling us how she does it.

Mattea gives me a pleading, "I've-got-this-under-control" look before gulping and turning her attention back to the feral girl. "Us and them *solamente buscano*. Through passing only with harm to not," she says with a slippery, wet accent that mimics the girl's.

"Her big *peligrosa*. And all *surgir* them."

Mattea risks a slight head shake. "Them's *mentiras*, lies and them."

The girl's arm relaxes a little more, and I take what I'm pretty sure is my first breath since this little caper began. Matholook and I exchange a side-mouthed smile of partial relief before I turn back to the girl, who still has the knife a bit too close to Mattea's throat for my liking. On top of that, she's got Mattea's wrist clenched in her other hand behind her back, so I'm not ready to let my guard down just yet.

I do a quick mental calculation of all the angles and possibilities I'll have to consider before deciding whether or not to whip one or both of my Serpent Blades at this girl and end her unprovoked attack...and possibly, her life.

Without breaking a sweat, I can have her on the ground before she knows what's hit her.

My fingers curl over the handles, the balance point of each weapon centered squarely on my palms. And then time seems to stop. And then it bursts forward in an explosion of motion.

In the center of that explosion, Mattea says my name. "Branwynne." She's not asking for anything or trying to get my attention. It's just like, in the sudden vortex of motion, she needs to be sure of me.

I don't have time to call back, blink, or react in any way.

The assailant's arm twitches, and the wrinkled skin swells from her elbow to her knuckles. Her fingers tighten around the handle of her knife. Almost too fast for my eyes to follow, she presses the knife harder to Mattea's throat, digs in, and draws the full length of the blade's razor-sharp edge across her neck in a blur of blood and black steel.

A seam in the skin covering the tendons and muscles in Mattea's neck slides open, and a burble of blood bursts out in a single mass, gushing like an egg yolk slipping from its shell.

2

HORROR

OUR COMBINED SCREAMS form a chorus of horror as Mattea slumps in a heap to the ground, her white shirt with the blue Academy crest under her combat jacket sopping up the dark red blood still pumping in thick pulses from her neck.

She gurgles, the dark browns of her eyes go milky white, and her body rips into a fit of convulsions. Her fingers dig into the top layer of coral-colored pebbles covering the arid earth, and it's like she's trying to claw her way back to life by digging her own grave.

Time freezes again, and something inside me snaps.

I'm not me anymore. Or Haida Gwaii. Or some sort of harmonious combination. I'm not Kress's pupil or the magical, missing puzzle piece to the mystery of Emergents and the war about to be fought over us. I've become something more and something less at the same time.

I am a pure, unleashed predator.

And just like that, I'm in a shambles and over the edge. Over the edge of patience, of restraint, of sanity. All the bits and bolts Kress has been teaching me about discipline and self-control go out the window along with what's left of any trace of intellect, sympathy, sensibility, or humanity.

I'm myself but at all different times in my life, from my first steps, thoughts, and curiosities to the vessel of pure rage I am now.

When I was younger, I used to have bleak dreams where I was fighting someone, and no matter how hard I hit them, I couldn't generate enough strength to keep them down for the count, to defeat them...to *end* them.

In those dreams, and as I later discovered in real life, death was never the total and absolute ending I once thought it was.

In my dreams, my enemy would just keep smiling up at me while I wailed and flailed until I was so exhausted, I thought I was *losing* the fight instead of winning it.

Killing this girl is like that.

I'm across the space between us faster than a blink or a breath, and she doesn't have time to take either one.

My hands are clamped to the handles of my pair of S-shaped Serpent Blades, their talon-shaped retractable knives flashing in the sunlight. I swing and slash as hard and as fast as I can. Over and over and over again. In front of my own eyes, my hands, my arms, and my weapons, melt into a dynamic blur of blazing-fast motion.

I strike and strike and strike, again and again, like some out-of-control machine.

And I don't care. I couldn't be *in* control right now if I tried.

Blood spraying, the girl's thrashing body starts to go limp under mine.

Eventually, she passes the point where I'm worried she might hang on long enough to tire me out or that she might get in one last lucky shot that turns the tables and ends with *me*, not *her*, bleeding out in the hot desert sand.

It's only in this moment, with my friends frozen in a semi-circle around me, that I realize how hard it is to kill a person, at least one who's fighting back and desperate to stay alive.

I don't mean the killing part is morally hard. I've got no problem with that. Especially when the person I'm killing doesn't have any morals of their own.

I've killed before. I've killed in defense of myself, and I've killed in defense of others. I've killed animals to eat, and I've killed fellow human beings who've wanted to eat me. (There's not much scarier in the world than knowing the fight you're in will end with you either standing over a corpse or else having your own corpse slowly consumed, digested, and eventually expelled into a steaming, putrid, waste-filled pit in some cesspool of wreckage that was once a dress shop, a corner store, or someone's overpriced flat in the heart of London.)

Just like back home, being an Emergent here in America comes with multiple pieces of baggage. Killing isn't one of them. Killing isn't baggage. It's not heavy, cumbersome, or unwieldily. Killing like this is light. And it's easy.

What's hard is the actual act of ending someone's life. To get them to stop breathing. To get their heart to stop pumping. To get their muscles to stop twitching. To get their brains to surrender and shut down. To get everything in them that wants to live to give up and stop fighting.

Human beings are resilient. They hang on. They struggle. They muscle through. Human beings cling to the last strips of life like it's something sacred.

It's what Mattea is doing now: spasming, kicking her legs while she rakes at the ground, and gurgling for a breath she can't take. I want and need for her to live, and I hope as hard as I can, even though I know it's hopeless.

"Human beings are defined by their capacity for hope." That's what Kress told me once during one of our rooftop training sessions at the Academy.

She told me never to rely on anything. "Except hope," she added. "It's the one thing that can keep you going and the only thing you can cling to when everything else is lost."

"If it gets to the point where all I have is hope," I told her with a smirk, "then maybe I should just give up."

"That's your choice," she advised me, before turning and calling for Render to fly over and land on her forearm. "Having that choice is the curse of what it means to be human."

I didn't need to remind her that I'm not a human being. Technically, like her and like Mattea and like almost everyone else in the Academy, I'm an Emergent.

Thanks to a confluence of events—a mysterious mixture of digital and biological codes, a natural evolutionary glitch, and a worldwide confederation of corrupt techno-geneticists—I wound up being who and what I am.

Not that I'm complaining. I don't think of myself as an outcast. I don't feel sorry for myself, and I definitely don't want or expect anyone else to feel sorry for me.

If anything, I feel sorry for everyone else. I may not have a Kress-level handle on my abilities. But knowing I could one day be as advanced and powerful as she is...that's more than enough hope for me to live on.

So, yes...sometimes, I feel sorry for Typics.

But not for *this* Typic, not for the one lying under me. Not for the girl whose skin splits into billowing crimson ribbons under my assault. Not for the murderer whose blood is now seeping in a drowning crawl along the soles of my boots and mixing with Mattea's blood among the wine-red stones and the hot desert sand.

I don't feel anything for killing this girl. Not fear, regret, remorse, or pity.

And that might just be the most horrifying feeling of all.

3

CRY

MATHOLOOK locks his arms under mine and drags me away from the dead girl.

He's not an Emergent. He's a Typic, like her.

Dressed in the white, black, and blue kit borrowed from the Academy, he's slim and about average height. But he's strong, and I feel helpless watching the heels of my boots cutting a pair of shallow trenches into the sunbaked ground of sand and stone.

I just unleashed a fury-storm and took the life of the girl who took the life of my friend. So why do I feel helpless? I should be flooded with power and burning with rage. I should be exalting, triumphant, and shot through with the thrill of victory and the satisfaction of finality.

Instead, I'm limp, and I'd be as prone and lifeless as Mattea and her shredded murderer on the ground if Matholook wasn't holding me up.

Where is the tingling buzz of combat? Where is the adrenaline rush? Where is the satisfying glory of victory? Is this what loss feels like? Is that why they call it that? Not because you've lost someone you cared about but because of the loss of everything inside of yourself that you never realized was holding you up?

Matholook drops to his knees behind me, his arms wrapped around my shoulders. His breath is warm in my ear, and with my back pressed up against him, I can feel his heart pounding in his chest. He's muttering something to me, over and over: "I've got you," he keeps saying. "It's okay."

But he doesn't have me. I don't even have myself right now. And as of this moment, *nothing* is okay.

Breaking out of their own frozen moment, Libra and Ignacio swarm past us and slide to a stop over Mattea's unmoving body.

The muscles in Ignacio's back and shoulders fire and twitch under his compression shirt as he hovers over our friend. Swinging around across from him, Libra barks at him to apply pressure to the gaping wound in Mattea's neck while calling for Sara to toss over her jacket to use as a bandage.

As if they've been hypnotized into action Ignacio and Sara follow Libra's orders.

I've always thought of Libra as the bubbly one of our Asylum, the gorgeous, dark-skinned girl with the perfect hair, the perky personality, the constant smile, and the endless, infuriating optimism.

I barely recognize the stern-voiced, authoritative girl directing everyone and making every effort possible to save our friend.

I don't know why she's trying. Mattea's life, without purpose, meaning, or even a few poignant last words—is over.

Could it be that the simple act of trying—no matter how intense and futile—is more important than succeeding?

Behind me, Arlo's voice sounds high-pitched and hollow as he says something about getting a med-kit before dropping his scythe to the ground and sprinting over to our cluster of Gripbikes.

Overhead, Haida Gwaii barks out a broken-hearted litany of

gurgle-clacks. I glance up to see her white feathers flutter and seem to turn shadowy-gray as she banks in a tight arc with the sizzling rays of the desert sun behind her. She tries to connect with me. Her voice is kind and insistent, like the voice of a doting aunt. I can feel her consciousness nudging its way into mine, but I resist.

~ *Let me in.*

I can't.

And I mean it. As close as she and I have been getting lately, as much of our consciousness as we've been sharing, it just doesn't feel like there's room enough for her and for the crashing waves of terror, regret, and grief roiling around in my head. My Emergent relationship with her is a door that swings both ways, and it feels like if I open that door now, the pain will just keep passing back and forth until it kills us both.

Sitting here in Matholook's arms, I'm panting, panicked, and sweat-soaked. Defeat envelops me like a weighted blanket. My white and blue compression top, my black military combat pants, the front of my red leather jacket, and my hands and forearms are splattered with blood. I can even feel the sticky droplets on my cheeks. I see everyone, and I hear everything they're saying, but none of it registers. I know they'll try to save Mattea, just as sure as I know she's gone.

We all know it. And, in the most unexpected and horrifying way, we're all gone.

In the space of a few minutes, we've morphed from a brash, confident crew, happily tearing around the desert on our Gripbikes and swollen to bursting with the thrill of adventure, into a hot mess of sorrow, terror, and doubt.

I don't know how long the flurry of motion goes on in front of me, how long Matholook's arms stay wrapped around me, or how many patient, soothing words he whispers in my ear.

When Ignacio collapses back and sits on the ground, his

dark, powerful arms around his knees, his head sagging low, I know it's over.

Returning with the med-kit, but slowing to a padding, defeated shuffle and then to a resigned stop, Arlo knows it, too.

Libra's curtain of thick, dark brown hair hangs in front of her face. She pushes it back over her shoulders and drags her arm across her eyes. Her whole core slumps, and all the life and vibrancy seem to have drained from her body. Her face, normally the smoothest chestnut-brown, has gone furrowed and fish-belly white.

Matholook helps me up, and I stagger halfway to my feet. It's like my muscles and bones have fallen into a deep sleep and have no intention or desire to wake up.

"Come on," he urges, his hand slipping over mine. "They need you."

They need me? How could anyone need me now? What good could I possibly be to anyone? "I need you." What used to sound like the ultimate compliment has turned into the most pointless, worthless joke.

As if driven by our shared distress and choreographed by grief, my friends and I wind up pressed together and kneeling in a tight circle on a bare patch of ground around Mattea's body. She seems to be staring up at the sky, like she's deep in thought. I want to reach over and close her eyes, but I'm scared. It seems like too intimate of a gesture, too final. I do it, anyway, telling myself I'm just helping her go to sleep.

As opposed to signaling the total and absolute end of her life.

On our knees, our arms around each other's shoulders, we huddle together with our heads tilted down in defeat.

With Mattea's body slumped and soulless in a horrific, unmoving heap on the ground, I don't know where to rest my eyes.

Distraught and disoriented, Libra can't stop crying. I can't start. It's not that I'm not sad. Sad doesn't begin to describe it. My jaw hurts from clenching my teeth so hard. My eyes are wet. My lungs are stone. My heart is broken. But I'm supposed to be tough. Indestructible. Unfazed. A leader.

I'm supposed to be like Kress.

Don't let the tears fall, Branwynne. Don't let them fall.

They fall, anyway, and a shudder rips through my neck and shoulders and sends a lightning strike of pain searing down the middle of my back. My chest is a tempest of convulsions, and I'm straining to draw even a sliver of breath.

We kneel like this for a long time. I don't know how long. Time doesn't matter anymore. Mattea is out of time, and I've lost all interest in measuring it.

Arlo is the first of us to stand.

Pushing himself to his feet, he tugs off his trademark hoodie, drawing it over his head and placing it over Mattea. The soft bulk of fabric covers her head and upper body. The intersecting patchwork of raised scar tissue cutting across Arlo's face and running down his neck are crisp and clearly visible in the midday sun.

Some of his wounds he got in combat. A few are from training. Most are from his time as a captive in the Processor in Valencia, Spain. He doesn't talk about those.

For him, the cuts and gashes covering his face and body are a reminder of every accident, injury, and battle scar from every enemy who tried to kill him and failed.

With his Emergent ability, he probably would have healed from the same slash across the throat that killed Mattea. I've seen how his skin magically puckers and closes up, taking minutes, or even seconds, instead of days or months to heal. Except he never *completely* heals. The bleeding stops. The skin seals. The bones mend. But the scars remain, and they just keep adding up over time.

It sounds sort of conceited to say, but I honestly believe that without the Academy's students and faculty, Arlo, left in the world on his own, would quickly transform into something unspeakably horrible. What does someone impervious to pain and so close to indestructible have to fear from the world? And, without fear, without any natural predators, someone like Arlo could easily become one of the many would-be gods we're in training to take down.

Why did that girl have to grab Mattea?

As if Arlo has just read my mind, he says, "It should have been me."

I slip my hand onto his forearm and tell him, "No. It shouldn't have been any of us."

And then we all start crying again.

With the six of us standing in a dazed bunch, our cheeks wet and our eyes red, Sara's got an uncharacteristic hesitance in her voice when she asks, "What should we do?"

Before the question is even all the way past her lips, something sad and soul-crushing occurs to me: We're not heroes. We're not indestructible or immortal. We're not even fully trained fighters or survivors. We're kids. Kids who just got a first-hand taste of our own fragility, of our own mortality, in the middle of a chaotic world we don't understand and can't possibly hope to control. And now I feel foolish for my eagerness to go on this mission and for my bravado in thinking it wouldn't be any different than one of our hundreds of training sessions. I'm embarrassed for the pride I had, for knowing our teachers trusted us, and for every smile and group cheer Math-olook and my Asylum and I shared grinding our Grip-bikes down here from the Academy as we went happily skimming from settlement to deserted settlement in search of clues we thought might help win an impending war.

How do Kress and her Conspiracy deal with moments like this?

How do they know what to do next? How do they even know they'll be able to go on?

"We could go back to the Academy," Ignacio suggests, his eyes sunken and dispirited as he gazes out across the sea of desert between us and our mountain. He wants to sound confident, but there's no hiding the tremor in his voice. Right now, nearly everything about him—his dark, narrowed eyes, the round knots of his muscular shoulders, the smooth lines of his jaw—they all seem a little softer, a little weaker, and drained of life and strength.

Libra shakes her head and says she's not sure how we'd even get back to the Academy now. She's still crying as she kneels down and adjusts Arlo's hoodie over Mattea's body. It's a sweet gesture, almost motherly. Which makes it even more heartbreaking. Libra's lower lip trembles, and it's like she's trying to talk while slowly drowning. "We can't take her with us. The terrain...the climb...How will we...carry her?"

I'm about to protest, but I realize she's probably right. We prepare and train for a lot of situations. We study combat, communications, weapons, history, politics, and diplomacy. And after all that, we're totally unprepared to handle the logistics of ferrying our murdered friend up a mountain on a Grip-bike.

"We can't leave her here," I object, my hands in defiant fists at my sides.

Adjusting her body harness of throwing darts, Sara points into the distance where the high, arched walls of another settlement glint silver in the sunlight. "How about there?" In the silence that follows, she fidgets with the feathered flights of her darts, twisting them in their leather sleeves like they're hotdogs on a grill. Unlike mine, her hands are delicate and clean, hardly the hands of a battle-tested warrior. "It could be our only option," she points out.

We've investigated four of these settlements so far—all abandoned—and we haven't found anything close to the kind of clues we're supposed to be tracking down and reporting on. The one in the distance, the one Sara is pointing to, is called Pueblo Outpost. It's a lot bigger than the settlements we've visited so far. Its curved, synth-steel perimeter walls must run four or five hundred yards in each direction, and they're polished to a high shine in a way the dusty, battered, wood, brick, and aluminum walls of the other settlements we scouted definitely weren't. Otherwise, though, it doesn't look any more promising. There are no vehicles around it, no lookouts in the six elevated sentry-posts we can see from here, and no exhaust from the three glass and chrome smokestacks jutting up into the sky from behind the wall. I'm not optimistic we'll find any signs of life there. And forget about finding help.

Wiping her eyes and nodding, Libra says she agrees with Sara. "She's right. We should go to the Pueblo Outpost. It's right here. And it *was* on our list of places to check out. Maybe we could take Mattea there. Maybe someone could help."

She doesn't say it out loud, but I know we're all thinking it: Even if we're lucky enough to find someone there who doesn't try to kill us at first sight, Mattea is beyond medical help. We're talking about something much more unimaginable: getting help giving her a proper burial and keeping her out of reach of the vultures and other desert scavengers that have claimed this mostly lifeless land as their own.

As if she's come down with a nervous tic, Sara continues to fiddle with the darts in her bandolier and adjusts the snug, X-shaped straps cutting across her torso. Sliding a lock of her short blond hair behind her ear, she squints into the distance. Her normally blue eyes are cold now and have gone pewter gray. "It *is* one of the places we're supposed to investigate and report about."

"You mean keep going with our mission?" Ignacio asks

through an incredulous snarl. His fists curled into hard, tight knots, he swings around to face Sara. He's tall and imposing, a boy who is going to rival Brohn in pure physical prowess someday. Despite his bluster, though, he doesn't seems to know what an intimidating physical presence he is. But that's starting to change as he grows older, more confident, and more aware of the potential for power he has over others.

In the Academy, Brohn is his mentor, and I'm guessing he has his hands full trying to keep Ignacio's confidence from spilling over into narcissistic arrogance.

Startled by Ignacio's hostile reaction to her suggestion, Sara steps back, and for a second, I think he might actually lunge forward and hit her.

Sara drops her eyes. Dancing in the light breeze, loose tendrils of her hair flit around her face. Although she's fair-skinned, the light and heat out here don't seem to bother her. "There's more riding on this than a single life," she says into her chest, her eyes returning to their normal, watery blue. "We need to be practical now, not emotional."

I pivot toward Sara, my voice a predatory growl. "Mattea was our *friend*."

"I'm not trying to be cold-hearted," she answers through a choking sob. She points a trembling finger in the direction of the open-eyed, blood-covered feral girl lying dead on the ground. "That girl probably wasn't out here alone. If we stay here—"

Frack. I hate it when she's right.

As if the cosmos decided to prove Sara's point, whatever she was going to say next is cut off by the grinding sound of Skid Steers and the advancing, unmistakable battle-cry shrieks of one of the small but deadly recon squads from the Army of the Unsettled.

4

CHASED

BOUNCING over the remnants of a cluttered and pock-mocked highway, the Unsettled Recon and Strike Squad—made up of four of those treaded, souped-up Skid Steers, four dirt-bikes, and a huge rust-red cube van with steel caging all around it and a roof-mounted grenade-launcher—bursts up from a canyon along with swirls of sand.

It's an alarming sight, and I feel like I've gone instantly from predator to prey.

With war-whoops and sporadic gunfire piercing the air, the fast-approaching patrol flies toward us through the undulating waves of heat rising from the ground. The fleet of pursuit vehicles bounces, skims, and rumbles over the rough terrain, leaving a sky-concealing cloud of dust and smoke in its wake. Their hurtling, churning caravan is lit up by dozens of muzzle-fire flashes. Bullets ping off the rocky ground and plunk into the low dunes of sand to either side of us.

The Unsettled usually rely on a combination of firearms, knives, and an arsenal of homemade spears, clubs, and swords. Just our luck, this group has guns while we're stuck with our dangerous but currently useless collection of close-range weapons.

"Get behind me!" Arlo shouts. "I'll slow them down!" Skidding to a stop and whipping around, he draws out his scythe and swings it in a swooping arc over his head.

The trick he's been practicing—he calls it casting an *Aegis Shield* —has saved us before. With his Emergent ability to affect the molecular density of the air, he has the power to create a sort of "bubble of thickness" that's been able to slow down attackers in the past.

I used to think his ability to affect the weight of the air was magical, bordering on impossible. It was Rain who pointed out to me how close to normal it is. "Everything from babies to cats," she explained, "has the ability to be heavier when they don't want you to pick them up."

Thinking she was joking, I laughed even though she didn't, and then I proceeded to spend the entire night awake in the Lounge with the weird reality of her statement pinballing around in my head.

With the knuckles on Arlo's blistered hands turning ivory white and his face in a compressed grimace, I brace myself for the inevitable "thickness" that will slow our attackers down and give us the few seconds we need to regroup.

Only...nothing happens.

Arlo waves his scythe again. When the steaming hot desert air doesn't react, Sara grabs him by his arm and shouts at him to get moving.

"I don't understand!" he calls out over the din of gunfire.

"Who cares?" Sara cries back. "Let's go!"

When Matholook, stunned in wide-eyed disbelief (or is it disappointment?) doesn't move, Sara clamps her other hand to his arm and yanks him as hard as she can until he snaps out of his petrified daze and starts running along with her. Stumbling and weaving, they sprint shoulder to shoulder, their boots kicking up a storm of red and gray sand behind them.

Ducking gunfire and vaulting their way over a small field of scrub brush, Libra and Ignacio dash over and scan their Grip-bikes to life. Matholook bolts over to the bike we've been sharing and gets ready to leap on, but I stop him and suggest we'll go faster if he takes Mattea's bike, instead.

As I say the words, I'm flooded with an instant wave of sorrow and guilt. Our friend died *minutes* ago. It's too soon to be dismissing her place in the world and turning her things over to someone else.

Focus, Branwynne!

While Matholook leaps onto Mattea's green Grip-bike and I clamber onto my yellow one, Sara and Arlo are busy sprinting toward their own bikes.

I'm frantically waving for them to hurry up when Arlo goes flying forward like he's been slammed between the shoulder blades with a sledgehammer.

I leap off my bike and scurry over with my head down to help Sara get him back to his feet.

A bullet has pierced the meat of his shoulder, and blood is already seeping through the chest and sleeve of his blue and white compression top.

Arlo grumbles that he's okay, but his voice is fuzzy and weak.

Sara and I help him onto one of the two black Grip-bikes. "You're sure you're, okay?" I cry.

"I'm fine," he growls, as blood continues to seep through his shirt and down his side in dark patches. "Let's go!"

Sara and I dash over and leap onto our bikes and slap on our helmets. With Libra in the lead, the six of us peel out, leaving our pursuers, our dead attacker, and Mattea's body behind.

Hurtling over the creased and uneven landscape and leaning into sharp, precarious turns to avoid the scrub-brush and jagged rocks jutting up from the ground, we race toward the giant silver wall surrounding the Pueblo Outpost.

It's a long shot. We have no idea if we can even get inside or who or what might be waiting for us if we do. But the uncertainty of the settlement is better than the certainty of what'll happen to us if we stay out here while the Unsettled use us for target practice.

Bouncing and jostling at breakneck speed, we power the bikes as fast as they'll go, with the Unsettled grinding along—shouting and firing their pistols and rifles—behind us.

Thankfully, they're not known as expert sharpshooters. Plus, their guns are pretty ancient, and it's times like this when I'm secretly glad the Wealthies have stockpiled all the best weapons in their skyscraping arcologies.

As for putting any sort of distance between us and them, we can easily outpace the Skid Steers and the lumbering cube van. But a quick look over my shoulder tells me just how fast their dirt-bikes are closing in. The Unsettled drivers, their sand-brown jackets and military-style cargo pants billowing in the wind, rev their bikes to a whirring, break-neck speed as they skim and bounce over the rough and rock-ribbed fields.

Even with my visor down, I'm squinting into the dust cloud and trying not to get blinded by the stinging bits of sand and debris being kicked up all around us, when the hair on the back of my neck stands on end.

Over the space between us, Matholook shouts out, "Did you feel that?"

I holler back, "Yeah! What was it?"

"I don't know!"

A second later, we find out as each of the small, magnetic reactors powering our Grip-bikes sends up a spray of electric-blue sparks.

As we shriek and flash our fingers over the accelerators in

the hand-bars, our six Grip-bikes glide for another few seconds before seizing up, sputtering, and grinding to a complete stop.

"What happened?" Libra cries, frantically slapping her palm pointlessly against the ignition pad on her bike's control panel.

"It's a Systems Diode Dampener!" Ignacio yells across at her, like it's her fault we've stopped. He presses his fist to his chest and winces. "I can feel it!"

"Come on!" I shout, slinging myself off of my Grip-bike, tossing my helmet to the side, and breaking into a run. "We can make it!"

I'm not nearly as confident as I sound.

The others follow suit, ditching their helmets and their Grip-bikes, and bolting along with me.

With at least two hundred yards between us and the settlement, we race on foot toward the wall as the bullets of the Unsettled continue to plunk into the ground behind us. No matter how many times it happens, in the Academy's training rooms or even out here in the real world, I will *never* get used to being shot at.

Although he's probably the strongest of all of us, Ignacio isn't very fast and is struggling to keep up. Matholook is also lagging behind, and Libra keeps shouting at both of them to keep moving.

With the bulky weight of her sledgehammer to deal with, even Libra is having trouble navigating the uneven terrain and all of the crevices and low rock formations standing between us and the possibility of safety. That leaves me and Arlo far up ahead with Sara, who's skimming along, light on her feet and falcon-fast, already almost at the wall.

"Can you try again?" I shout over the sound of gunfire, the shouts of the Unsettled, the revving of engines behind us, and the thunder of our boots on the hard ground, but Arlo's face slumps in defeat as the rest of our team finally catches up.

"I can't," he pants. "Nothing's happening!"

Joining Sara, the rest of us slam to a stop at the wall and duck as another spattering of gunfire dings against the towering barrier of overlapping synth-steel slats.

Breathing hard, Sara slaps her hand against the wall. "Now what?"

In my mind, Haida's voice says, *Follow*.

Overhead, the white raven drops down from the sky on a steep descent. Tucking her wings tight to her body, she dive-bombs straight at the wall about a hundred yards from where we're standing.

I gasp as Haida looks like she's on a suicide mission, but instead of smashing into the wall, she seems to pass clean through it, disappearing for a second before climbing high up overhead on the other side.

"There!" Matholook cries out.

With the rest of us racing along behind him, he sprints the hundred yards along the perimeter of the wall to where the silver pedestrian door Haida just flew through is sitting ajar.

I send Haida a mental *Thanks!* as the six of us slide to a stop at the heavy security door, and we can see immediately why it's open.

It's an automatic door—triple-hinged and as thick as the wall, itself. Built with an automatic closing mechanism, the door has been prevented from shutting all the way by the body of a man lying dead on the ground.

Whirring its gears and tapping against the prone man like it's trying to wake him up, the door is stuck in a futile attempt to close.

He's lucky. It must have a sensor that stops it from cutting him in two as it tries to complete its sealing and locking protocol.

Okay. Maybe he's not lucky. But there's something to be said for staying in one piece—even after death.

Dressed in khaki pants, a white linen shirt, and a pastel-pink blazer, the dead man looks like he's been attacked with a machete. *Recently.* He's got long, blood-soaked gashes in his clothes, and he's been nearly decapitated. The tendons and bones in his neck are exposed to the sun with a glossy, oval-shaped pool of his blood staining the sand around him. It's a gruesome sight, but also a welcome one since the body is all that's keeping this door open.

Questions flash through my mind: *Who is this man? Who killed him? And is his killer inside this settlement waiting to do the same to us?*

With the Unsettled closing in fast, we don't have time to consider any of that or worry about what happened here.

Jumping through the narrow opening between the door and the wall, Ignacio grabs the dead body by the lapels of its jacket and hauls it the rest of the way into the settlement.

In a crush, we scramble through the gap after Ignacio, and the door, completing its security program, shuts with a heavy clang and a relieved whoosh behind us.

With the Unsettled outside and a mysterious dead man lying at our feet, it's both a relief and a terror to be on this side of the wall.

5

OUTPOST

WITH THE DOOR CLOSED, I slap my palm to a fat, ruby-red button under an input panel attached to the interior of the massive, thirty-foot high wall.

In a fraction of a second that feels like a chunk of a year, I feel my pulse ease as we hear the clank of gears and the hiss of interior pistons slowly sealing the door shut. After one final *thunk* of what sounds like a magnetic lock, my friends and I find ourselves safely on one side of the wall with the Unsettled at bay on the other.

With their hands on their knees, my Asylum gushes relieved breaths while I check on Matholook to make sure he's okay. He's a guest, after all. And a Typic. And a teammate. But most important, he's a friend, a friend who probably didn't expect a small scouting mission like ours to morph so suddenly and so darkly into a mission plagued by death and mortal danger. He knew he had a solid chance of being reunited with the Devoted after this mission. But now, that chance seems to have thinned out considerably.

"Are you okay?" I ask.

"I was about to ask you the same thing. I don't know what I'd do if anything happened to..." His voice trails off behind his sparkling-eyed smile.

Wait? He was going to ask me if I'm okay? I admit it: this mission has gone to bloody shambles. But I'm a trained Emergent who's survived an apocalypse, escaped a Processor, and fought alongside Kress and her Conspiracy. Plus, I can talk to a raven, and I'm close to perfecting the art of walking through walls!

Before today, I might've been offended at the idea of Math-olook being worried about me. Instead, I'm flattered. Something is missing in me, and his presence alone seems almost enough to fill the gap. I'm also feeling like a daft cow for the way my heart flutters, knowing that after all we've just been through, he's got *me* on his mind.

I tell myself to shake it off. I'd rather leave the gushy princess stuff to Libra.

I may be in distress, but I'm sure as frack no damsel.

His chest still heaving and with a crescent of sweat darkening the back of his shirt, Matholook plants a hand to the wall. "This will keep them out?"

Gazing up at the imposing wall—thick, tall, and curved inward at the top—I assure him it will. I've seen walls like this in other parts of the country. I saw one just like it five years ago when I accompanied Kress and her Conspiracy on their road trip from Washington, D.C. to the mountains of Colorado where we worked together to finish building the Academy. That wall was around a city called Pittsburgh. The barricade there was bigger than this one and was polished to a mirror shine. It was the dividing line between the Wealthies inside and the Hell they worked so hard to let happen on the outside.

Keeping people out is what those walls are built for. This one may not have the drone patrols, perimeter pylons, high-tech detection systems, or an array of laser-wire barriers like the one around Pittsburgh, but it should do the trick. At thirty-feet tall, the polished silver wall is too strong for their weapons. There's no way the Unsettled can follow us. If it was Epic chasing us, I'd be worried. He has drones.

"Um...What if they have climbing equipment?" Matholook asks.

The rest of us freeze at the question and then, like a bunch of wary prairie dogs watching a golden eagle swooping overhead, we all turn in unison to stare up at the top edge of the wall. It's a possibility, after all. Without proper security in place like they have in the bigger, walled cities back east, what's to stop the Unsettled from throwing up a rope ladder or something?

"Maybe there's a proximity sensor at the top?" I suggest. "Or laser-wire? We had them back in the Tower of London."

Matholook says, "We can only hope," and then he tilts his head up, his hand pressed to his forehead as a visor.

Blinking up into the light, myself, I'm expecting to see grappling hooks clinking to the parapet, followed by a few dozen of the Unsettled clambering over the top edge of the wall and dropping down on this side to kill us.

Instead, on the outside of the wall, the sounds of vehicles grinding to a stop, the shouts of our pursuers, and the crack of their weapons are all muffled and feel a million miles away.

In my mind, Haida assures me we're safe.

Her assurance comes with a warning, though. When I try to ask her about it, her voice dissolves into little echo-y whispers in my head and then vanishes completely. I can see her flying over the middle of the compound, but I can't connect with her.

"I think we're okay," I assure my friends after a very lengthy sigh following an even longer span of holding my breath. "If they could get over the wall, they'd have done it by now."

"So we're safe?" Libra asks.

Although I'm not nearly as poised inside as I'm sure I sound, I promise her we are.

We're safe from the people outside the wall, anyway. But what about the ones who might be inside of it?

Ignoring the shouts and banging of the Unsettled, which are dwindling away to nothing anyway, we turn our attention to the settlement.

It isn't a makeshift town like the four other places we've seen. In fact, in many ways, it couldn't be much different. First of all, it's surrounded by a giant wall. And, instead of rustic, hastily assembled shacks and sheds, it's more of a collection of prefabricated, nearly spherical structures. Flat-bottomed and smoothly domed, the buildings have small round windows like portals on a ship and are each painted in a single color of pastel pink, blue, yellow, or green.

Combined with the steep curved wall running around the perimeter of the compound, it looks like we just stumbled into a nest of the world's most enormous Easter eggs.

I take a few steps toward the cluster of buildings before I realize my team isn't following me. I stop and turn around to see Ignacio with his shoulders pressed to the wall, his head lolling down.

"We left her," he mutters. "We left Mattea."

"We had to," Sara insists, her hand on his arm.

I walk back and put what I hope is a comforting hand on his other arm. "We didn't have a choice," I remind him in a rare moment of agreement with Sara. "If we would have stayed a second longer, we'd be just as dead."

It's a cold thing to say. The fact that it's true doesn't stop the lump from rising in my throat.

Kicking the toe of his black combat boot into the ground, Ignacio says he knows I'm right. "But being right doesn't bring Mattea back, does it?" He pushes himself away from the wall, only to turn back around and slam the side of his fist into it. The wall absorbs the impact and the sound, leaving us with a muted, unsatisfying thud. "We grew up together," he says, turning around, his eyes riveted to mine, his voice barely loud enough for me to hear. "Even before Libra, Sara, and Arlo got brought into the Processor. Even before them, there was me and her."

I know about many of the experiences my friends had in the Processor they were held captive in and experimented on over five years ago in Spain. But there are dynamics between them and the things they endured that I'm still only finding out about in bits and pieces. We've talked a million times over the past few months. Mostly we talk about our classes, our teachers, and Libra is always quick to lead us in a round of Academy gossip. But we rarely discuss our status as Emergents, and most of the kids shy away from spending too much time dwelling on their time as captive lab rats.

One thing for sure about growing up under such traumatic circumstances: you become a master of changing the subject.

I may not have grown up like most of my fellow Emergents, but that doesn't mean I don't sympathize with the rough ride a lot of them have had.

"It's like losing a sister, isn't it?" I ask quietly. "Like losing a part of yourself."

Ignacio nods, but he seems frozen, and I suddenly understand what people mean after a loss when they say they feel like they can't go on. There's something about having a connection get broken that guts you and immobilizes you beyond any type of restraint or confinement you thought possible.

We can't go on. And yet, we have to. Is that what Wisp meant when she gave us our mission of using our abilities to save a world that may be a million miles past hope?

"What now?" Arlo asks. He looks strange without his signature hoodie. His scarred face is open and unshaded. His white shirt is stained down one side and the blue Academy crest is blurred with blood, but he doesn't seem to be in terrible pain. I know he can heal fast—I've seen him recover from deep cuts that would've probably killed a Typic, or me, for that matter—but I don't know if he's ever been shot before. He rubs his shoulder like he's massaging a sore muscle instead of what should be a near-fatal wound. "We don't have our Grip-bikes," he grumbles. "And there's no way we can get back to the Academy on foot from here."

"Not without getting killed by the Unsettled," Libra adds. She's wringing her hands and toggling her gaze between the Easter egg-shaped buildings of the settlement and the towering wall.

Matholook runs his fingers through his straw and sand-colored hair. Fidgeting with the sleeves of his Academy-issued compression top, he passes an odd glance from one of us to the other, and it's like he doesn't know what to do with his hands or where to settle his eyes. When I ask him what's bugging him, he starts to say something but then shakes his head and clams up.

"What is it?" I press.

As if it's taking all his effort to creak his jaw open, he finally stammers, "You're Emergents."

"So what?" Sara asks through a defensive scowl.

"Can't you...I don't know...use your abilities? Like you did back at that ski lodge."

In a flash, I recall the time that Arlo and Ignacio saved us from a bunch of Epic's soldiers and a sky full of predatory drones. Arlo's ability to slow the enemy down combined with Ignacio's ability to tap into nearby electrical signals made them the heroes of the day. If they had hesitated, wavered, or if their Emergent abilities had gone glitchy, we'd have all died on that snow-covered field.

"I tried," Arlo snaps. He rounds so suddenly on Matholook I don't have time to stop him. Usually pretty easy-going, Arlo, snarling out of the corner of his scarred mouth like an enraged pit bull, has one hand on Matholook's throat and the other cocked and ready to swing. "I tried back there...*twice*...and it didn't work."

"It doesn't work like that!" Libra shouts at Matholook as she latches onto one of Arlo's arms while I grab the other.

Matholook wrenches free of Arlo's grip and stumbles backward but doesn't fall. Looking lost somewhere between fear and anger, he stammers out, "I-I don't understand."

"We're not magical superheroes or wizards or machines you can just turn on and off," Sara growls. Her cheeks flush red, and her pale blue eyes seem to bore into him. He takes a step back, and I think for a second that he might fall down just under the weight of her stare alone.

"It's like a muscle," Ignacio explains. "There's only so much we can do. There's limits."

"And we're not trained like Kress and the other teachers," Libra admits.

"Which means sometimes we can't do anything to stop our friends from dying," Arlo barks.

Matholook's eyes finally find a spot on the ground, and his head droops low. "I'm sorry. I didn't know."

Ignacio crosses his arms over his chest. "That's because you never thought to ask."

"Leave him alone," I say evenly from behind the menacing semi-circle my friends have formed around Matholook. And then, doing my best to reign in my anger, I push past them and repeat it. "Leave him alone."

Libra tilts her head forward and shoots me a steely glare. She's got a completely foreign-looking frown on her usually perfect and perky face. But the tightness loosens, and she turns away from me again to sigh an apology to Matholook. "It's not your fault, Math. It's ours. We failed to tell you, and we failed to save Mattea." The name of our friend sounds heavy as a stone in Libra's mouth.

Overhead, Haida gurgle-clacks before making a descending, corkscrew loop and lands with a flutter of her white feathers on my outstretched arm. She's not as big as Render, but she's still an imposing sight. I think of her as a white bird, but up close like this, she's an entire palette of shades and degrees of whites, faded yellows, and the tiniest bits of speckled gold. Her pink beak gives her the illusion of soft lips, which most of the kids back at the Academy find strange, but to me, it makes her that much more expressive and articulate.

After the last few weeks of dealing with fuzzy connections and then losing our bond completely a few minutes ago, it's refreshing to hear her motherly voice ringing again so clearly in my head.

~ *You need to keep moving.*

In my mind, I ask her if it's safe.

~ *No.*

In here or out there?

~ *There's no safety anymore.*

I don't know if I've ever heard her sound quite so sad. And scared.

I try to press deeper into our connection, but it's slipping in and out again in a grainy shambles, so the questions I want to ask fizzle away into nothing. Which is just as well because—with the known threat of the Unsettled on one side of the wall, the totally unknown on this side, and me and my friends caught in between—I'm not so sure I want to know the answers.

6

MOVE

THE DECISION about whether or not to explore the settlement is made for us.

Barely audible moans and what sounds like calls for help loft out from somewhere deep in the middle of the cluster of colorful domes.

Sara asks, "Did you hear that?"

"This place isn't abandoned like the last ones," Libra says.

"That could be great..." Arlo begins.

"Or terrible," I finish.

"Listen," Ignacio whispers, his hand cupped around his ear.

We pause, holding our collective breath as we lean toward the center of the settlement, trying to determine if what we're hearing is real, imaginary, wishful thinking, or a shared, group delusion.

"There it is again!" Matholook cries out, pointing toward the colorful domes. The cries are distant and muffled, wafting out in uneven waves, but the ghostly anguish in them is close and crystal clear. "There *are* people here. And it sounds like they might be hurt."

With steel in his voice, he sounds practically super heroic, and I half expect him to rip off his shirt, throw on a cape, and go flying into the compound to find someone to save.

Before I can weigh the pros and cons, I'm already stepping away from the wall and following him across a field of trampled vegetation and smooth, blood-spattered stones in the direction of the wails of agony.

For some people, cries like this are a stay-the-frack-away warning, a signal to run as fast as possible in the opposite direction. For Matholook, I think it's a siren song. Not because he craves adventure. And it's not that he's suicidal, an adrenaline-junkie, or lacking a sense of self-preservation. He's a Caretaker, by definition. That's his role in the Cult of the Devoted. He's pulled toward those who need help, which is noble. But it also means he's been conditioned to get sucked in by the deadly but alluring whispers of war. Which is terrifying.

I used to think I was destined to be someone like that, someone drawn heroically into battle. A warrior. More often, these days, I feel like I was meant to be something else. What, exactly, that might be, I honestly don't know. Epic seems to think I'm some sort of skeleton key that can unlock whatever door leads to the mystery of the Emergents. Kress thinks I'm destined to stop him and to save millions of people from the horrors of war and all the suffering it leaves in its wake.

Whatever I'm supposed to be, I'm not going to find it standing here.

I jog a little faster to keep up with Matholook, who is striding purposefully, shoulders back, his hair dancing in the light wind, and with way more confidence than anyone in this situation should ever have.

Rushing up from behind me, Libra clamps a hand to the crook of my arm. Her dark eyes are flared up with an agony of their own. Her thick, dusky mane of hair has fallen out of its loose ponytail and is framing her face in looping tangles. "Branwynne!"

She stomps her foot and balls up her hands like she's a two-year-old chabbie gearing up to throw a full-on tantrum.

"We can't go back," I remind her as gently as possible, my hand on hers as I start to move on. "And we can't just stay here." Pushing up the sleeves of my red leather jacket, I catch up to Matholook as we pass over the uneven ground toward the colorful domed buildings. Pointing in the general direction of the mournful cries that continue to tumble and limp along through the dry desert air, Matholook tells Libra over his shoulder, "Someone in there needs help."

"He's right," I call back to her.

She sprints after me and grabs my arm again. Turning me around, she points to the dead man on the ground back by the wall. "*He* probably needed someone to save him, too. Whatever he needed to get saved *from* could still be in there."

I unholster my twin Serpent Blades. "Then we'll be careful."

The truth is, I'm not being heroic, impulsive, or even curious. I just need to put as much distance as possible between me and the pain of losing Mattea. If that means charging headlong into danger side-by-side with Matholook, so be it. I feel like if I stay still another second longer—pinned between the Unsettled and the wall behind us and the fear of what might be in front of us—the weight of grief will become my new worst enemy, catching up to me and crushing me worse than all the pain of loss I've already suffered.

Tense-faced and looking helpless as she stands halfway between our divided Asylum, Libra calls back to the others and asks them to make me stop. "At least until we can figure out what to do," she pleads.

"I'm done figuring things out," I tell her over the space

between us, my voice ice-cold now and razor-sharp. "We need to move."

I know we shouldn't be split like this—with me and Math-olook charging forward, Sara, Ignacio, and Arlo waiting cautiously behind, and Libra in the middle trying to keep us all together. But standing around doing nothing is the worst of all possible options. Haida made that clear, and, calling back through cupped hands toward the wall, I tell my Asylum so.

"Branwynne's right," Arlo agrees as he breaks into a jog of his own, quickly covering the distance between us and catching up to me and Matholook. He slides his scythe from its straps and brandishes it in his tense fists. As if he's trying to massage it to life, he clenches and unclenches his fingers around the weapon's long wooden handle. "We need to move."

I don't know if he's talking about us or about the curved and deadly blade at the end of his scythe, but the deep squint of his eyes and the flickers of rage reflected in them tell me that he's as anxious about our situation as I am.

Behind us, the others nod, and I know they're also feeling what I'm feeling. A part of us just died. They can either stand there in the shadow of the high wall and keep suffocating in their grief, or they can get moving and join me and Matholook as we investigate this place and maybe, along the way, try to salvage what's left of our broken souls.

Libra, Sara, and Ignacio unsheathe their own weapons. Only Matholook is unarmed. That was Kress's idea.

"Whether he's with us or not," she cautioned me when she pulled me aside right before sending us on this mission, "he's still a Devoted. He's still a wild card. An unknown. Until we know for sure where he stands, I don't suggest turning your back on him."

I promised I wouldn't. But I didn't mean it like Kress thought.

Whatever connection drew me to Matholook in the first place is still intact and just as powerful as ever. Maybe even *more* powerful since I know Matholook feels it, too. Every look between us seems magnified beyond the level of any other human interaction I've ever known. He's taken up space in my head where I can't stop thinking about him. He's in my lungs where something as simple as his touch has the power to take my breath away. He *might* even be close to breaching the last of my internal walls and getting inside my heart.

Kress wanted me to be careful so I wouldn't get hurt by him. But that's not what I meant when I made my promise.

I won't turn my back on him, not because I'm afraid of getting hurt *by* him, but because I feel so powerfully pulled *to* him and because I'm not sure what's going to happen to my insides if he decides to detach and disappear.

Throwing caution to the wind, I snap out the retractable, talon-shaped daggers from one of my Serpent Blades and hand the weapon to Matholook. He takes it with reluctant disgust, like I just offered him a maggot-infested racoon pelt.

"I don't know how to—"

"Don't worry," I stop him with a raised hand. "I know you're not trained with it. But it's better than nothing. Whatever we find in here, I'm sure we'll be better off armed than not." We keep walking, and I give him a warning. "The blades are coated and sharpened with a laser-sheener."

"What's that do?"

"Ever see a laser beam slice through a merengue?"

"Um. No."

"Me, neither. But I imagine it's the definition of sharpness. So... try not to botch it up and cut your arm off. Or *mine*."

Offering up a weak smile, Matholook says, "Thanks. And when this is over, I'll make sure you get your Serpent Blade back."

"Great. I'll just have to hope you're handing it *to* me and not throwing it *at* me."

I'm joking. Sort of.

I may not share Kress's fears, but I haven't forgotten that Matholook is still a Devoted. Kress warned me there was more to them than meets the eye, and I'm willing to take her at her word. At least until all this is over, and we're safely back at the Academy.

Ignorant of the weapon's precise balancing point, Matholook grips the center handle of the Serpent Blade like he's carrying luggage, and I smile a little at how awkward—and slightly adorable—he looks. As a Caretaker of the Devoted, he doesn't get the same weapons training as his peers. Even if he did, there's no other weapon out there like my Serpent Blades, and I send a mental, long-distance "Cheers!" to Kress and Brohn for all the months of training they've done with me.

Libra shuffles up next to me and asks into my ear if this is such a good idea.

I make sure I answer loud enough for Matholook to hear. "You mean giving him one of my weapons or going *toward* the sound of screaming?"

"Either?" Libra shrugs.

"I think all the 'good' ideas have been used up. All that's left now is survival. And we're not going to accomplish that sitting around here."

Still walking along next to me, Libra hesitates and stares at the ground for a second before raising her eyes to meet mine. "Helping potentially dangerous strangers doesn't feel like the best path toward survival."

It's a good point, and I don't have an answer for her. But Matholook does.

He puts a hand on her shoulder. It's a slightly strange gesture of familiarity, but Libra seems to relax when he says, "Helping others is the best way to survive, yourself."

I have to admit, that's an even better point. And now it's got me thinking. In all the talk of helping others and saving the world, I never thought about surviving myself.

7

ZUGZWANG

Following the sound of the moans and the fading cries for help, we weave our way between the big pastel domes, jogging at times but inching along at others as we creep deeper into the settlement.

The compound is different than the others we've explored, and it's bigger than I would've thought from seeing it on the outside. We spend several minutes taking wrong turns and doubling back as we try to locate the source of the sounds of human voices, which rise to a high pitch and then, just as quickly, fade into next to nothing.

The space between many of the domed buildings isn't much more than dry, trampled earth. But in other places, great care has been taken to lay out walkways of smooth, brown and red cobblestones or square slabs of gray concrete embedded in the ground.

I try to concentrate so I can access Haida's vision and sense of direction. It helps a little, but it's not solid like it sometimes is. Instead of clear signals, I'm getting wispy feelings and a sort of mental static crackling around in my head. It's not a migraine, but it has all the tingly beginnings of one.

Sara was right about us not being machines. For the longest time, I thought my Emergent abilities would quickly grow to be one-hundred-percent reliable and exponentially more powerful with each passing day. But like all of us, I've discovered that, despite the training and teaching we're getting, true mastery over who we are and what we can do is a long way off.

Fortunately, Matholook seems able to home in on the echoing cries, so he stays in the lead with me right behind him and my Asylum scurrying along right behind me.

"Do you know where you're going?" I whisper up to him.

He says, "No" over his shoulder. "But those cries are fading. So wherever we're going, we need to get there fast."

He picks up his pace with the rest of us following in a crouch behind him.

It's hot out, but the smooth, round buildings are oddly cool to the touch. It's Sara who notices this, but it's Matholook who explains. In a muted whisper I think is still too loud considering the circumstances, he tells us about the Outposters. "Very smart. Scientists. Engineers."

"How'd they wind up out here?" Ignacio asks from behind me, and I shush him for also being too loud.

"They're pacifists," Matholook whispers over his shoulder to us as we continue to shuffle along. We take a wrong turn, hit a dead end, and have to double back. A ghostly moan comes to us from somewhere up ahead. Matholook puts his hand up and waits, but the sound stops. "They came out here decades ago," he continues as he starts walking again. "Even before Krug. They saw what was becoming of the country, and they didn't want any part of it. So they started building these settlements."

"Oh, wait," Libra says, forcing me to shush her, too. "I've heard about these people," she continues, thankfully dropping her voice a few notches down from its normal, squealing, high-energy decibel level. "They have Veiled Refractors, right? To hide their settlements."

"They *invented* them," Matholook confirms. "The idea was to stay hidden and survive while the rest of the world tore itself apart."

Cutting him off from any further explanation, an overlap of moans and the sound of shuffling, louder than before, comes at us from around a corner.

Whatever they were tying to hide from...it found them.

"We're getting close," Matholook whispers.

"Which might not be a good thing," Libra mutters in my ear.

In the front of our procession, Matholook comes to another sudden stop, causing the rest of us to crash into each other. Without looking back at us, he says, "The whole hiding out thing...I don't think it worked."

We step from the narrow laneway we're navigating and out into a wide, flat courtyard where we walk into the remnants of a massacre.

The open space is littered with *dozens* of bodies and patchy with blood. The people—most of them motionless but a few others writhing in pain as they fight to hold off death—are dressed in similar outfits as the one the dead man was wearing in the security doorway: pastel-coloured jackets, white linen pants, and matching white shirts, although with all the dirt and blood, not much of anything white remains.

Many of the people have been hacked to pieces. In some cases, literally. Scattered among the dead and dying, there are body parts bathed in pools of blood.

The moans we heard must have been the echoes—amplified by the configuration of domed buildings—of the few people still clinging to life.

Where I thought we might find hundreds of people calling for help and clinging to life, the opposite seems to be true: a few survivors, the last of them now slipping away before our eyes.

Libra is the first of us to start jogging out into the open, but Sara and Arlo grab her at the same time and haul her back.

"We don't know what happened," Sara snaps.

"Or if whoever did this is still here," Arlo adds. "Let Branwynne scout it out first," he suggests before turning to me. "Are you connected with Haida?"

"I've been trying. Give me a second."

Breathe, Branwynne. Focus. You can do this.

It takes longer than it should, but I finally feel my black eyes with the random white specks—Epic once called them "Galaxy Eyes"—gloss over as I link up with Haida. She was perched in the shade of a cluster of trees on the far side of the settlement but is now flying overhead, her keen eyes on the lookout for danger.

I can't always see through Haida's eyes the way Kress can see through Render's, so I still rely on Haida relaying information via our telempathic bond.

When she sends me vague warnings about the risks of leaping into this sea of misery, I try to get more out of her, but she seems overwhelmed by the carnage in the courtyard.

Welcome to the club.

"I'm not getting anything from her I can't already see with my own eyes," I tell the others as I let the bond disconnect. "If there were any Unsettled around, Haida would be screaming. I think we need to help these people. The ones we can, anyway."

We don't need special vision to see that nearly everyone in this courtyard is a million miles beyond help.

Matholook is the first to agree about helping and also the first to venture into the courtyard where he steps gingerly over a dozen dead people before stopping to kneel next to a woman, who reaches out a partially severed hand in an attempt to grab at the leg of his cargo pants. With several of her fingers dangling by splintered bone and white tendons and through a burble of blood, she begs him for help. As a Caretaker, he's got a strong protective instinct and an almost superhuman level of empathy. Without hesitation, he grabs a stray linen jacket from the ground and rolls it into a ball, which he tucks under the head of the mutilated, dying woman.

Following his lead, the rest of us move through the enclosed terrace. We scramble to save who we can, but we're too late and way out of our league. Our few months of field surgery classes aren't enough. I don't think anything would be enough at this point.

Still, we do our best. Wading through the sea of the dead and injured, we dash from person to person, offering consoling words to the two or three people still clinging to life, and making splints for compound fractures out of anything sturdy enough we can find.

"What are we doing?" Ignacio asks into my ear. "Helping these people is pointless. It's like an above-ground graveyard here."

Next to me, Matholook overhears him, and his jaw goes tight. "As long as a single person here is alive, there's hope."

For a split second, I feel like correcting him. I know from experience—and he does, too—that there's hope even *after* death. It's why his people were so keen to get their hands on Gwernna, the young Emergent girl, who supposedly has the power to raise up soldiers who have fallen in battle.

It's why Kress and her Conspiracy still talk in hushed, reverential tones about their friend Manthy getting killed on a rooftop in Washington, D.C., only to turn up alive and well in London, England, not long before they met me and agreed to bring me back here with them as the first official student of the Emergents Academy.

There's always hope, right?

They're encouraging words, but I don't say them out loud. How could I? Mattea is dead, and there's nothing we can do about it.

Instead, we brace ourselves against the carnage and take turns applying pressure to what are clearly fatal wounds in the few Outposters still struggling, with no hope in sight, to choke their way to one more breath.

I hate to admit it, but Ignacio was right. As gloomy and pessimistic as it sounded a minute ago, we're too late and too ill-equipped to save any of these people.

The sobs, moans, and breaths of the last of the living drift away, leaving us in a vacuum of silence.

I'm standing over Matholook as he leans down, his ear hovering over the nose and mouth of the last of the injured people to make a sound.

I put a hand on his shoulder, but he shakes his head and stands up. He keeps his back to me and stares out over the scene. I don't have to see his eyes to know he's crying.

"What now?" Libra asks. Her voice is hoarse—like the rest of ours—from offering whispered, consoling words to people who are too far gone for consolation.

"We leave," Ignacio grunts, his arms stretched out to encompass the calamity at our feet. "Before we wind up like them."

"And go where?" Arlo asks.

It's not a challenging or a rhetorical question but an honest one. If the Unsettled are still outside of the Outpost, we're dead. If they're not, they will have certainly taken our Grip-bikes and stranded us out here in the desert. In which case, we're dead. Whoever committed this slaughter could still be inside the compound, so if we stay here, we're dead.

In one of Rain's chess seminars, she taught us the term, "zugzwang."

"It's a German term," she explained. "It means 'an obligation to move.'" She went on to teach us how it's a situation where you're forced to take action and where any move you make is a wrong one that opens up a winning position for your opponent. The simple requirement of having to move leads to a loss.

It was frustrating in theory and annoying in a game. In real life, it's downright disheartening.

Everyone's eyes pivot to me.

I don't have an answer, and I don't have time to give one if I did.

Before I can so much as part my lips to say a thing, angry shouts startle us into a combined and panicked gasp.

My muscles fire up, but my heart still sinks. We're about to be forced into action. Can yet another loss be far behind?

8

DEFEATED

SPINNING around we find ourselves surrounded by a small group of armed Outposters.

There are four of them—two men and two women—spread out to form a wide arc with the two men in front of us and the two women taking up flanking positions on the sides. They seem too calm and composed, considering the situation. I can't tell if they're going to invite us in for tea or kill us on the spot.

They don't look angry. More like resigned, bordering on hopeless, and I don't which is worse.

I've been face to face with the Devoted, the Unsettled, and the Leftovers. Back in England, I had my share of run-ins with the Banters and the Royal Fort Knights. I've never met the Survivalists or the Cysters, but I know people who have.

The Devoted are creepily kind, all smiles and hospitality on the surface but with some weird traditions, a fanatical adherence to history, and an undercurrent of dread running throughout their desert city at the base of our mountain. The Unsettled, as I now know first-hand and with soul-shattering certainty, are roving, unpredictable savages and ruthless, relentless killers. The Leftovers—the group of survivors holed up in a bombed-out ski lodge in the mountains not far from the Academy—are paranoid, irrational, and defeated. The all-teen alliances of the Banters and the Royal Fort Knights of London only cared about building strong enough garrisons to keep everyone else out while they struggled to survive in their own closed-off communities.

It's a bunch of groups from two different countries on opposite sides of an ocean with nothing in common except the desperate terror of prey animals and a complete and total lack of hope for anything resembling a decent, easy future.

In my limited experience, there are only two kinds of hopelessness: the kind that curls you up into a ball while you wait for death and the kind that drives you into committing the most insane acts of depravity and violence.

Because, after all, without hope, who cares about consequences?

Two kinds of hopelessness: One, passive. The other, violently aggressive. Which sort of hopelessness are we facing now?

All I know about the Outposters are the smatterings I've overheard from Kress and her Conspiracy around the Academy. They didn't sound too worried about them, so I never got the sense they were anything to press the panic button over.

Of course, that was before my mates and I wound up off guard and facing four of them in a huge, open courtyard knee-deep in the bodies of their dead.

It's our unique but lethal weapons and our glitchy Emergent abilities against the four of them and the strange collection of small, black batons they wield like bladeless axes.

Gripping the eighteen-inch, glossy lengths of pipe, the four Outposters are dressed in sandals and wrinkled linen outfits with white or khaki pants and rumpled pastel button-down shirts. There's a breezy casualness to their style of clothes. It's the same kit as we saw on the first dead body in the doorway and on the newly dead bodies currently carpeting the courtyard.

I don't know what kind of weapons these Outposters are carrying, but at least they don't look like guns. In this open space, my friends and I would get mowed down before we could even *think* about defending ourselves and launching a counterattack.

Normally, I'd be overflowing with confidence and brimming with bravado. Normally, I'd put the odds in our favor. As Libra likes to point out, though, there's nothing normal about any of this.

Haida is circling overhead, but I'm having trouble connecting with her. Still, I can feel tiny tendrils of her natural abilities—her superior senses and reflexes—mingling with mine.

It's frustrating. After all these years and after all of the training, in times of stress or crisis—exactly when I need it most—my telempathic connection with Haida drizzles around in painful currents inside my head.

What's going on here? Why are Arlo and I both having so much trouble at the same time? It can't be a coincidence, right? Libra, Ignacio, and Sara haven't had to call on their Emergent abilities. When the time comes, will their experiences be as failed and frustrating as ours?

Of all of us, only Mattea's abilities worked like they were supposed to. And she ended up murdered before our eyes.

I clench my Serpent Blade but then try to relax like I've been taught. "They're your friends," Kress always reminds me during weapons training. "And we don't strangle our friends. Hold it like you'd hold a kitten: delicately, firmly, and ready to release it when it tells you it's time."

I ease up on my grip as my Asylum and I shuffle around to form a shoulder-to-shoulder defensive semi-circle like we've been taught. "Straight lines are for military training exercises and firing squads" is another one of Kress's famous lessons. "Think organically and be flexible enough to bend to your situation. Having each other's backs isn't just a metaphor."

With Kress's training and advice surging through me, I twist my boot heel into the ground, bracing myself and preparing for a battle to the death.

Matholook hands me my other Serpent Blade. "I really think you should take this."

"Let me guess...," I say out of the corner of my mouth. "You're a lover, not a fighter."

"I'm a Caretaker. I'm trained to prevent fights and to clean up after them. Everything in between..."

"Is *my* domain. I get it. Just stay behind me."

Matholook slips the Serpent Blade to me and inches around to stand behind my shoulder. He's an odd combination of brave and cautious. He's got the stalwart confidence of a warrior but the wary nature of a boy who believes in his cause, but who isn't quite ready to die for it.

When it comes down to it—when we're faced with having to choose between our convictions and our lives—which path will he choose?

"Arlo?" I whisper through the other corner of my mouth.

"I'll try," he answers, but he's not exactly brimming with confidence.

His face in a knot, Arlo once again attempts to cast his Aegis Shield.

This time, it works. Kind of.

For a second, it seems like the Outposters, stepping forward and raising those glossy black batons, are slogging through mud. I offer up a mental cheer for Arlo and prepare myself to go on the attack, but just as I'm doing that, the hazy bubble evaporates, and all four of the Outposters spring toward us at full speed.

Arcs of crackling green light snap out from their batons and engulf the six of us in a mesh of tingling electricity. It sort of tickles at first, and I'm chuckling inside at the weak attack as I get ready to hurl my Serpent Blades at the Outposters when I realize my arms aren't doing what I'm telling them to do.

In a flash, the electric tickle becomes an itch, the itch becomes a searing pain, and the searing pain knocks my feet out from under me and plunges me to my knees.

Libra, Sara, and Matholook collapse next to me. Arlo fumbles with his scythe before letting it clatter to the hard ground. He gasps and clamps his hands to the sides of his head and crumples down next to his fallen weapon.

Only Ignacio—tall and strong with his rippling muscles at the ready—is left standing.

Our attackers fire again, but he shakes off their attack.

Big mistake on their part. This guy practically lives on electrical impulses. They might as well be attacking him with a hail of cupcakes.

His face contorted but with a mocking smile behind his eyes, he brandishes his twin shillelaghs, spinning them around his hands. In a move too fast for me to follow, he lashes out at the nearest Outposter, covering the distance between them before the woman can even *think* about firing that electric stick of hers again.

His light but stingingly powerful shillelagh catches her on the jaw with a crack loud enough to hear from a mile away.

Her eyes rolling back so they're nothing but the whites, she spins into the arms of one of the men, who catches her but stumbles back in the process, sending both of them to the ground in an out-of-breath tangle of limbs.

Ignacio follows his initial strike with another that just misses the nose of the second man. The tall man smiles, seemingly pleased with himself for his quick reflexes. But Ignacio wipes the smile clean off the man's face with a sizzling, backhand strike with his other shillelagh that cracks the orbital bone under the man's eye and sends him pirouetting into the second woman.

Giving his twin staffs a helicopter twirl, Ignacio plants himself between us and the four staggered Outposters, daring them to take a step closer.

Two of them take a giant step back.

One of them, though, accepts the dare.

The brave Outposter—the shorter man with close-cropped hair and a marble-sized mole on his chin—turns a clicking dial on the base of his baton and fires it again at Ignacio.

Ignacio's grimace turns into a grin as he lashes out with one of his shillelaghs. The thin wooden stick with the titanium core strikes the Outposter right behind his ear where his jaw meets his neck.

His eyes roll back in his head, and his knees quiver and clack like a rattlesnake's tail before he drops with a groan to the ground.

Shaking off their own injuries and in frantic unison, the three other Outposters turn dials on the base of their batons and fire off another round of arcing green lightning at Ignacio.

Their electricity-shooting batons don't seem to affect him.

Unfortunately, a storm of tranquilizer darts do.

In a fluid, well-practiced motion, the two women holster their batons in exchange for small guns with red tips and a red, rubbery waffle pattern on the grips.

A hail of tiny silver barbs bursts from their toy-like weapons, and Ignacio pauses for a second—surveying his body and smiling at the dozens of quivering darts embedded in his combat gear but also in nearly every inch of his exposed skin, including the back of one hand and the palm of his other. His smile fades. He drops his shillelaghs with a tinny clatter and then follows them straight down to join his weapons and the rest of us on the ground.

We're in training to be a lethal reconnaissance, fighting, and infiltration force.

So how come we lost?

Holy frack! Did we really just lose?

Rolled onto my back by hands I can barely feel, I see and hear everything the Outposters are saying, but it comes at me in disjointed fragments. I can't move a muscle. I try and fail to blink. Staring up at the linen-clad men and women, I can feel my eyes drying out.

The taller woman, pale-skinned to the point of near translucence, hovers over me and stares with a worried frown into my "Galaxy Eyes." The three other Outposters join her, and together, their words drizzle down on us in a cold curtain of word-rubble:

"...invaders..."

"...guilty..."

"...revenge..."

"...interrogation..."

"...Emergents..."

"...impossible..."

Grunting with the effort, the four Outposters drag us by our boot-heels, one by one, through a cut-out, slide-away doorway in the lavender-colored dome behind them.

In my mind, I reach out to Haida Gwaii, but all I get back is a static-filled feedback of helplessness.

Is that coming from me or from her? Either way, this impromptu scouting and rescue mission of ours has just gone pear shaped.

Like bags of sand, my Asylum and I are dragged into the dome, planted into a line of mag-chairs, and our hands are bound behind our backs with some sort of electric cuff that feels like it's burning my skin.

The two men stand in front of us, and the two women are behind us, all of them with those black batons at the ready.

I have to give them credit for their respect of our abilities. We're bound, nearly paralyzed, and barely conscious, but they're not taking any chances.

With dull halo-bulbs spaced evenly along the walls and with natural light seeping in on steep angles from the round windows ringing the dusty space like a spider's eyes, the curved-walled room is a maze of sharp, angular shadows. The floor, seamless and milky white, sifts with distorted reflections.

Across from us, the taller of the two man stands with his shirt torn open halfway down his chest. He nods his head to the woman standing behind Matholook. The woman slips her arm under Matholook's chin, locking him in a tight stranglehold with her baton planted with concrete firmness to his neck. She pulls hard, and I think she's going to kill him.

"Leave him alone!" I shout, my voice strained and raw. I tug against my bonds and snap my head toward the door. "We didn't do that out there! We're not the Unsettled!"

"We know it wasn't the Unsettled," the man with the open shirt growls. He directs a hairy-knuckled finger at Matholook. "It was *his* people that got in here and killed everyone. Forget the Unsettled. Our people were murdered by the *Devoted*."

9

STORY

Next to me, Matholook gulps, and I'm pretty sure it's loud enough to be heard clean across the room.

"What are you talking about?" I growl in his defense, my head tilted toward the door. "The Devoted didn't do that."

I've been inside the Devoted's compound three times in my life. I'm not exactly an expert, but I feel like I know *something* about them. They were mostly kind, sort of serious, a little odd with some of their traditions, and maybe a tad tunnel-visioned when it came to their dedication to using how things were in the past as a template for how to live in the present and for what they wanted the future to look like. Sure, they have a reputation for being aggressively patriotic and a little intense when it comes to recruiting new members. And okay, they have some violent factions in other parts of the country. (I've heard ample war stories from Kress and her Conspiracy about the True Blue faction of the Devoted back east.) But the Devoted I've met, including their leaders, Justin and Treva, were reasonable and hospitable. They had teachers and administrators in their compound and a bunch of Guilds so everyone would have a role based on their interests and abilities.

People like that don't force their way into the multi-colored compound of a bunch of linen-wearing scientists in the most remote depths of the desert and brutally slaughter everyone in sight.

Do they?

Ignacio puffs up his chest. His eyes go narrow and dark with rage, and the muscles in his arms flex against his restraints. "That out there...*that* was the Unsettled."

Scowling at our captor, Libra narrows her eyes as well and hisses through her teeth. "We should know. We just barely escaped from them with our lives." She swallows hard. "And one of them killed our friend."

"And they would have killed all of us and the rest of you without thinking twice about it," I snap. "We were lucky to get in here when we did and to get your security door closed and locked behind us. If not for us, they'd have come in here and finished the job."

I don't mention the dead body blocking the door.

"We heard your people crying for help. We were just trying to give it to them," Arlo adds. He wrenches against the restraints, but one of the women lunges around behind him, clamps a hand to his shoulder, and places one of those black batons next to his ear.

"The list of the dead doesn't need to be any longer than it already is, kid." Her long, black hair brushes his shoulder. Her voice is husky and ominous in his ear.

"You know," Sara sneers, "the Unsettled are probably still banging around outside your wall if you want to go and check."

"Sure," I say through my most sinister smile. "Maybe invite them back in here for a cup of tea?"

The tall man chuckles at me and Sara before turning his attention to Arlo. With deep grooves forming on the bridge of his nose, the man looks like he might be about to ask Arlo about the scars on his face. (I wouldn't blame him. Arlo is a great guy, but, honestly, with the red waffle pattern of blistered ridges covering his face and body, he looks like he just got spit out stone-dead at the back end of a wood-chipper.) The man squints at him through one eye and then stops and shakes his head.

Stepping back and appearing to be deep in thought, he cups his chin in his hand and gives us a long look. Then another. Reaching over, he glides a mag-chair from the side of the room and spins it around backwards. Sitting down across from us, he folds his arms over the back of the chair and points to Matholook. "You're one of them, right? One of the Devoted. A Caretaker, I believe."

This time, I'm sure Matholook's gulp can be heard halfway across the country.

Looking between Matholook and the man, I ask, "How could you possibly—"

"It's important to know your enemy," the man says. Biting his bottom lip, he stares at us, his pale brown eyes lingering on mine for an uncomfortably long time. Clearing his throat, he introduces himself as "Simmons." He gives a sharp, military salute and then gestures toward the other man and the two women behind him. "This is Vander. His wife, Rosalind. Her sister, Fatima." Simmons drums his fingers on the top edge of the magchair and offers up a sort of ominous smile. "Out here, assuming everyone is an enemy is an absolute necessity."

"We're not the enemy," I object.

I don't actually know if that's true. Enemies seem to be a lot easier to make these days than friends.

Giving me a dismissive wave, Simmons sighs and seems to debate something in his head for a second before announcing with finality, "We were a colony of fifty-three. There are four of us left." He flicks his eyes toward the door. "Just outside...that courtyard. It used to be our meeting place. We talked about supplies, health, our plans for the future...everything that has to do with life. Now, there's forty-nine of our friends lying out there, pointlessly dead."

His voice trails off as if the reality of the math just landed on him with all its weight and is now taunting him with how close it's gotten to zero.

"Who are you?" the woman called Fatima asks, her unreadable dark eyes narrowed into either curious or furious slits.

"We're students," I tell her.

"Students."

"From a school. Up in the mountains."

I hope she doesn't press me on that. The story of our Emergents Academy, our complicated history, and our impossible future...well, I'd hardly know where to start.

Fortunately, Fatima seems more interested in a conversation than in an interrogation. "I mean what are your names?"

No sense lying about this part of us.

"I'm Branwynne." Gesturing with my head toward the far end of our queue, I introduce her to Libra, Sara, Arlo, Ignacio, and, finally, to Matholook, who's sitting next to me and staring daggers at Fatima and at the other three Outposters, who have just accused his people of a mass murder.

The pale woman called Rosalind points an accusing finger right at me. "What's with your eyes?"

"My eyes?"

"She means your 'Galaxy Eyes,'" Ignacio says out of the corner of his mouth.

"I don't know," I answer Rosalind with complete honesty. "They're just my eyes."

"Hardly," she scoffs. "You're an Emergent, right?" When I just stare, she adds, "Let me guess...you're telepathic."

"You think I can read minds?"

"Can you?"

"No."

"Then what *can* you do?"

"I can't do anything."

With her three friends tense-faced around her almost like they're suppressing smiles, Rosalind raises an eyebrow. "There's plenty of dead here. Let's not add 'Honesty' to the list."

Stretching against his restraints, Matholook manages to nudge me with his elbow.

"Fine," I say. "I can communicate with a bird. A white raven."

Our four captors exchange smug, very unsurprised looks before Simmons leans forward.

He rubs his bruised and blood-stained hand along his jaw and says, "If what you're claiming about trying to help is true... well, you're an unknown commodity, so don't expect any thanks just yet. But know this: We've lived here among the Unsettled for years. They pass by from time to time. Every few months or so. We don't bother them, and they don't bother us. The Devoted, on the other hand..." Simmons pauses for a long time, and I think he might be about to cry, but he runs his tongue over his teeth and tells us he knows we *think* we know what's going on in the world, but we really don't. "The story of the world you think you know...well that's a whole different conversation. Instead, I'm going to tell you a smaller story. If you'll be so kind as to indulge me. You tell me if any of it sounds familiar. Everyone comfy?" He smiles and says, "Good" before any of us has a chance to answer.

Simmons unbuttons the cuffs of his shirt and rolls the sleeves up past his elbows. There's the faintest trace of dried blood on the backs of his hands and up his forearms, and I wonder how many of his friends he tried to save before we showed up.

Clearing his throat and cracking his knuckles, Simmons begins his story:

"Once upon a time, a group of scientists left their settlement and went out into the desert on a geographical exploratory mission. There'd been some curious pyroseismic thermal activity—possibly related to other strange, biomagnetic energy signatures at or around the 40th parallel north —so they set out to investigate. They knew the area was a hostile place. Not unlike how the rest of world had become. Ungoverned. Lawless. Dangerous. So in addition to their research equipment, they took all the necessary precautions for such a mission: weapons, radiation detection gear, motion sensors, communications devices. These were smart people, and they were prepared for anything. Anything except for a man and a woman, unarmed, standing in the middle of an open field of desert grass and creosote bush, kind of like they were waiting for them. With all the appropriate caution and concern, the four scientists approached the perfectly pleasant-looking couple and asked who they were, what they were doing out there alone in the middle of the desert, and if they needed help. That in itself was an act of altruism and bravery. Stragglers like that tended to be sick and discarded, insane, chasing someone down, or else running from someone...or something. But this man and woman were clean, kind-eyed, and, well dressed for two desert stragglers. So...walking toward them instead of running away was a risk. But nothing untoward happened. Instead, there were friendly introductions and a brief conversation. They said they were from Denver. They said they didn't qualify for residence in the Goldsmith Arcology and that the rest of the city—with its distressed and dangerous communities of Cysters, Plaguers, and Survivalists—was too dangerous for people like them. The four scientists took pity on the couple and brought them back to their compound. They brought them right in through the security door even though there were a million protocols in place to prevent anyone from coming in without being properly vetted. After all, the world was a hostile and dangerous place, right? Drones. The Eastern Order. Cyst Plague. You never knew who might look like a friend but wind up an enemy."

Simmons scrunches up his face and asks if we're still with him. We answer with silent, icy stares.

"Excellent," he continues. "So...the two strangers are charming. Maybe *too* charming. Who can tell? The gap between kindness and killing is an easy one to bridge. The two strangers convinced the scientists to let a few more of their people into the compound. 'We appreciate any help you can offer,' they said. 'We're harmless,' they promised. Before you knew it, the compound was overrun with more strangers. Things didn't feel right to the four scientists. It was like the world had shifted. Just a little, mind you. Barely enough for them to notice. They were mostly themselves. *Mostly*. But there was another voice inside their heads. A voice that made it a little harder for them to doubt their well-dressed, well-mannered guests and a lot easier for them to doubt themselves. The four original scientists—the ones who first found the strangers and welcomed them in— were strong. They shook off the hypnosis. And let's face it. That's what it was. They helped the other scientists shake off theirs. Together, they fought. They were pacifists...in *theory*."

Simmons laughs to himself. "But they weren't stupid or without a sense of self-preservation. They knew when it was time to fight for their lives. So they did. They fought and fought, but the enemy just kept pouring into their compound. It was like they had an infinite supply of soldiers. And it turns out, they kind of did. You see, every time one of the invaders was killed, they'd magically come back to life and keep fighting. Get killed. Pop back up. Keep fighting." Simmons laughs again, but it's not a happy laugh, and his eyes are wet and red. "So the scientists fought," he continues. "And the scientists lost. How could they hope to win against an immortal army, a giant, a sharp-toothed savage, and one magical little girl?"

Simmons finishes his story, and we're all sitting there stunned.

He stands up and gives his mag-chair a little push. It glides across the room and settles into a gentle hover over its mag-pad docking station against the curved wall.

"'Once upon a time' started two days ago and ended this morning," Simmons says. "The people who swarmed in here were dressed in their red, white, and blues. We'd had dealings with them before. A long time ago. Back when they promised to leave us in peace to do our research. I assure you, it was the Devoted—*not* the Unsettled—who wormed their way in, slaughtered nearly everyone in the settlement, and left. They didn't even bother to raid our food rations. But they depleted our weapons supply. And they went out of their way to try and slaughter every last one of us...like it was their *duty* to kill us. An obligation. The only four people they left alive were the four original scientists who met them in the desert and invited them in." Simmons' finger does a slow point at each of his three friends before landing back on himself. "So. I'll ask again. Not rhetorically. Not hypothetically. Does any of that sound familiar?"

I don't mean to nod, but I do. I know the hazy feeling, I know the man and the woman, and I know the immortal army he's talking about and the sharp-toothed savage. I know the giant and the magical little girl. And I know Matholook knows it all, too.

Bendegatefran: the impossibly gigantic warrior from the Vindicator Guild of the Devoted.

Efnisien: his fanged, wolf-clawed half-brother.

Gwernna: the little Emergent girl with the power to bring the dead back to life.

Justin and Treva: the well-mannered, well-dressed, disarmingly persuasive leaders of the Cult of the Devoted.

Glancing over at Matholook out of the corner of my eye, I have to wonder: If the Devoted infiltrated this place as Simmons claims, could Matholook have been doing the same by getting himself invited into the Emergents Academy? Is that what the Devoted do? Offer friendship with one hand while the other one gets primed to stab you in the back? And if that's the case, could Matholook have been using the same trick to get himself invited into this friendship he's formed with me?

Simmons said the gap between kindness and killing is a narrow one. The Devoted stepped over it. Is Matholook getting ready to do the same?

Just outside of this building, there's a courtyard full of dozens of dead people, people who—if there's any truth to what Simmons is telling us—paid the price for inviting the Devoted into their compound. Is that what's in store for the Emergents Academy if we fail in this mission?

If we manage to survive this, is a school full of slaughtered bodies what we're going to come home to?

10

ZERO SUM

WITH CLAMP-JAWED DEFIANCE Matholook restores my faith in him and his people.

Sort of.

"It's not possible," he snarls, his head on a swivel, his green eyes bouncing between our four captors—the two men in front of us and the two women behind us. "We defend ourselves. We protect our own. We don't stir up trouble. We don't initiate attacks or violence." Like the rest of us, his hair is a disheveled quilt of dirt and sweat, with some of the longer strands toward the front sticking to his forehead or hanging limply over his eyes. Flexing the muscles in his shoulders and leaning in his chair, he gestures with his chin toward the door. His words are as solid and evenly spaced as railroad ties. "And...we...don't... do...*that.*"

Simmons and Vander, their arms crossed in identical poses, exchange a shrugged-shoulder look of disbelief. Walking around to stand on either side of them, Rosalind and Fatima drop their eyes, but I don't know if they're also in disbelief or if they're annoyed by the men's silent, dismissive exchange.

Simmons seems angry at first, but Rosalind—her long, pinkish-red hair in a pair of thick, frizzy braids—rests her hand on his shoulder, and the tension seeps from his face. He smiles up a "Thanks" to her before turning back to us, his eyes drifting from one of us to the other until they land with the weight of an avalanche back on Matholook. "Maybe you just don't know how little you know about your people, young man. Or maybe you're lying to me. Or to them. Or to yourself. Either way, your ignorance is fertile ground for the same violent declaration of war your people just subjected us to."

"We don't start wars," Matholook objects, the tendons in his neck tightening up and jutting out.

The other man, Vander, claps his hands together and laughs. His oversized Adam's Apple rises and falls in a rolling pulse. "*Of course* you start wars. The True Blues out east...we know about them. We know they're part of the Devoted. We know they nearly took down Washington, D.C. a few years ago. And today? We know about their plans to 'unite' the country by becoming its newest, post-Krug tyrants. We're here because we don't want any part of your war. Don't let this little situation we have here fool you." I can tell he wants to sound cold and brave, but the quiver in his voice and the glossiness at the corners of his eyes give away the searing freshness of his pain. He points toward the door, his hand in the shape of a gun. "Yes. We fought back against invaders. Yes. We killed. Or, at least we tried to. But we were just trying to survive. It's all we've ever wanted: to survive and to live in peace."

"So...you're cowards," Sara says, her lip curled into a canine snarl.

Shut up, Sara!

The cheeks of both men and both women flush through with matching splashes of strawberry red, but it's Vander, his gulping Adam's Apple now throbbing in a rage, who snaps around to face Sara. "That's one way to put it, little girl. Another way to put it is that we're sane, decent people who don't see the point of millions dying on the word of the very few who'll sit back laughing and raking in the resources while we're all busy killing each other."

Like Simmons did a minute ago, Vander rolls up the sleeves of his lime-green linen shirt and cuffs them above the elbow, exposing twin tattoos of a DNA double-helix on the inside of each forearm.

The tattoos make me think of Kress and how she's probably out there in the world somewhere right now, successfully completing her mission with her Conspiracy while my friends and I sit here, defeated, disheartened, and bound prisoners of our own failure.

Her voice cotton soft and flute-high despite her thick-shouldered, muscular build, the woman called Fatima holds up a finger and says, "Wait." She plunges her hands into her pockets and stares at me for a second. "You said the Unsettled killed one of you?"

"Mattea," I tell her. "Our friend."

"And you honestly think it was the Unsettled?"

"One hundred percent. She dressed and talked weird like them and everything."

Fatima takes off her rectangular, blue-tinted glasses and wipes the lenses with the bottom edge of her shirt. "Things aren't always what they seem. Neither are people."

"Sometimes, things and people are *exactly* what they seem," I fire back.

"I'll grant you that," she chuckles. "But the Devoted are tricky. Trickier than you might realize. They've spent *years* now on their newest strategy."

"Strategy?"

Fatima brushes her dark hair over her shoulder and jabs an accusing finger at Matholook. "He knows."

Controlling the frustration and fury I know must be boiling up inside of him, Matholook clenches his teeth. "I have no idea what you're talking about."

He sounds sincere, like any good friend. And like every good liar, right? So how am I supposed to tell the difference?

Simmons raises a skeptical eyebrow and pins his gaze to Matholook's. "You don't know about the infiltrations?"

When Matholook doesn't answer, Simmons' other eyebrow goes up.

What the bloody hell is going on? Does Matholook seriously not know what his own people have been up to? Or even what they're capable of? If he doesn't know, he's oblivious. If he does know...Well, if he knows that, then I sure as frack don't know him.

Neither one of the possibilities—that he's ignorant or else he's masterfully deceptive—is an especially appealing character trait, and I can feel a little part of my internal self taking a step back from the boy who's spent a long time drawing me forward.

Rosalind chuckles enough to send a blush through her pale cheeks and spreads her arms wide. "We're people of science. People of the *mind*. We don't value weapons."

"Those little black sticks of yours say otherwise," Arlo reminds her.

"Ah. Our stun-sticks," Vander cuts in with a proud smile. "We've got a whole arsenal of non-lethal weapons. Most of them of our very own design. Stun-sticks, gas pellets with a mild neurotoxin. Flash grenades. Tranquilizers."

"Forgive my friend," Simmons says. "He's our weapons master. And he takes his role seriously."

"You mean his role of coming up with ways of killing people?" Libra barks, her bold challenge brimming with snark.

"No," Fatima says with a finger wag. "The opposite. You see, we got sick of how the war had become zero-sum."

"Zero-sum?" Matholook asks, his eyes skipping from Fatima's to mine and back again.

"It's a term from Game Theory," Fatima explains.

"We know what Game Theory is," Ignacio protests.

Libra sighs and rolls her eyes, but I know she's happy to take over from Ignacio and show off her knowledge. "Zero-sum," she sighs, as if it pains her to have to share this information, "refers to an all or nothing theoretical proposition. It means one side has to win, and one side has to lose."

"Exactly!" Fatima exclaims, slapping her fist into her open palm. "But shouldn't there be another option? Why is it 'kill or be killed'? How about disarming your opponent so you're not drawn into that zero-sum scenario in the first place?"

"So you invented a different kind of weapon," I say.

"Exactly. Instead of Krug's drones that either sat idle or else exterminated entire populations, we came up with less deadly solutions to seemingly irresolvable problems."

"Sure. That's great in theory," Arlo points out. "But when they attacked, according to your own story, you killed the Devoted."

"No!" Simmons interrupts, clearly offended. "We *tried* to kill the Devoted. I'm sorry to say, but we really did try..."

"And we really did fail," Fatima finishes for him, her head and shoulders slumping in defeat.

Simmons draws the black baton from a loop on his belt. He slaps the glossy weapon three times in his palm. "We can set these to their maximum power range. Overload a person's neural synapses. It doesn't kill them, but it zaps their brains in spectacular fashion. Yesterday was the first time we ever did that. The first time we *needed* to do that. And it wasn't enough. Most of us have been in this outpost for nearly twenty years. For the first time, we were forced to open up our *other* arsenal."

"Other arsenal?" I ask.

"The one with the guns. The one we said we'd never use." He points to the wall behind us where the floor-to-ceiling doors of an empty cabinet hang open. The empty racks, hooks, and tiers of shelves are an ominous reminder of how many weapons they must have deployed only to be slaughtered nearly to the last person, anyway.

"You should let us go," Sara says, a smirky grin tugging at the corners of her mouth. Blond-haired, blue-eyed, and pale nearly to the point of ghostly, she's giving off some pretty devilish vibes, and I'm about to tell her to keep her mouth shut before she gets us all killed. But it's my own mouth that stays shut, and I'm suddenly and inexplicably at a loss for what to say or of any actual way to say it.

I literally can't gather enough air in my lungs or make my mouth move enough to say a word.

"We have a mission to complete," Sara continues, her voice distant and hollow. "And based on what you've told us, I don't figure you're the kind of people who go around kidnapping a bunch of lost kids, are you? Besides, you've suffered enough for one day." She looks over at the door and gives our four captors a sad shake of her head, even though she's still smiling. "Keeping us here won't do you any good."

After a pause, Simmons nods and tells the woman named Rosalind to let us go. Her eyes darting from one of us to the other, she edges around behind us, and there's an overlapping sizzle as she releases our zip-cuffs.

Scowling, we all rub our wrists, except for Arlo who I know doesn't experience pain the same way as the rest of us.

"See?" Sara beams. "Now isn't that better for everyone?"

Ignacio is the first of us to stand up. With short, soft steps, he inches over to the end of the stainless-steel table by the wall where our weapons are lying in a neat row. His eyes fixed on our four captors, he extends his hand out toward his shillelaghs.

When the four Outposters don't resist or even react, he finishes the motion, picking up the weapons and snapping the deadly twin staffs into his shoulder harness.

Libra does the same, hoisting her powerful sledgehammer up and returning it to its mag-lock harness on her back. She tosses Arlo's scythe to him. He catches it with one hand as she tosses my twin Serpent Blades to me and Sara's bandolier of throwing darts to her.

The six of us, armed again and with Matholook safely tucked behind me, are now standing in a line in front of the table with the four Outposters watching us curiously from the middle of the room.

"We're going to go now," Ignacio says. It sounds like an announcement, a guess, and a threat all at once.

"Yes," Rosalind agrees. "Of course."

"This has been fun," Simmons says with a clap of his hands. "It's a shame for a pacifist to admit, but, honestly, I'd kind of like to kill you all right now."

The tight knot in his jaw just below his ears and the flexed muscles in his forearms tell me he's not kidding.

Simmons catches my eye, and the tension in his face softens. He gives me a glum, humorless grin and tilts his chin toward Sara. "Your friend there is right. Keeping you here doesn't do you or us any good."

"So...we can keep our weapons?" Libra asks.

"Yes."

"And...you're really going to let us go?" she stammers.

"Yes." But in about two minutes, you might wish we hadn't."

"What do you—?" I start to ask, but he cuts me off.

"We can't risk having you betray us. It's happened too many times before."

Even before the last words are out of Simmons' mouth, Fatima has tapped a small button on the silver bracelet on her wrist. A lazy cloud of what looks like snowflakes drifts down in loopy swirls from the ceiling, encircling me and my Asylum.

How cute, I think. *A snowstorm indoors.*

And then, after a flash of movement from the Outposters, there's a bag over my head and what feels like a foot-long knitting needle jammed into my upper arm.

11

EVICTED

Lying on my side on the ground, I wake up in hot, steamy darkness.

Where...? What the frack just happened?

My head is throbbing. I can sense Haida somewhere nearby, but she seems to be reacting to my pain and is keeping her physical and mental distance.

Great. I need help, and she chooses this exact moment to get skittish and develop a thin skin.

I can't blame her for staying away. What I feel, she feels. And right now, wherever she is, she'll be as confused, uncertain, and as wracked with pain as I am, so she's probably wise to stay away.

I'm on my side with my cheek pressed to the ground, and I've got what must be the sharp edges of a dozen rocks digging like shark teeth into my legs and ribs. A pain-storm full of thunder and lightning rips through my body, and I can't tell if none of my bones are broken or if all of them are.

I blink my eyes to try to focus, but everything is still cloaked in a shadowy haze.

Oh, right. The bag.

I tug the musty cloth sack off my head, and the intensity of sudden daylight blasts my black eyes white. I cringe against the pain and take a split-second, internal inventory of my body from the cramped muscles in my legs, the spasms in my neck, and all the way to the dull throb in my upper arm from where those bloody frackers stabbed me with that needle.

At least they had the courtesy to free my hands first and let me have my weapons back. And I don't think the zip-cuffs burned my wrists too much.

Not a good sign when that's the best news of the day.

I chuck the hood aside as my eyesight rushes back. On the ground in front of me, Matholook and my Asylum are also squirming to life and pulling off their own hoods. Sitting but slumped over and with her legs splayed wide, Sara presses her fingertips to a cut on her cheek and pulls her hand back to examine the blood. Ignacio leans to his side and puts a fist to his mouth to cover up a hacking cough.

Libra asks me what happened, and I tell her that her guess is as good as mine. "Off the top of my head," I say through a groan, "I'd say we've just been evicted."

My jaw is slack, and my tongue feels like a useless slab of ham.

"And drugged?" Ignacio asks.

Obviously.

"Better than killed," Arlo grumbles, and I have to agree.

"About what that guy Simmons and those Outposters claimed," Matholook says, "about what they accused me...my people of doing..."

"Don't worry about it," I tell him. But inside, I'm thinking, the opposite.

Definitely worry about it.

Gathering myself, I realize it's cooler than it was before, and I turn back to see that we're sitting in the dark shadow of the settlement wall.

And we're not alone.

Gathered behind us, nearly invisible in the shadows and looming cold and quiet as a cluster of tombstones, are at least a dozen members of the Army of the Unsettled.

The boys and girls are armed with a deadly collection of homemade weapons, mostly metal shards, knife blades, bike chains, or lengths of rebar attached with wire and twine to wooden broom and mop handles. Some of the Unsettled have small cross-bows hanging from sagging rope-belts around their waists. Others are gripping pickaxes, hoes, shovels, and steel-headed rakes with hooked, red teeth. It looks like they've raided a hardware store.

Like almost all of the Unsettled we've encountered over the years, they're kids, our age or younger.

Startled into action, the six of us on the ground spin around and scramble to our feet to face the shabby, crusty-haired assembly of the Unsettled.

Different shapes and heights, the kids are lined up in a neat row, as tidy and still as pieces on a chessboard.

Stepping forward, a tall girl peels down the powder-blue surgical mask she's got strapped around her mouth and nose. Adorned with an Africa-shaped, toast-colored birthmark on her cheek, her face is pimply and streaked with gray creases of grime. Her eyes are struggling to be blue, but they're failing and are closer to the color of cold steel. Dressed in a dirt-brown hoodie, baggy cargo pants, and unlaced combat boots at least three sizes too big, she takes a second step forward and thrusts her spear—really just a two-foot wooden handle with a pair of rusty steak-knives tied to the end with black duct tape and a few loops of frayed twine—right under my chin.

She has a Glock nine-millimeter pistol clipped with a carabiner to her belt by its trigger guard, but I can tell from here that it's missing its magazine, so, assuming there's also no bullet in the chamber, I don't have to worry about getting shot. The knives under my chin on the other hand...

The girl taps the flat part of one of the two blades against my cheek. "Hers and hims *vas a venir con nosotras* troubling in times."

I blink up at her and offer up a simultaneous shrug and a frown to let her know I have no idea what she's talking about.

"Hers and hims—*venga, venga*—troubling in times," she repeats, casting her eyes over the six of us before letting them land back on me.

"I don't know what the frack you're talking about," I snap.

And your people killed the one person in our group who would.

I smack her bladed contraption away, but the girl makes an animal growl from somewhere inside her chest and returns the weapon to my cheek.

Inching up next to me on all fours, her eyes wide, white, and locked onto our new batch of assailants, Libra asks me what we should do.

"How the frack should I know?" Despite the pair of knives dangerously close to my throat, I risk looking back over my shoulder to my Asylum. "Anyone here speak Crazy?"

The beastly girl isn't amused. She jabs the blades forward just enough to make contact with the skin above my shirt collar. And now I'm totally brassed off six ways from Sunday. Mattea died like this—with a knife to her throat.

I smack the weapon away and reach for my Serpent Blades... which aren't there.

Oh, frack.

A shorter girl barks out for the tall, gray-eyed girl to stand down.

"It's okay, Mary. No sense killing them before they have a chance to get executed."

Ah. English. Wait. What? Executed?

Smiling through a set of spotty, domino-looking teeth, the shorter girl greets us and tells us the leader of the Unsettled (she calls him "the Governor") would like to see us. "He says you're the answer he's looking for."

"I think we're good," I tell her, rubbing my backside and doing my best to work feeling back into my aching jaw. "But please thank him for the offer."

"It's not an offer," the girl says, her rust-brown hair hanging limply over one shoulder. "It's an order."

"Well then, that's different. Thank your Governor for the *order*. But we'll still have to decline." I give her a modest, rolling salute. "*Respectfully.*"

Behind the girl, a boy slouches, his arm is hanging low under the weight of an army-green canvas duffel bag. Ignacio's two shillelaghs, the long handle of Arlo's scythe, and the shorter, thicker handle of Libra's sledgehammer are sticking out of its open top. I'm assuming my Serpent Blades and Sara's bandolier of throwing darts are in there, too.

Great. We get our weapons back from the Outposters, and two seconds later, another posse of buck-nutters snatches them away.

The boy, from under a surprisingly elegant head of curly, chestnut brown hair, catches me eyeing the bag, and he pulls it back and drops a protective arm down in front of it.

Let's assess this situation, Branwynne: We've been chased into a place we didn't want to be, kicked out just when we were getting answers, and now we're unarmed and at the mercy of the same people we were running from. The same people who killed Mattea. Talk about out of the frying and into the fire...and then, as only we seem able to manage, back into the frying pan.

A million questions, mostly about what the frack we're

supposed to do next, rush through my mind. Haida's voice, clear and protective this time as my mother's, rises out of the turmoil.

~ *You're in a storm.*

Thanks.

~ *You can fight it...*

Or?

~ *You can ride it out.*

You're telling me to surrender to these murderers?

~ *I'm telling you to be patient. A tempest is only as deadly as you imagine it to be. And no storm lasts forever.*

I need you. Where are you?

There's a crackling in my head, but I catch Haida's answer at first. I concentrate hard enough to give myself a monster of a headache, but at least I'm able to tune her in.

~ *I'm where you need me to be. For now.*

A flashing wave of dizziness whips through me as my perception changes from my own to Haida's. Instead of sitting here helpless on the ground, for a second, I'm high above the earth, soaring and banking on thermals and looking down at a spread out, cloud-covered caravan of construction, military, and recreational vehicles.

Haida severs our connection, leaving her cryptic advice and the overhead panorama of the endless motorcade of the Army of the Unsettled ebbing from my mind's eye.

The tall girl with the birthmark lowers her weapon and turns to face the other members of her gang.

Four or five of them launch into a hodgepodge of English and Spanish and a few words that don't sound like either. I can't follow it all, but I definitely get the gist. Two of the girls and one of the boys seem to be in charge as they debate about whether to kill us or take us back to their army.

I don't understand what they say about their final decision, but since we're not dead, I'm assuming they're taking us with them.

The short girl orders the boy with the bag loaded with our weapons to step forward. He complies, dragging the bag behind him.

"Put them in there." She points over to where one of their vehicles is resting in a skewed group about fifty yards away on top of a small dune of sand, scrub-brush, and a cluster of about two dozen bottle-shaped rocks. He gives her a slight bow before jogging off toward one of the Skid-Steers and tossing the clunky sack into its front-loader bucket.

"It's time," the short girl says, directing us to the collection of vehicles.

We groan ourselves upright. I want to fight. Even without Haida's abilities enhancing mine, I have a feeling that if we don't make a stand now, we won't have a chance later.

There are only two problems: We've got no weapons, and my muscles feel like watery banana pudding.

Whatever the Outposters injected us with is doing its job, and I have to hope it wears off, or else we're all going to spend the rest of our very short lives at the complete and total mercy of the Unsettled.

In a flash of white that nearly makes me puke, I get a second wave of sensory-images in my head from Haida Gwaii. The images are a blur, and I feel like I'm sensing more than seeing.

From my mind's eye, I watch myself and my friends, caged in glass and surrounded in the middle of a war. Only, we're not exactly surrounded. The fighting isn't happening around us as much as it's happening...below us? Arcs of silver smoke streak overhead. A burst of muzzle-flashes blinds me for a second. Gasping, I choke down a swell of doubt, fear, helplessness, and...betrayal?

I try to ask Haida what's happening, but I get feedback and a crushing migraine in response.

I don't always see what she sees, and I can't communicate with her like Kress can with Render. But something different is happening, something Kress hasn't taught me or talked to me about. I think Haida and I are starting to connect in a different way than we're supposed to. It's not visual. Well...it's not *only* visual. And it's not intellectual or emotional. I think it's almost... I don't know. Chemical? Molecular? That last flash had me in it, but in a place I've never been and in a situation that hasn't happened. At least not yet.

Could our connection even be...*temporal*?

Whatever it is, it's fading again, and I blink my eyes hard to refocus on the band of the Unsettled in front of us.

Arlo seems to have recovered already. But the rest of us are still doing our best to deal with our woozy heads and wobbly legs.

Three of the boys and three of the girls half-guide, half-carry us over to an aluminum-sided camper parked up on the road just past the Skid-Steers.

Domino-teeth flips up the latch on the rear door and ushers us up the two steel steps and into the dark, empty box.

We all climb up, except for Matholook, who's stopped by Domino-teeth's hand on his chest.

"The Governor is going to be happy to see you."

"I don't know any Governor."

"Climb on up," she says, stepping to the side and waving him forward. "By the time we get back to the Army, you'll definitely wish you didn't."

Looking back at her for answers she obviously has no intention of providing, Matholook joins the rest of us inside of the hollowed-out camper.

It's musty and steaming hot in here. The floor is made of

long wooden planks, riveted to the truck's base. The walls and ceiling are corrugated steel with horizontal ridges that make it look like an unfolded piece of origami. A small, slatted vent at the top lets in five perfectly parallel strips of light.

We all jump when the door slams shut behind us, and I can't speak for everyone else, but I know my heart sinks a little at the clunk of a lock being turned, sealing us inside this steel container like six raw fish sticks about to be baked to a crisp.

12

HELPLESS

NEXT TO ME, Libra latches onto my arm as the vehicle's engine putters to life and grinds forward. With no seats or benches, we're jostled against the ribbed steel walls and have to hang on to each other to stop from sliding around and falling arse over teakettle.

It doesn't help that whatever the Outposters drugged us with hasn't completely worn off.

"*I* feel fine," Arlo says through a totally inappropriate smile.

I know he's teasing us to lighten the tension, but my goopy muscles and foggy brain aren't in the mood.

I tell him to knock it off, but since my mouth and jaw are still limping their way back to normal, my command comes out more like a slurred bowl of mashed peas.

At least I'm not drooling. At least not much. And the leftover numbness in our bodies is keeping us from experiencing the full brunt of the jostling vehicle.

Like most of the world we've seen in our lives, smooth, paved roads are in short supply. I honestly can't tell if we're on the sand and debris-covered highway or trundling along over the completely raw, unpaved ground of the open desert.

The six of us drop to the floor, our arms wrapped around our knees or around each other, just doing our best to avoid being slammed to death against the walls.

It'd be a shame to die before the Unsettled have a chance to execute us.

I try to tap into Haida again. Thanks to the brief flash of vision I had before getting loaded into this truck, I know she's out there somewhere, but my connection with her hasn't been this weak since early on in our telempathic relationship back in the Tower of London. I get the sense she knows something, only I can't tell if what she knows and has been trying to relay to me is where we are or where we're *going* to be.

At the moment, instead of conversation, I get patches of feelings and emotions—sorrow, fear, anxiety, and helplessness—although I can't say for sure if it's her mind I'm reading or my own.

Finally, I breathe a relieved sigh when our interior voices connect.

Please tell me we're going to be okay.

~ I can't promise that.

Great.

~ But I can promise, when we fully connect, you'll be a lot better than "okay" for the rest of your very long life.

Fully connect?

~ We're not where or when we'll ultimately be. Not yet.

Where or when? What do you mean?

Haida and I get disconnected before she has a chance to answer.

Haida?

I can hear her calling back to me, saying my name, but our voices get muddled together until I can't tell which is which. And then, there's only me. Jostling around in the back of a truck with my five closest friends, I feel strangely alone.

Next to me, Libra breaks into a shuddering sob. "I'm so sorry for back there."

"Sorry for what?" I'm too sore, tired, and annoyed to offer words of consolation or even a supportive arm around her shoulders.

"I should have stopped us from going into the settlement. I should have dragged us all away."

"It was me," Matholook says glumly, his hand half-raised. "I can't hear suffering and not help."

"We're a team," I tell both of them. "We live or die together."

"Not Mattea," Sara mumbles into the air. "She died alone."

All at the same time, I want to tell Sara to shut it, to have faith, and to tell her she's right.

I wind up not saying anything.

Arlo asks Ignacio if he can do something to disrupt the vehicle's electrical system.

"Yes!" Libra squeals, clapping her hands and going from despondency to delight in less than two seconds. "You can do that thing you do! You've done it before." She hops to her knees, her hands clasped in prayer, her eyes pleading and wide in the dim light of the truck's shadow-spackled interior. "Come on, Ignacio. *Please* get us out of here!"

Partially illuminated by the meager strips of particle-filled sunlight from the ceiling vent, Ignacio's eyes are desert dry. But there are tears of frustration and futility in his voice.

"I can't feel…"

"Feel what?" Sara asks.

"I can't feel my abilities."

We're all quiet, and it feels like another one of us just died.

I swallow hard. I know exactly what Ignacio means. Three times in my life—twice with Kress next to me and once on my own—I've been able to pass through solid walls. It's a painful trick, and each time I've felt like I was being ripped apart and reassembled on a molecular level. (Which Kress later explained is a pretty good description of what's happening.) Right now, though, I don't feel like I could so much as pass through a stiff breeze. It's not that my Emergent abilities aren't there. I can feel them lurking around like lost ghosts in the back of my mind and wafting with slow, miserable moans through my body and limbs.

But it's like they're scared or defeated. Like they don't want to...emerge.

I tried to explain the feeling to Matholook once before. We were alone in the room Kress and Wisp set aside for him at the top of East Tower in the Academy, and he asked what it felt like to be superpowered. I thought he was teasing so I gave him a good swat, but he insisted he was serious.

"I just want to know what it's like to be..."

"Different?"

"No."

"Powerful?"

"No. Not exactly."

"What, then?" I asked.

"I like you," he confessed through an adorable blush. "And I guess I just want to know what it's like *being* you."

I didn't answer. I would have, but that's when he leaned in to kiss me, and the fact of my being an Emergent and him being a Typic suddenly didn't seem so important.

I don't have a lot of experience with Typics. But one thing I'm finding out is that, in the mind of the average Typic, there are two sorts of Emergent abilities: the sort they imagine we have and the sort we *actually* have.

In their minds, we're techno-genetically enhanced lab rats who have these weird and dangerous superpowers we can turn on and off like a light switch. Flick the switch, and you can do superhuman things. Flick it again, and you're just a regular person.

But that's not anywhere close to what it means or what it feels like to be an Emergent. (Unless you're talking about a malfunctioning, short-circuiting, grease-covered dimmer switch that toggles randomly and uncontrollably in the wide range between pitch dark and ultra-bright. Then, yes, it's a *lot* like a light switch.)

But no. Being an Emergent is more like being a professional athlete, like the kind my father used to be before his stint in the military. He loved telling the stories of his football days. "Some days, you're in the zone," he told me once, "and you feel like you can take on the world and do no wrong. Other days, it's hard work just to remember and realize a fraction of your training. Some days, you're sore all over, and some days, it takes ten times the effort it took to perform to the level you did the day before."

He puffed out his chest and looked over to make sure my mum wasn't paying attention. (She had an annoying habit of diluting his stories of his glory days with too much truth.)

"And some days," he added, fixing his eyes back on mine, "your body hurts down to your bones, and you just can't seem to get out of bed at all."

I used to think that Emergents like Kress and Brohn and their Conspiracy were invincible and in top form at all times.

It was only after Kress started mentoring me five years ago that I discovered that, like the rest of us, they have their good days and bad days. (They have a lot more good days than we do, but Kress promises me that I'll get there, too, someday... provided I keep training and concentrating and not going out of my way to get my stupid arse into trouble all the time.)

With my thoughts on Kress, I have a slow look around at Matholook and my Asylum, and I wonder just how much trouble we're going to get into before all this is over.

If we're alive when all this is over, that is.

Matholook rests his hand on my leg. I put my hand on top of his, and he squints like he wants to say something or ask a question, but he winds up pursing his lips and staring at the dust specks dancing in the empty belly of the truck. He's wise not to say anything. After what happened back there with the Outposters—after what they claimed his people did to theirs—he's got to be assuming that whatever he says right now will be received by the rest of us through a filter of suspicion and doubt.

And he wouldn't be entirely wrong.

THE REST of the trip is at least two hours of tooth-jarring, bone-rattling, and bum-bruising bumps.

We don't talk much. It's more than just the after-effects of the Outposters' drugs. There's a fatigue hanging over us. It's not that we're not used to challenges and setbacks. We are.

But this collection of setbacks is different. It feels like piling on. Like it's curveball after curveball, and we keep on swinging and missing.

And the specter of Mattea's lifeless body—faded of energy and color and already stiffening under the desert sun when we had to abandon her—hangs over us, weighing us down like a suffocating blanket we can't kick our way out from under.

Back in London, my mum used to talk about "closure." She said it was one of the worst parts of the Atomic Wars.

"People were vaporized, crushed by falling buildings...so many missing...no chance to say a proper goodbye."

I knew what she meant. Sort of. But now, losing Mattea like we just did and with no chance to pay our last respects or give her a proper burial, the idea of "closure" has taken on a deep, personal, and painful new meaning.

With no closure, all that's left are open wounds.

As the feeling finally starts returning to my body, I ask everyone else if they're okay.

With a chorus of feeble grunts, they all say they are.

Matholook rubs his arms and massages his shoulders. He taps the toe of his boot against mine. "We're going to get out of this, right?"

I'm tempted to tell the others about the images Haida sent me of us being trapped in glass, high above a war, and the haunting feeling that we'd been betrayed. But that would mean telling them that my telempathic bond with her may be going even beyond just glitchy. Or worse, that Haida has found a way to show me the future. And, with what we've been through already and what we're going through now, I don't think I can handle trying to get my mind around what *might* be yet to come.

So, instead, I lie and say, "Absolutely. We're going to get out of this just fine and be back at the Academy before you know it. This truck ride can't last forever, right?"

The answer not only seems to put my friends at ease, it also turns out to be mildly prophetic as, at that moment, the rig we're bouncing around in slows to a grinding crawl.

When the steel door at the back of the truck swings open, Domino-teeth greets us with the business end of a hunting knife strapped with barbed wire to a thick silver pole.

The truck is still moving, and she and her fellow Unsettled are marching behind it as she steps to the side and orders us out.

One at a time, we hop down from the steamy camper to the hot, hard ground, and it's like we just stepped into a towering city of moving, smoke-belching machines.

The panorama from East to West and the air from the blistered and pock-marked ground to the smog-choked sky, is filled with monstrous vehicles, churning along at a casual walking pace on thick studded wheels or on metallic, interlocking tank-treads—all of it thrumming at deafening levels in our ears and grinding deep ruts into the barren and bumpy earth.

The cloud hanging over it all is a molasses-thick mass of pinwheeling debris. Spreading in a slow-moving vortex across the expanse of sky, it's nearly enough to block out the sun.

Every one of us breaks into a simultaneous fit of coughing and hacking, with Ignacio doubling over, his hands on his knees, as he hocks up a wad of sticky green phlegm, which he spits into the caked dirt next to us.

I don't bother asking if he's okay. It's a safe bet none of us is.

In front of us, the truck we were just in continues to trundle along, oblivious to the fact that it's been emptied of its human cargo.

With her makeshift spear nudging me in the lower back, Domino-teeth announces with the grand flourish of a carnival barker, "Welcome to the Army of the Unsettled."

13

ARRIVAL

I'VE ALWAYS WONDERED how the Unsettled live. Now I know. And I *really, really, really* wish I didn't.

In addition to being an endless collection of every dinosaur-sized vehicle imaginable—all of them in constant, crawling motion—a noxious cloud of thick, gunmetal gray smoke rolls in burbling waves over us. Ashy flecks of dust, rust, sand, and oil-residue stick to my clothes, and I can feel a layer of grime already forming on my teeth, against my skin, and in my hair.

It's more than just walking through a cloudy spectrum of dirt and debris. It's more like walking through the entire *idea* of filth.

The sound of it all is deafening.

The feel of it is bone-quaking.

The smell is worse.

Overall, it's a sensory overload of the most putrid kind.

While Ignacio coughs, Arlo gives him a couple of light pats on the back.

Sara's mouth hangs open, which she quickly realizes is a bad idea as she inhales a lungful of wispy fumes and joins Ignacio in a fit of raspy hacking. Her normally pinkish-white cheeks go tomato-red, and Matholook reaches out to steady her and ask if she's okay.

She wipes her watering eyes and puts her hand on his. "Only someone as cute as you could get away with a question as dumb as that," she grins.

In my mind, I hiss at her not to touch him.

It's bad enough we have to be shuffling along at what's barely walking speed in this moving Hell on earth. I don't need Sara to be doing her flirty thing right in front of me at this particular second.

On my first day of classes at the Academy, Kress used me as a punching bag in her and Brohn's Unarmed Combat class. Seeing Sara and Matholook lock eyes doesn't hurt quite as much as that did.

But it's close.

Her unsubtle attempts to win Matholook over and my unexpected and unwelcome jealously aside, perhaps most disturbing is that Libra, the ultimate Miss Chatty Cathy, is totally speechless.

I wave my hand in front of my face to clear away a small vortex of smoke and sand. "It'll be okay," I assure her, doing my best to make myself heard over the commotion around us.

I don't know if what I'm promising is even remotely true. But I do know that I'll do whatever it takes to *make* it true.

At any other time and in any other place, Libra's feeble smile of thanks might make me laugh. Here, it makes me wonder if all of this—the deaths, the captivity, the uncertainty, and the fading sense of hope—will be too much for her, and she'll lose her perkiness and break under the weight of experience.

Snapping us to attention, Domino-teeth orders the six of us into a line as we continue to move along.

I scan the sky for any trace of Haida Gwaii.

She must have followed us, right?

But I don't see her, and, even worse, I don't *feel* her. Squinting with as much intense focus as I can manage, I reach out with my mind and try to open our bond, but I might as well be trying to grab a handful of air.

Resigned, I slip my black hair into a ponytail, partly to keep it from flying in my face but also partly to preserve some semblance of neatness and orderliness in this hellscape of pure chaos.

My Asylum and I are herded from a cluster into a queue, and two of the Unsettled boys, walking along on either side of us, clamp thick metal bands around our necks and slide a length of braided steel wire through loops welded to each band to link us together.

"Great," I mumble to Matholook, who's shuffling along behind me. "Just what I've always aspired to be: a giant, six-person charm bracelet."

He lets out a hearty laugh, which one of the Unsettled boys cuts off with a sharp jab to his ribcage.

Matholook responds with a glare that the shaggy-haired boy ignores as Domino-teeth shouts for us to keep marching. I turn to face forward, glad to see Matholook flash a little anger but also frustrated that the little row didn't escalate into a full-on fight.

I've got some serious anger to vent.

The ground under our boots is packed down and dug through with deep tread-marks that make us stumble as we're paraded between a shifting line of crawling vehicles.

Many of their whirring joints are glossy with black grease. Others are crusted over with layers of rust and lumpy red sand. The monstrous arms of a pair of excavators swing deadly close over our heads. On one side of us, there are smoke-belching tractors and white cube vans, each with a silhouette of a green vulture painted on the sides. A queue of front-loaders, their buckets big enough to hold a hippo with room to spare, rock and sway on tires that have to be fifteen feet high and as wide as I am tall. On our other side, rhinoceros-sized bulldozers—some automated, others with teenage boys and girls at the controls in the cabs—thunder along to create a series of crawling laneways. With the ash-covered rigs chugging forward in evenly spaced rows and columns to form a system of streets in between, the whole place feels sort of like London. Instead of skyscrapers, though, giant cranes dot the skyline, their crisscrossed metal frames casting a checkerboard pattern of shadows onto the clouds of dust hanging over every person and vehicle around us.

We all get startled and hop to the side as three Container Shuttle Carriers—each carrying the carcass of a dismantled and torn-to-shreds military jeep in its three-fingered claws—thunder past, one right after the other. Shaped like an upside-down "U" and cradling their cargo on huge iron hooks under their steel bellies, the carriers are enormous and wide with their glass-enclosed cabs high up on the top of the foul-smelling machines.

The boy behind the controls in the last of the three carriers spits out the window at us as he passes. As a group, we shout our objections, with Ignacio bellowing out some choice and vaguely sexual words about all the terrible things we're going to do to the boy's mother.

Domino-teeth snaps at us to keep quiet and stay in line, which we do as the three towering carriers cut at a sharp right angle up ahead and disappear down a lane between parallel rows of gold and gray campers, driving along, twenty-feet apart, in perfect sync.

With the constant motion of mega-tons of treads, wheels, and steel shuddering us to our teeth, the ground beneath our feet trembles in an ongoing succession of tremors I'm sure is going to split the earth in half at any second and swallow us down in one big, dusty gulp.

Risking a glance over my shoulder, I can see a fleet of identical, muck-crusted, yellow dump trucks about a hundred yards back, pushing the whole caravan forward like sheep dogs wrangling a flock.

Trying to think logistically like I've been taught, I make a mental note: *We must be toward the back of the fleet.*

In between the rows of rigs, boys and girls of the Unsettled zip around on puttering dirt bikes or on battery-powered wheelchairs, kicking up dirt clouds, and appearing and disappearing around and under the enormous construction vehicles of the armada.

Laughing, some of them buzz us, and one of the bikes ridden by a girl with foggy green goggles over her eyes and a braid of thick black hair looped around her neck, comes close enough to brush the sleeve of my red leather jacket.

I kick at her but hit nothing but air as she pumps her fist and tears off, laughing and high-fiving her fellow bikers.

As Domino-teeth pushes us along, some of the younger Unsettled throw pebbles and fist-sized balls of aluminum foil at us from the windows and rooftops of the RVs, campers, and tractor-trailers we pass.

Like the Devoted's hodgepodge of a compound and Epic's underground lab-city, there's more to the Unsettled than I first realized. Yes. Everything is dirty and coated with layers of sand on top of layers of dirt and a foundational layer of permanent grime. Yes. It smells of burning oil, mold, old vegetables, animal fat, and a swampy miasma of flatulence and body odor. But it's still a city. Shuffling along in the middle of it, I'm already able to see some method in the middle of all the madness.

In addition to the symmetrical gaps between the vehicles that form a network of roads, people are trading and haggling under kiosk awnings on the sides of vans, which appear to serve as a series of shops. We pass a place where little kids are running around on the back of an open flatbed, playing some kind of full-contact soccer game. The sides of the open trailer are lined with high walls of black mesh to keep the ball from skittering off into traffic. Right after that, we come upon a similar trailer, only this one has steel grating around its exterior, while inside, five boys and five girls are engaged in a full-on, no-holds-barred, bare-knuckles blood-brawl.

At first glance, I think it must be some sort of punishment. But all ten of the kids—through bloody lips and missing teeth—are smiling, laughing, and seem absurdly happy.

All of it—the shoppers, the soccer players, the fighters, the machines, and us—are in creeping but constant motion.

Ducking the little stones and various bits of garbage and debris—mostly finger-sized twigs, orange peels, and more crumpled balls of tin foil—people keep throwing at us, we shuffle along. Guided by Domino-teeth and with three of the Unsettled, each armed with a holstered hunting knife and a chainsaw carried rifle-style in both hands, marching stiffly along on either side of us, we move in a right-angled pattern through the makeshift avenues of the moving city.

It's hot out, and although the Unsettled are dressed in drab layers of what looks like heavy, itchy clothing, I don't think I've seen any of them sweat.

Part of me is hoping we don't make it out of this alive. I don't want to have to report back to Kress about what happened. After the stunt I pulled by slipping out of school and spending the day with the Devoted before letting Matholook follow me back to the Academy, I think her faith in me is hanging on by a thread as it is.

From the back of our procession, Arlo calls out, "Is anyone else hungry?"

One of our Unsettled guards reaches out and tugs at the metal collar around Arlo's neck. Since we're all attached, the rest of us stumble but manage to avoid dragging each other to the ground.

"You're just in time for dinner," the guard laughs.

To eat it, or to be it? I wonder.

We finally arrive at the rear end of a long, slow-moving tractor-trailer.

We don't stop, though. (Nothing here seems to *ever* stop.) Instead, two women—maybe fifty-years-old or so—lift the latch handles and swing open the double doors at the back of the moving rig.

Domino-teeth slides the thick steel wire out of the loops of our collars and wraps it in a neat, clunky coil. We all breathe a generous exhalation of relief.

We may not be free. But at least we're not shackled anymore. I guess there's more than one definition of "freedom."

Domino-teeth hands the coiled wire-rope to a slump-shouldered boy who clips it to a carabiner on his belt. Another boy collects the collars from our necks. We all rub our necks where the collars have left a perfect red ring in our skin. Libra's the only one who thanks the boy, and he glares at her for a second through a snooty squint like she just asked permission to spit in his breakfast cereal.

Turning his attention to Domino-teeth, the second boy gives her a little salute and sprints up toward the cab of the tractor-trailer. Jumping up onto the foot-rail, he leans into the passenger-side window and has a conversation with the driver we can't see or hear from this far back.

"Up you go," Domino-teeth says to us with a splotchy but rather pleasant smile.

Like she's inviting us in for high tea.

"Into *there*?" Ignacio asks, peering into the gloomy dark of the trailer's interior.

"It's called the 'Trial Barge,'" she explains, her face rosy with glee.

That definitely doesn't sound like a place where they serve high tea.

At the no-nonsense insistence of the guards, we're forced to climb into the steaming steel box, and the double doors close shut behind us with a metallic finality that echoes in our ears.

Inside of the deep, empty trailer, we bump against each other with the rocking sway of the rig as it continues along with the rest of the moving city.

"What is this place?" Libra asks. Her voice sounds smooth and soft in the trailer's humid interior.

"Looks like a jail to me," I tell her.

"Aren't jails supposed to have bars?"

"You spent most of your life in a Processor," I remind her. "Did you see any bars in there?"

Libra drops her eyes and offers up a meek, "I guess not."

"At least it's roomier than that last rolling prison," Matholook says, his palms up in a make-the-most-of-it shrug.

Sara, looking more annoyed than worried or afraid, has Ignacio on one side of her and Arlo on the other. Turning back and forth between the boys, she asks, "Can't one of you do something?"

"What do you suggest?" Arlo asks through a wrinkled frown.

"I don't know. Ignacio, can't you short circuit this rig?"

Ignacio shakes his head. "I think maybe there's too many vehicles and people around. All the electrical energy is over-riding my brain. I've never been around this many machines before. They're all giving off an electrical energy signature. I'm used to it in small doses from my training sessions with Brohn. But this is a total, and honestly agonizing overload."

To emphasize the point, he presses his fingertips to his temples and rubs them in a slow circle.

"Besides," Arlo adds, his voice a molasses drawl, his head lolling down in defeat, "even if he could somehow stop this truck, what would we do after that? How would we get out? Where could we go?"

"True," I tell him, doing my best to stay positive but failing. "But not especially helpful."

"What about you?" Sara asks, swinging around to face me. "Or that white raven of yours?"

"I don't know where she is. Ignacio's right. There's something...disruptive about this place."

"Maybe it's all the smoke," Libra suggests.

"Maybe. That might stop Haida from trying to find us," I agree, tapping my temple. "But it doesn't explain why I can't even connect with her."

I almost tell them about my last couple of connections with Haida and the fuzzy images of war and the feelings of confinement and betrayal she shared. But until I get it all sorted out in my own head, it's probably best to keep the uncertain, unexplainable rubbish to myself.

Biting her lip and pressing her hand to the corrugated steel wall, Libra asks, "What do you think they're going to do to us?"

"Nothing good, I imagine," I sigh.

No sense sugar-coating the obvious, right?

Arlo cups his jaw in his hand and squints at me through the darkness. "They could have hurt or killed us a million times over if they wanted to. The fact that they haven't...well, it's not the worst sign in the world, right?"

"Maybe they don't want us at all," Ignacio suggests.

"What do you mean?"

He flicks a thumb toward Matholook. "Maybe they want *him*. The Devoted are their enemy, not us."

"*Everyone* is their enemy," I snap back.

"The Devoted did *not* do that back there," Matholook insists.

"Those Outposters were wrong. Or else they were lying. We spend half our lives keeping an eye on the Unsettled. They're out of control. Violent. Look at this place. Look at where we are, what they've done already. What they still might do."

"The girl who killed Mattea...," Libra begins.

"What about her?" I ask.

"She *looked* like an Unsettled. She dressed like them..."

"But?"

Libra folds her arms across her chest and leans against the truck's hot interior steel wall. "I'm starting to think maybe there's more going on here than we thought."

"You said it yourself," Matholook insists. "She looked like them. She dressed like them. She was armed like them. What makes you think she was anything other than an Unsettled murderer?"

After a brief pause while she appears to gather her thoughts, Libra nods and seems like she's ready to surrender the point. But then she reminds us that the Unsettled are almost never out alone. They have a reputation for killing but not for murder. And the Outposters knew details about the Devoted, and they didn't have any reason to lie about the invasion. "Something just isn't adding up," she finishes.

Next to me, Matholook tenses up, and I swear I can feel the heat of anger steaming from his body.

Before he can react to Libra, though, and before I can react to him, we all jump at a series of bangs and clunks that fill the steel-walled trailer. The wall at the far end of the trailer near the cab groans, cranks up, and starts to rise.

As bad as being captured and trapped in this steel box is, it's way better than knowing that the worst is almost certainly still to come.

14

CHARGED

With an ear-splitting refrain of metallic clanks and rattling clunks, the wall of horizontal sections up front by the cab rolls up, a foot at a time, to reveal a huge wooden desk and a massive, wide-armed, high-backed chair. Trimmed in gold and with a queue of shiny, ruby-red stones around its top edges, the desk extends nearly from wall to wall of the trailer's nine-foot-wide interior. The chair—dark wood decked out in chiseled star and crescent moon patterns and with burgundy pads on the arms and a matching burgundy pillow for a headrest—looks less like a random piece of Unsettled furniture and more like a throne for one of the Wealthies.

Like everything else around here, the furniture shifts and shimmies with the uneven roll of the tractor-trailer. The chair keeps knocking against the desk like it's an annoyed dog scratching at the back door, desperate to get back inside of a locked house.

Two banks of flickering yellow lights on black tripods behind and to either side of the enormous mahogany desk cast rakish shadows throughout the interior of the boiling hot space. Spotlight-bright and lava-hot, the lights illuminate every scratch, scrape, dent, and patch of dried blood on the walls and covering the wood-planked floors of our moving prison.

For the past five years, I've been accustomed to the clear, white holo-lights of the Academy or the sizzling cherry-red sunlight of the outdoors.

In here, glowing furnace hot, the old-style incandescent bulbs burning from the two light-stands feel Hellish and pointlessly aggressive.

Matholook and my Asylum and I all squint, blink a whole whack of times, and drape our arms over our eyes.

"I think they're trying to broil us," Libra guesses, her cheeks flushed and her forehead shiny with sweat.

Personally, I think "broiling" is an exaggeration, but it's sort of hard to disagree when I can feel the hairs on my forearms getting singed off.

From behind the lights, an adult man cries out in a grandiose baritone, "Level Two for the Governor's entrance!" and, as if in answer to the prayers of my frizzled, crispy-fried skin, the intensity of the array of lights drops a couple of notches. It's not much, but it's enough to let me know we're probably not going to be roasted alive. Yet.

I look over and exchange glances with Matholook and Libra who are on either side of me.

"That's a *little* better," Matholook sighs.

"Everyone okay?" I ask the rest of my Asylum.

"I've been 'okay-er,'" Ignacio grumbles from just behind my shoulder.

Sara is standing next to him, unnaturally calm, like she's about to yawn. Her eyes lock onto mine. "I'm not looking forward to dying," she confesses, "but yeah, I'm okay."

"Arlo?" I ask.

He drags the back of his hand across his scarred face and

then rubs the heels of both hands in little circles over his eyes. "The heat feels kind of nice, actually."

I can't tell if he's kidding or not. "I think you have defective pain receptors," I tell him.

"My pain receptors are a million times better than yours," he teases, and I can't help but smile.

A rustle and a scrum of commotion cause all of us to snap back to attention. Squinting into the light, we spot the motion of shadowy human figures. From out of the darkness behind the lights, a boy appears.

Escorted by an adult man on one side and an adult woman on the other—both dressed in matching white, terrycloth bathrobes—the boy steps around one of the two light-stanchions and positions himself, chin up and chest out, next to the wide-backed chair behind the huge wooden desk.

The boy's glossy black hair is neatly combed with a tidy part on one side. He has the orangish-olive skin of many of the Unsettled, but he's cleaner and more polished than most of the ones we've seen so far. He's decked out in an odd combination of a yellow dress shirt, an oversized plaid sport coat, ironed blue jeans two sizes too big, and thick-soled work boots. He's got small, round reading glasses perched on his nose, and a pair of heavy canvas work gloves on his hands. Thin and short but not frail, he looks like a twelve-year-old who couldn't decide if he wanted to be a business executive or a construction worker for Halloween. So he decided to raid his father's closet and go as both.

The adult man next to him, blond and scruffy faced with a few days' worth of silvery stubble, moves away to stand at ramrod attention off to the side while the woman, her dusty brown hair falling in a cascade of tangles over her face, hauls the clunky, high-backed chair out from under the desk and steps back as the boy hops into it. He looks small and swallowed-up in the large chair. With a clear line of sight under the front of the desk, I can see his feet don't quite touch the floor of the trailer.

After slipping off his thick work gloves and setting them neatly to the side, he draws a silver pen out of a cylindrical, pewter holder on the desk and taps it a few times against his knuckles before scrawling something onto a piece of yellow, curled-edged paper at the top of a pad. Tearing the sheet off with magisterial flourish, he hands the paper to the silver-stubbled man behind him. The man takes it with a little bow and hands it to the woman who skitters off with it, disappearing with a hunched-over gallop into the darkness behind the bank of lights.

As we're all still rattling around and trying to keep our balance in the constantly shaking trailer, the boy turns his attention to us. Pushing his wire-framed glasses up onto the bridge of his nose and then lacing his fingers in front of him, his elbows planted firmly on the table, he announces with arrogant gravity, "My name is Governor Angel Fire."

"Did he say, 'Angel Fire'?" Libra whispers.

"*Governor* Angel Fire," I correct her.

"Silence!" he shouts from behind his desk, and I choke back a laugh. His voice is high-pitched and about as intimidating as the average piccolo.

My amusement fades, however, when Silver-Scruff, standing protectively behind him, reaches under the flap of his bathrobe and draws out a modern-looking ARX-160 assault rifle and levels it straight at us. With a telescopic stock, a sixteen-inch barrel, and a grenade-launcher mounted underneath, it's a beast of a weapon.

We know from our lessons that guns like that are hard to come by. The Wealthies have commandeered or stockpiled most of the best weapons, and there's no telling if the one aimed at us right now is even loaded.

I'm not in a hurry to find out.

I drop my internal grin, and I can feel my Asylum tense up and shuffle a few inches back in the face of the potentially deadly weapon being aimed at us in very hot, very close quarters.

Although it's hard to conceive of the six of us dying in a hail of gunfire right here in the back of this steaming trailer-office of the Unsettled, it's not entirely *impossible* to imagine, either.

If my imagination had fingers, I'd cross them right now and hope there's some better fate in store for us.

Governor Angel Fire adjusts his fat-knotted tie, slides down from his monstrous chair, and walks over to Silver-Scruff. Placing his hand on the barrel of the menacing gun, he shakes his head. The armed man, his jaw clenching and unclenching, lowers his weapon and takes a half step back, as Governor Angel Fire walks around to the front of the desk. Hopping up, he sits on its front edge, looking for all the world like a ventriloquist's dummy with his face waxy, his feet dangling, and his skinny ankles exposed above the top of his clunky work boots. His speaking voice is slightly deeper than his shrill shouting voice when he tells us, "Unlike some of you scavengers left in the world, we Unsettled obey strict rules and codes of conduct."

I'm just about ready to ask him what he plans to do with us, but he cuts me off with a glare and a firmly raised hand.

"You thought you were following us," he says with a smile, "but really, it was the other way around in reverse."

"Isn't that a double negative?" Libra whispers in my ear.

"I'm not about to argue semantics with this kid," I mutter back through the corner of my mouth.

"What's wrong with that?" Ignacio beams, leaning over my other shoulder. "There's always time for some antics."

I give him a backhanded whack, which he absorbs with a wincing, embellished cry and a big step back.

"You've been charged with a crime," Angel Fire announces, pointing directly at Matholook.

Matholook presses a fingertip to his chest and looks back and forth between me and Angel Fire. "Me?"

"You are Devoted."

"Um...yes?"

"Step forward, Devoted."

Matholook complies, edging his way to the front of our group.

Angel Fire makes a show of glancing at his fingernails before polishing them on the lapel of his jacket. "You attacked an Unsettled caravan. You killed innocent Outposters."

Matholook's fingers curl into white-knuckled fists at his sides. "I didn't do that."

"I'm sorry. Perhaps it's my misunderstanding. Didn't you just agree that you're Devoted?"

"I am. But I didn't do that."

"So you distinguish between yourself and your people?"

"Of course. I'm an individual, not an entire community."

"I think the leaders of your Cult would disagree. Or do you pick and choose when you're going to be a 'you' and when you're going to be an 'us'?"

When Matholook doesn't answer, Angel Fire writes something on another sheet of crinkled paper and hands it to Silver-Scruff, who, clenched-jawed and tucking his gun under the lapel of his bathrobe, turns and passes the sheet to a second, shorter man—this one stocky, bare-chested, and hairy as a bear—standing next to one of the banks of lights.

"You are being charged with murder and will be held as a prisoner of war," Angel Fire declares, turning back with dramatic grandiosity to face Matholook.

I'm tempted to step forward and correct him. Despite what he and the Outposters claim, I still say there's no way the

Devoted would have killed all those people like that. And they sure as frack didn't kill Mattea.

I think?

But I can't imagine that raising my hand and pointing any of that out would go over very well.

"That's *Matholook*," Ignacio growls. His voice full of impatience and annoyance, he toggles his thumb between himself, Libra, Sara, Arlo, and me. "He's Devoted. What about the rest of us?"

I want to tell him to shut it and let this play out. His bravado is amusing in the Academy and helpful in battle, but this is a delicate situation that calls for a bit more discretion and self-control.

"We have something special in mind for you," Angel Fire announces with what I think is supposed to be a cheeky grin, but from here, it just looks like he's got a bad case of gas. "You are nameless. Unable to hear yourselves. You are on the run from Death. It's a race you can't hope to win, and it's the trying to do so that will ensure your loss. Do you have the power to live?"

The power to live?

Sweating and still huffing for breath in the steaming, enclosed trailer, we can only answer with blank stares. While we mill in place trying to figure out what the frack this baby-faced chabbie is talking about, he raises both arms in the air, his oversized plaid jacket bunching up around his ears.

With even more emphasis the second time, he shouts out, "Do you have the power to live?"

He pumps his fists in the air a few times, but then stops and whips around to scowl at the woman behind him. "That's your cue, Zephora!" he barks.

Flustered and blushing, the woman called Zephora—her bathrobe falling partly open before she manages to clutch its panels together around her chest—says, "Sorry! Sorry! Sorry!"

and springs into action, grabbing the hand of Silver-Scruff as they both go bolting backward behind the bank of lights.

As the two of them disappear behind a heavy red curtain, Angel Fire turns back to apologize to me and my friends. "Don't mind Zephora," he grins. "She hasn't been the same since she got her head stuck in a radiator grill of a military utility jeep a few years back. Still, she's loyal, and nobody's better than her at running our enemies through the Death Games."

I'm about to laugh, but then the weight of what he just said hits me.

Um...Death Games?

15

SELECTED

THE WOMAN CALLED Zephora and the silver-scruffed man return right away, each wheeling an angled, seven-foot tall lollipop-shaped object covered in a glossy black cloth.

The man positions one of the tall objects on the floor to one side of Angel Fire's desk and presses his boot to a silver bar on the wheels, locking it upright and into place. The woman does the same with the second covered object, repeating the man's motion of standing the round-topped post upright and locking it down to the floor of the trailer.

Looking like a pair of tall, swarthy ghosts, the two, black-clad stanchions sway with the rocking motion of the trailer.

At Angel Fire's direction, accompanied by an overly dramatic roll of his hands, the man and the woman slide the black sheets off of the twin objects to reveal two crude-looking clocks, each attached to the top of a metal pole.

Except instead of twelve like with traditional clocks, these clock faces are numbered in a circle of lightbulbs up to six with the oversized numbers scrawled in yellow chalk in what looks like the handwriting of a small child.

While we're taking all this in, Zephora ducks down behind

the big desk and draws out a silver, ice cream cone shaped microphone from one of the desk drawers and slides it into Angel Fire's waiting hand.

Tapping the head of the cordless microphone three times, she breathes into it and whispers, "Angel, Angel, Angel... Governor Angel Fire," her voice bouncing off the trailer's steel walls and ceiling and echoing in haunting waves from behind, in front, and all around us.

Thanking her, Angel Fire gives another head tilt and gestures to the shorter, bare-chested, hairy man standing in the shadows back by the red curtain.

There's an explosive grind of metal on metal that has me and my friends, startled, scrunched down, and clamping our hands over our ears. To our shock, the steel roof over our heads magically starts to peel back, sardine-can style. With the steaming hot lights turned off now and folded into recessed pockets in its panels, the truck's long rooftop rolls open, a single section at a time and with a grating *clunk-thunk-chunk*, until the blazing sunlight from overhead fills the steel-walled trailer.

As we put our arms up against the burning sun beating down on us, the trailer's four walls roll down as well. Grinding down in rolled-up sections, the walls disappear into fifty-foot-long metal storage lockers running the length of the trailer's sides until we're exposed on the open platform of what has morphed from a boxed-in trailer to a wide-open flatbed.

As if it's being chaperoned, the flatbed is flanked to the left and right by a pair of similar, open flatbed trailers. Only these two escort vehicles are loaded with steep, steel bleachers, filled with cheering and jeering members of the Unsettled.

Together, the three trailers chugging along, side-by-side-by-side, form a sort of rolling amphitheater among the rest of the roving city.

With us smack dab in the middle as the main event.

The whole thing is deafeningly loud. Libra still has her hands clamped to her ears and her chin tucked down to her chest in a futile effort to turtle herself away from the throbbing, bone-rattling clatter.

"You live in a school," Angel Fire announces into the microphone. Peppered with static and feedback, his amplified voice pounds out from a dozen clunky black speakers—square as a nightstand and squat as a knot of toads—set up facing in and out along the four edges of our trailer and held in place with a combination of rope, black tape, and heavy links of silver chains that rattle against the sides of the trundling rig. "I'm sure you have all kinds of fun activities to go along with your classes. Well, here's one you might enjoy. We're going to play a game." He turns to Zephora. "Give them an intro."

Zephora, easily old enough to be Angel Fire's mother (and, with their thin bones, oil-slick hair, and pouty lips, they even sort of look alike), shuffles forward, eyes down. With trembling fingers, she takes the microphone from him like it's a live hand-grenade.

With the crowds murmuring on either side of us from their bleachers or from the ground around us, she casts her eyes to the floor for a full five seconds before raising her head to address us. "You have been selected by Angel Fire, Governor of the Unsettled, for execution," she announces. Sad-eyed, sallow-skinned, and doing her best to hold her bathrobe shut with one hand while she grips the microphone with the other, she says the words robotically and by rote. Her facial expression barely changes as she speaks. "You have been consumed by the Unsettled, the Purifiers of the Plains. Lords of the Lowlands. Disinfectants of the Deserts. However, in his great and magnificent mercy, Angel Fire, Governor of the Unsettled, has agreed to allow you the chance to settle your debts. Let it not be said that the Unsettled are savage or without mercy or reason. This game will end with a winner and a corpse. Which you end up as is up to you. You may select one of your group to represent the rest."

Angel Fire snatches the microphone from Zephora's hand and shoves her backward. She staggers into the arms of Silver-Scruff, who delicately escorts her into the backstage darkness behind the heavy, blood-red curtain separating the now-open flatbed from its smoke-belching cab up front.

It's odd seeing the kids in charge and the older Unsettled treated like kids. I thought that kind of reversal would sit well with me, but it doesn't.

Angel Fire lowers his head for several seconds while the crowds around us mumble and buzz. The few dozen spectators in the flatbeds on either side of us are joined in their murmuring by what must be a few hundred more teenagers, packed ten-deep and walking alongside of us.

"It's called...," Angel Fire drones for dramatic effect and then pauses. With a big, looping arc, he tilts the microphone out toward the escort trailers and their dozens of teen and pre-teen rowdy riders and the walking crowds around us, who all scream in unison over the roar of engines and the thrum of tires, "Debate! To! The! Death!"

"That's right!" Angel Fire cries, tilting the microphone back toward his mouth. "A game of fun, a trial for truth, and a debate to the death. You'll love it!" He promises. "Or hate it," he adds from behind his hand and to the whoops and cheers of the seated and marching spectators. "It all depends on how you do! Let's have some fun!" Turning to us, he adds, "If you're going to die, you might as well die playing a game, right?"

"How about if we don't play the game *and* we don't die?" Ignacio mutters from behind me.

"I doubt that's an option," I mutter back.

Angel Fire hands the microphone to a stringy-haired girl who can't be much older than ten or eleven years old. Her dress is a burlap sack cinched at the waist with a length of braided wire. She's barefoot, and the skin on her legs is patchy with ashy scales. Her voice is strained and mousy as she cheerily blasts off a list of rules, halting here and there as she struggles to pronounce some of the bigger words.

"The Governor hereby challenges your...repro...representative to intel...intellectual mortal combat. A Battle of the Brains. The Governor will present a topic for consideration."

(She badly botches the word "consideration," and it takes me a full three seconds to figure out what she said.)

"Your repro...representative will debate the topic with Governor Angel Fire," she struggles on. "Every point you win will get you closer to freedom. Every point the Governor wins will get you closer to being a snack for the vultures."

When I hear the word "snack," my heart does a little jump. We've heard about how the Unsettled sometimes eat people, so knowing our dead bodies might wind up in the gullet of a buzzard instead of chopped up as dinner for the Unsettled is a strange sort of relief.

"And now," the little girl announces with a grand squeak like a carnival barker on helium, "let the Debate to the Death begin!"

16

DEBATE

THE HOOTING KIDS on the trailer to the right of ours part way for twelve teenagers dressed head to toe in yellow robes with baggy sleeves and deep, oversized hoods.

One by one, the yellow-clad figures hop up onto the moving trailer and take their seats in the front row, stooping under a canvas shade-awning as they go and plopping down one at a time onto the long steel bench.

The girl in the lead is a tower of height, with traces of wild, purple and black hair bursting out in a frizzy mane from under her hood. Like motherless ducklings, the twelve teens waddle up, apparently arranged by height, with the last of the brood a wisp of a boy whose oversized robe seems to envelop him as he takes his seat at the far end of the silver bench.

Governor Angel Fire, microphone in hand, paces back and forth and prowls the edges of our flatbed, calling out to the assembled crowds all around us as he goes. "The Arbiters," he cries, pointing to the twelve ducklings, "are prepared to judge. Are you all prepared to bear witness?"

The seated crowds and the ones walking on the ground roar their confirmation.

"Debate!" Angel Fire shrieks into the microphone.

"To the death!" the audiences holler back.

He does this a whole whack of times, skulking back and forth on our flatbed like an undersized panther with a pelt of fur too big for his adolescent body.

He whoops the Unsettled on the two flanking rigs into a frenzy. (Except for the twelve hooded ducklings. Like all of us, they shift and jostle with the motion of the flatbeds, but otherwise, they stay stone-faced and stock-still.)

Angel Fire's voice competes with the grumbling engines, grinding gears, the whooping Unsettled spectators, and the thrum of thousands of treads and tires from countless vehicles spread out over miles of barren, red desert.

The speakers convert Angel Fire's thin, flimsy voice into a crisp, metallic roar.

"Today," he announces to the assembled crowds, "we will be debating the idea of Emergents. Not their existence, mind you. That's a *fait accompli*. A given."

The crowds boo and hurl pellets of crumpled aluminum foil at us. It's harmless, but disproportionately annoying, and I've got half a mind to leap across the few feet of space from our flatbed to one of the ones next to us and single-handedly separate the heads of a few of the obnoxious chuffers from their jostling, trash-throwing bodies.

Microphone clenched in both hands and pressed to his lips, Angel Fire continues to skulk around our flatbed. "Emergents have been rumors. They've been myths. They've been experiments. They've been a weapon in Krug's arsenal and a thorn in his side. And they've been hailed and feared as the harbinger of human extinction."

The boos and jeers of the crowds turn into a few light claps followed by a round of scattered, tepid applause.

"What Emergents have *not* been is judged."

Now, the crowds burst into a full-on, fist-pumping hail of rowdy shouts.

Angel Fire wags his finger. "Today, that will change."

He does a one-hundred-eighty degree pivot on his heel, toggling between the two flatbeds accompanying ours and then scanning all the fist-pumping spectators on the ground, who are shuffling along and pushing themselves up onto each other's shoulders to get a better view.

"Before the Port Grandstand," he says, facing the open trailer on our left, "and the Starboard Grandstand," he adds, facing the trailer on our right, "I will be arguing that Emergents—no matter how glorified—are more of a bane than a boon. More devil than angel. And more of a danger than they're worth. I will be debating for fun. The accused will be debating for their lives."

The crowds filling the so-called Port and Starboard Grandstands break into a coordinated chant of "For—their—lives!" and rain down another volley of aluminum foil balls at us.

Growling, Ignacio takes a step toward one of the flanking rigs. Even though he's not impulsive or dumb enough to try to take them on, Arlo clamps a preventative hand onto his collar and drags him back into our huddled group, just in case.

I slip my own hand into Matholook's before I even realize I've done it. His fingers curl around mine, and he draws me closer to him so my shoulder is pressed snugly against his upper arm. Although the flatbed continues to pitch and toss and despite Angel Fire sounding like he's about to sentence us all to death, I feel oddly secure.

Angel Fire trots over toward the Starboard Grandstand where he motions for the twelve hooded ducklings to rise.

Spinning back in a dainty pirouette to face us, he announces, "You will hereby be judged by the Jury of the Unsettled. They will ensure fairness throughout the debate."

"Right," I mumble. "Totally fair to get judged by the same people who've already condemned you."

Angel Fire paces perilously close to the edge of the flatbed with a gap of only a few feet of empty desert space between him and the twelve yellow ducklings. "Matholook is charged with murder," he informs the hooded jury. "The rest of the prisoners you see behind me are being charged with being Emergents."

"He's no murderer! And being an Emergent isn't a crime!" I shout across the space between us.

Angel Fire whips around to face me. "No," he grins. "It's *multiple* crimes."

He slaps the microphone onto his palm three times before raising it back to his mouth, puckering his lips like he's about to give it a sloppy kiss. "You have been accused of a crime. That makes you, by definition, a criminal."

The crowds around us boo and hiss. Some of them throw more foil and smooth white pebbles at us until they're told to stop by the guards of the Unsettled flanking them on either side.

Watching over the crowds, the guards are all adults—male and female and a few whose gender I can't tell at all—and are all olive or mocha-skinned like most of the Unsettled. Robust and muscular, they're all topless but are wearing rainbow-striped haram pants. They each have a black leather strap running diagonally across their bare chest with a three-foot machete hanging from their hip. Male or female or androgynous (in London, they'd be called "Sexbrids"), they're also all completely hairless. No head hair. No body hair. No eyebrows. It's hard to tell from here, but I don't think they even have eyelashes. Like the duckling jurors, their stoic focus stands in stark contrast to the rowdy crowds of teens around them. Their colorful pants scream fun and frivolity. Their knives and faces scream death.

Angel Fire paces in front of me and my five friends. He pauses in front of Ignacio and inspects him head to toe before giving him an impressed nod. Shaking his head, he plants himself directly in front of me. "You are violations of evolution *and* of technology."

I open my mouth, but he cuts me off with a raised finger. "You'll have your turn." One hand clasped behind his back and the microphone in the other, he turns his attention to the crowds around us. "By any definition of Fate, biology, or the intervention of God, Emergents weren't meant to be. They were created in labs from the synthesis of biogenetic and digital code and were manufactured as weapons of war." Switching his microphone from one hand to the other, Angel Fire makes two dramatic sweeps with his arms, taking in the now quiet and attentive crowds. "The fact that some of them don't know they were designed as weapons doesn't make them any less danger-ous...or any less guilty of violating every law of ethics and every rule of war known to humanity."

He lowers the microphone and takes a small bow as the crowds look on. He waves his hand at Zephora, who shuffles over to his desk and draws a second microphone out of one of the drawers.

"So," Angel Fire drawls, "who's it going to be?"

Almost without hesitation and definitely without consulting my Asylum, I raise my hand. "Don't worry," I assure my friends with a half-turned head and through the corner of my mouth. "I can handle this."

On cue from Angel Fire, Zephora swings her arm and tosses the second microphone underhand to me in a spinning arc. I catch it in a smooth scoop, with Angel Fire giving me an approving nod.

Calm as a clam, I lean forward, my lips to the head of the mesh-topped microphone. "There's a difference between *being* a violation and committing one."

Out of the corner of my eye, I catch the ducklings making

small motions with their fingers over a small black-mirrored pad each one has fixed to the palm of one hand.

There's a beat of silence, and I'm not sure anyone heard what I said. But then, from somewhere up front by the trailer's cab, a gong of some sort chimes out in a vibrating peal. Over on one side of Angel Fire's desk, the sharp-ended arm of one of the numbered stanchions toggles to the number "1."

Angel Fire's face drops into a melty pout. Next to me, Math-olook claps me on the back. "Nice going! We're winning!"

I answer with a shrug and a blush. "Nothing to it."

A little cheer goes up from the rest of my Asylum behind me, although it's quickly suppressed by a chorus of hisses from the crowds and a barrage of menacing glares from the bare-chested guards, who don't look too happy about my side taking an early lead.

For their part, the yellow-clad jurors—finished logging what I'm assuming must have been their vote—return to being rigid, unblinking, and pretty much expressionless. If they weren't rocking back and forth in their makeshift jury box, I don't think they'd be moving at all.

Angel Fire shakes his head, clearly unwilling to admit defeat, even of the smallest point. "Being a violation is far worse than committing one. The act follows the being. The corruption of the act reflects the corruption of the being. You are a corrupt being, a plague, a cancer, an origin of a path leading humanity away from itself."

Her chin on my shoulder, Libra whispers in my ear. "Did this kid swallow a philosophy textbook?"

I'd probably laugh out loud...if we weren't apparently on trial for our lives.

Libra's right, though. This Angel Fire kid is smarter than I thought. He must have studied a lot or maybe he's a savant or something. Either that, or else he's really good at faking it.

"But what if we're leading humanity down a better path?" I ask, stepping forward, trying to match his tone, confidence, and posturing.

The squat black speakers are barely enough to overcome the ambient noise sending shuddering waves through the air and vibrating my skin. I've never spoken into a microphone before, and I'm horrified at how high and whiny my voice sounds.

Not sure if the crowds—and especially the judges—heard me, I raise the microphone to my lips and repeat my question: "What if us Emergents are leading humanity down a *better* path?"

Angel Fire points past me toward Matholook, who's standing sheepishly behind my shoulder. "The Devoted can answer that. The cowardly leader pushes from the back. The despotic leader drags from the front. A *true* leader—the best and most ideal leader—guides from the side." The twelve ducklings fiddle with their palm-pads, the gong chimes again for Angel Fire's side, and the arrow-shaped arm on the other stanchion points to "I." Reveling in quickly tying up the score, Angel Fire spreads his arms wide. "There has never been a time in history when people with power didn't exploit that power."

"Kind of like you're doing now?"

A rumble of "Oohs" and a chorus of finger-snaps rises up from the jostling crowds on the ground and from the audiences seated on our two companion flatbeds.

Angel Fire smiles. "This is an inquiry whose end result will be justice."

"On your terms."

After tucking the microphone under his arm and adjusting the oversized knot in his tie, he offers up a dismissive shrug. "You've been given the right to defend yourself."

"A right given to us by you, which means you can also take it away. Isn't that the definition of unchecked power?"

The ducklings fidget, the gong chimes, the scoring clock dings, the arm moves to "2," and another point is added to our side.

Angel Fire scowls at the clock, now showing a score of two to one, like it's personally offended him before pivoting back to me. "Are you aware of the Singularity?"

"Yes," I sigh into the microphone, wondering where on earth he could be going with this. "It's when artificial intelligence catches up to human intelligence. And then surpasses it. Do I look like a self-aware supercomputer to you?"

Laughing, Angel Fire shakes his head and tosses me a condescending smirk before striding forward and pacing in front of me and my Asylum. "Scientists, philosophers, bio-technicians...they were right about the Singularity. They were just wrong about the two component pieces. It's not artificial intelligence and the human mind that were on a collision course. It was genetic code and binary code. The double-helix and the bits and bytes of ones and zeros. Long thought to be separate, they have turned out to be two dialects of a single language. And you are the Rosetta Stone."

I know from Kress a bit about the confluence of binary and genetic code. But Angel Fire must see the confusion etched in my face because he pauses and takes a long look around at the crowds, now mostly silent and leaning forward, although I can't tell if it's in anticipation or confusion.

Around us, wheels and treads continue to grind, diesel engines continue to cough up exhaust, and mag-generators continue to hum. But what was once an oppressive sensory overload has started to fade into the background thrum of life, and I remember something my mother said about a place she once visited in this country called Niagara Falls. "It's a thunderous, astonishing sight and sound," she gushed. "But people who live close to the Falls lose the ability to hear it."

Is that what's happening here? Are we getting used to the chaos of the Army of the Unsettled? And is that a good thing, or is it the worst thing imaginable?

"Do you know what that is," Angel Fire asks through a smug grin. "The Rosetta Stone?"

"I know it's something that used to be in the British Museum," I answer.

I know what I'm talking about. Unlike anyone else here, I've actually *been* to the British Museum. Well, I've scavenged in the rubble. Before I let myself get taken to the St. Paul's Processor, I spent a lot of my days exploring the city and seeing how close I could get to the Banters of Hyde Park or to the Royal Fort Knights of Buckingham Palace without getting caught, captured, or killed. Along the way, I foraged in the ruins of some of the city's museums, although I didn't spend too long inside any one of them. There were too many dangers, including from random gangs and from the very real possibility an entire building would fall down on top of me.

"The Rosetta Stone," Angel Fire explains with a snootiness that makes me want to punch him in the face, "was an ancient decree from around 32 BCE, written in hieroglyphs, Egyptian script, and Ancient Greek. The message in the three languages was rather basic. It simply said that the priests supported King Ptolemy. But out of that elemental proclamation came the key to unlocking countless ancient mysteries."

"Is this a debate or a history lesson?" Ignacio heckles from behind me.

But then he has to cover his head with his arms and duck as a hail of those tiny white pebbles rains down on us from the annoyed audience.

"In either case," Angel Fire continues, "you represent the culmination of technology and the end of humanity."

I risk letting out a little chuckle. "Maybe that's for the best. You've seen what humanity is capable of."

I expect a point for that, but the crowd stays quiet, and the numbers on our lollipop-shaped clock don't change.

Amplified over a high-pitched screech of feedback, Angel Fire's voice rises through the air, pushed along by the momentum of his confidence. "Humanity is capable of great ignorance, uncontrollable fear, and the worst depths of irrational violence. But we're also capable of growth and change. Emergents leap over that growth and change."

He glances at the ducklings, whose fingers skitter over their palm-pads. The arm of his clock ticks forward, the second bulb on his side lights up, his score pings up to "2," and the crowds belt out their most enthusiastic cheer yet.

Frack. Tied. Two to two.

Trying to counter his rather insulting claim about us being some kind of shortcut, evolutionary cheat-code, I decide to turn the tables on him. "Maybe our role as Emergents is to guide Typics in the right direction."

Damn! I shouldn't have said "maybe." It makes me sound unsure.

Angel Fire scoffs at this. "You say 'guide.' I say 'force.'"

The gong peals. His clock dings again as the arm points to "3," the third bulb glows yellow, and the crowds cheer, pumping their fists in the air or clapping their hands heartily over their heads in the anticipation of their leader's victory.

Leading three to two, he's halfway to victory, which means me and my Asylum are halfway to death. "We have the right to live!" I cry.

Frack. That sounded more like a whine than a reasonable argument.

"No more so than any other specimen from a lab," Angel Fire answers with breezy composure.

"Why do we scare you so much?" I ask.

"You don't scare me...you scare all of us."

"Why?"

"Because you represent...no...you *are* a harbinger of doom. You will either lead us, replace us, enslave us, or destroy us." The crowds around us growl their agreement. "In any case, your presence means our time on earth is over."

The gong clangs, the next bulb burns bright, and the arm on his score-counter ticks to "4" while my score stays locked at "2."

"It doesn't have to mean that," I remind him.

"It *shouldn't* have to mean that. But history tell us it can never mean anything else."

I know how desperate I must sound when I point an accusing finger at him. "Your people invaded the Devoted compound. You kidnapped a little girl."

"We attacked an enemy who had already attacked us, and we left with a weapon of war. And unless you've forgotten, you stole her from us and returned her to them so she could be used against us."

"A little girl is not a weapon of war."

"Said the little girl who is a weapon of war."

The crowds erupt in a mocking, "Oooooh!"

"I'm not a little girl," I object once the taunts and jeers die down. "And I'm definitely not a weapon."

"You are the worst kind of weapon. Unflinching. Unafraid. Deadly. And it doesn't matter what side you're on. You go in the direction you're pointed."

The gong sounds. The scoring arm ticks to "5."

Oh, frack. He's ahead five to two. This isn't good.

"We haven't been pointed in any direction."

"Even worse," Angel Fire laughs into his microphone, and the crowd laughs along with him. "And also very untrue. Your Academy is training you to put an end to us."

How does he even know about the Academy?

"Our Academy is training us to use our abilities," I say with a pout of righteous indignation.

"Right. To put an end to us."

"No! To put an end to war!"

"And how, exactly, do you plan to do that? Wars can't be defeated. Only the people waging them can. Don't kid yourself, Branwynne of the Emergents Academy. Every soldier thinks their side is the right side...to the degree that they think at all."

I don't know how to respond to this other than to press my lips together and scowl at him.

I glance up at the two scoring posts. He's way ahead, and I'm getting anxious. Behind me, Matholook and my Asylum mutter their encouragement. "You can do this," they assure me.

"Emergents are an abomination," Angel Fire declares. "You upset the balance of power."

"Good," I snap. "Power *needs* to be unbalanced. Otherwise, it becomes solidified and crushes all of us under its weight."

When I say, "us," I gesture, not just to me and my friends, but to the audiences around us and to the Army of the Unsettled, in general.

That gets me three seconds of silence and then a few bits of scattered applause from the spectators. The gong sounds, and the clock on our side ticks to "3." From behind me, Libra shakes my arm and whispers, "Nice job!"

Angel Fire lowers his head, and I feel a surge of adrenaline rush through me.

Maybe I can win this thing, after all.

When he looks up again, he seems sort of sad. When he leans into the microphone this time, I can barely hear him.

"Emergents are better than the rest of us," he concedes. "You're too strong. Too advanced. Too close to the ultimate goal of defying Death. These aren't things to be celebrated. These are things to be feared and expunged." He takes a deep breath like he regrets what he's about to say, but then he soldiers on. "Maybe someday we'd all get to where you are. But we're not there yet. You'll claim to want to take us with you, but you will outpace us and ultimately overpower us. What's going to happen when—instead of guns and the genocidal weapons of the Patriot Army—the next President Krug has an army of Emergents at his disposal?"

He drops his hand to his side, the microphone dangling from his pinched fingers.

Out of the corner of my eye, I see the ducklings entering their scores.

Oh, frack.

The long hand of the giant clock on Angel Fire's side toggles to "6," and there's a single second of cemetery silence before the audiences around us burst into a foot-stomping, chest-thumping thunder of explosive cheers.

Looking strangely downcast for someone who just won, Angel Fire turns his back to the raucous crowds and walks over to stand in front of me and my Asylum, covering the top of his microphone as he does.

"Don't tell," he says, looking even smaller than before as he takes a wide-legged stance in front of us. "But I was secretly rooting for you."

"That's great," Ignacio says, sidling up next to me and glaring down at the shorter boy in front of us. "So that means you'll let us go then?"

Angel Fire shakes his head. "Unfortunately, I'm as bound as you are by the rules of the Debate to the Death."

Turning to his adoring fans, he raises the microphone back to his mouth and announces for everyone to hear, "Thank you all for coming out to the Debate to the Death! The *debate* part is done. Only *death* remains!"

17

VERDICT

"THE TWELVE ARBITERS have done their duty. You lost the debate and lack the power to live. I hereby declare you guilty of all charges."

Angel Fire raises his arms and pumps his fists. The sleeves of his oversized sports coat drop down in crumpled wrinkles around his spindly, hairless arms.

The crowds sway and break into a chant of "Hereby guilty!" as the trio of flatbeds lurches and rumbles along.

Libra nudges her way between Ignacio and Arlo. "What's that mean?" she asks me, her hand on my shoulder.

It means we're about to die.

When I don't respond to her right away, she steps forward, her hands cupped around the sides of her mouth as she shouts out across the Trial Barge at Angel Fire, "What does that mean?"

"It means," Angel Fire proclaims, taking a few steps toward us, his mouth to his microphone, "that you five Emergents are hereby sentenced to death for being Emergents." The crowds applaud at this, to Angel Fire's clear delight. He waves them down and holds up a "But wait—there's more!" finger. "The

Emergents are sentenced to death for being Emergents," he repeats and then adds, "the Devoted named Matholook is hereby sentenced to death for war crimes committed in the name of his Cult."

"Death?" Ignacio barks out from behind me. "Isn't that a little extreme?"

Angel Fire shakes his head. "Not as extreme as letting any of you live."

He's rewarded with a cacophony of hoots and howls from his adoring fans.

"This guy *really* doesn't like us, does he?" Sara says from the back of our assembled Asylum. She inspects her fingernails before crossing her arms across her chest. "I can see wanting to sentence *Ignacio* to death...but the rest of us?"

Ignacio says, "Hey!" and I put a hand on his chest and reassure him that Sara's just taking the piss.

Ignacio clamps a hand to his crotch. "I've got a piss she can take right here."

"Nice," I say with a shake of my head, increasingly baffled by Sara's casual taunting. I dip my head and tilt my chin down, keeping my voice low so Angel Fire won't hear me. "Forget the joking around for two seconds," I mumble to my Asylum. "We're going to have to fight."

"We don't have weapons," Libra moans in a defeated whisper.

"And we're outnumbered about a million to one," Sara points out, sounding almost gleeful and with what I swear is a happy twinkle in her eyes.

Is she actually rooting for us to die?

Despite her constant porkies and pissing around, she's the least combative of all of us, so I can't imagine where this casual smugness of hers is coming from. She's either suicidal, naffing crazy, off-the-charts-indifferent...or else there's something else going on, and shame on me for not being able to figure it out.

Taking a split second to center myself, I do my best to connect with Haida Gwaii. She's out there. She's tracked us down. It's not wishful thinking. I can *feel* it. I don't need advice at the moment. What I *do* need is the opportunity to channel her abilities. We might not have our weapons, but Haida's speed, agility, relative strength, and heightened senses surging through me can more than make up for my confiscated Serpent Blades.

Ever since I was a little girl, I always felt more confident amid chaos, like I could take on an army if it came down to it.

It looks like it just came down to it.

Haida's consciousness trickles into mine, and I curl my fingers into fists, bracing myself for the surge of strength and adrenaline I'm about to feel. But then the trickle fades into a slow, drippy leak. And then, it's gone.

Ignacio's right. There's something affecting us here, and I don't think it's just the stress of captivity, the constant bumpiness and noise, or even the choking swirls of wind and sand that make simple things like talking and breathing a draining challenge. It's almost like there's a psychic energy hanging over this place. We all know about the Unsettleds' notorious Systems Diode Dampener, their go-to tool for stopping mechanical energy in its tracks. Could there be some sort of mental equivalent out there? Have they found some way of inhibiting our Emergent abilities? If so, we may be in more trouble than I thought. (And I already thought we were in the most serious trouble of our lives.)

"If we have to fight," Ignacio whispers, "we might as well go all in." Turning to me, he asks if I have any inspirational last words.

"I do," I tell him. "But our last words are going to happen a long time from now and far away from here."

"If only optimism were an Emergent ability...," Arlo chuckles, without a trace of amusement or humor and absently dragging his fingertip along one of the wavy scars running from just below his jawline down to his collar bone.

"Maybe we can get out of this without fighting or dying," Matholook suggests, barely loud enough for us to hear. He loops his fingers around my wrist and raises my arm up to his mouth so he can lean into my microphone. "We would like to invoke the Appeal Decree."

I get a pang of jealousy and embarrassment when his voice, belting out through the squat black speakers, sounds so much more confident and authoritative than mine did during my failed Debate to the Death.

What is it about guys that gives their voices such legitimacy? Are their deep, authoritative voices the reason why they keep winding up in charge of the world? Then again, Angel Fire has the voice of a slightly hoarse baby bird, and he seems to be running this entire desert army. So who knows?

As Matholook's poised and self-assured voice fades into the ether, the crowds go weirdly quiet, and Angel Fire's eyes grow comically wide. He's got the build of a malnourished, nine-year-old boy and the thin bones and small facial features of a spider monkey. So it's sort of hilarious to see his eyes expand into two white, perfectly round casserole dishes.

After the bug-eyed stare, he squints his confusion, which I share, and asks Matholook, "How—how do you know about the Appeal Decree?"

I was about to ask the same thing! Just when I think I've got Matholook figured out, he unveils some new knowledge or some new way of seeing the world and of understanding things no one out here has any business understanding. The mystery of him confuses, annoys, and attracts me in equal proportions.

Matholook is leaning over the microphone like he's going to say something else, but he doesn't.

The caravan is still chugging along with all of us swaying with the oceanic motion of the flatbed. The desk, lights, score-keeping clocks, and speakers are rattling as loud as before. But the silence of the once-cheering crowds seems to have dropped the total decibel level down about a hundred notches.

Angel Fire clears his throat. Twice.

"Are you invoking your right to a Forgiveness Hearing, here and now on the Trial Barge?"

"We are," Matholook says into the microphone, his lips close enough for me to feel the heat of his breath on the back of my hand. "As outsiders, it's the only way to exercise our rights to the Appeal Decree, correct?" He's asking a question, but it still sounds just as much like he's stating a fact.

Angel Fire walks all the way over to us, lowering his own microphone to his hip as he approaches. Matholook straightens up and smiles down at the slim, younger boy, who doesn't return the smile.

Angel Fire pushes up the sleeves of his oversized blazer. "You are a Caretaker."

"I am."

"Not a strategist or a warrior?"

"No."

"And yet you seem to know your enemy."

"I know a little bit about a potential friend," Matholook smiles.

Angel Fire leans in close, so his head is right between mine and Matholook's. His voice is a penetrating, serpent-y hiss. "The two of you don't fool me."

"No one's trying to fool you," I tell him. "We're just trying to get back home."

"Now that your spy mission has failed, you mean, right?"

"We're not spies," Matholook tells him. "We are survivors, like you. We have hope for a better future, like you. Branwynne and her fellow Emergents want to end the war before it starts. Just like you do."

"And what makes you think we want to end the war as opposed to *win* it?" Angel Fire asks.

Shrugging, Matholook asks, "Am I right?"

Tense and baffled, I snap my gaze back and forth between Angel Fire and Matholook.

"You've been sentenced to death," Angel Fire says at last, stroking his jaw and chin like he has a beard, which he most definitely doesn't. Slightly pimply, he's got to be another couple of years away from being able to boast facial hair. "And since you're dead," he drawls, "why should I bother negotiating with a ghost?"

"I'm not dead yet," Matholook says with a charming, brotherly smile. "And neither are you. Now...about the Appeal Decree..."

Angel Fire smiles back, and I expect him to be bitter or angry or something. But he grins and says, "I'm impressed" before turning back to face the curious, restless audiences surrounding us.

"The invocation of the Appeal Decree has been invoked," he announces into the microphone. When the audiences murmur their dissatisfaction, Angel Fire makes a pumping-the-brakes motion with his hand and tells the crowds how proud they should be. "Making and living by our own laws is easy. The sign of a community's success is when the enemy knows them and lives by them as well."

He's answered with a chorus of reluctant muttering, grumbling, and an assortment of headshakes and a few equally vigorous head nods.

In the audience, a girl with her head shaved on one side and a light-brown braid of hair on the other thrusts herself to her feet and calls out, "Appeal Decree!" Her voice is barely audible, but it has the desired effect. Her chant spreads like a desert brush fire until everyone in the two flatbeds is chanting it, and I'm doing a round of mental head-scratching as I try to determine what Matholook just did, how he did it, and if doing it is going to result in us being magically freed or, more likely, hacked to pieces by these nutters and left in the desert as a midafternoon snack for the vultures.

Laughing, Angel Fire gestures for the two crowds to keep it going, which they seem more than happy to do. Stomping hard enough to shake the steel bleachers under them, the crowds in the grandstands keep calling out "Appeal Decree!" until Angel Fire finally shouts out, "Okay! Okay!" into the microphone before turning his attention back to us. Well, back to Matholook, actually.

"You know our laws," he says, his hand cupped over the top of his microphone so it won't pick up his voice. "Some might say that makes you dangerous. Or a spy. We say it makes you aware enough to be given the benefit of the doubt." He scans Matholook up and down like he's a prize horse before raising the microphone back to his lips. "The Appeal Decree has been invoked by our enemy and accepted by our spectators. I hereby declare it will be done. The prisoners will be pardoned!"

Before I realize what I'm doing, I hurl myself into Matholook's arms and kiss him full on the lips. He loops his arms around my waist and lifts me a little until I'm on my tiptoes in front of him, my chest pressed to his, my arms draped over his shoulders with my hands clasped around his neck.

For a second (okay, more like ten glorious, heart-skipping, skin-tingling seconds), I forget where we are. I forget about the rest of my Asylum, Angel Fire, and the crowds of the Unsettled with all their guards and their yellow-clad, twelve-person jury. As far as I'm concerned, the world can finish going to Hell.

Just let me enjoy this moment of relief with Matholook!

I don't know which one of us pulls back first, but—with the Unsettled audience "oohing" and "aahing" their cheeky delight —I wipe my lips with the back of my hand, clear my throat, and turn to Matholook,

I *almost* say, "I love you," but I chicken out and go with an alternative that I hope is just as true. "You saved our lives!"

The burning sensation in my cheeks isn't from the sun.

Without taking his eyes from mine, he grins and reminds me that he's always happy to help.

"So...how does this work?" Libra asks, her eyes darting in suspicion. "Do we have to plead our case to a panel or something?"

"Or prove how we don't deserve to die just for being who we are?" Ignacio adds.

"Or...," Arlo drawls, "can we maybe just *go*?"

Angel Fire waves his hands back and forth. "No, no. Nothing like any of that."

"Then what—?" I start to ask.

"By our own rules, you are free to go."

"Really?"

"Well, no. Not really. There's a caveat."

"A what?"

"It's a set of conditions," Matholook explains.

"What conditions?" I growl, glaring at Angel Fire.

"To prove your worth," he responds, "and to satisfy our doubts, you'll need to prepare yourselves for combat."

At the word "combat," Ignacio taps me on the shoulder. "I don't like the sound of that."

Arlo thrusts himself between me and Ignacio, his arms draped across our shoulders, the scars around his mouth stretched back toward his ears along with his wide smile. "Don't be so glum. Freedom is the only thing worth dying for."

It's not the only thing worth dying for, I think, as the sweet warmth of my spontaneous, moderately embarrassing public kiss with Matholook continues to tingle on my lips.

18

MIND APPEAL - LIBRA

ANGEL FIRE SCANS us all once. Then twice. And then a third time.

He beckons with his finger for the first and last in the line of the twelve hooded ducklings to step forward.

Holding onto the guardrails of the small bridge extending out between their flatbed and ours, the small boy and the tall girl—she's got to be Ignacio's height plus another six inches—shake and wobble their way across the space between the two rigs.

As if they've never done this before, the boy and the girl approach Angel Fire with the delicate caution (bordering on quivering terror) of two field mice passing by a rattlesnake's burrow.

Agitated, Angel Fire hurries them over with a flurried back and forth wave of his hand.

Gathering up their yellow, gown-length robes, they scurry over to him.

He motions for the girl to lean down and for the boy to come closer and has a private, three-headed discussion with the two Arbiters, who gesture wildly with their hands and cast shaded looks at me and my Asylum before nodding and taking up flanking, straight-backed positions at either side of their boss.

Tucking his microphone into his belt and with ceremonial flourish, Angel Fire puts one hand on the shoulder of the smaller boy and reaches his other up to land on the shoulder of the much taller girl. The flatbed is the standard fifty-three-foot length, which is just long enough to prevent me from being able to make out much of the details of the girl's face at this distance. And her hood obscures most of her features, anyway.

But there's no hiding the stage fright she's got etched in her eyes.

With bored, sagging eyes, her smaller counterpart doesn't seem as openly frightened, although he's now chewing on the skin around his index finger with enough ferocity to make me think he might gnaw off his own arm if this little moment of Angel Fire's doesn't end straight away.

Angel Fire tilts his head back and closes his eyes like he's saying a prayer in church. The audiences to either side of us and many of the kids in the dense crowds walking along next to the flatbeds do the same.

His eyes darting side to side, Ignacio tugs on my jacket and asks me what's happening.

Before I can tell him that I have no idea, Angel Fire shoos the two Arbiters away. The two of them gather their yellow robes around themselves and lurch back across the swaying, bowed metal bridge between the two flatbeds to join the rest of their fellow ducklings.

"After consulting with the One and the Twelve," Angel Fire announces into his microphone, we have decided to make a slight adjustment to our Standard Operating Procedure."

The crowd murmurs, and a few of the kids in the audience let out some disapproving grunts we can hear from here.

"The Appeal is usually a single-step process," Angel Fire

continues, "a test of mind or body. Since we have six minds and bodies to deal with, the appeals process will be adjusted accordingly. Because Branwynne lost the Debate to the Death—"

The two crowds hoot and holler, but I honestly can't tell if they're booing or cheering.

Are they upset because I lost, or are they upset that I'm still alive?

"And since Matholook, a confessed member of the Cult of the Devoted, has been determined to be an enemy of the Unsettled..." Angel Fire elaborates before swinging around to face us. "That leaves four of you who are eligible to participate in the Appeal."

One at a time, with showy exaggeration and to the delight of our flanking audiences, he points a stabbing finger at Libra, Arlo, Ignacio, and Sara.

Libra's cheeks go dusky red. She bites her lip and locks her worried eyes onto mine. Sara is casually preoccupied with picking at a freckle on the back of her hand. Arlo takes a half-step back like he's expecting Angel Fire to whip out a machine gun and mow us all down right here on the back of this flatbed and dance naked around our lifeless bodies. Ignacio takes a bold step forward, his hands cupped around either side of his mouth.

Brassy as a tea kettle, he comes off as unintimidated and unafraid.

I know him well enough to know it's partly real but also partly an act.

"We can take anything you throw at us!" he boasts to Angel Fire and then turns to us for confirmation we can't possibly hope to offer. "We *can*, can't we?" he mouths in my direction, his eyes narrow and pleading.

What can I say? I'm so far out of my depth here, I'm likely to get the bends just thinking about coming up for enough air to answer him.

"Are you prepared?" Angel Fire asks.

At the same time, Libra, Arlo, Ignacio, and Sara—recoiled in a linked-armed cluster—answer with a resounding, "No!"

Come on guys. Don't embarrass me in front of the evil warlord!

"They're ready!" I cry out to Angel Fire.

They might not have faith in themselves, but I trust their abilities and expertise. Besides, what's the worst that could happen? I already failed my test. If they fail theirs, the uncertainty of our predicament will be over, and we'll know exactly where we stand. Of course, that apparently means our certain death, so I guess that's the answer to my question about what's the worst that could happen.

I need to stop asking myself questions whose inevitable answer is, "death."

"The first appeal," Angel Fires announces, "is the Mind Appeal. We are an army of intellectuals and problem-solvers."

They are?

"Prove that you, likewise, are an individual of intellect and problem-solving."

As my four friends look back and forth at each other, Angel Fire takes five big steps toward us and aims his finger like a gun right at Libra. "Are you ready to prove yourself?"

"And how...how do I do that, exactly?" Libra stammers.

"You must discover the four pillars of the Army of the Unsettled."

"Four...?"

"Pillars. Each pillar represents a primary bastion of our philosophy."

"What's a 'bastion'?"

Angel Fire freezes, his eyes in a deep squint, and I think maybe he's trying to use some sort of laser-powered telepathy to burn a hole in Libra's face. Reeling himself in, he tells her that a "bastion" is "a foundation and a cornerstone of our philosophy."

"And how are we supposed to know your philosophy?" Libra asks.

"You're not. That's the mystery for you to solve."

I'm not sure what he's getting at, but my guts aren't too happy, either way.

"Are you prepared to solve the four pillars?" he cries out.

Around us, the crowd chants, "Give them the riddles!"

Riddles? Is that all this is?

I nudge Libra and give her my best and biggest smile of encouragement. "I think all you have to do is solve a few riddles. That *is* your thing, right? Solving things. Figuring them out."

"Um…I mostly deal with mechanical systems and things like that. I *like* puzzles and stuff, but I don't want to die doing them."

"You won't die."

Overhearing us above the ruckus from the crowd, Angel Fire wags his finger at Libra. "You *will* if you fail."

Libra tries to swallow, but I think her mouth is too dry and her brain is short-circuiting, so her attempted swallow turns into a gagging gulp.

Angel Fire rounds on her, ignoring the rest of us as he stands, small but powerful, in front of her. Speaking into his own microphone and gesturing for me to pass her mine, he says, "Here is our first pillar: 'He speaks without a mouth, and he hears without ears. He has no body, but he surfs in the air.'"

I've never been good at this kind of mind-bending puzzle stuff, so I'm glad I'm not eligible to be the player. To my brain, riddles are gibberish with an answer I know is there but can't see or understand until it's explained to me. Which makes me feel twice as dumb as I did before I even heard the riddle.

(My reaction to the answer to every riddle I've ever heard is, "Oh! I *would've* gotten it if you game me more time.")

Why is it sometimes so easy for me to lie to myself?

In front of us, Libra paces like a prize-fighter, anxious to step into the ring. With all of her sweet and optimistic bubbliness, I sometimes forget that she's getting the same intense training as the rest of us at the Academy. She's taking most of the same classes, and War is her mentor for her personalized training sessions. Plus, she lived in a Processor and had to deal with any number of tortures and indignities before she got freed by Kress and her Conspiracy.

Could she be more of a proper tough than I ever imagined?

Libra stops, both feet together and her head on a steep tilt like she's been blasted by some sort of dry-ice cannon and frozen, mid-step.

She says something I can't hear at first and then, nodding her head in agreement with herself, she raises the microphone to her lips and calls out, "An echo."

An echo. Speaking with no mouth and surfing the air. Okay. That makes sense. So how come I couldn't have figured it out in a million years?

"An echo!" Angel Fire echoes into his own microphone.

"An echo!" all of the spectators echo back.

Angel Fire looks more happy than upset about Libra's correct answer, and I get the sense that his scrunched brow and slightly sinister squint are more for show than anything else.

Does this pint-sized, ankle-biter-warlord actually like us?

The crowd calls out for the second pillar, and Angel Fire nods to them and adjusts his fat-knotted tie like he's preparing for his wedding photos. Holding two fingers up in a "V," he pivots back around to stand nearly nose-to-nose with Libra. "Here is our second pillar: I belong to you, but everyone else uses me far more than you ever will."

Ugh. I hate this stuff. Riddles aren't fun. They just make you feel two levels short of a double-decker.

Don't get me wrong. I enjoy a good mystery as much as the next person. But riddles are different. You *solve* a mystery. A riddle is given to you by someone who already knows the question *and* the answer. It's a stacked deck, and they're holding all the cards with a couple of extra aces up their sleeve for good measure. And the whole point is to make you feel like a daft, grade-A tosser.

And then I feel even dumber when Matholook leans down and whispers to me, "At least this one's easy, right?"

"Uh, yeah. Sure. Easy-peasy." I'm trying to sound casually confident, but Matholook's skeptical squint tells me I'm not fooling anybody.

Libra paces again and then stops, her finger in the air like she's checking the direction of the wind. "Libra!"

Angel Fire does a half spin away from the audience and toward Libra, dropping to one knee at the end of his little maneuver and taking aim at Libra with his finger and thumb in the shape of a gun. "Excuse me? Is that your answer?"

"The answer is, 'My name.' It's mine, but everyone uses it a lot more than I do!"

Matholook nudges me with his elbow and says, "Easy, right?"

"Yeah," I answer with an eyeroll I hope he doesn't see. "Easy-peasy."

In front of us, Angel Fire leaps back up and turns to quiet the increasingly rowdy crowds.

Did he just smile?

He holds up three fingers and twirls in a set of three slow circles in the middle of the flatbed before skipping, school-girl style, over to Libra until he's standing a foot in front of her. "Used to threaten, used to defeat. Sometimes it grows, sometimes it shrinks. Used to conquer, used to protect. It marks your downfall and marks your wins. The true god of war, the creator of sins. What is it?"

Libra holds up a finger and mutters, "Give me a second."

"I'll give you *five* seconds," Angel Fire says with his hand up, his fingers splayed wide, and through a crooked sneer that I'm almost sure is just a poorly disguised smile.

One at a time, he starts curling his fingers down, one finger per second, until only his thumb remains, held aloft like he's about to hail a flying taxi.

As his thumb begins to drop to form a closed fist, Libra beams wide enough for the corners of her mouth to inch perilously close to her ears. Her perfect teeth are shiny, white, and symmetrical as blocks of ice in an igloo. The answer she gives is an answer I've heard a million times but never thought much about until now. It's an answer that Krug built his world around and that forms the fertile ground that enabled Emergents to exist. It's an answer encompassing everything Kress has been fighting against and training us to attain in a new, different, and more empathetic form.

Libra's voice is silky and completely static-free when she bends over her microphone and says, "Power."

Sensing Libra's success after my miserable failure, I slip my arm into hers and tell her she's doing great. Arlo and Ignacio aren't quite as subtle with their encouragement. Shoving me out of the way, they hurl their arms around her and call her their hero.

"That remains to be seen," Angel Fire admonishes, pumping the brakes on the boys' celebration. "Here is the fourth and final pillar: 'Some try to hide, some try to cheat, but time will show, we always will meet. Try as you might, to guess my name, I promise you'll know, when it's you I claim. Who am I?'"

"Do you know who the frack he's talking about?" I ask Libra out of the corner of my mouth.

She looks like she might cry when she nods and says she does. "We've seen him up close and personal, and I'm not eager for another meeting."

"Who...?"

Turning away from me and toward Angel Fire, Libra leans into her microphone. "Death."

There's a second of stunned silence from Angel Fire and the audiences trundling along next to us. All I can hear is the grind of the chugging city on wheels, which is a lot, but right now, with all that's going on in my mind, it sounds more like the delicate, background hum of a bank of fluorescent lights.

Angel Fire's squeaky, almost-masculine voice breaks the silence. "She has identified the four pillars!"

And then the crowds go balls-out crazy with the earth and air-shattering celebratory exuberance of a stadium full of football hooligans.

"Echo, Name, Power, and Death," Angel Fire rattles off as the cries die down, "are the four pillars of the Army of the Unsettled. Like all of us, you are the echo of Death's voice. It comes for you. It takes you. And it sends you back. You may not return as you were, but you will return." And then he looks down at the long, riveted floorboards of the flatbed between his feet and adds, "We're never the same, we're always in motion, and we *always* return."

The quiet confidence from the way he says this makes me almost start to cry.

In a flash, my mind whips me back to my childhood in the Tower of London. I see myself meeting Kress, leaving my parents behind, and coming with her to this country with nothing but Haida Gwaii and the clothes on my back. I see Kress and her Conspiracy, our challenges, our victories, and our losses. I see Manthy and Cardyn vanish hand-in-hand into the Lyfelyte on the rooftop of the Academy, and I watch as their friends—my teachers and mentors—suffer a collective heartbreak that I suspect may never fully heal. I see Mattea dying again right before my eyes. And it's all there, just like Angel Fire said: The *Echo* of my *Name* on Mattea's lips as she surrendered to

Death and the *Power* the rest of us needed to summon in order to keep moving when it would have been so easy to stop.

Combined, the four pillars of the Unsettled, reveal our place in a world where we can shrink into helplessness or else grow into hope.

Is that what the Army of the Unsettled is actually all about? The power to keep moving, knowing they can never outrun Death? Is that what they mean by, "The power to live"? Is it possible the Unsettled aren't the enemy I thought they were?

Unlike Angel Fire's riddles, this time, I think I know the answer.

19

BODY APPEAL - ARLO

SETTING aside his carnival barker voice, this time, Angel Fire speaks into his microphone with conversational ease.

"The second appeal is the Body Appeal. This is the appeal to your physical being. Billions have perished in the chaos and wars of the last twenty years. The ones who survived did so because of intellect, luck, or brute strength. Is there a brute among you? Is there someone unsheltered and unafraid?"

As if to stick the knife in deeper and emphasize our predicament, Angel Fire reminds the audience that we've already failed the first trial, the Debate to the Death.

Okay. I failed it.

On the other hand, Matholook's knowledge of the Unsettled and their rules opened the door for our appeal, and Libra succeeded in her challenge, so maybe there's hope?

"The Emergents have passed the first appeal," Angel Fire begins. And then, dousing my meager glimmer of optimism, he adds, "No one has ever passed—or even *survived*—the second."

Great.

"And what do we call those who fail?"

A repeated chant rises from the audience: "Buzzard bait!"

Doing another graceful pivot on his heel, Angel Fire returns his attention to us. "So...who's it going to be? Who is prepared to know the sensation of being digested?"

Arlo half-raises his hand. "Um...I guess I'll go?"

Ignacio stops his attempt to step forward with a wide-fingered hand slapped firmly to the center of Arlo's chest. "I don't think so. I've got the highest marks of all of us in War's Exercise and Fitness class. If this is a physical challenge, I should be the one..." Ignacio turns to me. "Right, Bran?"

I put my hands up in surrender.

No way I'm getting between these two guys. They're old enough to figure out for themselves which one of them has the biggest death wish. I'd take a shot at this appeal, myself, if I were allowed. But since I'm not...

"What about Sara?" Libra asks, turning to our perpetually aloof and annoyed classmate.

Sara looks up and frowns in response. "What *about* Sara?" she asks through an acidic hiss.

Backing down, Libra stammers, "Nothing. I just thought maybe you wanted to..."

"Volunteer to die? I don't think so."

"No one's dying," I promise, my voice low so Angel fire won't overhear. "Libra figured out those four pillars. And besides, I don't think these people really want us dead."

"Are you willing to bet your life to find out?" Sara asks. "Or are you happier betting mine?"

"I'm not betting anything," I say, my fingers in fists, my defenses fully up. "We're a team. An Asylum. We have to work together."

"By working *separately*?" Sara laughs. She gives a little flick of her head, tossing her short blond hair and taking one giant, very deliberate step back. She scans Arlo and Ignacio, licks her lips, and slips one of her arms into the crook of Arlo's arm and the other into Ignacio's. "It's called the 'Body Appeal.' I say we let the boys with the appealing bodies take care of this one."

The Unsettled might not want to kill her, but I'm starting to consider doing it for them.

"It looks like you've selected a champion," Angel Fire announces, his hand out flat and aimed squarely at Arlo.

"We sure as frack have," Arlo calls back. "Don't worry," he assures us, "I've got this."

"Welcome," Angel Fire belts out, "to the Body Appeal!"

I can't speak for the others in my Asylum, but I get tense and start looking around, waiting for whatever is about to happen.

When nothing does, Angel Fire blushes and waves his hands at us. "Oh, sorry. Stand back!"

The audiences laugh as we move away from the back of the trailer and gather in a clump in its middle.

Over on Angel Fire's desk, Zephora presses a button, and a large wooden panel rises from the floor like a drawbridge being raised. Snapping into place, the impromptu wall looms ten feet high near the rear bumper of the trailer.

It's peppered with small holes and stained with blood. A *lot* of blood.

On a signal from Angel Fire, Zephora waves her hand at the twelve teens in the yellow hoods.

Six of the ducklings, numbers two through seven this time, stand with ceremonial swagger. In a tidy queue, they approach the narrow steel bridge and make their way from their flatbed to ours.

"The Sniper Squad of the Arbiters will administer the Body Appeal."

Wait. The same kids who condemned us are now going to oversee this part of our appeal? I guess they don't believe in impartial juries.

Arlo brushes his palms along the sides of his combat pants,

pulls his fingers back in a stretch, and tilts his head from side to side. "I guess I'm up."

"That's great," Matholook says to me. "But up for what, exactly?"

Sneering, Ignacio tells him, "I doubt they're going to set up a tea party to test his social etiquette."

"Too bad," I mutter, my eyes on Arlo, who is standing alone in front of the high wooden wall. "I could go for a good cuppa right about now."

Zephora and the adult man whose name I still don't know disappear behind the red curtain and re-emerge seconds later pushing a rack of polished black and gray weapons.

"Those are compressible carbon-compound hunting bows," Sara says from behind us, clearly impressed. "Overdrive binary cam system. Exchangeable modules. Dovetail mount. Split limb. Single pin sight. Fixed, triple-blade broadheads..."

When we all stare at her, she acts like we're a bunch of daft cows. "Granden's been teaching me."

As if he's whispering sweet nothings into the ear of his invisible lover, Angel Fire—his eyes closed, a playful smile on his lips—purrs into the microphone. "Will our Sniper Squad please approach to gather their weapons?"

One by one, Zephora and the man distribute the six compound bows, one to each of the six ducklings.

At the same time, four of the hairless guards—two men and two women—cross over from their flatbed to ours. They surround me and my friends and herd us behind Angel Fire's desk, leaving Arlo standing alone in front of the blood-stained wall and facing a queue of the hooded archers.

With a half-curious, half-sadistic grin tugging the corners of his mouth, Angel Fire calls for the Body Appeal to begin.

From here, all we can see is their backs as the archers draw their bows and, one after the other in rapid-fire succession—

without fanfare, warning, or a single word—fire their volley of deadly arrows.

I shout out, "Wait!" but no one is listening. Every scrap of everyone's attention—from the audiences in the grandstands and on the ground to Angel Fire and me and my Asylum on the Trial Barge—is locked onto Arlo.

Before our astonished eyes, the arrows slow down. At first, I think I'm imagining it. But from here, I can actually see the ruffle of the arrows' flight feathers as the shafts push their way through the soupy air. They're still moving fast. But not with the near-invisible velocity a well-shot arrow should.

With the graceful, half-speed of a ballet dancer practicing his routine in the empty, open space of a studio, Arlo slides left, right, forward, and back, as he allows each arrow to go streaking harmlessly past.

One by one, each of the arrows plunks into the big wooden wall behind him.

Except for the last one.

That one proves to be one too many for Arlo to avoid. And even a slightly slowed-down arrow is plenty fast and deadly enough to do damage.

Which this one does.

Arlo has just slid down to allow the fifth arrow to zing past his ear.

But the sixth and final arrow finds its mark, piercing his throat just to the side of his Adam's Apple. The arrow lodges in place, the arrowhead-half of its shaft sticking out the back of his neck, its flight-end quivering in the front.

The simultaneous gasp from the audience is so loud I can barely hear my own breath of horror escape my lips.

I was just about to celebrate—not only Arlo's victory but what looks to be the return of his Emergent abilities. And now...

Arlo drops to one knee. A small river of blood pumps down

his neck, staining his shirt, and I'm nearly knocked backwards from the memory of what happened to Mattea.

Are we all cursed to die in the most gruesome way possible?

Down on all fours now, Arlo coughs up a glob of blood, and a shudder ripples through his body.

Libra tries to run toward him, but one of the guards latches onto her wrist hard enough to make her cry out as he twists her shoulder on a weird angle.

Side by side, Matholook and I charge forward and start to clamber over Angel Fire's giant desk, but the guards grab us by the collars of our jackets and sling us backward. We slide on our backsides and plow into the heavy red curtain at the cab-end of the trailer.

In front of us, Sara is just standing there, although she takes the time to put her chin on her shoulder and look back at us with a disdainful, "you're wasting your time," eyeroll.

Surging past her, Ignacio elbows one the guards in the ribs and vaults Angel Fire's desk. Shouldering straight through the team of archers, he sprints the length of the Trial Barge, sliding to a stop next to Arlo while Matholook and I shout and flail in the unrelenting arms of the guards.

We both stop struggling and stare as the uproar from the crowd plummets into a muted groan.

With Ignacio's help, Arlo stands up. Looking around like he's just woken up from a long sleep, he nods his thanks to Ignacio and gently pushes him a step back.

With everyone staring in heart-stopping silence, Arlo reaches behind his neck and locks both hands onto the arrow's shaft. Grimacing, he pulls the arrow clean through his neck and holds it in front of his face like he's a duck hunter showing off a fresh kill as blood drips from the arrow's flight feathers and begins to pool on the wooden deck around his boots.

Waving his hand with a "shoo fly" flourish, Angel Fire orders the guards to release us, and we scramble over to surround Arlo, pat him on the back, and marvel at his impossible accomplishment.

"I guess that's going to be a new scar for you," Ignacio giggles.

Arlo makes me gag a little when he slides his finger back and forth into the raw, puckered hole going straight through his neck. "It's for the best," he grins. "I was looking for a new place to keep my pencil."

Sara says, "Gross," smiles, and crosses her arms in a defiant huff.

Microphone in hand and squeezing his way through us to throw his arm around Arlo's waist, Angel Fire says he agrees with Sara. "Definitely gross. But quite impressive!"

Leaning into the microphone, he announces to the now-cheering crowds that we have passed the Body Appeal.

"Arlo's got his abilities back," Matholook whispers to me, his head low and his lips barely moving. "Are you able to...?"

"Reconnect with Haida?" I squint and tell him, "It's patchy."

"Enough for us to try to make a run for it?"

"Yes. But not enough to keep us from getting killed in the process."

"Where does that leave us?"

"Here," I sigh. "Unfortunately."

Matholook gives my shoulder a supportive squeeze. "But one step closer to *not* being here."

I put my hand on his, grateful for a pleasant thought in the middle of so much carnage but also worried that pleasant thoughts alone might not be enough to get us through whatever happens next.

20

CHARACTER APPEAL - IGNACIO

THE ARCHERS SLIP around us and grunt as they pry their arrows out of the wall.

As soon as they're done, they head back to their grandstand while the huge wooden wall starts to crank back down, and my Asylum and I shuffle out of the way to avoid being crushed as it folds with a clunk and a steamy hiss back into the floor of the Trial Barge.

"The third appeal," Angel Fire announces to us and to the crowd, "is the Character Appeal." He stalks across the flatbed to stand in front of us. "In this Appeal, your answers will let us know if you're the kind of person who should be trusted and spared...or else cast off the Trial Barge and run over by a cement-mixer."

I'm waiting for the crowd to laugh. When they don't, I realize the taunts and applause from the audiences have died down to next to nothing. And then I realize *he might be dead serious.*

Angel Fire summons Ignacio forward.

Full of macho brio, Ignacio strides out to the middle of the Trial Barge. He may be ready for whatever's about to happen, but I'm sure as frack not.

His microphone to his mouth, Angel Fire glides in a slow circle around Ignacio.

"I'm going to walk you through a scenario. The more honest you are when you answer my questions, the better your chances of walking off this Trial Barge with your head and limbs still attached to your body. Do you understand?"

"No."

"Good. Close your eyes."

Ignacio looks over at us, and the five of us shrug in unison.

Sighing, Ignacio closes his eyes. Kind of.

Angel Fire leans in close until he's nearly nose to nose with Ignacio. "No peeking."

Ignacio groans, "Fine" and clamps his eyes shut all the way as Angel Fire's voice wafts out again from the black speakers posted around the flatbed for everyone to hear.

"Imagine an empty room."

"A room?" Ignacio asks, his eyes closed, the sleeves of his white military jacket rolled up to the elbows, his hands thrust deep into the pockets of his black tactical combat pants.

"An *empty* room."

"Okay."

"Describe it."

"I don't know. Big."

"Go on."

"Okay," Ignacio's shoulders droop, and he huffs out a resigned sigh. "I can barely see the ceiling or the walls. I know they're there. They're just far away." He pauses, and when he starts up again, his voice rolls out in serene, almost surprised-sounding waves. "*Really* far away. And there are dangerous parts of the room. Little pockets where it's too cold or too hot. I can't see them, either. But I know they're there."

"Imagine a cube in the room. Describe it."

Ignacio scrunches up his face, but his eyes stay clamped shut. "A...cube?"

"Yes. Describe everything about it. What it looks like. Its size. Where it is in the room."

"Okay. It's a big cube. Not huge, though. It's floating a little. And rotating, but it doesn't want to. It wants to be still, but something is keeping it moving."

"Imagine there's a ladder in the room. Describe it."

"It's close to the cube. No. It's *part* of the cube. And it's not just one ladder. There are six of them, each running along one of the faces of the cube."

"Now, imagine a horse in the room."

"A horse?"

"You know. The big animal."

Ignacio's eyelid twitches, and he peeks out at Angel Fire. "I know what a horse is."

"Describe it. And close your eyes."

"Fine. The horse...it's got a serious side and a playful side. It's beautiful. And...it's hurt."

"And finally, imagine a storm in your invented room."

Ignacio's hands tighten into fists at his sides. "It's horrible. Loud. Churning. But I can control it. No. I'm not controlling it. I'm *partnering* with it. I can't stop it. But I can kind of move with it. It's not so bad, anymore."

The crowd gasps as Ignacio drops to his knees, and my Asylum and I automatically get ready to sprint over to him, but we're stopped by Angel Fire who holds his hand up, palm out, and shakes his head.

With uncharacteristic tenderness, he steps over to Ignacio and rests a hand on his shoulder. Ignacio looks up at him with either strained, puzzled, angry, grateful, or else totally hypnotized eyes. I honestly can't tell.

Guiding him to his feet, Angel Fire helps Ignacio balance with a steadying hand on his forearm.

"It's called the Cube Test," Angel Fire says into his microphone once Ignacio can stand on his own. "Its origins are unknown." He puts his hand up next to his mouth like he's revealing his deepest, darkest secret. "Personally, I first read it about a year ago in an old college textbook on Relational psychology."

Dropping his hand back down, he goes on to tell us, "Some say the origins of the Cube Test are from the Sufi religion. Others says it's just an urban legend about a parlor trick used as a means of social seduction. Or it could be like one of the personality tests in a Japanese book called *Kokology*. That's Greek for 'the study of psychological games as a guide to human behavior.'"

With a second conspiratorial whisper from behind his hand, he tells us, "I found that one in what was left of a library in Amarillo."

Pausing, Angel Fire seems to notice that the audience is still there, leaning in and hanging on his every word. They all seemed rowdy but otherwise perfectly happy watching me lose the debate and watching Libra and Arlo succeed at their appeals challenges. I get the sense this whole business about the Cube Test is as new to them as it is to us.

Angel Fire rounds on Ignacio, standing toe to toe with him and taking one of Ignacio's hands in his.

"As your spiritual guide through the many rooms in the house of you, I'll interpret your answers." Angel Fire suppresses a giggle, but it might also be a sneeze.

"The room," he begins, "is how you see the world right now. The cube is you. It's your ego, your sense of self. You said your cube was solid. That's your strength. You described it as floating. A little. That's your bits of humor and whimsy breaking through an otherwise serious soul. And dark. That's your secret. The ladder represents your friends. The distance between the ladder and the cube reflects how close you are with your friends. Your description was...unique. You and your friends are...intertwined. Mostly. Your bonds are unbreakable. Nearly. Most of you support each other. In some ways, some of you *are* each other. The horse is your ideal romantic or spiritual partner. The storm...that's your obstacles. It's all the things in your way, whether they're put there by chance, by someone else accidentally, by someone else on purpose, or, most significantly, by you."

Ignacio blinks hard and stares down at his hand in Angel Fire's before asking, "Why would anyone put up their own obstacles?"

"The same reason anyone does anything evil, cruel, or stupid: *Fear*."

Angel Fire holds the microphone up between himself and Ignacio, so both of their voices can be heard.

"So...," Ignacio asks. "Did I pass?"

"You are a young man of great physical strength, high moral character, and a fascinating blend of confidence and insecurity. Your forces are in balance. Barely. That's what makes you dangerous to some, helpful to most, and compelling to all. And yes...you passed."

Angel Fire winks at Ignacio, and the crowds burst into a frenzied round of applause as Angel Fire drops Ignacio's hand and raises his own fist in triumph.

Although I'm not quite sure what he could possibly be celebrating.

Ignacio just won, right?

Still a bit shaky, Ignacio makes his way back over to our Asylum where we greet him with hearty pats on the back that I think nearly knock him over.

The six of us square up to face Angel Fire, but he's now busy leaning over the side of the flatbed, high-fiving the kids in the front row of the Port Grandstand.

Ignacio is standing on one side of me. I tug his sleeve and lean in so only he can hear me. "I get the room, the cube, the ladder, and the storm. That all sounds like you. But the horse?" I ask. "The partner. What was that one all about?"

"I don't want to talk about it."

True to his word and despite just having scored another victory for us, he sulks his way between me and Matholook, nudges past Libra, Arlo, and Sara, and takes a quiet stand by himself at the back of our Asylum.

21

SOUL APPEAL - SARA

ANGEL FIRE FINISHES FRATERNIZING with the grandstand audiences and pivots back around on his heel to face us.

"The fourth and final appeal, the Soul Appeal is the discovery of your inner essence, the part of you deeper than action, instinct, or intellect. The Soul Appeal is your last and only chance to render your own verdict for or against yourself."

"I guess you're up," I say to Sara, hoping this won't be the last time we all see each other alive. Just because there's no love lost between us doesn't mean I want to see her fail. Especially if her failure means *our* death, too.

"So," Sara sighs at Angel Fire, her whole body brimming with *frack-you* attitude. "What do I have to do? Dodge a bullet? Eat a bug? Assemble a jigsaw puzzle with my feet? Demonstrate my knowledge of the quadratic equation?"

"You'll wish it was that easy," Angel Fire answers with a cool, easy laugh.

Reacting to Angel Fire's silent nod, the Unsettled guards surround the rest of us and march us to the edge of the trailer. With a chorus of warbled grunts, they herd us onto the small metal bridge spanning the distance between our trailer and the one next to us.

The spectators on the trailer cheer and chant as they shuffle back in a crowded clump to the last rows of the steel bleachers to make room for us. Some of the hooting kids reach out to us— possibly to hit us, or maybe just so they can go home and say they touched real-live Emergents.

Either way, the guards order them to back off and brandish some menacing looking bladed weapons to show they're not joking around.

Turning their focus back to us, the guards force us to stand in a line behind a metal restraining bar, leaving Sara standing alone in the middle of the Trial Barge.

She sways and rocks along with the motion of the trailer, and her short blond hair is whipping all over the place, but she doesn't seem to notice any of it. There's a cloak of calm over her, a calm that shouldn't be cloaked around anyone in her situation.

Angel Fire hops up onto his desk. For a kid on the shortish side, he's agile, and he makes the high leap look easy.

Taking his microphone from where it's tucked in his belt, he pins his eyes on Sara. "You and your friends over there are running from a horde of Survivalists," he begins. Matholook and I share a confused look and a simultaneous shrug.

"You're running," Angel Fire continues, "and you find a good place to hide. But you have a baby with you. You know it's about to cry and that if it does, it'll give away your hiding place. If that happens, you and your friends—and the *baby*—will all be killed. You have two options: Kill the baby and save everyone, or let it cry and condemn you all to death."

He points to one of the men by the tall score-clock behind him. The man sets the arm of the clock to "6" and the hand starts moving right away, inching its way backward toward "1."

Sara puts up her hands in a spiritless shrug. "Am I supposed to tell you what I'd do?"

"Your answer will tell us all we need to know about you. And based on that, we'll know what we need to do with you and your companions over there."

"What's happening?" Libra asks into my ear.

I shoo her away and tell her to stop breathing on me.

Matholook is more charitable. "It's a moral dilemma," he whispers over to Libra. "There's no right or wrong answer."

"Then how will Angel Fire know if he should—?"

"Kill us or not?" Matholook's voice drops to a husky whisper. "I wish I knew."

Alone on the middle of the flatbed, Sara seems to be lost in thought, while the crowds behind us and on the flatbed on the other side of the Trial Barge sit back in silence, waiting for her response.

I know what she must be thinking: *Is it worth killing a baby to save six people?* And I can imagine the follow-up questions Angel Fire might be sadistic enough to ask: *What if it weren't a baby? What if it was a cat? Or an unusually loud bug? What if it was someone you knew and loved who just couldn't stay quiet? Or someone you hated? What if it was a hundred people being saved instead of just five?*

The arm of the clock continues its march, taking a few torturous seconds to move from one number to the next. Just as the thin, tapered black arm is about to click over to the "1," Sara opens her eyes wide and plants her fists on her hips.

"You have your answer?" Angel Fire asks from his wide-legged perch on the top of his desk.

"I do."

"Present your answer, and we'll see if you live or if you die."

I don't know how I'd answer, and I definitely don't know if Sara is going to say she'd kill the baby or sacrifice all of us.

It's a no-win situation, and both answers seem horribly wrong.

I guess that's why they call it a "dilemma."

"First," she says, leaning into her own microphone and ticking off numbers on her fingers as she goes, "I track down the psycho who thought coming up with such a sadistic, no-win hypothetical situation would be in any way helpful in determining the state of my soul. Second, I pull his oversized sport coat over his head and get my friend Ignacio over there to short-circuit the electrical synapses in his pea-brain. Third, I gather up my friends, and we get the frack out of here, leaving the drooling psycho-boy and his huge, smelly, rolling army to rot away in the desert." She has her head tilted down as she grins and glares at Angel Fire through the tops of her eyes before adding, "Hypothetically speaking, of course."

She's now standing, alone and exposed, in the middle of the Trial Barge, facing Angel Fire. She's got the microphone clasped in both hands and that cheeky grin still plastered on her face, while Angel Fire stares at her hard enough to burn holes in her forehead.

It's a frozen moment in time.

The Army of the Unsettled keeps moving along, of course. But everything else—the shouts of the crowds, our thoughts, and Angel Fire's orders and pronouncements—come to a stunned and screeching halt.

He stares down at her from the top of his desk. I don't know if he's swaying from the motion of the rig or if he's just gone catatonic. He doesn't say anything. No questions. No snappy patter. No comeback.

Sara stares right back. No. Not exactly. She's not staring. She's waiting. She's watching. It's the look Rain gets when she gives us chess lessons and we take too long to move. Sort of amused. Sort of impatient. But also brimming with confidence.

After all, if we're taking *that* long to react, our opponent knows she must have done something right.

Angel Fire finally blinks, and that seems to snap the rest of the world back into motion. The crowds boo and jeer. Next to me Matholook's breath is light as gossamer in my ear. "What did she just do?"

"Not much," I shrug with a sigh. "Just condemned us all to death."

Angel Fire works his jaw around a few times and clamps his thin fingers into strained, white-knuckled fists at his sides. His eyes seem to be fighting between the urge to open wide in surprise or else scrunch down into squints of fury.

He settles on saying something to two of the Unsettled guards behind him, but since he doesn't say it into the microphone, I have no idea what he's up to.

It doesn't take long to figure it out.

The two Unsettled—one boy and one girl—step forward from their sentry positions behind him.

Each of them is brandishing one of those five-foot-long wooden handles with a meat cleaver duct-taped and tied with twine to the end.

"Two against one? And she doesn't have weapons? That's not fair!" Ignacio shouts over the din of the raucous, taunting crowd around us. His hands are clamped in a vice-grip on the steel railing in front of us that separates this flatbed from the Trial Barge.

This time, Angel Fire leans down and speaks into the microphone, his entire face puckered with rage. He points an accusing finger at Sara but then turns his full attention to me and my Asylum. "You have already been found guilty. But you have been miraculously successful in three of your appeals with the fourth now left unresolved. If your champion can survive the final

Bonus Appeal, you'll go free. What could be more fair than that?"

"How about you and me, one on one?" Ignacio cries out over the thrum of machines and people.

I don't think Angel Fire hears him. Which is just as well. We're maybe two minutes away from being free or dead, and I'd rather not have Ignacio tipping the scales of Fate, or the mercurial wrath of Angel Fire, in the wrong direction.

The two teenagers from the Unsettled circle around from behind Angel Fire's desk and stride toward Sara, who doesn't seem to care what's happening one way or the other.

In fact, with her tired eyes and her arms hanging loosely at her sides, it looks like she might be gearing up to...*yawn*?

Whatever she has in mind, the two Unsettled attackers don't seem to care. The boy, short but powerfully built, slams to a stop right in front of her. He raises his spear and plants his feet into an attack position on the deck of the flatbed.

And then...he attacks.

Sara ducks the whooshing swing of his spear and pivots around behind the boy. Lashing out at the same time with a sweeping leg kick, she uses her momentum to drive the heel of her boot into the boy's knee. He cries out as his leg folds backward in the complete wrong direction, and he falls to the ground.

But he doesn't stay down.

We all shout at her to watch her back, but she can't hear us. The downed boy presses himself to his feet. With Sara now engaged with the girl, he's got an open shot, and he takes it.

He swings his bladed spear. Fortunately, the trailer lurches just enough so the strike catches Sara in the shoulder instead of in the head where he was clearly aiming.

And then, two of the strangest things I've ever seen happen

right before our eyes. (And I've seen some *stonking* strange things.)

Sara moves in toward the boy, almost like she's going to slip into his arms and invite him to dance. He stares at her, smiles a sweet, appreciative smile. And then, he turns and limps down the length of the flatbed, leaps off the back end of the trailer, crashes through the crowd of walking spectators, and disappears in the distance in a hobble-sprint between two moving columns of treaded bulldozers.

As for the girl, she stops in her tracks. Her eyes glaze over, and I think she's about to launch some kind of last-ditch desperate attack against Sara.

Instead, she scoops up her spear, bounces it twice in her hands, and hurls it...*right at Angel Fire.*

22

TREASON

THE MAKESHIFT SPEAR sticks with a *thunk* right into the wooden desk in front of Angel Fire. The wood splinters out in a starburst array with the crackling crunch of a tree getting struck by lightning.

I can only imagine what that weapon would have done if it had hit human flesh and bone. Especially flesh and bone as flimsy as Angel Fire's.

Snarling and frothing at the mouth, the girl, with the rabid desperation of someone starving and eager to have a taste of food, charges toward the desk to get at Angel Fire.

She has blind rage in her narrowed eyes and is screaming like a ferret in a bear trap.

Angel Fire shrieks and drops down behind the huge desk. Even though there's not a ton of space between the bottom of the desk and the floor of the flatbed, it's more than enough for us to see Angel Fire curled in a fetal position, his knees tucked to his chest and his arms clasped around his legs.

The girl grabs the spear and works it out of the desk like she's pumping water from a well. Getting her feet under her, she leaps up onto the top of the desk, spear in hand, her thick-soled boots hammering out thunder as she thrusts the spear forward with one hand while making big circles with her other arm in an effort to maintain her balance.

Clamping the spear in both hands, she raises it above her head, point down, a feral snarl at the corner of her lips, her eyes laser focused on her target. I think she's about to plunge her spear straight down through Angel Fire's cowering body, but then she wobbles as the truck hits one the millions of deep fissures in the ground.

From next to me, Ignacio calls out, "Whoa!" and reaches out a hand like he's going to magically steady the girl from thirty feet away. (I don't know why he'd want to, anyway.)

Even over the rumble of the expansive fleet of vehicles, I can hear the audiences around us gasp.

Melting the frozen moment, Zephora leaps out from behind the heavy red curtain. She surges forward, her own spear in hand. She rams her weapon into the girl's chest just under her solar plexus with enough force to turn the traitorous girl instantly into a human kebob and skewer her all the way through, from chest to back.

In a feat of unexpected strength, she lifts the impaled girl clean off her feet and flips her down to the flatbed where she lands in a twisted heap of limbs with the spear—its blade end coated in a glistening layer of blood—halfway through her body.

Angel Fire's head appears from behind his desk. With the darting eyes of a desert pocket mouse, he glances around and apparently assesses the situation enough to know it's safe. Silver-Scruff on one side and Zephora on the other reach down, hook his arms in theirs, and lug him fully to his feet.

Straightening his tie and standing with his feed wide apart, he signals for his microphone. Leaving Zephora to work her spear out of the crazy dead girl, the male guard picks the microphone up from the deck of the Trial Barge and hands it to him.

Taking it with the delicate care of a boy taking a bone from the mouth of a rabid dog, he addresses the crowd. I expect to hear a nervous tremor in his voice or an angry rant, but he acts like he gets spears thrown at him every day.

"The appellants have been successful in their appeal. I hereby decree that a pardon has been granted."

The crowds cheer and starts chanting "Granted! Granted! Granted!"

From our scrunched-together line behind the gate of the escort flatbed, Ignacio's mouth is still hanging open. "What the frack just happened?"

"That girl with the spear...," Matholook starts to say but then trials off.

Arlo shakes his head. "I don't know why she did that."

"I do," I tell them.

Ignacio curls his fingers around my shoulder and whips me around. Leaning down, his nose an inch from mine, he asks, "Do you mind sharing with the class?"

I tell him, "Sure."

Libra and the three boys lean in like I'm about to tell them the secret of the universe or something. But it's not anywhere close to being that complicated, I promise them.

"Every organization has its brainwashed, its true believers, and its doubters. That girl just happens to be someone strong and brave enough to stand up to injustice, even when she knows she's bucking the party line and will likely get punished as a result. She did a noble thing—standing up for us like that against a dictator like Angel Fire. We should be thankful."

After a wordless moment of verification with each other, Libra and the boys nod and hum their lukewarm agreement.

I let out the breath I've been holding, happy they were at least partially okay with my explanation.

But I was lying.

I'm not ready to bet my life on it, but gun to my head, I'd say what just happened here has something to do with Sara.

The guards usher us across the metal bridge and back onto the Trial Barge to join her. The six of us stand there in a cluster, wondering if we just succeeded or if we just failed once again in spectacular fashion. The flatbed continues to roll on, and even though it's a smoother ride right now than it was a few minutes ago, we still bobble together in a huddle, waiting for whatever might come next.

From in front of his desk, Angel Fire takes a full minute to survey his chittering audiences.

Leaning toward Sara and doing my best to keep my lips together, I whisper a question to her: "For that moral dilemma... what would you have *really* done?"

She doesn't blink or turn to face me when she answers. "I'd have killed the baby."

The way she says this, quick and casual, makes me think she would've killed the baby even if her life and ours *weren't* depending on it.

23

CHOICE

With carnival barker pomp and over-the-top grandiosity, Angel Fire issues a proclamation:

"Our prisoners have proven their merit and have warranted their innocence. I hereby decree that they are free, now and *in perpetuity!*"

"In what?" Arlo asks.

"It means 'forever,'" Libra giggles.

Angel Fire's smile stretches far enough across his face that I think his lower jaw might plunk off and land at his feet. He makes a ceremonial adjustment to his ill-fitting tie and then, turning in each direction to face the crowds, he rolls his hand in an exaggerated royal salute.

In unison and rolling along with the trailers like sailors on a rocking boat, the crowds in the Port and Starboard Grandstands start chanting, "He hereby decrees! He hereby decrees!" while pumping their fists in the air and stomping loud enough to drown out the grumble and grind of the engines and the crunch of rubber tires and steel treads on the rocky tundra all around us.

Ignacio looks around at the rowdy crowds, over to Angel Fire, and then to me. "We're free? We can go?"

I'd answer except that I was about to ask the same thing.

Ignacio taps our microphone, which causes a screechy cascade of feedback to ring through the steaming hot air. "We can go?" he asks, leaning forward, his eyes locked onto Angel Fire.

"You can," Angel Fire declares from behind his own microphone, his skimpy chest puffed up enough to *almost* strain the buttons on his dress shirt. "But I would prefer it if you didn't. At least not yet."

Libra raises her hand halfway, like she's afraid if she calls too much attention to herself, he'll change his mind and execute all of us on the spot. She steps up next to Ignacio, nudging in front of him and taking the microphone from his hand as he takes a hesitant step back. "You want us to stay here?"

"For your own safety," Angel Fire answers.

"I'm sorry," Libra smirks as Ignacio and Arlo assume protective flanking positions on either side of her. "Do you seriously think we're going to stay with someone who just tried to have us killed?"

"I tried to have you *tried*," Angel Fire grins. "There's a difference. Justice and vengeance are sometimes the same. Not this time. Our ferocity in battle is absolute. As is our reliance on fairness and our uncompromising forgiveness. Once convicted, you die. Once acquitted, you're forgiven. Instantly. Forever."

My Asylum gathers around me and Matholook to form a loose huddle.

"What should we do?" Libra asks, her palm cupped over the top of the microphone to muffle our voices.

"We get the hell out of here," Ignacio snaps through clenched teeth. "Of course. I mean, look at all the people. Any one of them, or *all* of them for that matter, could be our very own potential future murderer." His eyes are zipping around so fast I think they might eventually pop right out the sides of their sockets.

"Okay. I'm with you," I promise. "Angel Fire is just as likely to change his mind and make us box a cactus or play a game of chess to the death or something else insane."

Sara slicks back a lock of her short blond hair and looks past me and over to Angel Fire, who is waiting patiently while the six of us confer, our heads nearly pressed together in our tight, conspiratorial circle. "I disagree," Sara coos. "I think we should stick around for a while."

I give her an eyeroll I'm sure she can feel. "I hope you're kidding."

Tossing her hair and with an easy confidence, she gives us all a little smile and a helpless, "what-choice-do we-have?" shrug. "We're not on the mission we were sent out to do. But we *are* on a mission. If we can gather some intel to bring back to the Academy…"

"You're assuming this isn't some kind of trap," I point out. "You've seen what they put us through. That kid is into mind games and manipulation. He says they're all about the rule of law. But look at this place."

Arlo squints like he's in pain and shakes his head. "No. Sara's right. If we miss this chance to find out everything we can about the Unsettled…well, that's a lot of intel to leave on the table."

"I guess it makes sense," Libra concedes. "We don't want to get back to the Academy empty-handed, right?"

"If we *can* even get back," Sara adds, toggling her finger between Arlo and Ignacio. "Their abilities are still glitchy. Arlo's lucky to be alive. And you don't seem to know where Haida Gwaii has gotten off to, and without her, we don't have any chance of finding our way. So…I say we stay."

"It's the top of that mountain," I remind her with a stab of my finger in the direction of the far-off, snow-capped peak where the Academy sits, invisibly overseeing the world below. "How hard can it be?"

"How about 'next to impossible,'" Libra sighs.

"Impossible has never stopped us before," I snap, and then I take a breath and rein myself in.

I'm not angry at her. Technically, she's right. But whether or not we know the way home won't matter if we stay here and end up dead. We've lost too much on this mission already.

No. What I'm irked about is the fact that Haida's disappeared, and I don't know why she left, where she is, or what I'm supposed to do about this weird gap in my brain where her consciousness usually takes up shop when we're bonded. And, on top of that, I've got my Asylum looking for excuses to stay when we're lucky we've even survived this long.

Matholook raises his hand halfway. "I hate to bring it up, but I'm not exactly one of you. Everyone in this army thinks I'm the enemy, and they seem to have a wide variety of pretty unpleasant ways of treating their enemies. So I'm all for taking Angel Fire up on his original offer and getting the frack out of here."

"And where would you go, exactly?" Sara asks. "Back to the Academy with us? Back to the Devoted?"

I know what Sara is really asking: *Are you with us or against us?* It's kind of a rude question to ask the bloke she knows I'm into. But it's also, I have to admit, a pretty good question.

Face to face with Sara, Matholook blinks a bunch of times and runs his hand along the light stubble coming in under the sharp slope of his defined cheekbones.

I ask him what he's thinking. He grits his teeth and shakes his head before answering. "No. Sara's right. We should stay. At least until a better opportunity presents itself."

I plant a stiff gaze on each of my friends before asking if

they've all gone completely off their nut.

Behind us, Angel Fire leans into the microphone and clears his throat. "Have you made a decision?"

Sara and I nearly bump heads as we both lean into our microphone with Sara saying, "Yes!" and me saying, "No!" at the same time.

"At least let me show you around," Angel Fire offers. "Before you go."

When we don't answer right away, he pleads with us. "There are dangers in the desert you don't know about. There's a war on its way. If you leave now, *it* could find *you*."

When we still don't answer, he sweetens the pot. "I'll take you to your weapons. They're in an ammunitions truck in the Security Garrison." He points off into the distance. "Up that way. Toward the front of the convoy."

"Security...?" I start to ask.

"Security Garrison. Our army is divided into eight districts called Garrisons. My good friend Revelle oversees security. She'll make sure you get your weapons back."

"It would be nice to have our weapons back," Libra admits under her breath. "Maybe it's worth the risk. After all, what's the worst that could happen?"

It's the kind of question I'm perfectly happy to leave unanswered.

"Yeah," Arlo agrees. "We'll feel better once we're armed again."

Nodding his agreement, Ignacio says he's also leaning toward staying. "For a while, anyway. Angel Fire's right about the dangers out there. And I don't want to end up like..."

He doesn't finish, but Mattea's name, like her memory, hovers ghostlike in the air around us.

"So you all really want to stay?" I ask. "At least until we get our weapons back? And then we'll definitely leave, right?"

I'm answered with glazed eyes but enthusiastic nods.

What's happening here? All we've been talking about was getting free and getting back to the Academy, and now, after two minutes of debate, my friends have gone from desperate to leave to eager to stay.

Even Matholook shrugs. "Sara's right. I don't know where I'd go back *to* if we left. You all need your weapons. And your intel. I need to figure out if I'll even be welcomed back by the Devoted. So...I guess it makes sense to stay."

"Okay," I sigh as my friends stare at me, waiting for me to weigh in. I straighten up and turn to address Angel Fire, who is waiting patiently about thirty feet away, rocking, his hands clutched behind him, in a kind of rhythmic, almost hypnotic sway as the flatbed continues on its course with the rest of the Army. "We...um...accept your offer," I mumble into the microphone.

Beaming and snapping to full attention, Angel Fire springs to life. He pumps his fist to the delight of the crowds. Dropping his microphone to the deck and letting it clatter with a clunk and a blizzard of jarring feedback, he charges across the length of the flatbed.

Sliding to a stop in front of us, he throws his arms around us, hugging us one at a time and telling us how happy he is to have us on his side.

We're not on your side, and we're keeping our guard up until we're a long way away from here.

"Come on!" he beams, his warlord aura giving way to the hyper, happy boy underneath, eager to impress his new friends. "I'll show you around on our way to the Security Garrison."

A changed man—well, *boy*—Angel Fire promises to escort us through their expansive caravan.

Could Sara be right? Is this our chance to do real recon behind enemy lines? Will Kress think we're heroes or a band of complete ninnies? Or, worse, will she think we've legit lost our minds?

It's hard to think. I try to remember the lessons Rain taught us about how to strategize under pressure. She compared it to chess (her go-to metaphor in our Puzzles, Codes, and Game Theory class). "Cultivate small advantages. In most cases, acting is better than reacting. Play *your* game. Breathe. Focus. And don't do what your opponent wants you to do."

It all made sense at the time. At the moment, however, all I can see is the chaos of the chessboard, the haze of infinite possibilities, and the tempting clarity of all the wrong moves.

Make a move, Branwynne. Even a wrong move is better than standing here like a bloody tosser.

"Okay," I tell my Asylum. "We'll go with him. But just to get our weapons back. After that, we'll slip away if we can, or else we'll fight our way out of here if it comes to that."

And I have a bad feeling it's going to come to that.

24

ESCORT

ONE AT A TIME, we hop down from the back end of the moving Trial Barge.

On either side of us, the two flatbeds containing the Arbiters, the audiences, and the bare-chested guards start to empty out. Laughing and jostling now, the Unsettled hop down from the moving trailers and begin to disappear, along with the deep crowd of pedestrian spectators, into the low-hanging clouds of dust between the rows of churning, chugging vehicles.

Angel Fire strides right through my bunched-up Asylum, marching along the pockmarked ground with the towering vehicles of the Unsettled rolling along at walking speed next to him.

"Come on! Come on!" he insists, the enthusiasm of youth beaming from his wide grin and twinkling eyes.

He has the same gleeful tone this small boy had back in London when he came across me while I was checking the perimeter sensors outside the Tower of London when I was nine years old. He couldn't have been more than six or seven, himself. It was rare to see someone so young out there alone and even more rare to see someone like that out there *alive*. He begged me to follow him to a nearby building where he said he and his puppy had been hiding from the drones. Even though I knew my mum and dad would knock me arse over elbow, I couldn't resist. I was used to being around the ravens but was always fascinated by the idea of dogs. (Thanks to drone strikes, leftover toxic radiation from the Atomic Wars, and being a last-ditch source of food, the dogs in London were all dead, dying, or feral, and I could never get my mind around the idea that people used to let these wild, sharp-toothed predators live right in their flats with them.) I followed that small boy to a fifteen-foot-high pile of wood beams and broken bricks that had once been a pub. I suspected a trap, but the surprise I got when I let him lead me inside was way worse. The puppy was real. It was also dead. But the boy cradled it in his arms and kissed its brittle, gray nose, beaming at me about how cute it was.

Angel Fire has the same look as the boy with the dead dog: Misplaced pride. Irrational happiness. Sort of like he's bragging about the oh-so important role he has in this bombed and blitzed-out world because…well, it's all he has.

We've already seen some of the Army. There was more to it than I ever suspected.

And now that we're being guided on a tour instead of being marched to our deaths, we're discovering that what we saw before was only the tip of a very large, very loud, and unexpectedly metropolitan iceberg.

I can't speak for the others, but personally, I'm dazzled.

In the space of less than five minutes of walking, we pass rows of shops—including clothing stores and small, mobile cafés. There's a huge camper with a red cross and the word "Clinic" painted in crisp, stenciled capital letters on its side. A small cube van with no glass in its windows chugs along with a polished metal sign on top advertising eyeglasses for sale. A comically large pair of glasses—made from two bicycle tire rims connected by a wooden broom handle—hangs over the van's sliding door. Right next to the van and moving at the exact same speed, a man in the back of a forest green pickup truck sits in a chair while another man stands behind him, cutting his hair with a flashing pair of silver scissors. (I'm sure there are plenty of things I'd get a thrill out of doing in a state of constant, slow, but jarring motion. Getting my hair cut isn't one of them.)

Next to me, trying to keep her voice quiet but failing, Libra has morphed into an overstimulated little girl and keeps pointing out, well, *everything*.

"They've got restaurants! Look! A shoe store! Over there—gardening supplies! And a water purifier truck!" Shrieking about a nearby city bus with one wall missing and rows of steel shelves filled with pillows, sheets, quilts, and blankets, she grabs my arm hard enough to nearly knock me over. "That bus has bedding!"

I pat her arm and give her my best, maternal, "Yes, Libra. I know. I see it."

"Bedding!" She jogs a couple steps ahead to get a closer look before turning back to the rest of us and squealing about how they've got a whole bin full of stuffed animals, too.

I think she might be about to cry.

Matholook leans in and says he think she might have lost her mind.

"That happened a long time ago," I assure him with a snicker. "This is just Libra finally getting a chance to express her true, inner crazy."

"Sometimes, I don't know how you deal with her."

"I grew up mostly alone in a thousand-year-old prison castle. I go to a hidden school run by a bunch of techno-genetically enhanced heroes who want to save the world. And I share a mental bond with a bird. I'm not exactly normal, myself."

Grinning along with me, Matholook throws an arm around my shoulders and plants a warm kiss on my cheek.

"What was that for?"

"For not being normal."

He combs his fingers through his hair and beams me his perfect, pretty smile. I want him to kiss me again. Or possibly let me leap into his arms. But now's not the right time or place.

But the second we get to the right time and place...

Breaking my train of thought (or is it a train of *heart*?), Libra turns to pester Ignacio and Arlo, who—pointing and wide-eyed, themselves—seem to be catching her fever of unbridled excitement.

As overenthusiastic as always, she *is* right about one thing: This place isn't what we thought it was. What I always assumed was a collection of random, roving, pollution-belching vehicles, is actually a...city?

"You seem a little puzzled," Angel Fire says to me as we walk on.

"Not puzzled," I assure him. "Mostly surprised."

"This...," Angel Fire says with a casual flick of his hand. "Is nothing. Just the outer rim of the Commercial Garrison. And not a very exciting part. But down this way," he says, pointing to the side and cutting sharply into a laneway between two long lines of chugging front loaders, "Is the Leisure Garrison. A good place to relax and have some fun before getting on with the business of not dying."

"I feel like we're always about two seconds from getting run over," I confess, leaning in close so he can hear me and gesturing to the array of moving vehicles surrounding us on all four sides.

"That's because we always are. Which is also why we pedestrians have to stay in constant motion. It's the only way to stay alive. And don't worry," he adds, catching my unsatisfied frown, "all the primary vehicles go at a carefully calibrated walking speed." He waves a hand in the general direction of the lumbering front loaders. "You'd have to be pretty dumb, clumsy, or unlucky to get run over."

Great. In the past few hours, I've been all three.

"What about our weapons?" Ignacio asks, leaning past me to get Angel Fire's attention.

He sounds a little snide. Not that I blame him. Less than an hour ago, Angel Fire had pretty much condemned us all to death. But I don't want to start pressing this kid's buttons just yet. As far as him returning our weapons to us, I'm willing to take him at his word. Until he gives me reason not to.

"It's okay," I assure Ignacio, reaching up to plant a reassuring hand on his muscular shoulder. "I'm sure our host will honor his word."

"Spoken like a true warrior," Angel Fire laughs.

"Thanks."

"But be careful," he advises, holding up his finger. "Honor is subjective, words can be misinterpreted, and warriors often end up dead."

Matholook and I exchange a glance of panic, which Angel Fire interrupts with a high-pitched, red-cheeked laugh.

"I'm kidding!" he squeals. "Come on. Let's go get your weapons."

Pressing past me, Sara says she wants to see more of this so-called Leisure Garrison first. She rubs her hands together like she's warming them over a fire and pins her eyes to each of ours in turn. "We might as well relax and have some fun while we can!" she declares with a broad grin and a loud clap of her hands.

Around me, my friends belt out their hearty agreement.

"You're all sure?" I ask.

As if she's secretly confessing something intimate to me, Sara leans in close enough for me to feel her breath in my ear. "We're supposed to be gathering intel, right? Imagine how impressed Kress will be when you come back to the Academy knowing every inch of this place and every bit of inside information about Angel Fire and the Army of the Unsettled."

"I don't—"

"Have any objections? Good." Her voice is weirdly warm and soothing, even after she's pulled back and announced our intention to take Angel Fire up on his offer to do some more touring.

Angel Fire cries out, "Great! Let's go!"

Matholook brushes his hair back and squints like he does when he's nervous or worried, and a small crease forms between his eyes. The rest of my Asylum, on the other hand, is all smiles and cheers.

I'm conflicted, but I'm also outnumbered. Letting out an exaggerated sigh, I tell everyone, "Okay, okay" and continue to follow Angel Fire along the rocky path between all the thrumming and trundling rigs.

In the meantime, I'm wracking my brain trying to figure out how to leave while also trying to figure out why my friends suddenly seem so eager to stay.

25

LEISURE

Before I have a chance to consider this in more detail or plot out our next move, I'm washed through with an interior wave of warmth.

The mental fizzle I've been feeling for the past hour or two evens out to a dull thrum and then morphs into the familiar, protective voice I've been hearing in my head since I was a little girl.

Haida!

~ *I've been scouting.*

Where?

~ *Not a place. I've been scouting a time.*

Her voice is much clearer now, but it's also hollow and strained, and it's as if her mind is out of breath.

I don't understand.

~ *I don't totally understand, either. But I'm afraid.*

Afraid? Of what?

~ *Our bond. It may be changing you.*

I sensed that.

~ *It's changing me, too.*

For the better, I hope.

~ Not if "for the better" means the ability...no...the curse to see things at their possible worst.

You sense danger, don't you?

~ Not yet. Now now. But somewhere...no, some when *up ahead.*

Some...when? Something's wrong. My head...it hurts. Why does it hurt?

At that second, my knees hit the ground, and someone grabs the sleeve of my jacket, hauls me back to my feet, and drags me to the side. I snap myself back into focus to find Matholook peering into my "Galaxy Eyes" while guiding me forward and asking if I'm okay.

As if I've been jarred from a deep sleep, it takes me half a second to shake off the fog. The inside of my head is swirling with flashing, overlapping images and pulses of strange, unfamiliar sensations and a spate of unnamable emotions. "What?" I stammer. "Oh. I was just talking with Haida."

Matholook points ahead to where a band of four girls on dirt bikes are zipping off into the distance, leaving four funnel-shaped clouds of spinning desert dust and debris in their wake. "They almost ran you over," he says through a wheezing cough.

"Is Branwynne okay?" Angel Fire calls back to us from up ahead where he's still walking along with the rest of my Asylum.

Matholook coughs again and gives him a thumbs up through the fading haze before turning back to me. "You *are* okay, aren't you?" He bends at the waist in front of me and leans in. "You know, it's impossible to read your eyes."

"Part of the mystery of me," I laugh.

"And you're really okay?"

"Just a little dizzy," I promise. I blink hard, massage my temples for a second, and then brush the film of powdery sand from the sleeves of my red leather jacket. "It's like Haida had to use all her strength just to connect us."

I let myself lose focus on Matholook while I search around in my head for Haida. It takes a second, but I find her.

Nearly getting run over...is that the danger you were talking about? I ask her.

~ *No. In fact, that might be about the least dangerous thing that's going to happen to you today.*

I can't tell if she's joking or if I misheard her, so I settle on conveying a single, simple truth: *It's good to have you with me.*

Our connection fades again before I can hear her answer, so I turn to Matholook and thank him for saving my life.

"Hardly," he chortles with a modest shrug as he plunges his hands into the hip pockets of his cargo pants. "I don't think any of those little dirt bikes of theirs could have done much damage. At best, I might have saved you from a few bumps and bruises and maybe some facial tire-tread marks."

"Well, thanks for saving me from *that*."

"Any time."

"Don't forget," Angel Fire shouts back to me, "The big rigs move at walking speed! The scouts and couriers, well, as you just found out, that's a whole different story!"

I thank him with a wave while I cough out bits of dust and spit grains of sand from my mouth.

Re-focused on the present and with a weird, crystal-clear, hyper-detailed impression of our surroundings (the colors, sounds, and scents seem more varied and vibrant than before), I can't help but gush to Matholook. "I can't believe what a *city* this place turned out to be."

"Come on," he urges, tugging the sleeve of my jacket again. (Only gently this time and not like he's trying to yank me out of a crocodile-filled river.) "Let's catch up with the others."

We follow Angel Fire and our Asylum around the front fender of a moving neon-green, pink-trimmed garbage truck, and Matholook says, "Whoa!" as a rolling line of double-decker, forty-five-foot-long buses rises up on either side of us. The churning wheels on each of these gargantuan rigs—ten on the cab and another set of six pairs under their bodies—are spray painted bright blue and are studded with jagged rows of triangular white spikes like the teeth of a prehistoric shark.

The windows along both floors of the massive, golden buses are scratched up and smoky, but we can still make out the silhouettes of dozens of people inside—on both the first and second floors—all of them jumping and dancing around to bass-heavy music thumping out through the vibrating glass.

Who'd have thought we'd find a dance club in the middle of a city-sized army on wheels?

"This is Leisure Garrison," Angel Fire calls out over the thunderous music that's loud enough to drown out the grind of engines and the hum of mag-transports all around us.

"You guys actually have leisure time?" Arlo shouts over the din of rumbling wheels and the thumping, window-shuddering music.

"Our lives don't revolve around war," Angel Fire snorts through a hand cupped around his mouth. "Unlike some people."

He looks right at Matholook when he says this. Matholook squints back at Angel Fire, his fists balled, before averting his eyes and uncurling his tense fingers. It's not a concession. I know Matholook will defend the motives of the Devoted to the death. But as a guest and a recently exonerated enemy combatant, he's being extra careful with how he reacts to our young host's in-your-face challenges. Plus, as a Caretaker, he's especially sensitive to the ways of others and all the things they're forced to be and all the things they're forced to do in order to survive in a land of countless dangers, few resources, and less hope.

"Our lives don't revolve around *anything*," Angel Fire clarifies, giving what I think is an approving nod to Matholook for refusing to escalate. "That's on purpose. It's why we're always on the move."

"A rolling stone...," I begin.

"Gathers no moss," he finishes with an impressed smile.

Gazing up at the nearest bus, Libra points back and forth between its first and second-floor windows, which are rattling hard enough to make me think they might explode at any second and shower us with shards of glass. "They're...they're really dancing in there?"

"It's the Midday Mingle," Angel Fire explains, as if it's the most normal thing in the world and shame on us for not knowing about it. "For us, for the Unsettled, being stagnant, locked in, clamped down...to a place or to the past, well, that's when fossilization happens." He taps a fingertip to his temple as we tighten our circle around him so we can hear. "The mind needs to keep moving. It's the only way to stop the worst parts of ourselves, the parts we hope at our best to leave behind and hope to hell they never catch up."

"Are we going in there?" I call out, pointing up at the trembling walls and windows of the rolling dance halls.

I breathe a weighty sigh of relief when he says, "No."

I may have been outvoted when it comes to getting out of here and trying to find our way back to the Academy, but that doesn't mean I'm anxious to jump into one of their traveling discos.

My first job was to keep my friends alive. I didn't just fail. I failed in spectacular fashion, and I know as sure as I know anything that I'll be carrying the last images of Mattea with me wherever I go for the rest of my life.

My second job was to gather enough intel to help us survive an inevitable war. Now, I'm walking through the Army of the Unsettled, amazed by everything I see but with no real knowledge about their location, destination, motives, weapons capabilities, or strategic plans I can bring back to Kress.

In the same instant, my heart locks up under clamps of grief, fear, curiosity, regret, and sorrow. I feel as if someone came along and sliced my brain up like a lemon drizzle cake, and I gasp at the overwhelming sensation of being pulled in a dozen different directions.

"I feel guilty," I confess to Matholook.

"Because of Mattea?"

"Uh huh."

He flicks his hand toward the pulsing, whale of a bus and scoffs. "It's not like we're going to go in there are join in their dance party."

"It's not that. Well, it's not *just* that."

"What then?"

"This place...this Leisure Garrison. The idea of being leisurely, of relaxing, reveling, having fun...It all seems so carefree."

"Being carefree is better than being worried, isn't it?"

"Maybe. But care*free* is a little too close to care-*less*. And I don't want to be careless with Mattea's memory."

I feel the pressure of tears behind my eyes, but I fight them off. I can't afford to lose my edge. Not here. Not now. Not like this.

Matholook puts his hand on the small of my back. In any other time or place, we'd find a nice, quiet corner to sit alone and talk. But sitting and being alone are out of the question, and there's not much that's nice or quiet about where we are.

So I settle for enjoying the light, reassuring pressure of his hand.

26

CHEERS

OUR NEXT STOP in the Leisure Garrison (not that anything here ever really stops) is at a section of the Unsettled army made up entirely of repurposed food and ice cream trucks. The once-white trucks still bear the faded text and images of a colorful array of logos, pictures of popsicles, and cartoon drawings of brownies, overflowing milkshakes, ice cream cones, and fully-loaded banana splits.

"Aww...This garrison looks so sweet!" Libra gushes, giggling at her own joke.

Shaking his head, Angel Fire holds up his hand, palm out. "This is the Dungeon District."

"Oh."

Walking through the garrison, thankful to be able to hear again after leaving the music of the so-called "Midday Mingle" behind us, I'm expecting jail cells and criminals in chains.

I'm partly right.

A lot of the people here *are* in chains. Strapped into leather cuffs and nearly cocooned in overlapping links of silver mana-cles, there are teenage boys and girls and a few people, whose gender is a mystery, all partially bound or strapped into patchy recliners and modified barber's chairs. But they're not prisoners. "It's one of our sex dungeons," Angel Fire explains, pointing to one of the larger, windowless white vans he says is called "the Palace of Pleasure." (We don't go in. I'm willing to take his word about what goes on in there.)

Sara lingers the longest and actually hops up onto the steel step and pokes her head into the van before Libra screams at her to "Get the frack down from there!"

"This Garrison is run by the 'S and M'ers,'" Angel Fire informs us as Sara—looking comically sad—jogs back over. "We've long ago given up on stopping them from doing whatever it is they do in there. Live and let live, and if it feels good, do it, right?"

"Too bad we can't have a visit," Sara sighs, giving her lips a long, exaggerated lick. "Sounds like it could be fun."

"Sure," I sneer. "If you don't mind chafing in ass-less chaps."

Sara sticks her nose in the air. "All chaps are ass-less," she corrects me and then asks Angel Fire about the lights coming from an expansive caravan of wide-bodied silver rigs up ahead.

Angel Fire says, "Ah. You've got good taste, my dear. That's one of our Coupled Cabins."

I'm about to ask what that means, but as we get closer, it's easy enough to figure it out on my own.

The tractor-trailers we've seen so far—the Trial Barge and the Port and Starboard Grandstands, included—have all been the standard fifty-three feet long, thirteen-and-a-half feet high, and just over eight feet wide.

(The lorries in London were a lot smaller, not that there were many intact or working ones left.)

These so-called Coupled Cabins, unlike the long American trailers, are two or, in some cases *three* of those single rigs welded together side by side.

Instead of a single tractor-trailer, the fused together trailers form enormous steel boxes on a system of shared axles and multiple sets of wheels. They look for all the world like rolling, aluminum-sided bungalows.

"We remove the interior walls," Angel Fire explains as we approach one of the huge, trundling rigs. "So they're plenty of roomy inside. Kind of like a lodge on wheels."

Picking up his pace enough to overtake the nearest of the trio of fused-together trailers, he leads us up a short set of metal steps and onto the back of the middle section of the Coupled Cabin. The boxy structure is framed on three sides by ribbed steel walls. But its back end is made up of huge panels of thick canvas in muted blues, dusty yellows, and phlegmy greens, most of it held together with zippers, metal latches, or else tied together Frankenstein-style with a crisscross stitching of thick, mustard-colored threads.

Angel Fire makes a grand show of unlatching and pulling back one of the rear panels and ushering us inside.

We step into the moving vehicle, and I glance up to where a giant mosquito net has been drawn over the top and is doing a surprisingly good job of keeping the heat out. (This might be the first time I've felt remotely cool since leaving the Academy.) The distorted pattern of squares cast by the long, sagging net on the murky interior makes the place feel like the inside of a beehive.

True to his word, the Coupled Cabin is brillie roomy.

Ignacio lets out a long, low, "Wowwww!" that makes Angel Fire laugh.

"It's huge," Arlo gushes.

"It's amazing what a vehicle can look like when you're not limited by the width of roads," Angel Fire brags.

The open interior of the three banded-together trailers is dotted with wooden tables and leather-topped barstools, all of them bolted to the floor, where twenty or so teenagers of the Unsettled are chatting happily over metal cylinders of some sort of drink that they raise to their lips and then plant down on magnetic pads embedded in the round tops of the bistro tables.

The metallic-pink liquid sloshes along with the rocking motion of the Compound Cabin, but the cups stay fixed to their silver mag-pads.

Unlike the previous two stops on our tour, this one doesn't have the rollicking chaos of frenetic dancing or the lascivious display of teenagers with whips, ball-gags, riding-crops, fishnet stockings, and high-heeled, black leather boots.

Libra nudges me with her elbow and directs my attention to the bar set up in front of the long side wall.

"Nice," I nod. "It's practically a proper pub." I direct her attention to the mesh-top ceiling. "If they replaced the netting with some oak beams..."

"Yeah," Libra agrees. "That'd be nice."

"Think they'll pour us a pint?"

Libra licks her lips and says she sure as frack hopes so.

Standing shoulder to shoulder around a table, we bump and jostle against each other like commuters on an overcrowded passenger train.

Matholook slips his hand over mine and gives it a little squeeze. "Can't have you falling over," he grins. "Again."

I tell him, "Thanks" and curl my fingers around his hand, grateful for the gesture of support but also for the warmth of his touch and the feeling of security it gives me.

Although I don't exactly have a ton of hand-holding experience, and I'm hardly the most touch-feely girl in the world, there's something about Matholook that makes it easy and warm just being in his orbit. I'm embarrassed at the stupid, gushy giggle I let out when he releases my hand and slips his arm around my waist, drawing me a little closer.

He's still a Devoted. His people could well be war-mongering murderers. Matholook could be the enemy. But even if he is, one thing's for sure: His arm feels amazing around my waist.

I'm tucked under his arm like a baby bird, and I hate that I like it.

"This is Sendahl's Saloon," Angel Fire announces, leaning over the table to make sure we can all hear him. His cheeks have the rosy glow of a teacher's pet who's been tasked with showing the new kids around. The smile is sweet, smug, and almost...cute?

Unless there's a whole committee of army generals we haven't met yet, as far as we can tell, this barely-pubescent kid commands every boy, girl, and adult of the entire Army of the Unsettled. In the short time we've been here, he's held us captive, put us on trial, bombarded us with challenges and mind-games, and may be responsible for instigating an upcoming war. He's powerful, mischievous, and kind of adorable all wrapped up in a cloak of cheeky charm and an ill-fitting suit.

Is this what it feels like to have a bratty little brother? Argh. What is it with me always getting charmed by the enemy? I've been called an "adrenaline junkie." Is there also such a thing as an "adversary addict?"

First, I feel an irresistible pull toward Matholook, whose Cult of the Devoted is dedicated to wiping out Emergents. And now, here I am, sitting next to him (with his arm pleasantly looped around my waist and his fingers drumming absently on my hip) and across from Angel Fire, whose Army of the Unsettled might *also* be dedicated to wiping out Emergents.

What is wrong with you, Branwynne? What kind of a nutter keeps going out of her way to get so cozy with Death?

Angel Fire drums his fingertips on the table and then rubs his hands together hard enough to make me think he's trying to start a fire. "Best drinks in town."

"I don't suppose they have fish and chips here?" I ask with a sassy smile.

"Unfortunately, no."

"Bangers and mash? Beef Wellington? Shepherd's pie?"

"I don't know what any of that is," Angel Fire confesses. He flicks his thumb in the general direction we just came from. "But 'Bangers and Mash' sounds like something they'd do back there in the Dungeon District."

Laughing, I reach over and give his forearm a playful swat with the back of my hand. Probably not the wisest thing to do to the leader of a monstrous, moving army, but something in the air keeps nudging at me to let my guard down. Unfortunately, it's becoming easier to do with each passing minute.

I fall back into my own head for a second to remind myself what's important: *Mattea. My mission. My friends. Our survival.*

With Matholook next to me, Angel Fire across from me, and my Asylum looking way too relaxed with their big smiles and with their elbows on the round tabletop, it's hard to stay in my head for long.

Pulled back into the bizarre reality of our situation, I let out an easy breath of relaxation as Angel Fire waves to the tall girl behind the bar. He makes a swirling motion with his finger at the six of us at the table. The girl—bald, bug-eyed, and skeletal enough under her baggy jumpsuit to walk through a harp—nods and starts pouring frothy pink liquid from a huge glass pitcher into a row of wide-mouthed, pewter mugs.

By the time she brings the drinks over—beaming a sparkling, toothy smile at each of us in turn—we're already slipping into our own little side conversations. Angel Fire is explaining more about the Army of the Unsettled to Sara, who is drinking in every word like the covert spy I know she wants to be. Libra, Arlo, and Ignacio are on the far side of the table from me, hunched together in their own three-person confab and talking far too loudly about how different the Unsettled are from what we were told or ever imagined.

Matholook must notice me toggling between relaxation and disengagement because he leans in close to ask me what's wrong.

I tell him, "Mattea," and my chest tightens up, and I feel like I might burst into tears right here at this table and in front of everyone. "She should be here. Or else none of us should."

I expect Matholook to lean away or get weirded out or something. But instead, he leans in, those soulful, emerald-green eyes of his gazing into mine. A few tendrils of his brown-blond hair fall across his face, but he doesn't slide them away or tuck them back the way I've seen him do so many times before. It's like he doesn't even notice and all he sees right now is me. "She's not a casualty of war."

"What do you mean?" I say, snapping him a pre-offended glare.

"I don't mean that in a bad way," he answers with a whoosh of hurried breath. "What I mean is, you're a warrior." He swings his eyes around the table at Angel Fire and our friends who are all oblivious to us and immersed in their own conversations. "All of you are warriors," Matholook explains. "But Mattea didn't die in a war. Or in battle."

"That wouldn't have made losing her any easier."

"No. I know it wouldn't. But it would have been in line with the life she was living and the lives you've all been in training to protect."

"I don't—"

"It's like the Devoted always say about history. The course of history flows like a river with all the events acting as rocks along the way."

"And we're all just leaping from one to the next."

"And sometimes, you just land the wrong way on the right rock."

"You're saying her death was destined?" I say, leaning back with a scowl. "Or that it had some kind of purpose or meaning?"

Matholook puts his hand on top of mine. I'm tempted to pull away, but there's something magnetic about his touch, so I leave my hand where it is. He gives it a little pat before drawing away, himself. He locks his sorrowful eyes onto mine. "I'm saying Mattea is now part of that chain. And you will be stronger, smarter, and better able to take your own next steps thanks to her."

"Small consolation," I grunt into a shallow sip of the pink drink in front of me.

"I wasn't trying to be consoling. There's no way to return from what happened back there. There's only going forward." Matholook offers a feeble half-smile. "Like the Unsettled do. They don't ever stop. And neither should we."

The way he's looking at me and the wink he offers up makes me wonder who he means by "we."

The Cult of the Devoted?

Our Asylum?

Me and him?

"So...," Angel Fire drawls, tapping me on the shoulder. "What do you think?"

"I think this place is the weirdest normal thing I've ever seen," I call out over the boisterous laughs, the hoisted pints, and the happy buzz of conversations going on around us.

Everything and everyone in here is shaking all the time, but it doesn't take too long to get used to it. It's how I imagine it is to be on a boat on the open ocean. (In my time exploring London after the last big wave of drone strikes, I once navigated the corpse and garbage-filled River Thames on a raft of wood planks that had broken off from a pier under Tower Bridge. I strapped a toilet lid to a broom handle to use as a paddle and steered as best as I could. With a small group of the Royal Fort Knights deciding to fire arrows at me from the riverbank, I only made it as far as London Bridge—or, what was left of it—before I had to bail. And that's as close as I've ever been to being on an actual boat.)

Angel Fire raises his mug and leads us in a toast. "On behalf of the Unsettled, I'm so glad we didn't kill you!"

We all raise our mugs and clink them over a chorus of, "Cheers!"

The pink drink (Angel Fire calls it "mineral beer," but it's grainy and tastes like malted sweat) is still surprisingly refreshing and gives me a tingle I can feel in my toes.

Or is it Matholook's arm slipped back around my waist that's doing that?

Drawing me close, he gives me a playful squeeze. Directly across the table from us, Libra beams us a goofy smile while Sara's lip curls into a mean snarl, which morphs into a pouty frown.

Sara's looked at me in weird ways before. Sometimes, it's been impatience. Sometimes, curiosity or contempt. A lot of times, it's been condescension. Now, it's pure hostility.

Her dull blue eyes dart back and forth between me and Matholook. At first, she doesn't seem to notice or care that I'm fully aware of her angry little gaze. Then, she averts her eyes and turns her attention back to Angel Fire.

What—are you jealous? Maybe you'd have a boy who likes you too if you weren't always being such a skanky little b—.

27

SHOSTAKOVICH

THE REEDY BARTENDER glides over again with another round and whispers something into Angel Fire's ear.

His eyes wide, he presses his palms together as if in prayer and says, "Really?"

The girl nods, and the two of them exchange a happy, slapping high-five before the girl retreats to her bar to dole out more rounds of bubbly pink beer to the patrons.

I've been in battle before. I've fought on my own and with a small team or two. But I've never been part of an entire, city-sized army. Is this what it's like before a war? Shopping. Laughing. Drinking. Joking. Happy high-fives?

"We've got a treat for you," Angel Fire announces, breaking my train of thought. "A classical music concert."

Wait—is the Army of the Unsettled getting weirder or more normal right before our eyes?

Adjusting his tie and squaring his shoulders under his over-sized blazer, Angel Fire directs our attention to the far end of the trailer, past the drinking and chattering kids, to where a barefoot boy, dressed all in black, is setting up four steel-framed folding chairs in a semi-circle on top of a low wooden platform.

A series of long glass tubes embedded in the trailer floor flash white and metallic blue. The crowd settles down, and then the entire trailer falls into a muted, almost impossible silence. The constant ping of pebbles and dirt, the dinosaur-thunder of truck tires, the gravelly blast of dirt-bikes, the chatter and busyness of all the people we've encountered so far...it all fades, leaving only the rhythmic thrum of the vehicle's magnetic propulsion system.

Across from me, Angel Fire sounds modest, almost to the point of being embarrassed, when he tells us, "Only eight percent of the fleet has been retrofitted with the Mag-Catalyst Conversion System. We used dry milled corn ethanol for years... until the last of the crops disappeared. Biofuels are hard to come by without a biosphere, right? So we rely on our harvested stores. I'd show you the big silo trucks, but they're on the far side of the fleet." He brightens up when he adds, "Oh, and we're working on radiothermal generation and thorium as potential energy sources."

I'm about to ask him more about their power sources and fuel consumption (not as a spy this time, but more out of genuine curiosity), but he puts a finger to his lips and directs our attention back to the small stage.

Out of the surprising stillness, four teenagers emerge from between the panels of an inky black curtain hanging behind the wooden platform.

I jump a little when the Unsettled around us, Angel Fire included, burst into a hearty round of loud, spontaneous applause. Although we don't know what they're clapping about, my Asylum and I join in, hoisting our glasses in the air and laughing when the pink liquid sloshes from everyone's mugs.

On the stage, the four teens take a little bow and ease down into the padded metal-framed chairs.

The two boys in the quartet are each sporting an ill-fitting tuxedo jacket over a starched white shirt (complete with ruffles running down the middle), a crisp black bow tie, and a ribbed, red cummerbund slung snugly around their waists. Instead of matching black pants or highly polished shoes, though, they're wearing faded, powder-blue jean shorts with frayed edges and grungy leather sandals on their feet.

The two girls, slick-haired and with their swarthy skin glistening with a sheen of sweat, are each decked out in a sleeveless black cocktail dress with an apple-red bandana tied around their necks and bright yellow, hole-filled stockings covering their legs. Their feet are enveloped in mismatched, dusty hiking boots with the laces dragging in loose coils on the floor.

They're an oddly dressed bunch. Wealthies on top. Beggars on the bottom.

Isn't that always the way?

At the Academy, we have a standard kit, uniforms that are color-coded according to which Cohort you belong to. I know from history class that armies throughout time have relied on strict uniform codes. This is to inspire camaraderie, encourage team spirit, and to differentiate your army from the enemy. Even the Cult of the Devoted draw on their patriotic palette of reds, whites, and blues.

Sitting here in our matching black tactical cargo pants, black military boots, and our white compression tops with the blue Academy shield on the upper chest, my friends and I must look like a squad of leftover Patriot Army special agent operatives.

Other than my trademark red leather jacket (and our accumulating layers of blood, sweat, and dirt), we're a fairly coordinated bunch.

But the Army of the Unsettled...well, let's just say that the apocalypse didn't only wipe out cities and huge swaths of the human population. Here, it seems to have wiped out any sense of style or uniformity along the way.

And I'm not so sure that's a bad thing.

"We're lucky," Angel Fire beams. He plants one hand on Libra's shoulder and the other on Ignacio's and gives them each a little shake. "We got here just in time. They're scheduled to play one of my favorites: Shostakovich's Quartet Number Three in F Major, Opus 73."

We all stare at him for a second, but he's too buried in glee to notice.

His eyes on the four musicians up at the front of the trailer, he mumbles, more to himself than to us, "For this piece, Dmitri Shostakovich originally titled the five movements but retracted the titles after 1946 for some reason."

Too startled to offer up any brilliant commentary, I say, "Oh," and leave it at that.

Up on the low stage, one of the boys, tall but lanky nearly to the point of being malnourished, has a cello clamped between his bony, dirt-creased knees. Looking like it's been attacked by a mountain lion, the hourglass-shaped instrument is pockmarked and scarred, with deep, dark trenches dragged through its surface. Whatever luster it once had has long since faded, ravaged no doubt by its exposure to desert dust-storms and to the wind and the scorching sun searing over the open plains and barren prairies out here in the American West.

The two boys and two girls break into a random flurry of dragging their bows across the strings, which they pluck while they reach over to fiddle with the rows of little white tuning pegs.

"*This* is classical music?" Ignacio asks, his palms pressed to his ears. "It sounds like an alien howler monkey massaging a crying baby with a carrot-peeler."

"They're warming up, Dummy," Arlo says, with an elbow to Ignacio's arm and accompanied by a swooping eyeroll.

"Oh."

"I'm glad Ignacio said it," I confess to Matholook from behind my hand. "I was thinking the same thing."

The lack of access to music is one of the things we all have in common. My parents used to talk about music all the time: Jazz. Rock and Roll. Classical. Postmodern Fusion. Neuro-Algorithmic Arrangement. I've seen pictures of various instruments, and I know about music, of course, but I never actually heard any of it. Libra, Arlo, Ignacio, Sara, and Mattea grew up in a Processor. Their lives were a series of experiments, tests, and tortures. The Cult of the Devoted are all about history, politics, and the art of war. Kress and our other teachers are tunnel-visioned about training us to save the world. So...not a lot of extra time for music, dance, or any of the arts.

So now, sitting here while the musicians warm up and Angel Fire glows in anticipation, I'm brain-deep in an inexplicable flood of regret. I've always thought of our mission as being all about saving people. Maybe even saving structures and institutions. I never thought about us saving the Arts. I was never exposed to any of that directly. And now, two minutes into a discordant warmup, I feel a protective surge of urgency about needing to save it.

Is it possible to miss something you never had?

After a moment of silence, the four teens lock eyes and then break into an overlapping round of rapid-fire notes. The music —a dizzying spectrum of volumes, pitches, and tones—multiplies, overlaps, thunders forward, sneaks back, and loops around and around. I follow the refrain, but then I lose it, and it's like the four instruments are teasing me, goading me on, and then forgetting about me altogether before finding me again and calling out for me to follow them. It sounds right goofy to say, but the music makes me feel wanted, like life has meaning.

Not my life, necessarily. Just life in general.

Matholook's arm is still around my waist with his hand

curved over my hip. I tuck my hand over his and pretend that something caught my eye on the other side of the room.

I don't want him to see me cry.

I always figured—with how I grew up, who I am, and with all the things I've seen, done, experienced, and survived—I'd know pretty much every feeling, sensation, and emotion there is. But this is a surprise. It's been five minutes, and I feel like I'm hearing, seeing, and feeling for the first time.

The boy behind the cello works feverishly, his nearly shoulder-length mop of half-dreadlocked, sun-bleached hair flopping up and down with the sway of his body and left and right with the humming, still slightly uneven wobble of the trailer.

Next to the cellist, the other boy has a violin clamped under his jaw. Unlike the cellist, his body is rigid as a rock. But the fingers on his left hand are a blur over the tapered neck of his little instrument, and his right hand is a dynamic piston as he skips the bow over the fluttering strings.

The girl on the other violin—her scraggly hair cut in a bob, her unlaced boots twitching and kicking hard enough to make her shoelaces dance—plays with the stern ferocity of someone out for revenge. As if carved in stone, her face is tense, furious, and stern.

The other girl has what looks like a larger violin, which Angel Fire tells us is a viola. I've heard about them, but I've never seen one in real life. This girl is a composed figure of spectacular beauty. Bare-armed, dark-haired, and fair-skinned, she leans into her instrument like someone playing a frenzied game of tug-of-war with their small dog. Her body dances in a push-pull rhythm, and she seems to be sitting in place in her chair and moving in five different directions at the same time.

When one of the violinists starts plucking at the strings, I think maybe she's upset and trying to snap them, but Angel Fire leans over the table and tells us what she's doing is called "Pizzicato."

"It's an Italian term," he explains in as much of a whisper as he can manage. "It means 'to pinch.'"

It's a proper good sound but sort of chilling, too, since it reminds me of the sound of stay bullets plinking into fields of desert sand and stone.

At each brief pause in the performance, Angel Fire leans over and whispers to our huddled group.

"That was the Allegretto. Very playful. The original title was 'Blithe Ignorance of the Future Cataclysm.'"

"Gloomy title," Matholook says.

"But true," I add.

In class at the Academy, Brohn once told us there are three ingredients in evil: fear, ignorance, and insecurity. "Every injustice you see in the world stems from one or more of those."

I wonder if this Shostakovich bloke knew about the horrific power of "blithe ignorance." I wonder if he knew the world was going to look like this nearly a hundred-and-fifty years after his birth.

After a heartbeat of a pause, the quartet launches into the next movement, which Angel Fire informs us is called "The Moderato con Moto."

"It was originally entitled, 'Forces of War Unleashed,'" he adds.

He closes his eyes, and his finger does a little conductor's wag above the table. "Listen to the skipping rhythm of the waltz as it strains to be allowed to cut loose. There's potential energy behind the notes. Like they're being held back but are ready to explode."

With that index finger of his bopping in the air in time with the beat, he's a boy-warlord with a connoisseur's passion for classical music, and I'm impressed with his combination of knowledge and keen affection.

Matholook drums his fingers in light taps against my hip, and I glance over at him to see that he has his eyes closed. He nods and says, "I can feel it."

Feel what? The music? My heart telling me how nice it is to be nestled up against you? Or my brain, shouting at me to run like hell?

I try to listen harder to hear what he's hearing, but I'm having trouble concentrating. The music is fast and complex. But that's not what's throwing me off. It's the arm around my waist, the fingers curved over my hip, and the tapping of Matholook's foot I can feel against my own. It's like he's in sync with the music, and I'm in sync with him. Which I should *not* be allowing to happen.

Bugger-all, Branwynne. The Unsettled said it themselves: He's a potential traitor, spy, and enemy combatant!

But he's also modest, painfully good-looking, and he always says the right things to make me feel the right ways...plus, his eyes are like Arctic Ocean water, and I'm feeling the impulsive urge to join the polar bear club.

Angel Fire must sense that I'm losing focus, because he locks his eyes onto mine before flicking them back to the quartet. "That was the Allegro non troppo. Also known as 'Rumblings of Unrest and Anticipation.'"

Story of my life.

After a few minutes, he whispers around the table, "That's the Adagio. 'In Memory of the Dead.' Listen for the resonance of the cello and the lamentation of the viola."

Across from me, Libra is smiling and crying at the same time. On either side of her, Ignacio and Arlo put their arms around her, and I know—I knew the second Angel Fire said the words, "Memory of the Dead"—we all have exactly one word, one thought, one person, and one memory on our minds:

Mattea.

It's a painful but fleeting feeling that evaporates almost as quickly as it formed.

She just died. So why the mental fog? Why am I having so much trouble remembering? Is it because I don't want that image in my head ever again? I feel like someone slipped a filter in my brain, and it's weeding out memories, desires, my connection with Haida, and my thoughts of Mattea.

After a brief pause in the music, Angel Fire tells us "The composer's final command is *morendo*. It's where the sound slowly dies away."

"It's very pretty," Libra says, wiping tears from her cheeks with her fingertips.

"This is the last part coming up...it's the Moderato. Also known as 'The Eternal Question: Why? And for What?'"

Those are very good eternal questions.

In my mind, the plan was to stay here for a few minutes, tops, and then get moving to the Security Garrison to pick up our weapons and get the frack out of here before Angel Fire and his Army of the Unsettled changed their minds and decided to eat us after all.

But "a few minutes" has morphed into half an hour as the waves of music continue to wash over us.

A couple of seconds of silence snap me to full attention. I wonder if maybe the performance was worse than I thought, and the Unsettled in the audience are expressing their quiet disapproval.

And then, with a roar that drowns out every grumble, rumble, and ambient sound around us, the Unsettled in the moving, make-shift pub-slash-concert hall explode into a full-on round of standing, thunderous applause.

I can feel the vibrations of their ovation in my bones.

Flanking me, Matholook and Libra start laughing, and then I realize that Sara, Arlo, and Ignacio are laughing, too. And so am I, and it occurs to me that we're all experiencing the same wave of relief. Not just about being alive, but because—after being swept away by the mastery of these four musicians—it feels like now we have something unexpected but vitally important to stay alive *for*.

I make a mental note to talk to Kress about adding some Fine Arts to the Academy's courses if...*when* we get home.

28

FRIENDS

WITH THE CONCERT OVER, Angel Fire weaves between the high-top bistro tables as he rushes forward to embrace the four musicians.

The five of them leap into each other's arms, bouncing and jumping around to the whistles and cheers of the rest of the Unsettled audience. With all the foot-stomping, chest-bumps, and happy shoulder punches combining with the slight but still noticeable shifts and shimmies of the rig, the place has the feel of a jubilant birthday party in the middle of a mild earthquake.

Jumping to our feet, my Asylum and I join in, cheering and clapping, with Ignacio climbing up onto his barstool, pumping a fist and whistling through his fingers as he ducks down to avoid the shade-netting sagging over his head.

"Get down from there, Dummy," Arlo warns, reaching up to keep Ignacio from being flung down by the jostling crowd of celebrating teenagers.

Libra joins Arlo in helping Ignacio clamber back down. Blushing, Ignacio says, "I guess I got carried away."

"I can't say I blame you," Libra tells him. "I've never heard anything like that."

High-fiving everyone in the crowd as he passes, Angel Fire makes his way back to our table. He dabs sweat from his forehead with a folded white handkerchief, which he refolds and tucks into the breast pocket of his oversized blazer. "So...," he pants, "did you enjoy that?"

Libra plants both hands on his chest, and for a second, I think she might be about ready to kiss him. "What *was* that?"

"It's called chamber music," Angel Fire laughs. "Joseph Haydn was one of its pioneers. He helped music become a kind of conversation, as much about socializing as about performing. It requires a balance of skills and personalities where all the players at every moment in every measure need to know when to be assertive and when to turn over command to someone else. It takes something that has the potential to be divisive and balances it to form something harmonious, intimate, and potentially life-changing. Kind of like what we're doing now." He tugs his handkerchief back out and gives his forehead a second wipe before telling us it's time to move on. "A fun fact," he adds, peeling back the canvas panel-door and hopping down from the moving pub, "it used to be called, 'the music of friends.'"

At that, Matholook and I, hand-in-hand, follow him out, with the rest of our Asylum hopping down to the ground right after us.

"Where are we going now?" I ask.

Angel Fire pauses long enough to give me a quizzical stare, and for a second, I think maybe I have something on my face, a pink beer moustache or something. "You want to get to your weapons, right?" he says at last.

I blush, embarrassed about forgetting what should have been the most important, pressing thing on any of our minds.

There's that fog again.

According to Kress, the Cult of the Devoted have the ability to recruit people into their ranks through a sort of subtle, communal brainwashing.

"I'm not sure how it works," she confessed. "But you need to be on your toes. Sometimes it's hard to tell if you're doing what you're doing because you *want* to do it or because someone else is manipulating you into doing it."

And now, I'm wondering if something similar could be happening here. I've got a specific mission to finish, and there are countless dangers between me and success. Nothing is more important right now than getting our weapons back.

Could the mental haze be because of the music? If so, is music the best thing in the world, or the worst, for making me forget?

WE'VE BEEN WALKING along for a while, and I've already noticed how we keep automatically adjusting our speed to that of the moving vehicles around us.

Maybe it's just chance. Or maybe my Asylum and I have synched up out of a sense of self-preservation. After all, slowing down or speeding up too much around here could easily end with a person crushed under a set of wheels or treads and left to rot among the rocks and the crispy, straggling weeds.

I don't care what Angel Fire says about how slow these things go. I'll take my chances against pretty much any person— or even multiple people—in a fight. Most of these rigs, though, are a few dozen tons of something else entirely.

"You know," I say to Angel Fire, "the Unsettled are different from what we heard and a *lot* different from what we expected."

"Then maybe you shouldn't believe everything you hear. Or put too much faith in your expectations."

We all nod our agreement, and Angel Fire tells us we need to keep moving. (That seems to be their mantra around here.) "There's more to see between here and the Military Garrison at the front of the fleet," he boasts, "and I'm sure you won't feel comfortable until you have your weapons back in hand. I know I wouldn't."

As we continue marching along, various adult men and women queue up behind us and shuffle forward, one by one, to ask Angel Fire about one thing or another.

Despite being surrounded by the six of us—all total strangers and only recently released from a very public penalty of death—they don't seem too concerned about secrecy or privacy.

Often shouting to be heard over the rev of nearby engines, the clunk of gears, the clang of slamming metal doors, or the putter of darting and dashing dirt-bikes, the adults hurl questions at Angel Fire before sprinting off to enact his orders.

A man with a head of thick, woolly hair sprints up first with a floppy spiral notebook in hand. "The Advanced Scouts have updated reports of troop movement for the Devoted."

Angel Fire wrinkles his nose and fires a hostile glance at Matholook who responds in the only way he can: with a blush and a helpless shrug.

Dipping his head back around to face the messenger, Angel Fire seems relaxed as he strides along, issuing orders, his hands clasped loosely behind his back. "Dispatch two Strike Squads. Make sure Callie leads one of them. Have them take four of the good Skid-Steers from the Search and Rescue squad. Callie'll know which ones."

The man says, "Yes, Governor," before jotting some notes in his notebook with the nub of an orange pencil. He rolls the pad closed, tucking it into his back pocket, and sprints off the way he came.

A woman, her hair braided through with silver and golden wire, pops out from between a row of garbage trucks moving along next to us. Striding into the wind, her long, brown trench coat billows out around her like a cape. She draws the belts around from the sides and ties them off as she approaches. (And it's a good thing, too. Otherwise, I'm pretty sure she might catch too much air and go sailing off like a human kite.) The trench coat lady asks Angel Fire what she's supposed to do next.

Calling out over the crunching of the treads from the pair of backhoes next to us, he tells her, "Get the weapons inventory results from Varetta in the Military Garrison. Make sure she includes the new and repaired stock. And tell her we're on our way."

"Yes, Governor." And then the woman sprints off, her rubber flip-flops slapping against her heels, her trench coat whipping along behind her as her belts come undone and she cuts at a right angle and disappears into a crowd of pedestrians.

The next woman shuffles forward, and Angel Fire greets her with a friendly nod. The woman asks him something I can only partly hear about energy efficiency or some such thing.

He tugs on the shoulder of the woman's faded, silvery coolant tunic, drawing her in close. "Tell Galisteo to consult with Canova about the upgrade to the solar cells. And remind her about tomorrow's Navigation Committee meeting."

"Yes, Governor."

The woman dashes off and is replaced by a shirtless man with a broad, red chest.

"Ethanol production was down another fourteen percent as of yesterday," Angel Fire says to the man. "Tell Straton and Colby I want to know why and what they plan on doing about it. Make sure they consult with Minden. She should still be in her lab in the Tech Garrison."

"Yes, Governor."

It goes on like that as we walk, grown men and women of the Unsettled, rattling off reports, asking questions, taking orders, and rushing off to do Angel Fire's bidding.

There's a sort of chaotic efficiency to it all. Back at the Academy, I've seen teachers and students pouring into Wisp's office to ask her questions of one kind or another. I've been in Kress's office when we've been interrupted by students seeking dispute resolution or one of the other teachers needing information or guidance about lessons, combat training, or facility maintenance issues. But in those cases, there were walls and desks, and the person being sought out sat and listened and solved the random problems that came popping up over any given day.

Here, even strategy sessions happen on the move.

My mum used to tell me about how you used to be able to see the stars at night. "Our planet is rotating on its axis while it revolves around the sun," she said, her eyes on the lofty wood and stone ceiling back in the Tower of London. "And the sun is in constant motion at the center of the solar system that's spinning around other solar systems throughout the galaxy that's also spinning. So you see," she finished, "the key to the universe is motion. We're always in it, even when we think we're not."

Watching Angel Fire in action is like that: objects in orbit around other objects in orbit around even more objects in orbits of their own, and on and on it goes.

"I've got to give the Unsettled credit," Arlo says from just behind me. "They've got this place running like a well-oiled machine."

"Look around you," Libra corrects him with a laugh. "This entire place *is* a well-oiled machine."

"How many of you are there, exactly?" Sara asks, sidling up next to Angel Fire.

"Looking for a tactical advantage?" he grins, along with a knowing wink.

"Just curious."

"You know what curiosity did to the cat, right?"

Sara rakes her fingers through her hair and shakes her head. "Um. No."

"It killed it."

"She was just making conversation," Libra apologizes on Sara's behalf. Tugging Sara by the sleeve, she gives her a *shut-the-frack-up* look. Sara scowls and yanks her arm out of Libra's grip and shuffles ahead to keep plying Angel Fire with questions.

She asks him about the size of the army, their inventory of food and water rations, their navigation systems...everything.

To my surprise, he answers every question. And not like he's being interrogated. He seems proud of his army and is clearly happy to share its specs with a bunch of teenagers I think he's starting to think of as friends.

As it turns out, he's a gifted multi-tasker. He continues to field questions from his own people, offer suggestions, and solve problems as the men and women of the Unsettled approach him like autograph hounds descending on a celebrity. At the same time, Sara asks him some more about the different Garrisons, the general history of the Unsettled, the way their army is structured...and he keeps on telling her everything she wants to know.

Is he a careless, unsuspecting, and piss-poor excuse of a general? Or is Sara a more convincing spy than I thought? Either way, if he wants to give us a huge tactical advantage, who am I to stop him?

As confident as a conductor, Angel Fire continues to keep tabs on everything around him. But there's more to it than control. He has a balanced relationship with his own people, and he seems committed to developing a harmonious one with us.

As we walk along, the tension in my body and the weight on my heart seem to lighten. Taking in Angel Fire and my Asylum, I feel like maybe—just *maybe*—we're all becoming players in "the music of friends."

29

EXPLANATIONS

SHUFFLING ALONG SO his long strides don't have him outpacing the rest of us, Ignacio tosses in a few questions of his own.

Angel Fire responds to him, too, while he's also, apparently, running the entire army by himself as we continue to walk along next to the rolling fleet of vehicles.

"We didn't always live like this," he explains. "How much do you know about the last twenty years?"

"We learn about history in the Academy," Ignacio boasts.

"And this guy's people are *all* historians," Arlo adds, clapping a hand to Matholook's shoulder.

"So you know about Krug, the Patriot Army, the Eastern Order, the Drone Strikes, the Atomic Wars?"

We all nod, and Libra gushes about how he can ask us anything, like she's excited to show off her knowledge for a teacher before the big test.

"I believe you," Angel Fire laughs. "And how much did you know about *us*? Before today, anyway."

This time, there are no nods and no cocky claims about our knowledge. Instead, we respond with an embarrassing, humbled, and slack-jawed silence.

"The truth is," I tell him finally, "we heard *some*."

"And we assumed a lot," Arlo admits.

"But I guess we didn't really *know* all that much for sure," Libra confesses with a resigned sigh.

"Don't worry," Angel Fire reassures us. "This isn't a test. You've already passed all of those. Our secrecy has been part deliberate, part accidental. It was deliberate because our founders were trying to escape our country's self-inflicted apocalypse. And it *was* self-inflicted. Make no mistake. Any enemy you might have heard about was just a fearmongering fiction to cover for Krug's real enemies."

"Who were his real enemies?" Sara asks.

"Anyone who was honest and unafraid. Anyone who refused to sit still. Anyone with the courage to ask questions or challenge their own convictions. Our founders discovered that not only is a moving target—even one that grew to be as big as ours —hard to hit, it's also hard to get to know."

We continue padding along in a cluster around him as he navigates the laneways, waving at his fellow Unsettled, asking questions about their health or their families, and exchanging friendly greetings as he goes. He seems to know everyone's name and everything about them. "Nearly twenty years ago," he says, turning his attention back to us, "the floodgates to greed and selfishness opened. Everything that had kept them back— empathy, charity, compassion—wound up being disposable. So Krug disposed of them."

"Not just Krug," Matholook offers. "There were a lot of complicit people: politicians, law enforcement, civilians..."

"All true," Angel Fire agrees, "but Krug makes such a great scapegoat, wouldn't you say?"

"I don't think—"

"I'm kidding," Angel Fire interrupts with a pleasant laugh. "It's just easier to blame everything on one person than to admit that it takes millions of people—either through action or inaction—to enable evil to flourish. The founders of the Unsettled, they didn't want to be part of the problem, and they didn't want to be part of the solution. They just wanted to *be*. For our founders, the world didn't go to Hell. Hell came to them. So they moved on. What started out as an abstraction—the whole 'rolling stone' metaphor—evolved into a reality. Our oldest members got the idea of staying in constant motion. The drones were mostly attacking cities and high-value infrastructure targets. They weren't being programmed to go after desert nomads. So that's what we became. It was the only way to stay safe. And we scooped up followers along the way. People were desperate, and we took them all in. It didn't matter to our founders how you lived or what you thought. As long as you could commit to being in constant motion." He makes a sweeping, general gesture at the army and presses a fingertip to his temple. "Out there or in here."

"That's pretty enlightened of them," Libra says with a surprised but approving grin.

Angel Fire agrees. "The original Unsettled were kids, like all of us. Untainted, unprejudiced, and scared to death of staying still. And it's been this way ever since. Don't get me wrong. *Knowing* your roots is great. Being locked in place by them...well, that's something our founders decided was too high of a price to pay."

I catch myself riveted by his history lesson and by the bits of philosophy he sprinkles in. But it's more than that. I'm amazed at how much he seems to know for someone so young. He sounds smart—maybe even wise—but not pretentious or condescending. He looks twelve, acts fifteen, and talks like someone who's lived five lifetimes.

"Isn't it hard living like this, though?" Matholook asks.

"The Devoted live out here, too," I remind him.

"But we have a secure compound. We're building and grow-ing, expanding out. Being on the move all the time like the Unsettled...I just can't get my head around it."

"Fuel shortages are a problem," Angel Fire admits. "That's why we've been working on developing solar and magnetic propulsion and a host of other alternate energy systems. And then there's water shortages and Dust Devils."

Ignacio scrunches up his face. "Um...Dust Devils?"

"Vortexes of sand and wind. Like a cyclone or a tornado. They pop up out here all the time. It's the result of radical temperature fluctuations. The Earth has natural freeze-thaw cycles and atmospheric balance. It didn't take much more than a couple hundred years of human interference to throw it all off and then another decade or two to thoroughly knock it completely out of whack. So now it's hot where it should be cold, windy where it should be calm, and chaotic all over. We Unsettled...we stopped *fighting* the chaos. Now, we *ride* it."

Laughing, he makes a wavy, dolphin-like motion with his hand, like it's surfing on the air.

"The kids run the Unsettled," Libra says. "I get that. But what happens when you get older?"

"This." Angel Fire's broad hand-sweep nearly knocks me over. "This is Retirement Garrison."

He directs our attention to a huge collection of nearly iden-tical motorhomes, all chrome and white and startlingly clean considering the constant clouds of dust swirling around, through, and over the constantly moving city.

"How do you keep them so clean?" Ignacio asks.

Angel Fire slaps his open hand to the slick side of one of the lumbering behemoths and then, just as quickly, says, "Ouch!" and snaps his hand back. "Synth Steel but coated with a magno-static, polytetrafluoroethylene particle repellent. Makes it hot as hell, but it keeps the dirt and dust and such from sticking." He gazes up into the side window of one of the motorhomes as we pass. Inside, a man with thick gray dreadlocks presses his palm to the glass and nods at us as we walk along. Angel Fire tips his head in return and goes on to tell us more about the fleet of motorhomes in the Retirement Garrison.

"Forty-one feet long. Leveling jacks. Double awnings and slide-out generators. Eight batteries. Gravity water fill. Leather seats. Full kitchen and dinette. Bedroom. Bathroom. These are condos on wheels. The first Unsettled 'liberated' most of them from a bunch of dealerships in Denver long before the city got bombed and walled off."

"Liberated?" Matholook asks.

"Pilfered," I explain. "Filched."

"Filched?"

"You know: Nicked."

"Who the frack is Nick? And why the frack do you want to pinch him?"

"Wait. Are you having me on?"

Matholook's lips are straight, and his eyes are expressionless. "Maybe."

And then it's like his whole face bursts open into a belly-clutching laugh.

I shove him hard enough to stagger him into Ignacio who growls and pushes him back into me. Pretending Matholook is about to fall, I throw my arms around him and say, "Whoa!"

"You saved me," he pretend gushes.

"You're worth saving," I answer, speaking the real and total truth. And then, sadly, I release him from my unnecessary bear hug as Angel Fire leads us along.

On either side of us, all the motorhomes have low, wrought-iron fences encircling their rooftops. Adult men and women sitting in lawn chairs on the tops stare down at us with what I can only imagine is a combination of confusion and curiosity. While most of the Unsettled are dressed in their hodgepodge of mushroom-colored clothes, my Asylum and I are still sporting our Academy kits.

"I hope they don't think we're the spearhead to an invading army," I sigh. "We must look like a military squad. Or maybe a biker gang."

Libra says she doubts anyone is that suspicious of us. "Especially with Angel Fire leading the way." She bites her lip as she scans the rooftops of the motorhomes, returning the gaze of the dozens of staring faces. "They don't look all that old."

"Don't let looks fool you," Angel Fire cautions her. "All of them are over twenty. And some of them," he adds with a semi-horrified gasp, "are in their *forties*."

The rest of my Asylum doesn't seem to find this even a tad odd, which I guess makes sense. They spent most of their lives in captivity. At least I had a mum and a dad.

I *have* a mum and a dad.

"Why do you do that?" I ask. "Why do you separate out the older people?"

"Honestly, it's mostly because of the Cyst Plague. Anyone can get it. But it's at its most contagious after around the age of twenty or so. That's when we go from having symptoms to being a human disease-bomb with a very short fuse. Without isolating the symptomatic adults, we'd all be dead inside of a month."

We all must look shocked because he tells us not to worry. "It's what human beings have always done. There are specific stages of human development. We've determined that our physical and cognitive abilities peak at around the age of twenty-one or so, anyway. That's when the symptomatic adults start getting assigned here. It's for their own benefit but also for ours. We're a community constantly on the move. Which means we're only as strong as the slowest of us. So the adults who test positive for Cyst Plague—even if it's just as a carrier—get moved to the Retirement Garrison. And, of course, for breeding. Don't worry. They have good lives."

In my ear, Matholook asks, "Is he joking about the breeding part?"

"If not," I whisper back, "this so-called Army of the Unsettled should change its name to Army of the Reproductive Endocrinologists."

I can't tell if Matholook wants to kiss me or punch me.

"It was my nan's job," I shrug.

"Just when I think I've got you figured out," he chuckles.

Tapping my temple, I warn him, "Don't try to get inside here. You might not get back out."

Angel Fire points down a laneway between two lines of the retirement motorhomes to a cluster of huge white, windowless cube vans. "That's the Infirmary Garrison." He sounds sad when he adds, "I won't take you there."

About ten feet ahead of us, Sara returns to plying Angel Fire with questions. "Seriously," she asks as we all turn down a new laneway between two rattling and very smelly rows of angle-armed backhoes. "How do you all not get run over?"

"The RVs, cube vans, construction vehicles, tractor-trailers, and pretty much the entire fleet stays in sync through a propulsion guidance system," he explains. "The Advance Teams scout the terrain. The graders smooth out what they can. And GLOPS keeps them all talking with each other and making speed and navigational adjustments in real time."

"Glops?"

"It's what we call our Geo-topographical Locator Piloting System. That's our off-grid network that keeps us from getting lost, crashing into each other, or plummeting down a canyon like lemmings on wheels."

"You have that kind of tech?" Sara asks, flicking a wide-eyed glance back toward the rest of us.

Angel Fire puts a finger to his lips and winks.

As we continue on our way, we cut to the left where we're slowly overtaken by a row of long yellow school buses, each with a green crest adorning its hood and another one emblazoned on each of their sides. The shields are neatly stenciled and have Latin writing in a banner with the silhouette of a vulture in the middle.

"*Motus liberi vivit*," Arlo says, reading the Latin motto out loud.

"It means 'freedom lives in motion,'" Angel Fire translates.

Jogging up to the nearest bus, he taps his knuckles on the glass door. The driver—not more than twelve years old and with his small, bare arms spread wide as eagle wings on the tire-sized steering wheel—gives a thumbs up and the double-paneled door whooshes open.

"I didn't know you were in the Education Garrison," the boy stammers, beads of sweat coating his forehead. He swipes his hand over his head of hedgehog hair and wipes his palms on the leg of his jean shorts.

Dressed in a honey-brown pantsuit, an only slightly older girl in the front seat of the bus leaps to her feet and makes a noble, frantic, and ultimately futile effort to pat down her lion's mane of frizzy blond curls. "Governor...I didn't...I mean...I don't—"

"It's okay, Nylssa. I'm just giving our recently liberated former criminals a little tour on our way to the Security Garrison." Angel Fire urges us to cluster deeper into the bus as he introduces us to the two dozen, wide-eyed children sitting in either rigid terror or bent-forward curiosity. "This is one of our schools."

"You have schools?" I ask.

"Yes."

"Here? In the Army of the Unsettled?"

"Yes."

"But what do you teach?" Ignacio asks, slipping in front of me. "I mean...why bother?"

Angel Fire surprises me by laughing at this. Ignacio is strong and has the Brohn-like build where it looks like he's been chiseled out of polished stone. But he's also a rough-around-the-edges boor with no sense of diplomacy or decorum.

But Angel Fire doesn't skip a beat. Doubled over, with one hand on his knee and the other gripping the back of one of the bus seats, he continues to laugh out loud. "It's not always going to be like this," he guffaws, rising up to wipe happy tears from his eyes. "It wasn't always like this. Things were bad before Krug, but people got by. The older folks talk about it all the time. Everything was five steps forward and four steps back. It sounds like a frustrating way to live, and it's no wonder everyone was stressed to the gills and anxious to the core. It's one of the many reasons why we keep moving. One step forward, no steps back. That's our motto. Forward motion. Inertia conquers all. The country was built once. It can be built again. There'll be roads again. And water. There'll be enough room for all of us inside the arcologies and safe places outside of the Wealthies' walls. It'll be good again. And we need to make sure we're prepared for when it is."

Arlo squishes past me to stand next to Ignacio. The kids in the front rows gasp at his scar-covered face. Arlo returns their stares with a clenched-jawed growl and the fingers on his raised hands curled into predatory claws.

The kids snap back in their seats and squeal with feigned terror while Arlo flips his hands up in surrender and promises he won't kill them.

Instead, he clucks his tongue at Angel Fire. "It all sounds so happy and, I don't know...foolishly optimistic."

"What's so bad about 'happy'?" Angel Fire asks, dropping his pleasant grin. "And there's nothing foolish about optimism. Believe me, one day, the world will be better."

"Funny," Libra says. "It's kind of our job to make sure that happens."

30

HAIDA

A LITANY of rubbery beeps sounds from behind us, and we edge to the side as four small, canopied golf carts trundle by. Each toad-green cart is driven by a young girl dressed in all white, with an assortment of passengers—a few teenagers but mostly much younger kids—sitting sideways and shoulder-to-shoulder on the outward-facing bench seats.

The drivers shout their greetings to Angel Fire as they pass, and he answers back with a flutter of two-handed happy waves as the carts go bouncing off into the distance.

"Our internal transport carriers," Angel Fire explains. "People-movers. It's one of the ways we get around the different Garrisons when we're not walking or tooling around on dirt-bikes."

"I wish we could have hitched a ride," Ignacio whines. "My feet hurt."

"But then you wouldn't get the full experience of the Army of the Unsettled," Arlo explains with a helpful swat to the back of Ignacio's head.

Ignacio grunts and pretends to stumble forward like he's been shot, which makes us all giggle.

At the same time, Angel Fire—still operating as our personal docent and shouting to be heard above the noise of some of the louder vehicles we pass—continues to point out different parts of their rolling city and promises we're now only about fifteen minutes from the Security Garrison where our weapons are being stored.

If this is a delay tactic...or a trick...or a lie...

But, oddly enough, my suspicions fade, and I'm feeling unusually relaxed, which is maybe why I'm so startled by the white flurry of motion I catch out of the corner of my eye.

Everyone ducks as Haida curls through the air around the braided wires of a nearby truck-mounted crane before dipping low and alighting on my outstretched forearm.

Where'd you come from?

~ More scouting.

Checking out the future for us?

~ Not this time.

Why not?

~ I think I've seen as far as I can see.

And?

~ I just wanted us to be together at the end.

Wait. What do you mean? What's "at the end"?

~ I don't know the "what," only the "when." And the "when" is soon.

Desperate for answers, I try to maintain our connection, and I can feel her trying to do the same. But the bond between us fizzles, and I'm left staring dumbly at the white raven on my forearm, her curved talons pressing little divots into the sleeve of my red leather jacket.

Haida has hinted about treachery and danger waiting for us sometime in the future. Now, she's talking about "the end." But the end of what, exactly? The end of our time here in the Army of the Unsettled? That wouldn't be so bad. Although I'm enjoying our tour, I'm still focused on getting our weapons back and getting out of here.

Could she mean the end of the war before it even starts? We know there's a huge conflict looming on the horizon. But that doesn't mean it's inevitable. Maybe the Devoted and the Unsettled are going to declare peace instead of war.

Or could Haida mean something simpler? The end of our adventure, maybe?

Or is it something more ominous, something too paralyzing for her to convey and too catastrophic for me to hear? Could she be talking about the end of my Asylum? The end of me and Matholook? The end of the Emergents, our Academy, and our mission to save the world?

I try to reach out to her again, but my Asylum has crowded around, and everyone is taking turns reaching out to run their fingers along the top of her head and down the sides of her body. As they do, Haida makes velvety, purring sounds from deep inside her chest.

She usually doesn't like being touched like this, so I'm equal parts surprised and worried that she's sitting so still while everyone greets her.

Is she letting them say goodbye?

I try to shake the most negative possibilities from my mind.

After all, things could be worse. The Unsettled haven't been the savage cannibals we expected. Angel Fire, despite not being any older than the rest of us, is turning out to be an interesting sort of bugger who handles leadership like it's a baby bird he needs to nurture before it leaves the nest. We may be deep behind enemy lines, but the ideas of "lines" and "enemies" is proving to be less binary than I ever thought.

"And who is this?" Angel Fire asks over his shoulder.

I quicken my pace until he and I are walking side by side.

"This is Haida Gwaii. She's a white raven and has been my friend for as long as I can remember."

"A white raven."

"She's not an albino, if that's what you were going to ask." I put my finger under Haida's beak and lift her head a little. "See. You can tell by her eyes."

"Black."

"A true albino raven would have pale or pink eyes. Haida only has partial pigmentation loss. It's called *leucism*."

Angel Fire nods and repeats the word. "You're from England, right?"

"London. Not that there's much of it left."

"Out in the Pacific Northwest, there's a story about how ravens got their color."

"I know the story. The first raven was white. Gray Eagle refused to share the natural elements of the world, so the white raven snuck into his lodge and stole them. The raven flew away, but he dropped water and fire to the earth, and the smoke from the fire rose up and turned his feathers black."

There's a cheeky twinkle in Angel Fire's eyes when he smiles and points out that Haida is white.

Matholook and I exchange a glance before I ask, "Yeah? So?"

"It means," Angel Fire laughs, "that Haida, unlike all the black raven, didn't drop the fire." He pauses for dramatic effect before adding, "Don't you see?" When Matholook and I don't answer, he elaborates with a happy grin. "She still has it. The fire. Fire can both burn and blind. But it also provides warmth and vision. In the story, fire represents healing, wisdom, and the miracle of spiritual revelation." He pauses again while the rest of my curiosity-filled Asylum nudges in close. "Haida," he says, his eyes on mine, "has something to show you."

I flash back to the visions she shared of me and my friends

encased in glass in the middle of a war, and I wonder if maybe she already has.

Angel Fire continues strolling ahead, whistling, his hands in his pockets, as if he just announced the weather as opposed to dropping a mystical wisdom-bomb.

31

VULTURES

WITH HAIDA's premonitions and Angel Fire's interpretations baking my brain, I jog to catch up with Angel Fire. He leads us around the next corner where we run straight into a bustling, open-air market, filled with kids, haggling, buying, and trading.

I can't speak for the others, but I'm stunned, impressed, and a little saddened by this chaos of commerce.

"This is Market Garrison," Angel Fire announces, pointing at a neat progression of open-sided, eighteen-wheeled heavy-haulers. Loaded with white canvas tents and rows of wooden bins, the long, flat-backed rigs move in perfect coordination over the ridges and creases of the crusty desert floor.

"Are we going to go shopping?" Arlo asks, eyeing the dozens of vending stations.

Angel Fire tells him, "Unfortunately not. The Security Garrison is five minutes up this road. Come on."

"I've been meaning to ask." I tell him, pointing to more of the stenciled shields we keep seeing all over the place. "What's with all the vultures?"

"You mean the heraldry? It's our logo. We adopted vultures as our mascot about ten years ago. The First Generation of the

Unsettled liked the bobcat as their symbol. But when the bobcats all died—"

"Died? All of them?"

"They wound up affected by radiation in the ground water. It didn't take more than a few years before they went extinct. The Second and Third Generations of the Unsettled liked the mountain lion. But then those all disappeared, too. So the Fourth Generation adopted the last of the semi-predatory animals left: The vulture. They're nomadic. They're survivors. And their natural heightened resistance to bacterial toxins helped them survive when other animals, and even the water and air, turned deadly after the Atomic Wars."

Impressed, Arlo gives a long, hearty whistle, but walking along next to him, Ignacio wrinkles his nose. "They're such ugly critters."

Libra elbows Ignacio who says, "Ouch" but doesn't seem to get the hint about not insulting our host as he adds, "Plus, they eat dead stuff."

"So does Haida," I remind him.

As if to confirm the truth about that statement, Haida hops up to my shoulder and does a little shimmy as she leans over and clacks out a mocking snap of her beak at Ignacio.

"That's different," Ignacio says, his voice softening after being chastised by my bird. "Haida's...different. Haida's...pretty." I can practically hear his boots digging into the ground as he tries to backtrack.

"So are *they*," Arlo says, pointing to a row of vultures perched wing-to-wing on a thick wooden dowel stretched across the back of a metallic-blue pickup truck. "If you look at them from the right point of view."

Ignacio squints at the mangy collection of bald, pimple-headed clumps of hissing and hacking birds. With their red heads, scabby necks and with their plum and dirt-colored feathers dusty and splayed out in random directions by the wind, they're not exactly a flock of idyllic sparrows twittering away in a tree.

"To other vultures," Angel Fire reminds us, "I'm sure they look—and smell—very pretty."

"While *you*, on the other hand," Sara sneers at Ignacio, "look butt-ugly from the point of view of any species on the planet."

"So...," Ignacio drawls, sliding his fingers through his hair and puffing out his chest. "You've been checking me out, eh?"

After an exaggerated bout of coughing, Sara pretends to be about ready to offer up a sloshy serving of pavement pizza. "I've been checking out the number of ways you repulse me."

"Ha! You know I'm the best-looking guy in the school. Why don't you just admit you can't take your eyes off of me?" Ignacio flexes his arm muscles (which I hate to admit *are* sort of impressive), but Sara answers with a finger down her throat and an open-mouthed gag.

For as long as she's been at the Academy, Sara has never been one to shy away from an opportunity to be a total, agitating prat, always on the lookout for a chance to insult someone or stir up trouble. Ignacio, always a glutton for the spotlight, doesn't seem to care one way or the other, as long as *someone's* paying attention to him. Although Sara tends to annoy me with her not-so-passive aggressive digs, it's Arlo who looks the most upset at the moment. One of the scars running vertically from his hairline down into the middle of his eyebrow compresses into an accordion wrinkle as he frowns. Usually, it's me or Libra who's willing to tell Sara to knock it off.

Grinding his teeth, Arlo barks at her to quit picking on Ignacio. "Or else the only number you'll be checking is how many of your teeth I've knocked out."

Sara responds with a stunned stare, which I'm pretty sure matches my own. Sure, she can be annoying and pointlessly hostile, but Arlo looks like he's about ready to hit her in defense of Ignacio. (Who doesn't need anyone to defend him since, frankly, he's usually the instigator of these little rows.)

"Down, boy," I whisper to Arlo.

His face melts from knotted to sheepish, and he tries to laugh the moment off. "I just don't like her picking on...people," he mutters.

Libra, ever the peacemaker, restores the mood. "I think Arlo's right," she coos, her eyes on the line of vultures like she's scoping out a litter of wayward puppies. "There's something kind of charming about them."

"Charming?" I laugh. "Is that honestly the most accurate description you could come up with?"

"No. I'm serious. Okay. So they're not peacocks. It's like they don't care what they look like. They're just happy being who they are. There's something attractive about that."

"They're survivors without the weakness of self-awareness," Angel Fire muses. He pauses to give us a chance to take in the queue of fat, slouching animals, and I forget for a second that he's just a boy.

As we continue through the Market Garrison, I start noticing more and more vultures. Not just the birds, although there seem to be plenty of those—in windows, on the rooftops of many of the campers, and swaying and wobbling on cylindrical wooden or steel perches drilled into the aluminum sides of many of the RVs, flatbeds, motorhomes, and vehicle transport carriers.

In addition to those and to the few wide-winged vultures soaring and banking overhead, there are also vulture images all over the place.

Apparently Matholook notices, too. Following Libra's lead, he starts pointing out objects sitting on shelves, in bins, on windowsills and in display cases as we pass: vulture-shaped mugs, handmade vulture-headed walking sticks, fat canvas bags with white drawstrings around their necks and a green silhouette of a vulture on their sides, and, of course, all the vulture crests that are stamped, embroidered, or branded into half of the surfaces on the crawling vehicles.

"What is it about having something on your mind that makes it start appearing everywhere you look?" Matholook asks.

"Maybe you're manifesting it," Sara half-jokes, giving Matholook an elbow to the meat of his upper arm. "Maybe the fact that you're thinking about them is exactly what's making them appear everywhere. Maybe you're an Emergent, after all."

Sara starts walking ahead with Angel Fire while Matholook and I drift toward the back of our procession.

"That wouldn't be so bad," he says after a minute of quietly plodding along together, my shoulder against his arm.

"What wouldn't be so bad?" I ask.

"Being an Emergent."

"I couldn't say. As far as I know, I've never been anything else." I take a deep breath and decide to see if Matholook will let me ask him something a bit more personal.

"Sure," he grins, as if he's flattered by my question. "Anything."

"What are we going to do after this?"

"You mean after whatever war is coming?"

I don't answer because I don't need to. As a Caretaker with the Devoted, Matholook has an uncanny level of empathy, and I can feel how much he gets me.

"I don't know," he sighs, reaching over to take my hand. "I'm a lot of things. Worried isn't one of them."

"Easy for you to say. You don't have an evil albino preparing to blow up the world just to get his veiny, chalky hands on your genetic code."

"I didn't mean I wasn't worried about *me*." He pulls my hand up to his lips and kisses it. "I meant I wasn't worried about *us*."

My face and neck go glossy with perspiration, and it's not from the heat.

"Besides, Epic's not evil," Matholook insists. "He's just trying to survive. Like all of us. Like all of you up at the Academy. Like the Devoted. Like the Unsettled." He sweeps his arm at the ominous lineup of four vultures, perched gargoyle-like on the edge of a pick-up truck's tailgate. The birds shift and sway along with the motion of the truck and seem almost hypnotized into a gruesome stupor. "Like them," Matholook says. "They may look like alien-dinosaur pillow stuffing, but they don't wake up in the morning thinking about how they're going to take over the world. They just want to survive."

"Ugh," I groan with an eyeroll. "I hope you're not defending Epic. If my Asylum hadn't gotten me out of his underground lab, I'd probably be hooked up to a dozen machines right now while he plays shuffleboard with my DNA."

"I guess I just mean I don't think I'm worried because I still have faith in all the positive possibilities."

"Like what?" I laugh. "That it's *possible* the Devoted and the Unsettled kill each other before Epic has a chance to kill all of us Emergents? Or that it's *possible* that Kress and the rest of my teachers at the Academy can somehow restore this wasteland to its former glory?"

"No," he says softly, "None of that."

"What, then?"

"I think *we're* possible."

I beam and blush and give his hand a squeeze.

What is it about everything he says that makes me want to get closer to him?

"Hey lovebirds!" Ignacio calls back. "Keep up, or you're going to get run over!"

Heeding the advice but ignoring the "lovebirds" taunt, Matholook and I pick up our pace and reunite with Angel Fire and the rest of our Asylum.

As we near the end of the long and frenetic Market Garrison, I do a double-take and point at the squat, pink-beaked vulture sitting by itself, mascot-like, on the hood of an oversized blue pickup truck. The lone, swaying bird has got an oversized beak and a neck like a bleached garden hose. Until just this second, I thought that all vultures looked pretty much the same and were sort of anonymous Gothic monsters. But this one—scaly-headed, blister-faced, and prickly-necked, with flecks of bile green and murky purple streaked through the tips of its coat of leathery-looking feathers is actually familiar.

"Holy frack!" I shout, grabbing Matholook by the arm. "I think that's *Jeff!*"

32

JEFF

Everyone—and I mean all five members of my Asylum plus Matholook and Angel Fire—say, "Jeff?" at the exact same time.

And then, slowing down to a shuffling walk, they proceed to stare at me like they're two seconds away from fitting me with one of those white canvas jackets with sleeves that buckle in the back.

"Did you say, 'Jeff'?" Libra asks, her eyes darting back and forth between me and the vulture.

"Remember?" I ask in a spirited huff. "Jeff. That vulture War is always going on about back at the Academy!"

"What about it?" Arlo asks, leaning over Libra's shoulder to catch my eye.

I stop in my tracks as the caravan of the Unsettled continues to grind along all around us. Because of the way the army moves, it's perfectly possible that we'll all get run over by some giant, lumbering rig or another, but right now, I don't care. Either I just saw the most unexpected familiar face, or else I'm going banana-pants crazy.

No. I know what I'm seeing.

"That's him!" I insist with a stomped foot and a stabbing

finger. I start walking again and match my pace with the blue pickup truck and its squat, avian accessory. "That's Jeff!"

"Wait a minute," Ignacio asks through a mocking grin and with a wag of his finger in the vulture's direction, "you're saying you think *that's* War's long-lost pet?"

"No. I don't think it. I *know* it. And War wouldn't be too happy about you calling Jeff a 'pet.'"

"It's true," Libra says in a sharp aside to Angel Fire. "War gets mushy talking about his *friend*."

Angel Fire squints hard enough to bring his hairline down close to his eyebrows. "You really think that could be the same vulture?"

"I don't see why not," I gush. "We lost track of him after a big fight on our way here from D.C. over five years ago. We never did find out what happened to him."

"And he means that much to you?" Ignacio asks, his face plastered with skepticism.

"Well, no. Not exactly. But he means that much to War."

"War is one of our teachers. He's about the size of that dump truck over there," Sara informs Angel Fire. We all stare at her for a second, and she shrugs. "Just trying to give our host some context," she smiles apologetically.

"I don't know where that particular vulture came from," Angel Fire confesses. "But I know someone who will. And he's on our way to the Security Garrison. Just over there, actually." Pointing to a cluster of four campers driving in a diamond pattern, Angel Fire urges us along.

He takes a sharp turn between a pair of smoking, pebble-spitting asphalt-spreaders and beckons for us to follow him. "His family's been with us since the beginning," he calls out through the dense smoke and the roar of engines. "Whenever anyone needs help with any of the vultures, he's the go-to guy."

The smoke clears as we jog along, and I ask Angel Fire who this person is, exactly.

"He's our resident Vulturemaster."

"Vulturemaster? You mean like a Ravenmaster?"

"What's a Ravenmaster?" Angel Fire asks.

"She is," Sara says, giving me a small push to the shoulder as we round another bend. "She controls ravens."

"I don't do anything of the sort," I pout. "I have a partnership with them. Well, with one of them anyway." I run my free hand along Haida's back, and she bobs her head in appreciation.

"Don't be so modest," Sara teases. "Show him."

"Show me what?"

"She and the white raven kind of share a brain," Arlo offers.

I remind him that that's not entirely true. "But it'll do for now," I say with a smile.

Tapping into Haida Gwaii, who's now tucked like an American football in the crook of my arm, I'm happy to find her receptive to our telempathic bond. As my Asylum and I have discovered, something strange has been going on lately. There's been a sort of static shield, a disruptive force that seems to act as a dampener on our Emergent abilities. I don't know what it is, or if it really even exists. Or, if in our state of stress and grief, we're all just imagining it.

Angel Fire ducks as Haida—her white feathers a stark contrast to the grime and grimness of the endless fields of moving machines—launches herself from my arm and rises high into the pink, sizzling hot sky. At my request—which I call out inside my head and repeat out loud for the others to hear—she banks, dips, and climbs even higher before embarking on a brillie series of overlapping barrel rolls before plummeting down from the sky and skimming just over Angel Fire's head and alighting again on my outstretched arm.

He says, "Impressive!"

"I'm in training," I announce, with royal grandeur, my voice rising to compete with the churn of a fan-blade land-skimmer next to us, "to be a Ravenmaster."

Angel Fire makes a little bow toward me and then to Haida and says he's "honored to meet a Ravenmaster and a *Human-master*," and we all laugh when Haida answers with a harsh bark and a wet gurgle-clack.

"She says, 'Knowing *yourself* is ultimately the only mastery that matters,'" I interpret as we slow down to a brisk walk and then to a shuffling stroll next to a giant camper with alternating green and white stripes running in V-shaped chevrons down its side.

Angel Fire says, "This is it" and raps five times with his knuckles on the door.

We walk along next to the camper for a minute, and I'm starting to think maybe this wasn't such a grand idea, after all. We're still unarmed. We're still technically behind enemy lines. We're still being led along by a boy who might very well be stalling while he figures out what horrible things he's going to do to us. My Asylum still doesn't seem to be appropriately panicked about any of that. And I may have just sealed our fate. And for what? Just because I think I might have recognized my teacher's long-lost bird?

Angel Fire knocks again. Just when I think no one's home, the latch clicks, and the dusty white door swings open with an angry, grating screech.

A boy—small and round and with his bulbous neck polished and smooth as a river stone hanging over the open collar of his unbuttoned, short-sleeved linen shirt—retreats a full step back in startled surprise at the sight of us.

"G-G-Governor," he stammers. "How...why...I wasn't expecting..."

"Take it easy," Angel Fire says from behind a raised and calming hand. "These are—"

"The Freed!" the boy exclaims. "I heard over the Waves, not more than ten minutes ago."

Angel Fire's eyes dart inside the camper. "Can we—?"

"Come in! Yes, of course!"

The boy waddles backward, summoning us all in with big circles of his pink, hairless arm.

Following Angel Fire's lead, the six of us hop up, one at a time, into the oddly small and cramped room of what, from the outside, looked like a football-field sized camper, "The Waves," Angel Fire clarifies, "is our communication system."

"I could hardly believe it when I heard," the boy gushes, his cheeks blushing rosy-red with undisguised delight.

"The Waves never lie," Angel Fire reminds him. "If it's not true and verified," he explains, turning to us and joined by the boy who echoes his words, "it doesn't make the Waves."

"Bondo," the boy says, introducing himself and reaching out to give each of us an energetic handshake. His fingers are thick, soft, and weirdly warm. "My name is Bondo. I'm the Vulturemaster. This is my Aviary." Turning, he skims his hand over a holo-panel floating six inches above a narrow, silver lab table. The shimmer from the panel lights up his fingers (and their unexpectedly manicured nails) with a soft turquoise glow.

With a clunky grind, the corrugated steel wall behind Bondo rolls up, one long segment at a time like a giant garage door, to reveal the rest of the camper. The length of the container is divided into two columns of glass cubes stacked three high with a walkway down the middle and small, neatly organized work-stations set up every ten feet or so.

Bondo skims his hand over another input panel, this one embedded in the camper wall, and the gloomy length of the long vehicle springs to life under an instant, blinding white light.

Illuminated all at once as if by magic, the glass cases—all riddled with even rows of small breathing holes—reveal their contents with each one containing a single, shuffling, grumpy-looking vulture.

"They're not pets," Bondo insists. "These are incredible survivors with intricate social structures and some higher-level thinking we're only beginning to fully understand."

"That's a huge flock," Libra says, scanning the impressive collection of birds.

Bondo makes a disapproving clicking sound with his tongue. "They're not a flock. When they're eating, a collection of them is called a 'Wake.' Otherwise, a group of them is called a Committee."

"Hey!" Ignacio exclaims. "I knew that one!"

"We have a Committee of Vultures back at the Academy," I explain to Bondo, apologizing for Ignacio's giddy, over-the-top enthusiasm.

"The students at the Academy are divided into Cohorts," Arlo adds.

"Usually about six students per Cohort," Libra chimes in with a goofy grin, and now I'm wondering if she and Ignacio are competing to see who can be the most idiotically gushy. "We're the Asylum of Loons," Libra says proudly, her thumb pressed to her puffed-out chest.

"Each Cohort has a bird as its symbol," I explain, stroking the smooth feathers on Haida's head. "And one of our teachers used to have a vulture named Jeff."

Angel Fire gives Bondo a showy wink and a loud whisper from behind his hand. "And Branwynne here thinks she just saw him."

"Who?" Bondo asks. "Her teacher?"

"No," I tell him. "Jeff. His vulture."

Bondo looks around at all of us and then finally over to Angel Fire who nods his confirmation.

"And you want me to tell you if the vulture you saw is the same vulture that used to accompany your teacher?"

"I know it sounds strange," I admit. "But yes."

"I know every vulture in our army," Bondo brags. "I think I can help you."

We all hop down from the moving camper, and Angel Fire leads us back to the market where Jeff—and I'm even more sure now than ever that it *is* Jeff—is still perched in a squat lump on the hood of the blue pickup truck.

Bondo runs a hand along the side of the vulture's body. It makes a quiet, rolling buzz, somewhere between a kitten's purr and a rattlesnake's hiss.

"Incredible miracles of evolution," Bondo beams with fatherly pride. "There are seven New World vultures. Here, we have mostly California condors and Turkey vultures. But we also have two types of yellow-headed vultures and three full families of Black vultures. And we have a whole trailer full of Old World vultures—Andean condors, Himalayan griffons, African white-backs—mostly from abandoned or destroyed zoos."

"So...," I ask. "Is this Jeff?"

"I remember when he came to us," Bondo says absently, as if he's reminiscing about some old childhood memory. "I could only feel one thing from him. I could only hear a single thought passing from his mind to mine."

"You can hear his thoughts?" I ask.

"Sometimes. Mostly it's just feelings. Moods. Things like that. Being a student of their behavior enables me to read them like most others can't."

I know Angel Fire could probably just order Bondo to hand Jeff over, but he seems to be enjoying watching the red-cheeked boy fret over the possibility of turning one of his vultures over to six total strangers.

Bondo goes on to rattle off a long litany of unsolicited trivia about vultures: "Turkey vultures have the best sense of smell in the animal kingdom. A vulture's stomach acid is more corrosive than acid from a car battery. If something fits in their mouth, they can probably digest it. Andean condors can have an eleven-foot wingspan. Cape Griffon vultures, like this one here—the one you call 'Jeff'—are part of the Old World species and live mostly in the southern and central countries of Africa."

He presses the tips of his fingers to his temple and squints deep enough to make his round face look like a throw pillow someone punched in the middle.

"Oh," he says, snapping out of a daze and turning back to us, "since you asked, yes, this particular vulture *is* Jeff."

I pump my fist and gloat over the accuracy of my guess.

Fueled by my triumph, I'm determined to get Jeff back to the Academy to be reunited with War. After all we've been through and after our many failures in what was supposed to be an easy-peasy mission, I feel like we could use a win.

But there are some major obstacles. We've got no money. Without our weapons, we don't have anything to trade. Not that we'd trade our weapons, anyway.

"War's going to be so disappointed," Libra semi-sobs.

Bondo scootches up until he's toe to toe with Libra. "Say that again."

Now, Bondo presses even further forward. "He's going to be so disappointed," Libra says through a confused stammer.

"Who?" Bondo asks, his voice and his whole body pressing aggressively forward. "*Who* is going to be so disappointed?"

"War," Libra says, leaning away from the encroaching boy. "Our teacher's name is War."

Whipping around toward me, Bondo raises his head, his face

lit up in wide-eyed revelation, and he says, "He's yours. No charge."

"Wait," Matholook says, his voice dripping with suspicion and disbelief. "You're just going to give him to us?"

Bondo tilts his head toward Jeff. "He's not mine to give. None of them are. These are wild creatures, always on the move. It's how they survive. Sound familiar?" Jeff flexes his long talons and ruffles himself up into an alert stance from his perch on the hood of the truck. He stretches his wings out to an impossible length, and I can't tell if he looks more like a skydiver who just released his parachute or the auto industry's most ill-conceived hood ornament.

"Besides, and I'm quoting Jeff," Bondo says with a knowing wink, "He just said to me the one thing—the *only* thing—he's been saying to me for five years, the one thing I thought was his way of saying he was hungry for battle. Or that maybe he was just being overly hostile. Or that he was a shell-shocked veteran. Or else he was just plain crazy. But of course, none of that's true, and none of that is what he meant at all. I get that now. After over five years, I finally get it."

"So what is it?" Sara asks. "What's the one thing he always says?"

"He says he misses War."

33

HERE

JEFF BURSTS INTO THE AIR. But it's not the easy, graceful flight of Haida Gwaii.

No. Jeff heaves himself up, his enormous wings kicking up a plume of stray feathers and a vortex of dust and sand. With his rubbery legs dangling below his round, sooty belly, he rises up over our heads, blocking out the sun along the way, and then he surrenders to gravity and plummets.

Dropping like a skydiver with a broken parachute, he slows at the last second to a near-frozen, mid-air hover—wings spread wide, legs extended stiff as an airplane's landing gear—and then plops down with a heavy thud onto Matholook's shoulder.

Matholook lets out a squeal as one of the bird's massive wings smacks him in the head and ruffles his hair. (Matholook has somehow perfected the art of stylish bedhead, but the impact of the snake-necked bird's powerful wings takes it to a new level of mussed-up cuteness.) Matholook's knees buckle under Jeff's weight, and the tips of the vulture's dirty yellow talons press deep into the fabric of Matholook's compression top.

Our Academy uniforms are made of a synthetic carbon fiber

matrix and have a paper-thin layer of built-in armor plating in a waffle pattern on the upper chest and down the arms. It won't stop a bullet or anything, but it's enough to prevent Jeff's talons from going clean through the rounded chunk of Matholook's shoulder.

The combination of surprise, pain, and embarrassment (plus, what I think I'm safe in assuming is the unnerving fact of being landed on by a vile-smelling, twenty-pound scavenger) knocks Matholook into a helicopter-armed stagger, and the vulture tilts to nearly horizontal and almost falls off before digging his talons in even harder. The rest of us, still shuffle-walking along in pace with the moving city, look on, terrified at first, but then we burst into peals of laughter as Matholook, wide-eyed and red-faced, struggles back to his feet with Jeff hissing into his ear and hanging on for dear life.

It's not a graceful moment—either for Matholook who groans upright and scrunches his head to the side to make room for the thick-bodied beast or for Jeff, who inchworms his way down to Matholook's outstretched forearm, clenching and clamping the fish-hook talons on the ends of his pink, segmented feet along the way in an effort to find a steady purchase.

He's used to perching on War's Rocky Mountain mogul of a shoulder or clamped to his sequoia forearm, and poor Math-olook, slender and toned, just doesn't have the same amount of real estate.

"Looks like you have a friend," I point out.

"A *heavy* friend. I thought they were supposed to be hollow-boned."

"He's a hefty fellow," Bondo agrees. "For scavengers like him, the Atomic Wars, spiking temperatures, and the tribal conflicts that killed off so many people as a result, turned much of the country into, well...a buffet."

Matholook makes a gagging noise, and he squints his red, watery eyes. "Ugh. Great. And on top of that, he stinks."

Bondo puts his hand next to his mouth and pretends his shout is a whisper. "That's his excretion you're smelling."

"Excretion?" Libra asks.

"His urinary and defecatory discharge."

"I'm sorry. His *what*?"

"His pee and poop."

Matholook looks around on the ground, snapping his head left to right and raising his boots one at a time off the ground and inspecting them for vulture excrement.

"No, no, no," Bondo says, shaking his head hard and snorting up a chuckle. "You didn't step in anything. It's called *urohydrosis*. Basically, he urinates on his legs."

"What!?"

"To cool off. Some vultures urinate on their legs as a way of redistributing or suppressing heat."

Matholook grimaces but otherwise takes this revelation in stride.

Ignacio, on the other hand, isn't nearly as poised. Shrieking like a bunny in a blender, he flaps his hands and high-steps as he continues forward, asking over and over, "Why? Why? Why?"

It's funny watching him perform the miraculous, instantaneous transition from tall, oily-muscled warrior to hyperactive, squidgy nipper.

"Everyone does what they need to do to survive," Angel Fire reminds him.

"If I ever wind up getting to the point where I'm pissing on my own legs to survive," Ignacio says, "go ahead and let me die."

"Will do," Sara promises.

"Don't worry," Arlo tells Ignacio. "I won't let her kill you."

He says it as a joke. But I believe him.

WITH HAIDA on my shoulder and with Jeff on Matholook's forearm, we're getting even more stares than before as we continue
along.

At least no one's whipping those stinging little white pebbles
or balls of aluminum foil at us like they did when we first
arrived.

"How much longer to the Security Garrison?" Libra asks.
Her ponytail has come undone, and her thick, dark hair is
speckled with golden flecks of sand.

Angel Fire points to a narrow laneway between two rows of
yellow and green, rhino-sized machines, all of them grinding
along on studded black treads. "We're near the very front of the
fleet. Security Garrison is just up ahead. Past the lane of
Compactors and Levelers over there. See that armored truck?"

Libra shields her eyes with her hand. "The big gray one?"

"Yes. That's where your weapons are."

As we reach the top of a slight incline in the desert terrain,
a girl and a boy—no more than ten or eleven years old and
both with thick black glasses and long blond hair in matching
French braids—scurry up frantically, skidding to a stop
directly in front of Angel Fire. They walk backwards, eyes
wide, as he leans forward, and the boy whispers something
into his ear.

Angel Fire stops in his tracks, causing all of us to stop, too.

Since we're walking between vehicles and in the general
direction of the moving army, we have a few seconds before the
row of treaded Excavators behind us runs us over.

Angel Fire's sudden stop is such an abrupt break in what has
been our nearly constant motion that Libra, walking just behind
him, slams into him hard enough to stagger him forward a full
two steps and knock him into the blond boy. Blushing and apol-

ogizing, she reaches out to steady Angel Fire and asks if he's okay.

He doesn't seem to hear her and instead asks the girl and the boy—he calls them "Grace" and "Reece"—for confirmation. They answer with a vigorous nod, and he asks a second time if they're sure.

"Being only slipping past," the girl stammers, looking back and forth between Angel Fire the boy, who are both a full head shorter than she is. "*Mucho trampa éjercito.*"

"*Muy peligrosa,*" the boy whispers. His lower lip quivers, and he doesn't seem to know what to do with his hands. "Military Garrison *permiso* mobilized? Very *rapido!*"

The campers, rigs, and RVs continue to move around us. It's a disorienting feeling to be standing still and even more disorienting to feel like the world is still moving around us.

"What's going on?" Arlo asks.

Angel Fire's mouth moves, but no words come out. He clears his throat and tries again. He even adjusts his fat-knotted tie, as if the length of cloth is constricting his neck too much and impeding his ability to say what he's trying to say. When he does speak, this time, the authority and the eccentric personality spectrum—from threatening to joyful—we've seen in him so far is long gone. For the first time, he sounds like he looks: an inexperienced, isolated, in-over-his-head fourteen-year-old boy, who just got overwhelmed by the size, scope, and the reality of the rest of the world. "It's here," he announces from his frozen-in-mid-step stance.

"You said the Security Garrison was just over there." I'm more than a little anxious now, and I seem to be the only one interested in getting ourselves armed and out of here before it's too late.

"No—no. Not that." He points straight ahead. Up until now, our line of sight has mostly been limited to the trucks, towering cranes, buses, RVs, campers, motorhomes, construction vehicles, and the other wheeled and treaded rigs all around us. Being near the front of the fleet, though, we can now easily see the open desert—with its buttes, mesas, canyons, open plains, and wavy dunes—laid out before us.

The endless thrum of the vehicles behind us and the sweeping expanse of the exposed wasteland in front of us makes me feel like we could take a few steps past the single line of giant, vanguard motor-graders in front of us and fall off the edge of the world.

"That war...the war you've been hearing about...," Angel Fire mutters, directing our gaze toward the vast valley ahead and the steep, flat-headed mesas on either side.

"Yeah?" Ignacio asks, peering into the distance. "What about it?"

"It's here."

34

ENOUGH

Next to me, Ignacio says, "Uh-oh."

Coming from someone as die hard and gung-ho for battle as Ignacio, those are probably the two most terrifying syllables I've ever heard.

Libra squeaks out a pathetic, "What? What is it?" as she tries to peer past Ignacio's broad-shouldered body. She even reaches out a hand to try to nudge him to the side, but he's frozen in place, and doesn't budge.

Next to me, Matholook tenses up enough to cause Jeff to go all hissy and quivery on his forearm. The bulky bird opens and closes his talons, nervously kneading his curved claws into Matholook's arm.

On my shoulder, Haida raises her head and gurgle-clacks a litany of agitated barks toward the sky.

Even Sara, usually indifferent at best and unapologetically scornful at worst, clenches her fists and her teeth and lets out a sort of half-groan.

Arlo reaches back for his scythe, which, of course, isn't there. He turns to me with a blush and a helpless shrug.

I can't do anything but share in his helplessness. Angel Fire just announced the beginning of a war, and here we are, oblivious, weaponless, and strolling casually along as tourists without a care in the world.

Until that single word "war," that is. That's about the biggest care in the world anyone can ever be unlucky enough to have.

Everything we've done over the past twenty-four hours was supposed to do one of two things: prevent a war from happening or else prepare us for when it did. And yet, here we are, unprepared, and we've apparently prevented nothing.

We shouldn't be here. We should be a million miles away. We should be sitting in front of Kress and her Conspiracy right now, rattling off all the intel we acquired after our easy-peasy successful mission. Instead, we're on the front lines of the Army of the Unsettled, without Mattea, without weapons, and without any contingency plan for getting away.

Shostakovich's *Eternal Questions*— "Why? And "For What?"—rattle around unanswered in my head.

When I was growing up in the Tower of London, my dad used to have this funny phrase for being embarrassed at being surprised. He called it, "Being caught with your pants down."

I always thought that was kind of a dumb saying. If you get caught doing what you're not supposed to be doing, you probably have more important things to worry about than whether or not your pants are up or down.

But now, standing here like a bunch of idiots, the phrase finally makes some sense.

I really do feel naked. Vulnerable. Exposed.

As we all freeze in a cluster around Angel Fire, we inch closer to each other, as if out of some primitive protective instinct as we follow the index finger at the end of his extended arm.

"It's here," he repeats, louder this time. "They're here."

Because we're on the top of a slope toward the front of the

moving army, with most of the larger vehicles far behind us or fanned out in flanking positions on the sides, our view is mostly unobstructed.

In the distance, under a slowly rotating cloud of churning smoke, the silhouettes of hundreds of jeeps interspersed with thousands of marching soldiers come into focus.

At first, I blink my eyes hard, thinking I'm seeing the space between low-hanging clouds and a long chain of jagged desert rocks. This country is big enough to have illusions where you can't tell the tops of mountains from the bottoms of clouds.

But no. This is no illusion. It's an army. A big one. And it's on the move.

"It's the Devoted," Libra says.

I say "Matholook?" out loud as if his name were a question, but I don't actually ask him anything.

"This is it," he mumbles. When I ask him to say that again, he gags on his breath. "This is the move we've...they've...the *Devoted* have been planning. It's their next stone in the river. The next step. Their path forward from the conflicts of the past. This is the war they've been hoping for. Waiting for. This is the war they've been fighting for."

"What the frack do they want?" Libra cries.

Matholook shakes his head. "Not much. Just...*everything*."

It's a single word, but the way Matholook says it—filled with fear, regret, confidence, and desperation—it might as well be an entire dictionary.

Without taking his eyes off the terrifying phalanx curving all around along the horizon in front of us, Arlo asks what he means.

Matholook doesn't answer, but I think I know.

Like all the Devoted, Matholook is a historian. So I know he's read, studied, talked about, and analyzed everything about every war that's ever been waged. I once sat in one of their classes, so I've seen their methods in action.

At the Academy, we're being trained to understand the scope and limits of our Emergent abilities. We're being prepped to fight for those who can't fight for themselves. And, perhaps most important of all, we're being taught who and *why* we are so we can do our part to wrench the world from the grip of all the dictators and self-serving despots, who would just as soon see the planet and everyone on it suffer and die before risking losing their hold on power.

Not the Devoted. They see themselves as part of a chain. That's how they always describe it: stepping stones going across a river of violent rapids and unpredictable currents. The more they know the path, so they say, the better they can follow it.

Unlike most people in the world, they don't follow a leader or a cause. In many ways, their approach is even more dangerous. They follow what they consider to be an eternal, unwavering course, a course that leads from stone to stone, from war to war.

The Unsettled move so they can live from one day to the next. The Devoted live to move from one *war* to the next.

And we've just gotten sucked along with the Unsettled right into the jaws of the *next* war.

We weren't supposed to be here for this. We were supposed to steer clear of this whole mess.

"But if we can't," Kress explained to us before we set out on this mission, "if we can't steer clear, then we need to be sure not to get so caught up in the middle of it that we lose our advantage of distance."

With what appears to be an infinitely large army advancing before our eyes, whatever "distance" Kress was talking about is about five minutes away from being completely gone.

There's no avoiding it anymore. Angel Fire is right. It's here.

But so is my Asylum.

Six unarmed teenagers, a raven, and a vulture with the Army of the Unsettled all around us, the Cult of the Devoted closing in, and the fate of what's left of a broken nation hanging in the balance.

Staring forward into the distance, Matholook takes my hand in his.

It feels almost comforting.

Almost.

This time, though, I don't think simple comfort is going to be enough.

35

DEVOTED

I DIDN'T KNOW there were so many Devoted in their Cult. Hell, I didn't know there were so many Devoted in the *world*.

When I visited their compound, Matholook gave me what I thought was a pretty thorough tour. We walked around the town, and he told me some of their history, introduced me to some of their members, and showed me the buildings where they lived, went to school, cooked, relaxed, and trained. I got the feeling he wasn't showing or telling me everything, and I suspected there was more to the Cult of the Devoted than met the eye.

But I never suspected *this*.

Before my eyes, what I always thought of as a fringe group of a few hundred reclusive brainwashers has morphed into a dense army of *thousands* of armed soldiers. Even from here, I can make out their arsenal of guns, swords, spears, and a wide variety of very unfriendly bladed weapons.

It's a maddening moment. The Army of the Unsettled, with us swept along with them, is still moving forward, right toward the Cult of the Devoted. At the same time, the Cult of the Devoted continue their own march toward us.

It's two armies playing a game of chicken, and we're about to be barbecued right along with them.

As the Devoted continue to advance along the valley floor in front of us and take strategic positions on the walls of the canyons on either side, it occurs to me what an odd-looking army they are.

I'm used to London's Royal Fort Knights and the clothes they pilfered from various museums and costume shops around the city. They were deep into the Medieval aesthetic. And then there were the Banters and their cobbled-together gear from their raids on every sports and athletic equipment store left standing. Here in America, I've seen the pastel kit of the Outposters, and, of course, there's the Unsettled with their hodgepodge of mushroom-colored cloaks, drawstring pants, tuxedo tops, and scruffy hiking boots.

But the Devoted army...I've never seen anything like it.

Rank after rank of men and women (and some children, too, I think), all dressed in crisp, dark blue dress pants, white button shirts, red ties dotted with white stars, and navy blazers—all under what looks from here like American football gear: shoulder pads and body armor, spray-painted bright red, highlighted with spatterings of bright white stars.

They look like they're dressed more for a board meeting—or possibly an old-style American football game—than for a war.

"Are they in suits?" Arlo asks.

"And body armor," Matholook explains. "It's the battle gear of the Devoted. Eighteenth-century Prussian general Carl von Clausewitz said, 'War is the continuation of policy by other means.'"

"And what does *that* mean, exactly?" I ask, my eyes locked onto the encroaching army.

"It means," Matholook says with stern gravity and flicking his hand in the direction of the legion of his own people marching toward us, "that the Devoted see business, commerce, and negotiation as just other versions of war. And they dress for it."

"So...," Arlo drawls. "They're insane."

Matholook shoots Arlo a vicious glare but then takes a breath and holds his hands up in an "I'm sorry" gesture, even though it's Arlo who's the one out of line.

Matholook's voice goes slow and measured, and, from the mouth of the boy he is, I can hear the voice of the man I know he's going to become. "It's not complicated," he says evenly. "Horrible, maybe, but not complicated. Everything everyone has ever done in the course of human history—from relationships and trade to exploration, politics, and murder—is built on the idea of trying to convince others to think like you. War is no different."

"Yeah," Ignacio sneers, his eyes swinging from the advancing army and then back to Matholook. "But that kind of 'convincing' out *there* comes at the end of a weapon."

"Whatever it takes," Matholook says, and I can't tell if he's sad or proud.

"They'd look nice," Libra offers, planting her hands on her hips and gazing out at the assembly of deadly soldiers in their armored red, white, and blue business suits. And then with a blush and downcast eyes, she turns and adds, "I mean if they weren't about to kill us and all."

Haida belts out a few urgent gurgle-clacks to get my attention. I whip around and, sure enough, there are even more of the Devoted behind us and on either side. Lined up in tight rows hundreds of yards deep, they have troops stationed on every slope, hill, cliff, outcropping, and rocky ridge running along the sides of the valley we're in and in a huge crescent around the cratered field in front of us.

But the scarier part is what happens next.

By the hundreds, all around us, the tractor-trailer gears grind down. The excavator arms fold back. The chalky scratch of bulldozer and crane treads softens and fades. The skinny dirt-bikes sputter to a stop in the lanes and alleys branching out behind and to the sides of us. The RVs, campers, cube-vans, pickups, dump trucks, and the rest of the smoke-belching vehicles go quiet and still as a cemetery stone.

And, for what Angel Fire tells us is the first time in nearly a decade, the perpetual motion of the Army of the Unsettled comes to a dead stop.

As large and as unstoppable as the Army of the Unsettled is, the Cult of the Devoted have somehow both surrounded them *and* stopped them.

It's an impressive, baffling, and terrifying accomplishment.

We're surrounded by the Unsettled, who are surrounded by the Devoted. And just when I thought the shite we're in couldn't get any deeper...

With all of us frozen in our tracks, Ignacio swivels his head around to the sides and glances over his shoulder to take in the hundreds of eerily still vehicles. I'm sure he wants to say something profound, maybe offer up some inspirational bluster. But all that comes out is, "Ummmm..."

I know the feeling.

"You seem pretty relaxed," Sara says, her voice laced with accusation as she swings toward Angel Fire. "I mean, for someone who just led his troops into a full-on ambush. What happened to all of your high-tech navigation and communication systems?"

Staring out at the Cult of the Devoted, Angel Fire doesn't answer, and I think maybe he's gone catatonic from fear.

Without turning around, he flicks his thumb backward over his shoulder. "Grace and Reece...they're two of our Heralds. They said our navigation system's been infiltrated." I can barely

hear him when he adds, "They say there've been deaths."
Shaking his head, he repeats, "There've *already* been deaths."

Libra repeats the word out loud. "Deaths?"

Angel Fire nods. "There's not much in the world that's more
relaxing than inevitability," he mumbles, his eyes riveted on the
enemy army, half of it positioned in ominous attention on the
top of the steep escarpments on either side of us, half of it
marching confidently forward through the open valley ahead.

I find myself staring at him. He just found out the safety and
security of his whole world have been compromised, and he's
not even breathing hard?

With a shake of his head, Angel Fire rouses himself from his
daze and snaps back into the decisive leader we've quickly come
to know. After apologizing to us, he barks out orders to the
nearby boys and girls of his crew, who suddenly don't seem
nearly as intimidating—or as competent—as I once thought.

In their wide eyes, Angel Fire's panic is magnified and
multiplied.

Some of the kids around us form a cluster to defend Angel
Fire. Others dash down laneways between trucks or leap into
the larger construction rigs, even though nothing is moving
anymore.

From every window of every vehicle in the now-stopped and
gridlocked fleet, the heads and torsos of the Unsettled appear.

Wielding some very old looking rifles, they start firing into
the distance at the swarming masses of the approaching
Devoted.

Too soon, I think. *Let them get closer!*

But caught by surprise, the Unsettled seem to have given up
on anything resembling military strategy.

With fearless intensity, other squads of Unsettled soldiers—
mostly adult men and women—burst out of large transport
carriers. Brandishing makeshift spears and with raging battle

cries, they swarm around and past us, sprinting at top speed toward the Devoted attackers, who are now sprinting at top speed toward *us*.

A company of Unsettled troops, dressed in matching brown and green camouflage hunting gear, bursts past us, and we have to leap to the side to keep from getting trampled.

The churn and grind of engines, wheels, and treads has been replaced by wails of agony, shouted orders, and blasts of gunfire coming from behind us, deep within the Army of the Unsettled.

Startled, Haida and Jeff—the white raven on my arm and the purple-and-cream spackled vulture on Matholook's shoulder— rise as one. They beat their wings with frantic desperation as they surge up and bank on a steep ascent away from what's instantly turned from a motorcade into a battlefield.

I call out, "Hey!" but I can't blame them for leaving. If I had wings, I'd probably be long-gone, too.

The two birds fade into the soot-filled sky, leaving us on the precipice of the chaos and in the literal middle of a war.

36

CLIMB

THE CULT of the Devoted are relentless.

They're also unending. There are literally enough of their army up on the flat clifftops to surround the entirety of the Army of the Unsettled with a ring of troops twenty soldiers deep.

I want to ask Matholook where they all came from—how did they manage to turn a small compound of eccentric historians into...*this*?

But the question twists into a spiky bur that lodges in my throat.

Is that because I don't want to know the answer? Or is it because I'm afraid Matholook has known the answer all along?

In orderly rows now, the Cult of the Devoted are pressing forward.

At the same time, the members of the Army of the Unsettled continue to pour out from every door on every RV, camper, motorhome, tractor-trailer, pickup, cube van, excavator, bulldozer, dump truck, and construction rig in their fleet.

The metallic screech of steel on steel vibrates through the air as van doors—hundreds at a time—slide open on rusty, dirt-crusted rails.

Soldiers in the Army of the Unsettled—mostly kids but some adults, too—spill out from the laneways and clamber down from ladders, their boots touching down like thunder and kicking up clouds of red dust.

The contrast between the two armies couldn't be more stark.

These are two rivers—one crisply clean and red, white, and blue; the other choppy and shadowy brown—on a collision course, with me and my friends about to be swept up in the resulting rapids.

Overhead, a distant whistle grows louder, and we all look up in unison. Wavy spirals of silver exhaust streak in huge arcs through the sky.

I can't speak for Angel Fire or the Unsettled, but everyone in my Asylum knows exactly what we're looking at.

It's Libra who says it out loud. "Synaptic Atomizers."

We learned all about them—and the havoc they caused around the world—in Granden's World History class and in Terk's seminar on Demolitions and Explosives. Harnessing electrical impulses from the earth's natural magnetic fields, these weapons disrupt synaptic signals in the human brain. A much more powerful version of the Unsettleds' own Systems Diode Dampeners, they are dangerous and unstable. That's why Krug stopped using them after they kept wiping out entire companies of his own Patriot Army before they could even transport them off their military bases to be deployed against the invented Eastern Order.

Horrific, unpredictable, based on incomplete science, and built on dodgy technology, they are a last resort weapons of war.

So why are the Devoted deploying them as a *first* resort?

Whatever their reasons, the impact of these weapons is an apocalyptic level of deadly.

The sounds of the huge desert caravan, now frozen in place, have been replaced by the screams of the Unsettled—somewhere behind us and deep in the middle of the armada—being dismantled on a cellular level from the inside out.

"The eyes are technically part of the human brain," Granden once explained. "Which is why they go first when an atomizer is deployed."

He went on to show us archival footage of Cyst Plague survivors living in slums around one of the country's big cities as Krug's walls and the arcologies of the Wealthies were being built up. By the hundreds and all at the same time, those people in the holo-projection pressed their fingers to their temples as if in the throes of a communal headache. Only, instead of squinting in pain, their eyes opened wide, and it was like they were being forced to stare into the sun. The glossy wet of their eyes crystalized and went veiny and gray before shattering like glass and cascading down their faces in powdery clumps.

"Their brains literally turned to dust," Granden told us through a choked-off whisper as he leaned heavily on his glass-topped podium at the front of the classroom.

The physical damage he described didn't happen in an instant, either. The whole process took a few seconds. For me and my appalled Asylum, watching the writhing spasms second-hand from the safety of our classroom, it felt like an eternity. I can't begin to imagine what it felt like for the victims.

Here, out in the distant middle of Angel Fire's army, a wall of crackling silver-blue flame surges skyward, only to collapse back down and spread out in a rolling blanket of dust and heat.

We can't see the results of the detonations from here.

I can barely stand to imagine it.

Because the Devoted now have their own soldiers flooding the area, they're unlikely to deploy any more of those horrific atomizers. But that's small consolation for the hundreds of the Unsettled who just died.

Ignacio cries out, "Our weapons!"

Angel Fire points to where a cyclone of electric blue fire is swirling over a dozen armored trucks, their chunky, gunmetal gray bodies smothering under a storm of sparks. "They're in there!"

"We've got to get them!" Ignacio shouts and starts to bolt toward the conflagration.

Arlo grabs his arm and hauls him to a stop. "We need to stay alive!"

Barking out his agreement, Angel Fire shouts out for us to follow him. "I can get you to a safe spot!"

Hypnotized by the appearance of so many Devoted, by the resonant rumble of so many boots vibrating the ground, and by the sudden burst of chaos around us, I'm stunned into a state of complete immobilization.

So much for fearlessly leaping into action.

Matholook grabs my hand and tugs me along as Libra, twenty feet ahead, whips her hand around in a blurry circle and screams at us to hurry.

"We're right behind you!" Matholook shouts out as he and I duck a volley of gunfire. "Keep going!"

Scrambling and dodging, we all break into a top-speed sprint and follow Angel Fire down a laneway of smoking, paralyzed pickups. Almost musical, the ping of bullet-fire riddles the exterior steel plating of the vehicles around us.

Angel Fire calls back over the blast of a concussive explosion that tips over a yellow and rust-colored road-grader parked in a line of similar, thick-tired construction vehicles only about twenty-five yards away.

Normally, the graders are menacing-looking machines with six wheels—four under their huge cabs and the other two extended forward at the end of a curved, steel prow. They've got a row of indestructible teeth that are designed to drag along behind them for purposes of leveling out stretches of dirt and stone to pave the way for the rest of Angel Fire's city-sized army.

In motion, they look like a horde of monsters grinding through the shared nightmare of a bunch of terrified kids.

Upside down—its wheels slowly spinning while it coughs up black smoke from its shattered underside—this one looks like a wounded animal that can't get off its back.

After another full minute of sprinting, Angel Fire slides to a stop at the base of what's got to be one of the tallest vehicles in the Unsettleds' army. Its treads are over ten feet high, with interconnected plates of steel linked together with rivets as long and as big around as Ignacio's arm.

"It's a Lattice Boom Crawler Crane," Angel Fire explains, catching our collective, open-mouthed stare. "Bullet and shock-proof glass up there in the cab."

His words avalanching out, he rushes us to mount the narrow, towering steel ladder leading up to the cab of the crane.

When no one moves, he adds, "You'll be safe up there."

"What about you?" Libra asks. Only Libra could be standing here in the middle of a war and be wide-eyed and worried about a boy like Angel Fire.

In less than half a day, he's been our captor, judge, executioner, pardoner, protector, and tour guide. And now he's become our...savior? Or, even more incredibly, our friend?

"I've got to lead. It's what leaders do." He sniffs and drags his jacket sleeve across his sweaty forehead before swinging around to face Matholook. "You were supposed to be a prisoner of war."

I start to object, but Angel Fire clamps one hand on my wrist and his other hand on Matholook's. His grip is as vice-like as his staring eyes.

"You've proven yourselves. You earned your appeal. The Unsettled...we believe in second chances."

Matholook mouths a feeble, "Thanks," but Angel Fire

shakes off any hint of gratitude. "It's not out of the goodness of our hearts. It's out of our hopefulness for humanity." He drops my wrist and instead locks his hands onto Matholook's shoulders and leans in with a crinkle-nosed stare. "We believe in second chances. Not *third* chances. If you betray us...or *them*," Angel Fire adds, pointing at me and my Asylum gathered at the base of the ladder, "I'll make sure you wind up getting shat out by six different vultures."

Another explosion from less than a hundred yards away punctuates his threat, and a roiling cloud of foul-smelling smoke bursts from under the hood of a metallic-green pickup truck we can see and smell from here. The flames climb high and then collapse in a mushroom-cloud vortex with a burst of heat I can feel from here.

"Go!" Angel Fire shouts, rattling the steel ladder with his hand.

"No way," Arlo objects. "We're going to fight with you."

"Then you'll also die with us." He shakes his head and drags a sleeve across his red, worried eyes. "You'll have plenty of fights of your own. But this isn't one of them."

We all start to object, but he cuts us of, his watery eyes now on the sky before coming back down to lock onto me. "Haida has told you where you need to be, hasn't she?"

I open and close my mouth.

How does he know?

"She didn't drop the fire," he reminds me. "She's revealed something to you, some truth. And you need to trust her."

He rattles the ladder again and shouts "Go!" a second time, and this time, no one hesitates.

One by one and right on each other's heels, we start to scamper up the hot, thirty-foot steel ladder riveted to the side of the crane. It rattles hard as the pulse of another explosion vibrates the air around us, and I think for a second that we all might plummet down on top of each other and die in a heap at Angel Fire's feet.

Arlo is in the lead. I glance up in time to see his foot slip on the melted, patchy rubber grip-pad on one of the ladder's rungs, and it looks like my premonition might come true.

In a flash, he reaches up and clamps his fingers to the ledge leading into the cab. Hauling himself the rest of the way up, he opens the cab door and climbs in, offering a helping hand to each of us as we reach the top of the ladder.

As the last one in, I look down to see Angel Fire below, his hand shielding his eyes as he looks up at us and waves. I wave back and call down, "Thank you!" but he's already turned and started sprinting toward the middle of the worst of the fighting, shouting out orders to his scattered troops along the way.

Explosive, concussive waves ripple through the air around him, and the fleets of trucks and vans to either side burst into splinters of lightning-blue flame. He covers his face with one arm and scoops up a little girl in the other. I think it's the blond messenger girl—one of the two Heralds—with the French braid from before, only her braid, along with half of her face, has been melted to a blistering, resinous mess.

A tall boy, his arm wrapped in a blood-soaked bandage, races over to help, and he and Angel Fire—holding the limp and unconscious girl between them—race on and disappear into a cloud of dark smoke.

Part of me wants to bolt back down and follow them. Even without weapons, my Asylum and I are no slouches in a scrape. We've been training all year in unarmed combat, and we've even had our chances to use our skills out here in the real world. But those were minor skirmishes. One-on-ones. Or us against a few others. Emergent or not, if we leave the cab of this towering crane, we'd get killed before our boots hit the ground.

Besides, Angel Fire was right: This isn't our war. I don't even know what side we'd be fighting on. The Unsettled have proven to be a good lot. They're fierce, rowdy, and unpredictable. They're also fun-loving, knowledgeable, and honorable. But Matholook isn't an Unsettled. He's a Devoted. He's with us, and I want to be with him. The Devoted raised him. Kress and the Emergents Academy took him in. And the Unsettled forgave him. If it comes down to it, I don't even know which of the three sides he'd fight on.

With no better options, I close the door.

Up high and enclosed in the glass-walled cab, we're helpless, stranded, safe, and cornered at the same time. We're warriors, high up and disconnected from the war.

37

WORSE

IN THE CRANE, staring out through the scratched and smoky glass, Libra slips her arm into mine. "We should be down there, not up here."

"This isn't a classroom battle-sim," Arlo says from the other side of the cab. "If we go down there, we'll die."

"We're just as likely to die if we stay up here," Ignacio mutters. "If the Devoted win, they're not going to be shy about coming up here when they're done down there."

Leaning with her back to the glass, her arms folded across her chest, Sara looks inappropriately pleased. "We'll be fine," she assures us.

"And how on earth do you know that?" I snap.

She answers with a quiet smile. I step forward, fully ready to smack an answer out of her, but I'm stopped when a blast from below rocks the entire crane and sends us all sliding to one side where we smash against the glass. The crane goes into a teetering correction where it tilts the other way, and we go sliding across the floor and crash into the opposite window. Thankfully the glass is strong enough to withstand the impact. But the weight of Ignacio's body slamming into my back knocks the wind out of me, and I wind up gasping for breath as the crane steadies itself and regains its proper vertical position.

Gathering our wits and patting ourselves down to check for bruises or broken bones, we wait for a second explosion—one that will destroy this crane and all of us along with it—but we're lucky, and the majority of the fighting seems to have moved toward the interior of the fleet.

From thirty feet up and inside the glass-walled cab, we can witness nearly all of the war surging below.

The battle is like nothing I've ever seen before.

The two armies—the Devoted and the Unsettled—melt together.

The patriotic colors of the Devoted in their dressy reds, whites, and blues mix in with the baggy earth-tones of the Unsettled.

It's a dance, a choreographed ballet. Like the ones in London my parents went to see before the Atomic Wars.

"The Royal Opera House was the most beautiful place in the world," they promised, reflecting back on their times of basking in culture. "The music. The dancing. Simply sublime."

(During one of my many exploratory outings—always without my mum and dad's knowledge or consent—I personally explored the ruins of the Royal Opera House. Covered head to toe in protective layers of my lead-lined haz-mat suit, I went out to see what all the fuss had been about. Like everything else in and around Covent Garden, the place was a ruined mess of steel and concrete, packed with dead rats and dying people puking up the linings of their internal organs as they suffered through the aftereffects of radiation poisoning and the unforgiving assault of the Cyst Plague.)

This dance happening down below, while we watch on like a bunch of little kids spying on the grownups at a cocktail party, is like the dances my parents described: an overwhelming sea of intertwined bodies and a symphony of rolling motion.

Only this sea of motion is bathed in blood.

Crimson spray mixes with war whoops, shouted directions from field generals, and the screams of the wounded and of the soon-to-be dead.

Fire belches up in thick bursts throughout the Army of the Unsettled. The victims of impact grenades, four jeeps and one of the smaller RVs hop into the air and land on their sides as the Unsettled drivers leap out and dash for cover. Not more than two hundred yards away, the steel arm of an excavator sweeps sideways, swatting at a small platoon of marching Devoted soldiers, who duck and unleash a flurry of gunfire at the young driver in the cab of the burning construction vehicle.

The rigid rows of the Unsettleds' moving city are in disarray. What had been roads and laneways only minutes ago are already a jagged mess of confusion, with driverless dump trucks grinding to life, backing up on their own, and slamming into each other while the young soldiers of the Unsettled army try to keep their balance under an unending barrage of enemy gunfire.

"The Devoted have control of the fleet's nav-system," Matholook observes. "The Unsettled can't move. And if they can't move, they're going to lose."

It feels like we all might drown as the simple truth of that statement floods the cab.

Down below, the Devoted swarm through the Army of the Unsettled in unrelenting waves. To their credit, the Unsettled give almost as good as they get.

It might even be beautiful. If it weren't for all the death.

"Oh my God," I whisper.

Matholook asks me what's wrong.

"This...this is what Haida saw."

"What Haida saw...?" Arlo repeats.

"It's what Angel Fire was talking about down there. Haida told me where we needed to be. She shared a vision with me. A premonition. All of us, trapped in glass, floating above a war. She called it 'the end.'"

My friends stare at me, but I don't have anything more to tell them.

In the space of my silence, Libra opens and closes her mouth before finally asking, "What else? What else did she see?"

I know what she's asking. As a fellow Emergent, she doesn't need to ask me how I'm able to read Haida's warnings. And she doesn't challenge the truth or validity of my statement.

But the part of the premonition she's really asking about is too scary for me to answer out loud, so I clamp my teeth together and keep that final question to myself:

Could the "end" she was talking about be our death?

THE ARMY of the Unsettled have always been known for being in constant motion.

But now, playing out for us on the fields of rocks and desert sand below, it's the Cult of the Devoted who can't be stopped.

Ignacio stalks from window to window inside the cab. He keeps firing sinister glances at Matholook each time he pivots and gets ready to resume his pacing.

"It's your boyfriend's fault," he snaps at me.

"How the hell is any of that down there his fault?" I snap right back.

Boyfriend?

"Angel Fire was right. The Devoted don't call themselves a cult for nothing. One of them is just as bad as all the rest."

I've seen this before. When frustration, anger, and helpless-

ness have nowhere else to go, they go to whichever target is closest. In this case, that means Matholook is the target in Ignacio's
sights.

"It wasn't the Unsettled who killed Mattea," Ignacio says,
pointing out what we've all been suspecting since our encounter
with the Outposters. "That girl was a Devoted, wasn't she?"

Matholook shakes his head.

Ignacio responds by lunging forward, his fingers curled into
a tight clench on the edges of Matholook's jacket just below his
neck. "Your people infiltrated the Unsettled, didn't they?" His
forearms come together as he presses Matholook to the glass
with Matholook's feet now nearly off the ground. "How else do
you explain how this entire army could come to a sudden stop?"
He lets go of Matholook's jacket with one hand and snaps his
fingers in his face. "Just like *that*."

"Let him go!" I shout.

I clamp my hand on the crook of Ignacio's arm, but he
doesn't budge.

"It's what you do, isn't it?" he sneers to Matholook. "You lie.
You brainwash. You infiltrate." His white-knuckled fists are now
planted squarely under Matholook's chin. "It's what you've been
trying to do with us all along, isn't it?"

Matholook seems weirdly calm as he curls his own fingers
around Ignacio's wrists. He says, "I'm not the Devoted," and, at the
same time, twists Ignacio's wrists, causing him to release his grip.

It's the first display of physical strength I've seen from Matholook, and I'm stunned, proud, and terrified at the same time.

*Where is this raw power coming from? Where has it been up until
now? And do I have to worry about him using it against me someday?*

Another blast from down below rocks the crane's cab, shakes
the windows, and, in the distance, sends a mushroom cloud of
dust somersaulting high into the air.

"Stop it!" I shout, swinging myself all the way in between Ignacio and Matholook.

The two boys are staring daggers at each other over my head, and I've got one palm on each of their chests. I breathe a sigh of relief when I literally feel the tension drop a notch in each of them.

I've been in plenty of fights. But for about a dozen reasons I can think of off the top of my head, I don't want to wind up in the middle of this one.

"I can't take sitting around like this," Sara complains.

"I'd hardly call this 'sitting,'" Arlo says, making his way over to Ignacio's side.

Another blast rips through the air, and we rush to the big side window. Our hands pressed to the pock-marked glass, we stare out in horror at the small group of the Devoted marching their way from the back ranks of their army toward the scrambling, screaming heart of the Army of the Unsettled.

Standing out among the rest of the Devoted, this group is led by an unmistakable warrior:

Bendegatefran.

Towering above the next tallest soldier, the giant swings that mammoth axe of his in slow, swooping arcs.

The blade end slices two of the Unsettled at a time, and the hammer end catches two more on the way back.

Marching along in his wake, a second small group, only eight people in all, is made up of figures in dark hoods with their eyes burning orange from a piercing, electric glow we can see from here.

Unarmed, the figures nevertheless stalk in a confident march as the rest of the Devoted army parts for them.

Bendegatefran steps aside, and the eight hooded people with the orange eyes scatter in different directions.

Not running. Not fleeing or trying to outmaneuver or outflank the Unsettled.

No. These eight are on a mission of pure destruction. And they have the power to do it.

Peeling open their hooded cloaks, they reveal bodies clad in orange-trimmed black armor, layered with pockets, sheaths, and clips to hold multiple knives, grenades, and throwing weapons. They're all teenagers, like us. Unlike us, they stare out from behind soulless, inhuman eyes.

Four of the hooded teens have military sniper rifles strapped to their backs. Two of them have simple bo-staffs. Two of them don't look armed at all.

But as they separate in eight different directions, they whip their hands around, lashing out with wavy energy pulses, and something becomes crystal clear: they *are* weapons.

"Wait," Libra says, rubbing dirt from the inside of the glass with the sleeve of her jacket. "Those aren't Devoted."

"Then who the hell are they?" Arlo asks.

Matholook says something too quiet for any of us to hear.

"What'd you say?" Ignacio snarls.

"They're with Epic," Matholook says, louder this time. "That psycho who kidnapped Branwynne and Haida. They're what he's been after all this time. They're why he wanted Branwynne in the first place."

"But who are they?" Libra demands, her hands on her hips, her voice simmering with impatience.

"They're like you. Only...worse. They're Hypnagogics."

Ignacio rounds on Matholook, grabbing a fistful of his shirt in one hand and pressing him to the window, harder this time. "And you knew about this?"

Matholook shakes his head. "It was just rumors."

"Let him go," I shout at Ignacio, but Ignacio doesn't budge. "Rumors?"

"Emergents, Hypnagogics...whatever you want to call them. It's what Epic cares about. It's *all* Epic cares about."

"Let him go!" I shout again to Ignacio. This time, he glares at me over his shoulder, but I'm not about to let him hurt Matholook. Locking my hand onto Ignacio's wrist, I give his arm a sharp turn, causing him to lose his grip on Matholook's shirt. In a single, smooth motion, I sling Ignacio backward, sending his shoulders and head cracking against the glass on the far side of the cab.

"That's not war!" Libra shouts. "The Devoted are *murdering* people down there!"

"They're warriors," Matholook responds with way too much calm. "Whether it meets your definition or not, this is war. They're doing what they were trained to do."

I still can't tell if he's sad or boastful when he says things like that.

Technically, following me to the Academy has made him a traitor to his own people, so maybe he doesn't know, either.

Kress once told me, "There's nothing worse than not knowing who you are."

Standing here, not knowing if I might be in love with a boy who may or may not have had a hand in starting a war, I'm pretty sure I found something worse.

38

WITNESS

WHAT HAPPENS next shocks us all to our bones.

The eight hooded boys and girls—all teenagers like us—wade into the fray. They're different sizes, colors, and shapes, but they have plenty in common: Their sleek, armored black military gear. Their fearlessness. Their ferocity. Their deadly purpose. And those orange, burning eyes.

Forming a wide arc, they lead the Devoted army around and over the monstrous vehicles of the Unsettled. The matte-black armor of the eight teens appears to absorb the heat and the kinetic energy around them. The orange seams of their uniforms glow bright enough to make me squint, while Libra, standing next to me in rigid disbelief, gasps and clamps her hand over my forearm.

She repeats what we already know. "Hypnagogics."

I nod my confirmation, and Arlo asks what we should do.

Sara's abrupt chuckle startles me, but not as much as what she actually says. "Why *do* anything? We have the best seats in the house." With all the appearance of a Wealthy casting an amused condescending eye on the commoners below, she saunters closer to the window on the opposite side of the cab. "Let them kill each other down there. We're safe."

Safe? We're powerless and weaponless in a glass box thirty feet above Hell.

Scowling, I whip around to confront Sara. She gives a slow, deliberate turn away from her window, and I know in an instant that I'm nothing in her eyes. Just a nuisance. A prop. A tiny gap in the ground she's happy to step over to get to where she wants to be.

I move toward her, anyway, but she stops me with a raised hand, and it feels like I've just slammed face-first into a synth-steel wall. "I know you want to take it out on me, Branwynne," she says, her voice going satiny soft in my ears. "But I didn't kill Mattea. And it wasn't the Unsettled. Those Outposters were right. It was the Devoted." Her eyes do a skipping dance from mine to Matholook's and back to mine. "It was *always* the Devoted. But they're not just the annoying instigators back East or the quirky little community out here you thought they were. And now you've got a nice seat in the front row of the balcony where you can see that for yourself." She sounds sad when she adds, "We all can."

Matholook puts his hand halfway up like he's about to object, but Sara stops him, too, with a shake of her head. "No sense denying it, anymore," she smiles. She directs our attention to the outside of the crane's lofty cab where thick plumes of smoke are bursting up around us as far as we can see, and it looks like the entire desert of scrub brush, red rocks, deep canyons, and the entire Army of the Unsettled are being blitzed by a relentless meteor storm. "There are only two possibilities. In ten minutes, we'll either be dead, or else we'll be the last ones standing. If we're dead, our problems are over." Her bootheels thudding as even as heartbeats on the cab's steel floor, she steps forward and stops in front of Matholook, planting a hand on his shoulder. It's not an aggressive move or a flirtatious one. It's more like the way a mother might reach out to her petulant child to keep him focused, to make sure he knows she means business. He looks down at her thin, delicate fingers on his shoulder and follows her arm up to her dull, blue eyes. "If we're alive," she tells him with a happy shrug, "*your* problems are just beginning."

She drops her hand and lowers her head, and I can't tell if she's about to laugh or cry. She does neither. Instead, she sighs before gathering herself and lifting her eyes to meet all of ours. Her gaze settles on me, and a zippy little shiver skitters down my neck. The corner of Sara's mouth parts, barely enough to let the words out. "It's like Rain says in her chess lessons, isn't it? The most effective attack will come from the enemy you thought was a friend."

My own lips part, but anything I might have said is cut off by Ignacio, who calls out, "Hey!" loud enough for his voice to echo in the confined space of our elevated cab.

Startled, we all spin around to see that he's got his back to us and is staring out of the window. "Something's happening."

"What is it?" Arlo asks, as we turn our attention away from Sara and gather in a huddle around Ignacio.

He doesn't say anything, but he does press the tip of his finger to the glass.

The five of us circle around him, also pushing forward and doing our best to peer down through the scratched, foggy window into the dust storm swirling over the clashing armies.

Below us, most of the eight, black-clad Hypnagogics have faded into the battle. I can only see two of them from here. One of them—a girl with honey-colored skin and short, glossy pink hair visible under her hood—is holding up the front end of a cobalt-blue pickup truck with one hand and dragging a kicking, screaming teenage boy out from underneath with the other. The truck bounces on its front wheels as she drops it back down. She slings the boy with one hand, and he smashes back-first into the side of a second pickup truck, this one gunmetal gray with its doors and hood painted white. His head cracks and explodes in a splatter of blood. We can't hear the sound of bone on steel from here, but it feels like we can.

The other Hypnagogic—also a girl but shorter and with her hood down to expose her stringy brown hair and a face full of freckles—is leaping with inhuman speed, balance, and lethal accuracy from the roof of one of the stalled yellow dump trucks to the next and firing deadly rounds from a pair of enormous Action Express, fifty-caliber Desert Eagles that look like golden canons in her small hands.

But the Hypnagogics aren't the "something" Ignacio summoned us over to see.

It's not the Unsettled army, who have regrouped and are now launching their own counterattack of rifle fire and precision strikes from entire battalions of archers, spear-throwers, and hundreds of soldiers wading fearlessly into battle with nothing more than hockey sticks, aluminum baseball bats, and long-handled, curve-bladed gardening tools.

And it's not even the Devoted, who fall by the dozens, bloody and screaming in agony under the defensive stand by the brave soldiers of the Unsettled.

Instead, what draws our full, riveted attention, are the *resurrections*.

As we watch, fallen soldiers from the Cult of the Devoted—gashed, bloody, and fish-belly pale as life drains from their bodies—gather their feet under themselves, stand back up, and, shaking off what looks from here like some kind of zombie daze, charge back into the fray.

"Are you seeing this?" Ignacio asks, his voice high-pitched

with disbelief. As mesmerized as a little kid at a snake cage in the zoo, he's leaning forward with both palms on the glass now.

A woman in Devoted battle gear, her patriotic colors now soaked red with blood, stands up and, hunched over and apparently oblivious to the gaping wounds in her face and neck, searches around among the rocks and the desert thorn bushes for a weapon. A few feet away, one of her fellow Devoted soldiers stares down at the brown handle of the twelve-inch hunting knife protruding from his chest. Drawing a pistol from a holster in his boot, he makes a beeline toward a flustered regiment of the Unsettled, firing his weapon as they flee or fall.

Next to him, Arlo mutters, "It's the zombie apocalypse."

"Zombies are a movie invention," Libra protests, her hands planted in defiance on her hips but her eyes locked, like the rest of ours, on the impossibility of what's happening below. "That... down there," she insists with a stab of her finger toward the scene below, "isn't possible."

Her black hair hangs in curving waves over her face, and I can't make out her expression. But I know her well enough by now to know she'll have her eyes narrowed and her jaw set in defiance. Libra is a grounded, down-to-earth girl. Her comfort zone is only as big as what she can get her mind around. And, right now, the burning world outside of this cab is a million times bigger than any thought she could ever hope to hold in her head.

Through the swirling fog of battle below, we continue to watch as the Devoted—the living *and* the dead—refuse to break off their attack in the face of whatever stand the Unsettled attempt to make.

Even though what we're seeing is technically impossible, whether Libra wants to believe it or not and in spite of my deepest desire for this not to be happening, I trust my own eyes. They've seen too much for me not to.

When a fleeing group of the Unsettled cause the smoke around them to clear, we see the very last sight anyone would expect to see in the middle of a war:

A young girl.

Not more than ten-years-old, she's wearing a kid-sized version of the Devoted military gear. Smiling, she moves among the dead Devoted placing her small hands, her fingers splayed out like starfish, on the temples and chests of the fallen soldiers.

And, one by one, like the man and the woman we personally saw rise from the dead, those same Devoted—bloody and very dead, themselves—stand up, shake off the fog like deep sleepers after a long nap, gather their scattered weapons, and rejoin the fray.

Brushing back her hair, Libra looks over her shoulder at me, her eyes dark with a question whose answer I think she already knows.

At the same time, Matholook and I say, "Gwernna."

Gwernna. Ten-years-old. Cute. Quiet. A cherished and protected member of the Cult of the Devoted. And possibly the most important Emergent in the world.

The Devoted swept in like an ocean tide. The Unsettled pushed back in a surge of their own. And now, the tide that *was* the Devoted has swollen into an endlessly reviving and unstoppable wave.

"We have to help!" Libra cries.

Like the rest of us, I'm sure, her loyalties have automatically latched onto the Unsettled. Although Matholook is our friend, new classmate, and member of the Cult of the Devoted and, although I've personally met and been treated with great kindness and hospitality by the leaders of the Devoted, what we're seeing now makes any alliance with them out of the question.

The Unsettled are ferocious in battle, but they have rules. The Devoted are merciless killing machines. Before our eyes, they swarm through the ranks of the Unsettled, firing high-powered rifles and disemboweling the wounded with serrated, arm-length blades and laughing and high-fiving each other the entire time.

They're not just soldiers on a mission. They're not civilians lured into a fight. And they're definitely not a community of historians who've been recruited into a battle against their will.

They're enjoying this...as if there's no place else they'd rather be.

"What do you suggest we do?" Ignacio asks Libra with a curt snap. "Even if we had our weapons, there's thousands of people fighting down there. And with that girl in the mix, the Devoted could keep fighting forever!"

He's right, and the desperation of helpless futility in his voice hits me as hard as any punch I've ever taken.

While we watch and hope no one happens to look up, Gwernna—the delicate-looking little girl I once personally rescued from the Unsettled—walks in a casual stroll through the clashing, fighting, and dying bodies, reviving them one at a time before moving on to the next.

For all their civility and commitment to hospitality and history, the Devoted—the living and the recently revived—are ruthless, fearless fighters.

And why shouldn't they be? With Gwernna wandering in the middle of their army bringing the dead back to life, they're immortal.

The fallen soldiers of the Devoted continue to clamber to their feet and stretch like people waking up from a refreshing sleep.

The giant Bendegatefran, his upper body still visible even though he must be a quarter mile away by now, continues to swing that tree-sized axe of his in big, swooping arcs. It's covered in more blood each time it reappears above the low-hanging clouds of smoke and ash above his head.

Faced with an indestructible enemy, the Unsettled instantly doubt their ability to succeed. I can see it from here. We all can. The way they halfway engage or else scurry for cover...whatever game plan they had for this war has gone completely out the window. I don't know what their plan was or what they expected, but I'm betting it wasn't *this*.

The Unsettled are going to lose. And we won't be far behind.

Libra's crying on one side of me with Matholook slowly backing away on the other. He shakes his head like he can't believe what he's seeing. Or, more like he's trying to will away the fact that what he's seeing is one hundred percent real.

Their own eyes glistening with tears they're trying hard to hold back, Ignacio and Arlo turn to me for answers. They ask me about a game plan of our own. They beg me to try again to connect with Haida Gwaii. They ask if I think we can climb down from here without being seen and maybe find our way back to the Academy.

"Or find our weapons," Libra suggests through a choked sob. "So we can at least have a fighting chance."

On the far side of the cab, with her shoulders pressed to the glass and her arms folded, Sara grunts, and I realize she's resigned to our fate. Live or die...I don't think she cares one way or the other.

Arlo clamps his fingers around my wrist just below the cuff of my jacket. The waffle pattern of raised scars on his face takes on a blistering red blush. "There's got to be *something* we can do," he pleads. It's a suggestion that lands somewhere between hope and terror.

But I've got nothing to offer. Nothing but my own fear and my own indecision, two of the last things any warrior could want.

And yet, trapped in here with the riptides of war churning

below and ready to drag us down into its unforgiving undertow, they're all I have.

39

SURRENDER

AFTER ALL THAT, we're up here in this cab for...fifteen minutes? Half an hour? A year?

What's happened to my sense of time?

It occurs to me then: War doesn't just claim buildings, equipment, vehicles, land, and lives.

War takes away time.

The time to think. The time to learn and grow. The time to be at peace with yourself long enough to know your own mind.

Over however long it takes for the fiery apocalypse to play out below us, Sara and Matholook both inch their way back into our Asylum. We're no longer a confused, suspicious bunch of bickering, anxious kids. We've returned to being a collection of six teenagers with a shared sense of regret about what's come before and a terrifying uncertainty about what might happen next.

I've faced impossible odds before. Hell, I grew up isolated in the Tower of London while millions died outside the stone walls of the ancient prison-castle. But these feelings I've got now—helplessness, uncertainty, and insecurity—well, those are brand new. And I'm not a fan.

Standing behind me, Matholook loops his arms around my waist and rests his chin on my shoulder. "It's going to be okay," he whispers. "We're all going to be okay."

With the tension in here and the bloodshed outside, it doesn't take a mind-reader, which I'm not, to know he doesn't believe any of that, himself.

But I give him credit. He's trying.

And not totally without results. I know his arms aren't enough to keep me safe. I know his words of reassurance aren't enough to stop the fear or quell the pain. But his chest against my back and his breath in my ear feel...*amazing*. His hands are clasped together at the bottom seam of my leather jacket with my hands resting on his. He's enveloping me as sure as if he were a human shield, and I get a little heart flutter I've felt less than a handful of times in my entire life. (And Matholook has been responsible for nearly all of them.) I'm all of a sudden out of breath, even though all I've done is stand here in terror, pretty much waiting to be discovered by the Devoted and, eventually, killed.

Within the Branwynne-Matholook bubble, the world is okay at the moment.

This is what I need: Me, Matholook, and nobody and nothing else.

It's a split-second moment of blissful, utopian perfection. And that's the problem with split-seconds: *They never last.*

Her voice far too loud for the small cab we're in, Libra cries out, "Look" and points to a spot in a square clearing between a dozen parked excavators about a hundred yards from the base of our crane.

In an area not any bigger than the size of the average football pitch and surrounded by the rust and black bodies and arms of the construction vehicles, Angel Fire steps forward, his head bloodied, and his once over-sized but pristine business suit smudged with dirt and ripped to shreds.

He climbs up on top of the cab of one of the excavators and signals his troops to stand down.

We can't hear the words from here, but the slump of his shoulders and his downcast eyes make his intentions crystal clear.

I'm no lip-reader, but it *feels* like I am—like all of us are—as we watch him order his Unsettled troops to surrender and give up their positions and their weapons.

Like rodents emerging from their underground burrows after a predatory threat has passed, the Unsettled emerge from every vehicle, shadow, and laneway.

Everything about Angel Fire screams defeat: The bowed head. The loose arms and fidgeting fingers. The lack of anything resembling strength or confidence in his eyes. And he looks more than ever like an undersized little boy in an oversized business suit with no idea what to do now or what comes next.

I don't know what he thinks will happen. But what actually happens is a hundred times worse.

As we watch him watching the Cult of the Devoted and their immortal army, Bendegatefran and Efnisien, Bendegatefran's half-brother, shoulder their way through the crowd of gloating Devoted and the dozens of the Unsettled they currently have on their knees, their wrists zip-cuffed behind their backs.

Justin and Treva, the leaders of the Devoted, edge their way through the crowd as well and stand in front of Angel Fire in high-shouldered triumph. They're not alone.

Each of the two leaders has a child in front of them. Justin stands behind a small boy, while Treva stands behind a small girl.

Justin and Treva exchange words with Angel Fire we can't hope to hear from here, and I'm about to breathe a sigh of relief and suggest we use this break in the action to make our escape when the mirrored flash of a dark blade glints in the air above Justin's head. It's a black-coated, twelve-inch Bowie knife.

The exact same kind of knife that girl in the desert used to kill Mattea.

In a horrific moment of déjà vu, Justin plants the knife under the trembling chin of the small boy.

Libra, both palms pressed to the glass, stares down. "You don't think he'd—"

The knife slides in a long even stroke along the boy's throat, and a spray of blood fans out from the side of his neck.

We all scream at the same time, with Libra collapsing to her knees, her tear-stained cheek pressed to the cab's glass wall. She says, "No, no, no" until the single, small word fades into her sobs.

Down below, Justin hands the knife to Treva who plants it under the chin of the little girl.

From his knees, Angel Fire raises both hands, his own screams muted by distance and by the glass walls of our makeshift sanctuary.

In a deadly mockery of the motion we saw in the classical music concert, Treva drags the knife along the little girl's neck like a musician drawing her bow over violin strings. The girl's head lolls to the side, and she slumps down to a blood-soaked heap at Treva's feet.

Ignacio bangs the sides of both fists on the glass and echoes our own screams of devastated disbelief.

We all collapse to the floor, our eyes fixed on the pair of executions we just witnessed. We stay like that for a long time while we watch Justin and Treva continue to pace in front of Angel Fire.

"What should we do?" Libra asks.

"We can surrender to them," Matholook suggests. "They might be..."

"Merciful?" Ignacio snarls. "Did that look merciful to you?"

If Matholook planned on answering him, he doesn't get the chance. Arlo says, "Look" and draws our attention back down to where four of the Devoted are each dragging another pair of small children along with them. They toss the stumbling kids to the ground between Angel Fire and the two Devoted leaders.

Down in the clearing, Angel Fire, his head sagging low to his chest, points a weak, trembling finger in our direction.

"They know where we are," I say out loud. Not that it needed to be said at all.

Led by Bendegatefran and Efnisien, a small battalion of the Devoted march between smoking rigs and over the lifeless bodies of the Unsettled to arrive at the base of the crane we're in. With his axe on one shoulder and his other hand cupped around his mouth, Bendegatefran bellows out for us to come down.

"What do we do?" Libra asks.

"We fight," I snap. "Unless you feel like dying."

"We'll die if we fight," Ignacio says, pointing out the obvious.

"If they even let us get to the ground alive," Arlo adds.

As if our situation weren't already desperate or impossible enough.

There are six of us, weaponless and thirty feet up in the glass cab of a crane against a legion of cold-blooded killers, a giant, and his savage half-brother, all of them backed up by the entire might of the Devoted army and an Emergent with the power to keep them coming back from the dead.

Sara offers up an annoyed grunt and shoves past us to the cab door. She lifts the heavy latch and opens the steel door a few inches—just enough to let her voice be heard by the enemy troops below—and calls out, "We're coming down!"

"Wait!" I snap. "We didn't decide that!"

"Yes, we did," Sara says evenly over her shoulder and turns

around to start the backward climb down the ladder. "When we decided not to die."

Going down there into the arms of the enemy doesn't seem like a reasonable thing to do at the moment. But it's better than being a treed cat.

Isn't it?

Sara leads the way with Libra, Ignacio, and Arlo following close behind. I'm about to step out onto the ladder when Math-olook locks his fingers around my upper arm and tugs me back. I turn and lift my head just in time for his lips to meet mine.

It's not the best or the longest kiss we've shared (there was one in the middle of the night back at the Academy that made me sure my heart was going to sledgehammer its way out of my chest), but it might be the most important...since it might also be the last.

Which is exactly what Matholook tells me when he pulls back, a wry smile on his extraordinarily kissable lips. He tilts his head toward the cab door and in the general direction of the assembled army that might very well be about to double as our executioner. "Sara's right," he says. "The Devoted are more than they seem." He steps through the cab's open doorway and turns to face me before starting his descent. "But so am I."

I'm the last of the six of us to hop down to the ground. We stand there, surrounded on every side by deep crowds of the Cult of the Devoted, and I have an instant awareness of what it must have been like to be a slave about to be fed to the lions for the amusement of a Roman emperor.

BENDEGATEFRAN AND EFNISIEN are accompanied by their personal entourage of Devoted soldiers, most with handguns and all with holsters full of serrated, black-handled hunting knives strapped over top of their once-white dress shirts.

Efnisien flexes and unflexes his big-knuckled hands. His sharp-tipped fingernails are glossy as a raven's talons.

Practically as big as an excavator arm, Bendegatefran towers over everyone in the open area of empty desert at the base of the crane.

Behind the two half-brothers and their personal security detail, more of the Devoted are stepping over the bodies of the Unsettled and herding the survivors into small groups to be zip-cuffed, processed, and passed off to small teams that begin leading away their prisoners of war.

The platoon led by Bendegatefran and Efnisien ushers me and my Asylum into a line and starts snapping buzzing zip-cuffs to our wrists.

They get Libra first. And then Arlo and Ignacio. They pause at Matholook, who offers his hands, his fingers curled into loose fists, for them to administer the restraints. The Devoted soldier hesitates, so Efnisien snatches the cuffs from the woman and snaps them onto Matholook's wrists, himself.

Efnisien doesn't bother to lower his voice in the least when he leans in close to Matholook and hisses, "Traitor!" in his ear.

Behind him, his axe glossy with blood and resting on his shoulder, Bendegatefran scowls, but I don't know if it's because of Matholook's actions or because of Efnisien's *reaction*.

His sharp incisor teeth protruding over his lip, Efnisien snarls at the rest of us and then snaps a gloating grin out of the corner of his mouth at Libra, Arlo, and Ignacio, who are squirming helplessly in their cuffs.

I know from experience that zip-cuffs tingle and feel almost soothing. But then they tighten the more you resist and ramp up a painful energy pulse by design.

With the exact same grimace on their faces, my three friends struggle and wince against the restraints. I know the energy cuffs don't affect Ignacio as much as they do Typics or other Emergents, so I suspect his knotted face is more about having to surrender like this, the indignity of being a prisoner, and the knowledge that we just secured a total, embarrassing, and epic failure.

The guards reward my friends with smug smiles and a reminder of what happens when you struggle. "Don't worry, though," they assure us all with a mocking laugh. "There's plenty more pain to come."

For some reason, they don't make a move to cuff Sara at all.

When a female soldier—one of the shimmering blue-white zip-cuffs dangling from her finger and thumb like a garter snake —shuffles over to me and orders me to put my arms out, a floodgate opens in my mind, and it feels like every emotion I've ever felt in my life has turned into a live hand-grenade and exploded in my head.

Haida Gwaii!

The consciousness of the white raven blasts into my brain with a single word. I don't know if it's meant as a warning, a suggestion, or an order. But the word itself is unmistakable:

~ *Fight.*

So that's exactly what I do.

40

FIGHT

WITH A STRIKE I know is too fast for the woman in front of me to follow, I drive the heel of my hand into her nose, breaking it in an explosive spray.

Her head has barely snapped back when I'm already executing a reverse leg sweep on the Devoted soldier next to her. The man's legs fly up, and before the back of his head cracks against the jagged, rocky ground, I'm already on to Efnisien with a flying knee to his sternum.

Drooling, ferocious, and as savage as ever, he shakes off my attack and slashes at me with those sharp, talon-like fingernails of his. He misses my neck with one strike, and he gets close enough with a second shot for me to feel the breeze of his hairy hand whipping past my face. There's a bumping, scraping clink as his nails rake over the ridged waffle-pattern of armor plating in the shoulder and upper arm of my jacket.

I glance down to see the bloody git's managed to rip a hole in the material.

This jacket and I have been through a lot. I swear...I'm going to survive just so I can make him watch while I mend it with thread I personally make from his entrails.

He tries a quick follow up with his other hand, but he's off balance, and that slicing attack brushes harmlessly off my forearm deflection.

We each fire off a string of stinging strikes. His shots are as wild as mine are controlled. It's his savage unpredictability versus my enhanced, surgical precision. I plant a boot to his shin and execute a *hiza-guruma* throw that lands him flat on his back. He rolls away from my follow-up knee drop and clambers to his feet.

After another lightning-fast flurry while his stunned mates look on, he comes out on the short end of an exchange of blows:

I get a few scratches on my arm. *He* gets the wind knocked out of him and an express, nose-first trip to the rough ground where he lands in a spread-legged sprawl among the rocks and a patch of scruffy gray-brown shrubs.

While I allow myself an inner celebratory cheer, a dark shadow falling over me blocks out the sun and chills me to the bone.

Still bound and with a Devoted guard holding him by the collar, Matholook shouts out for me to watch my back.

Whipping around, I clench my fists and dig the heels of my boots into the rocky ground.

I've faced Bendegatefran before. Twice. And I won. Both times.

A head taller than most of the motorhomes we've seen in the Army of the Unsettled and backed up by the Devoted, he's an intimidating spectacle to behold.

Staring up at him, I feel like I might as well be getting ready to fight a tree.

The giant towers over me, and I get the impression he could just step on me or lash out with one sweep of his arm and send me spiraling off across the desert.

I don't plan on giving him the chance to do either.

Grinning their confident smiles and cheering on their colossal comrade, the Devoted step back, leaving me face to face with their real-life, axe-wielding Goliath in the circular clearing.

Leaning in, he swats at me with a hand the size of a car door. He misses, but the wind alone is enough to send me spinning and staggering backward.

Moving faster than I thought possible for someone his size, he catches me in the side with a follow-up punch that compresses my ribcage and vibrates my spine like a tuning fork.

"Stay close!" Matholook yells.

Close? I'm planning on staying as far away from this human sequoia as possible!

"He needs space to fight!" Matholook reminds me.

The guard behind Matholook order him to be quiet and kicks him in the side of the leg, dropping him to one knee.

And now I'm *really* pissed off.

Turning now to his weapon, Bendegatefran swings that Paul Bunyan axe of his with enough speed and force to slice through a truck.

But I'm no truck.

With my reflexes and predatory instincts jacked up to super-human levels, I easily dodge the swing and step in close to Bendegatefran until we're nearly toe-to-toe. (Considering the size of his boots, each of his toes must be as big as my entire foot.) I know from experience that he's as deadly by himself as any army. But Matholook is right: he has weaknesses. Well, *one* weakness: He has no idea what to do with an enemy who is within arm's length.

Sliding in close, my face barely even with his navel, I release myself to Haida Gwaii, who guides my leaping uppercut to the giant's sternum followed by a quick side kick to his patella.

I leap back, expecting him to buckle and go limp as his kneecap succumbs to the ramped-up strength of my attack.

That doesn't happen.

Instead, he growls loud enough to blow back my hair and swings a backhand at me hard enough to level a mountain.

Fortunately, I'm able to dodge the blow. Kind of.

His fist catches my shoulder, and I go flying twenty feet through the air, hit the ground, slide another ten feet, and come to a crashing stop with enough force to gouge a *me*-sized trench into the rocky terrain.

Overhead, Haida gurgle-clacks a way-too-late warning for me to watch out.

I send her a sarcastic, telempathic "Thanks" and roll to the side just as Bendegatefran's axe comes swooshing down, its bladed edge lodging two feet deep into the hard-packed earth.

Wedging it out, he prepares to take another swing. That split-second of preparation is the opening I need to launch my go-for-broke counterattack.

Yes—he's big. Fortunately, though, giants have the same weaknesses as the rest of us.

I slide under Bendegatefran's legs, scooping up a charred, forearm-length of desert mesquite as I go. It's not much of a weapon—barely kindling—but then again, the eyes aren't exactly the toughest spot on the body to get through.

It takes me three full vertical steps to climb high up enough on his back to reach his meteorite-sized head.

With both knees pressed into the middle of his back and one arm looped under his chin, I raise the spike high in front of his face and bring it down hard and fast.

The sharp end of the wooden splinter pierces his eye, and I make sure to dig it in deep enough so he can't shrug this off.

I'm expecting squeals, shrieks, and hopefully even a moan of complete and total surrender.

I get none of this.

Instead, he acts like I did nothing more than serve him up a minor, inconvenient nick.

With his free hand, and with the shard still protruding from his eye, the giant reaches behind his head and snags me by my collar. With my red jacket bunched between his fingers and with his brick-sized knuckles digging in between my shoulder blades, he drags me off his back and holds me in front of himself like I'm a disobedient puppy who just shat on his favorite area rug.

I kick and thrash with every bit of strength I have left (which isn't much), but Bendegatefran has me locked up tighter than a puma on a possum.

I try to tap into Haida again, but nothing happens. At first, I think maybe she got scared and abandoned me. Or else she realized the futility of my trying to fight a human mountain with a few thousand members of his army backing him up.

But then, I realize the horrifying truth:

Haida hasn't abandoned me. Out of the corner of my eye, I see her white-feathered form blasted by a Devoted sniper who's kneeling on the rounded hood of a nearby tractor. His shot screams through the air, and Haida does a downward spiral about fifty yards away. She disappears behind a massive, green and yellow earthmover, and just like that, her consciousness fades from mine, leaving me more helpless, vulnerable, and plagued by a guilt big enough to rival the guilt I feel over losing Mattea.

In my mind, I scream loud enough to split my brain in two.

My bond with Haida goes both ways. She can lend me her abilities. But she can also experience my pain. And I can experience hers.

I try to say her name out loud, but Bendegatefran, looking like a mutant unicorn with the wooden spike still buried in his eye, locks me in his grip, and the breath in my lungs is squeezed out of me in a rushing torrent.

Clamping my arms to my sides with one hand, Bendegate-fran holds me still while Efnisien, brushing dirt from his face and spitting a gob of bloody saliva to the ground, slips around behind me and tugs a pair of zip-cuffs as tight as he can around my wrists.

Now, bound the same as my friends—except for Sara who remains uncuffed—the six of us are shoved into a tight clump in the middle of the clearing.

Also locked up with humming zip-cuffs, the troops of the Unsettled kneel around the perimeter of the circle with a ring of the Devoted soldiers standing guard behind them.

The crowd parts as Justin and Treva step forward. But the real surprise is right behind them.

Just as the troops of the Devoted parted for their two leaders, those leaders now step aside, themselves, and offer small, deferential bows as three people—two men and a woman—stride forward to stand, feet wide and fists planted on their hips, in gloating victory.

One of the men is bald and looks carved out of marble. His iris and pupil-less eyes, the exact opposite of my "Galaxy Eyes," are white with tiny black dots sprinkled in. The other man is thin, bug-eyed, and curved as a question mark. The woman is exotic-looking, with honey-colored skin, hair as smoky as raven's wings, and a pair of metallic legs with a built-in propulsion system that generates an air wave distortion as she half-walks, half-glides forward.

I know all three of these people. How could I not?

It's Epic, Micah, and Aubrielle: the trio who kidnapped me and Haida and who would have certainly dissected both of us down to our DNA if my friends hadn't help us escape. They call themselves a "Triumvirate."

His coppery-brown hair, a spiky, disheveled tangle, Micah seems closed off and sad, a sagging, slump-shouldered, husk of a human. He's Kress's brother, but I think a mum and dad are the only thing the two of them could possibly have in common.

The other two members of their Triumvirate look supremely happy, only I can't tell if it's because they're on the winning side of a war or if it's because they're about to get their scurvy little claws into me for a second time.

41

BETTER

WHILE EVERYONE else tends to turn some shade of red under the hot desert sun, Epic's bald head somehow stays milky white, with just enough of a spiderweb pattern of thin, pale blue veins running under the skin to save his skull from looking like the world's largest pearl.

Unlike the patriotic kit of the Devoted, he's dressed in canary-yellow scrubs that manage to look baggy and comfortable while still making him look evil and scary. His veiny, muscular arms are fully exposed under his short-sleeved shirt. Even his shoes—glossy white with black trim and a golden backwards "E" emblazoned on the side—have managed to resist the red scuffs brought upon most surfaces out here by the scorched desert sand.

Sculpted and robust, he's a figure of confidence, vigor, and lethality. Not the kind of guy you'd want to run into in a dark alley.

Or a light alley, for that matter.

It's quite the magic trick, one replicated by Aubrielle, whose hearty, athletic build and elegant curves seem out of place in a world plagued by starvation, war, disease, and death.

Behind Epic and Aubrielle, his dark, soulless eyes pinned to the cracks and crags of the ground at his feet, Micah has the defeated, distressed expression of a scolded toddler.

His side just won. What does he have to look so glum about?

Snapping his fingers and tapping his foot to some tune I guess only he can hear, Epic takes a mini-stroll in front of me and my Asylum. He shakes his head like we've disappointed him somehow before planting himself in front of Justin and Treva, who don't seem to know if they should be hugging Epic, attacking him, or running from him in fear for their lives.

I don't blame them for the puzzled expressions on their scrunched faces. This guy is part techno-geneticist, part pit-bull, and all psycho.

"It's okay," Epic promises the pair, a cottony-soft smoothness and a hint of condescension on his pale blue lips. "We'll take them from here."

With the type of silent communication possible only between two people who know each other intimately, Treva and her husband exchange a look I can't read. Exuding a closed-off, "this is nobody else's business" aura, the energy passing between them is secret, private, and palpable.

Is this how it looks to others when I connect with Haida? Do my friends examine my blank face and my "Galaxy Eyes" and guess at what's happening in my head like I'm doing with Justin and Treva right now?

I do a mental scan for Haida, but I don't feel anything. There's no connection. Not even a flicker.

Don't panic, Branwynne. Your connection's been glitchy for days now. I'm sure she's fine.

I know it's wishful thinking, but that's the only kind of thinking I can allow myself right now. Anything else is sure to drown me in a crippling helplessness from which I may never return.

Forcing myself to focus on what I *have* instead of what I've lost, I turn my full and furious attention to Justin and Treva.

Their mental exchange complete, Treva pivots her body toward her husband, but her eyes stay fixed on Epic, and I get the sense that even here and now, allied and victorious in battle, she doesn't want to turn her back on him. Not that I blame her. Even for someone as clearly ruthless as Treva, taking your eyes off of that guy is a good way to wind up in an underground lab with a bunch of wires suction-cupped to your head.

"I don't know if that's such a good idea, after all," Treva says, half under her breath.

Justin puts a hand on her forearm. I think it's supposed to be a gesture of comfort and reassurance, but Treva draws her arm back like she's been electrocuted.

In their matching red, white, and blue battle gear, the two of them stand side by side, Justin, pink-cheeked, balding, and with a matte-black, polymer combat rifle leaning against his shoulder, and Treva, scowling and still looking like she's crunching on a mouthful of rocks. All they need is an oil-painted, peaked-roof house behind them and they could be a mid-21st century version of that "American Gothic" painting.

Clearly amused, Epic huffs up a shiny-toothed laugh in the face of their somber stillness and reminds them both that "a deal's a deal."

"What deal?" I chime in through a dribble of blood pooling at the corner of my mouth. My face still stings from where Bendegatefran backhanded me. I lean over, my eyes on Epic, and rub my jaw against my shoulder to try to dull the pain. It sort of works, and I'm relieved.

At least the giant arse didn't dislocate my jaw.

"It's about as easy of a deal as you can imagine," Epic says, his eyes still locked in some sort of long-distance battle with

Treva's. "I help the Devoted win the war. They get the Unsettled. And I...well, I get you."

Great. The only thing worse than being a pawn is being a captured *pawn.*

"The deal we made was before we saw what you turned *them* into," Treva says, an accusing finger raised in the direction of the eight Hypnagogics, who are lined up and sitting, kneeling, or squatting in gargoyle crouches along the hood, roof, and tailgate of an oversized, twenty-three-foot Crew Cab pickup truck.

From blonde to brunette and ivory-skinned to mahogany brown, the Hypnagogics are a range of skin tones and body types. Perched on the truck with their smoky black battle armor and its orange edging, their equally orange eyes, and their stony, unreadable faces, their outlines blend into the distant mountain ranges beyond the far edges of the Army of the Unsettled. The eight of them look, for all the world, like a murder of giant alien crows.

"They're not your concern," Epic warns Treva with a finger wag of his own.

"They're *everybody's* concern," Treva insists, her lips tight and the muscles in her jaw pulsing and tense. "If you're planning on turning the Emergents into...*them*..." She points once again to the Hypnagogics, whose electric orange eyes are now flashing with amusement as they take in the scene.

"That's not my intention at all," Epic coos. Treva's fists unclench, and the "V" between her eyes relaxes and evens out. "I can't turn Emergents into Hypnagogics," Epic goes on to explain. "It doesn't work like that. But I *can* turn them into something a lot better. A lot more powerful."

"You see?" Treva cries out to Justin. "He wasn't helping us. He was helping himself. How long before we're just another nuisance to him and he turns those...things...against us?"

"He won't," Justin answers with cool certainty. "We want different things."

"Your husband's right," Epic agrees. He makes a contemptuous *pfft* sound with his lips and offers up a wide, general sweep of his hand, taking in everything in the vicinity: the smoke billowing from under the hoods of hundreds of vehicles, Angel Fire kneeling with his head down and his wrists cuffed behind his back, the victorious Cult of the Devoted, and the defeated Army of the Unsettled. And, of course, me and my captured friends.

"If you want this country," Epic tells them, "it's all yours. My guess is that you'll come to the same fate as every despot before you. You'll revel in your victory here. You'll extend your reach too far. You'll fall under the weight of your own empire and the added weight of your ego and ignorance. So, yes. Take the country back. But these kids," he adds with a wry smile as he turns that swooping hand toward me and my Asylum, "are mine."

Treva's lips part, but Epic anticipates her interruption and cuts her off.

"I just handed you a victory over your one and only rival for power," he says through what somehow manages to be a charming snarl. "Handing me a few stray meddlers in return... well now, that's not too much to ask, is it?"

We all swing our heads in unison to await Justin and Treva's response.

I'm half-hoping they'll stand up to Epic and renege on whatever deal they had. I know we'll be as good as dead in the hands of the Devoted. But in Epic's hands...we'll certainly be subjected to something a *lot* worse.

42

VOICE

"Time for you to come home, my little orphans," Epic says, his pink gums and ham-slab of a tongue flashing against the backdrop of his bleached and veiny-blue skin.

He's not an albino. His eyes aren't pink. Could he be leucistic like Haida? And is that just a coincidence, or is something else going on here?

"Where are you taking us?" Libra asks.

Epic smiles at her, his voice breezy, as if he's inviting us all back to his flat for high tea. "Back to Sanctum. Only this time, we won't be letting you get away so easily."

"We won't be letting you get away at all," Aubrielle adds. Like Epic, this woman is seriously fit. I can see every striation in the sculpted muscles of her exposed arms. Of course, it'd be easier to admire her if she weren't part of an evil cabal bent on dissecting me.

"It wasn't easy," Ignacio growls with a lot more confidence than I have at the moment. "We had to break in and slip past a dozen of your gutless guards."

"And we must've knocked out at least two or three more," Arlo adds, piggybacking his bravado onto Ignacio's. "Plus, we freed Branwynne and got out before any of you idiots had a chance to blink."

Everything they're saying is true, but I give them both a silent "Shut it!" glare before they antagonize this lunatic into going completely off his trolley right here and finishing what he started.

Flanked by Aubrielle and Micah, Epic orders a handful of his Civillain Sentinels to get us moving.

"And don't let them out of your sight along the way. Even without weapons, they still have...*weapons*."

I wonder if he knows just how glitchy-at-best our so-called "weapons" have turned out to be.

Yes, we all enjoy firearms and bladed-weapons training classes in the Academy. But the one-on-one mentoring sessions —when we get to explore and learn to harness our abilities as Emergents—*that's* where we get the biggest thrill. Classes are mostly about camaraderie. But at night, when we're done being put through our paces, that's when camaraderie morphs into competition.

I can't count how many hours we've spent decompressing in the Lounge, bragging—sometimes with passive-aggressive subtlety, sometimes with undisguised bluster—about who's been able to do what on any given school day.

Ignacio will brag about how he worked with Brohn and was able to short-circuit a bug's brain from twenty feet away. Libra, usually more modest, will quietly explain how easy it was to dismantle and reassemble one of War's magnetic propulsion pads or reconfigure one of Wisp's prototype telecommunication beacons. Arlo proudly shows off his newest scars, bragging loudly enough for everyone in the Lounge to hear about how the injuries he shrugged off during his training session with Mayla would have killed anyone else in the room.

Returning from a mentoring session with Rain, Mattea used to ask us to challenge her. "Give me any language," she'd boast, "and I'll speak it for you right now." So the younger kids in the newest Cohorts to the Academy would go skimming through their wrist-mounted research-ports and then call out, "Swahili! Liki! Ishkashimi! Pawnee! Unsettled!" And, sure enough, she'd launch into a full recitation in whatever language they wanted. (Of course, since I don't speak any of those languages, I could only *assume* she was doing as she claimed. For all I know, she was faking the crunched-face facial strain and making up every syllable on the spot. Still, it *sounded* impressive. Plus, she'd accompany each performance with a parenthetical little history lesson. "Liki was spoken in a small part of Indonesia until 2032. Ishkashimi from Tajikistan in central Asia is a spoken-only language and doesn't have a written version. Pawnee is an Indigenous language from Native communities around the Platte River in the American Midwest. Not too far from the Academy, actually. And Unsettled is a patchwork of English, Spanish, and a bit of Pirahã, a language of a small community of native Brazilians who used to live along a tributary called the Maici River in the Amazon."

Sara—now that I'm thinking about our brag-filled exchanges in the Lounge—almost never joined in. I know she can do something manipulative with her mind. But whatever it is and the degree of power and reliability she possesses...well, she keeps that a pretty closely guarded secret.

As a Typic, Matholook doesn't possess any special abilities, unless you count being kind, empathetic, and heart-thumpingly handsome. While those are great qualities in a potential suitor, they don't offer a lot in combat situations.

That leaves me. A seventeen-year-old Emergent who has, in the past, built a strong telempathic bond with a white raven, survived drone strikes and the Atomic Wars that turned London into body-filled badlands, and who has passed through solid walls...three times.

And who, in the present—terrified, immobilized, and disconnected from Haida—is about as deadly as a paralyzed puppy.

I reach out to Haida again, sure we'll connect this time.

I need you.

Nothing.

At least let me know you're okay.

Still nothing.

I'll take anything. A word. A feeling. A breath.

When I'm answered with more nothing, I get angry at the tears trying to surge their way out. I order them back and tell them they'll have to wait.

Not yet, I command in my mind. *There's plenty of time for worry and sorrow. Now isn't it.*

As we're shoved into a forced march, all around us, the Army of the Unsettled are sinking even deeper into their own defeat.

On one side of us, three teenage girls are dragged by their hair from a small camper and are thrown to the ground where the Devoted soldiers kick them in the ribs, zip-cuff them, and then stand with one boot on the girls' backs in triumph, while four more of their mates gather around in fist-pumping celebration.

On the other side of us, six screaming boys and girls—none older than about ten or eleven—scramble out from underneath a smoking pickup truck and try to run, but one of the Devoted whips out a Desert Eagle with a ten-inch barrel and fires a spray of bullets at the fleeing kids. A few of the stray bullets whiz over the heads of the limping children, plinking against the solid steel exhaust vents of a giant combine harvester. The rest of the bullets *thunk* into the kids' backs, and all six of the young Unsettled sprawl to the ground.

Next to me, Libra gasps.

But there's no time to contemplate, complain, or mourn.

Epic's Sentinels lead us past the outer edge of the Army of the Unsettled on a forced march. Less than five minutes later, we're in a desert clearing with five military escort jeeps parked in a protective huddle around an enormous matte-black truck. The ten-foot high, mostly windowless rig is thick and powerful, with synth-steel reinforcements around its body, armor plating on its doors, a silver sensor spike on its hood, an angry-looking metal grill on its front end, and four heavily studded wheels holding it all up.

Boxier, uglier, and nearly as big as the Terminus, it's pretty much a rhino on wheels.

"This is the BearCat," Epic announces with a pride-filled smile. "Our recommissioned riot-control Armored Evac Personnel Carrier. It'll be your home for the next few hours while we take you back to Sanctum."

Sanctum. The name of Epic's town, with its rustic-looking surface and its high-tech underground labs, sucks the air out of my soul.

Don't cry, I remind myself. *And don't panic.* "*Worry*" *isn't a strategy.*

"You're not a revolutionary," I snarl at Epic. "You're just another version of Krug."

"You couldn't be more wrong," he laughs. "While we're waiting for the BearCat's cells to recharge, let me enlighten you."

Epic paces a little in front of us, but Micah shuffles backward a few steps while Aubrielle stays stone still, her hands clasped in front of her as Epic "enlightens" us.

"Krug had it wrong. His vision for the world was the vision of a child. He thought of you Emergents as some kind of saviors, a missing puzzle piece, a tool, and a weapon. But you're not any of those things. Do you know what you are?" He tilts his head like he's waiting for us to answer. When no one does, he steps directly in front of me and grins. "It's good to see you again, Branwynne." (If my mouth weren't so dry, I'd spit in his face.) He pivots from me to face the others. "You're a *warning*. Your abilities, the things you can do...it was all an experiment. But you know that. What you don't know is that the experiment failed."

I glare at him, hoping my stare will be enough to bring him down but also knowing that it won't.

"We're not a *failed* anything," I growl.

"Of course you are," he laughs. "And not just because you allied yourself with the losing side of this war. No. Your failure is your absurd idea that you can fix the world. Did it ever occur to you that the world doesn't need to be fixed? Every species has a hierarchy, a system of order to keep itself healthy and in balance. With your infantile dreams about some utopian future, Emergents upset that order. Only by preserving what is best and sacred about the nation we *were* can we ever hope to become the nation we were destined to be. Today is the first day of what will one day be known as a glorious history. Today, the Devoted will begin the districting of the Divided States." His voice peaking with pride, Epic makes grand gestures to the left and right. "Even as we speak, the walls are being built. The coasts can live out their remaining days of lawless decadence until they crumble to ash like all those that have come before."

"And what about them?" I ask, my eyes planted on the eight hooded Hypnagogics skulking in a semi-circle around us.

"Ah...them. They're a necessary evil."

"Evil is *never* necessary."

"I forget sometimes how young you all are. 'Evil' is just an arbitrary label people apply to anyone who refuses to agree with them. What you call 'evil' isn't only necessary, it's inevitable. But don't worry. These Hypnagogics are just the beginning. They'll protect the Devoted while I scour the world for more of them."

"You can't just make the Unsettled do your bidding. They'll fight you."

"They just did. And they lost. Don't get so caught up on the ideal of freedom. Like evil, it's all in the way you choose to look at it. What's so great about freedom, anyway? Freedom is chaotic. It's messy. It leads to anarchy, confusion, and entropy. Freedom is the enemy of order."

"You won't get away with this," I snap. "The Devoted should know better than anyone. Despots ultimately fail. Empires always fall."

"What's to get away with? It's a done deal. The wheels are in motion. The walls are already going up. The Unsettled have been stopped, and the Devoted are in place and dug in." Epic offers up a self-satisfied, gloating smile. "The Wealthies control the arcologies. But now, the Devoted will control them. And once Justin and Treva and their Devoted army have secured the country, they'll expand their borders until the world finally looks like they think it should."

"But that's *their* dream, not yours."

"Their dream will help mine come true."

"You're helping them succeed just so you can have the power to take them down someday?"

"Ha! I never looked at it like that. But yes."

"Someone will stop you."

"Who?"

I part my lips, but no sound comes out. I don't have an answer. So I'm startled when someone I can't see calls out, "Us!"

I recognize the voice before I even figure out where it's coming from. It's a voice I know better than my own, a voice that's guided me and trained me for the past five years.

Kress!

43

CAVALRY

STEPPING out from the laneways spoking out all around us, Kress and her Conspiracy appear as if by magic, and I wonder if I have some sort of secret Emergent ability even I didn't know about that enables me to summon a savior—or, in this case, seven saviors—with nothing but a thought.

Or maybe—win, lose, or draw—Kress just works hard to be in the right place at the right time. And who knows? Maybe that's exactly what makes her and her Conspiracy heroes.

Dressed in black tactical combat gear with white piping, Kress is a human bird of prey. Render, onyx-black and just as fierce, loops around her in banking, protective circles: the world's deadliest guardian angel.

He *kraas*! a warrior's battle-cry into the sky as he plunges, talons-first, into the chest of one of Epic's guards. The man swats at the air and staggers back, dropping to the ground and shuffling in a terrified, scrambling crawl underneath a nearby Septic Tanker.

Surging forward, Kress slaps the heels of her hands together, and the full set of five-inch, razor-sharp blades snaps out in a curving arc over each of her fingers on both hands.

She's got her talons buried in the exposed neck of one of Epic's Sentinels before he even knows she's there.

And then, in half-a-heartbeat, she's already moving on to her next flailing, bewildered target.

Only a step behind her, Brohn leaps onto the hood of a disabled, half-burned and flat-tired pickup truck. Landing with the grace of a gazelle and the power of a Belgian stallion, he's got his knee down and his arbalest primed, raised to his shoulder, and firing all in one single, impossible motion.

Four of the personal guards from Epic's team dive for cover but not before two of them spiral to the ground, taken down by Brohn's deadly bolts.

He tags the third Sentinel—a woman with a perfect black braid of hair extending down from under the back of her helmet —right in the meat of her calf muscle. Gasping for breath, she drags herself by her fingertips to find shelter with her fellow Sentinel underneath the Septic Tanker.

Fanning out from behind Kress, Rain slides to the ground while firing a swarm of tiny silver barbs from the Dart-Drivers strapped to her wrists. Most of the razor-tipped quills plink against the guards' armor, but enough find their mark to send a bunch of Epic's men shrieking and falling over each other in their disoriented scramble for cover.

Towering over everyone else in the clearing, Terk swings his morning star in a swooping arc. The Sentinel closest to him is nearly as tall as Terk but about half his weight and a fraction of his intensity. The tall man stands frozen and wide-eyed. His Kevlar vest is technically bullet-proof. But he's finding out Terk's massive Medieval weapon is deadlier than any measly bullet. The heavy spiked ball at the end of the chain embeds itself into the man's chest, and he goes flying back with five blood-red holes in his bullet-proof vest.

With lethal, pinpoint accuracy even most machines could

only hope to possess, Kella fires her Desert-Tech bolt-action sniper rifle from what feels like ten different positions at once. Her blond hair tucked under a black bandana, she's a blur of motion. She seems to be behind the four-foot-high treads of an armored bulldozer, crouched down between a cluster of sage brush, and laying down cover fire for the rest of her Conspiracy from behind Terk's piston and gear-filled body...*all at the same time.*

Decked out in a chainmail vest underneath thick, armor-plated battle gear and a helmet with an impact-resistant ballistic face-shield, War charges in to take on three of the Sentinels, who are regrouping and reloading their weapons. Tossing the Sentinels aside as easily as I throw blankets on my bed, War is somehow even bigger and more superhumanly strong than I remember.

Put a set of treads on him, and he'd fit right in with one of the bull-dozers of the Army of the Unsettled.

In a blurry crouch behind us, Mayla slides past, slicing off our zip-cuffs with a pair of laser shears.

My Asylum and I are desperate to jump in, but Libra stops us. Not because we're unarmed and outnumbered. And not because we'd probably just be getting in the way if we tried to help our teachers.

No. She stops us because of the ravens.

Dragging me into a crouch and barking at the rest of our Asylum to "get the frack down!" (as she so politely puts it), Libra points to the small storm swooping out from a low-hanging dust-cloud and descending on the clearing.

Except that it's not a storm.

"Ravens!" I shout.

Because that's what they are. Five ravens. And I recognize them instantly. War, Jr. and Cheyenne are oily-black. Apache is mottled with a striking black-and-white cheetah pattern.

They're accompanied by two white ravens, Arapaho and Shoshone, with one more white raven—a streaking missile who also happens to be their mother:

Haida Gwaii!

I shout her name, and I don't know which shout is louder: the one in my head or the one bursting from my mouth. Either way, the presence of my oldest friend has flipped me—with just a few beats of her powerful white wings—from helpless to completely and totally empowered.

A group of ravens is called a Conspiracy. I've known that since I was old enough to know anything. Growing up in the Tower of London with a pair of Ravenmasters for parents made knowing everything about ravens second nature.

I don't know what the term is for a single family of ravens, all of them working as a coordinated unit, swarming with the ferocity of a school of piranha on a capybara, and dive bombing the holy hell out of Epic's startled, scattering soldiers.

Including Render and Haida, there are only seven ravens in all. But, in terms of pure ferocity, seven angry and overprotective ravens might as well be a pride of lions.

My internal cheers are interrupted by the shouts of another platoon of Sentinels, who come charging out from behind a line of stalled excavators.

"Here!" Mayla shouts from behind War. "We thought you could use these!"

Unslinging the bulging sack from her shoulder, Mayla dives down into the bag and starts hauling out our weapons.

It takes some effort, but she chucks Libra's sixteen-pound sledgehammer to her. Standing as she catches it, Libra beams a shiny-toothed "Thanks!" and bounces the hammer in her hands, reveling in its heft.

Arlo does the same with the long-handled scythe Mayla

lobs to him. Without his signature hoodie, he doesn't look quite as much like the Grim Reaper as he usually does. But it's a start.

Mayla calls out, "I think these belong to you!" and slings a leather bandolier loaded with throwing darts over to Sara, who catches the harness, slips it over her head, and buckles it across her chest in one deft motion.

Next, Mayla tosses Ignacio's twin shillelaghs underhanded. He catches them on the run, already spinning them with helicopter intensity as he charges at our enemies.

And, finally, my Serpent Blades. The twin weapons spiral through the air from Mayla's hands and land in my waiting, open palms with a satisfying smack.

Standing over the empty bag, Mayla holds up Mattea's set of Bear Claws.

Pausing for a split second before entering the fray, I skid to a stop in front of Mayla and shake my head. "Mattea didn't..."

Over a blast of gunfire and Ignacio's squeals of glee at being able to fight, Mayla tells me, "We know" and tosses the weapons to Matholook. "He'll have to do the best he can!"

And just like that, we're an armed army again. We're few in number, and Matholook and my Asylum are still far from trained and battle-tested like Kress and her Conspiracy. But together, at least we stand a chance against Epic, his eight Hypnagogics, and his band of Sentinel bodyguards.

Haida and her offspring dodge, barrel-roll, climb, and dive-bomb the Sentinels in choreographed waves. Their claws and *kraas*! intimidate a handful of the Sentinels into bolting for cover. A few more of Epic's guards try to make a brave stand, but it's like they're firing and flailing at ghosts. With Render joining the fray, that's seven angry, determined, and deadly ghosts to deal with, and Epic's men don't stand a chance.

Practically before we even know what's going on, Kress and

her Conspiracy have already taken out half of Epic's Sentinels and nearly all the Devoted escort soldiers.

"We can't let them have all the fun!" I shout.

I sling one of my Serpent Blades at the Sentinel bearing down on Brohn from behind. The spinning blade glints in the sunlight, its curved steel talon nicking the man in the neck just under his ear.

It's not a kill shot. It's not supposed to be. Just enough to distract the guy while Brohn unleashes a flurry of bolts from his arbalest. The razor-tipped arrows lodge six inches deep in the man's chest. The soldier staggers back and smashes to the ground, kicking up a cloud of desert dust.

Brohn gives me a salute and calls out "Thanks!" before pivoting back around to rejoin the battle.

In the scrum, Matholook and I stay close. I do the first-order dirty work of spinning and slashing my way through the Seninels, and Matholook cleans up by finishing off the stragglers with Mattea's Bear Claws.

He's nowhere close to skilled with those things, but to get out of here alive, we don't need to be pretty or even accurate—just desperate.

Which we are.

A hand clamps onto my shoulder, spinning me around. I'm about to launch a ferocious attack with my Serpent Blades when I realize it's Libra. Her eyes wide, she points over to where the eight Hypnagogics have broken out of whatever daze they've been in and are starting to walk, with the casual leisure of someone strolling through a park, into the clearing to join the battle.

We've seen them in action from the safe distance of a crane's elevated cab. The last thing we need is to see them in action up close.

Lucky for us, we don't get the chance.

Epic barks out for his guards to protect the eight mysterious hooded and orange-eyed teens. "They're all that matters!"

Breaking away from Kress's Conspiracy and my Asylum, the remaining Sentinels—as yippy as a team of border collies—surround and wrangle the eight Hypnagogics into a tight cluster.

Despite their powers and their obvious delight in using them, the Hypnagogics are unexpectedly compliant. Following the orders quickly and without question, they let themselves be turned back around and herded toward the BearCat.

When the dust settles, Epic's remaining Sentinels are a bloody mess.

But he climbs into the huge transport rig, along with Aubrielle, Micah, and the eight mysterious, orange-eyed Hypnagogics.

From the opposite direction, an entire company of uniformed, heavily-armed Devoted soldiers—at least a hundred men and women strong—barrel toward us.

"Uh, oh," Ignacio says. "They've sent reinforcements."

Brohn grabs me by the back of my jacket hard enough to lift me clean off the ground. "Let's go!"

With Render, Haida, and their five offspring streaking ahead, Kress and the rest of her Conspiracy shout out for us to follow them to the Terminus.

"Come on!" I urge Sara, who's lagging behind.

She trots a couple steps toward me but then stops.

"What are you doing?" I cry out as I try to take her by the hand. "We need to get the frack out of here!"

She tugs her hand out of mine and takes a full step back. "I believe in Epic's mission."

"He's going to try to take over the whole bloody world!"

"Someone's got to do it," she shrugs with a sad smile. "And I can do things, Branwynne. I can do things that'll help him succeed."

Gunfire explodes around us and turns the door of a nearby jeep at the edge of the clearing into Swiss cheese.

Sara and I both drop to a knee, ducking under a second volley.

"Don't worry," she smiles, her pale blue eyes locking onto mine. "We'll meet again."

It's not an abstract hope or wishful thinking. It's not even a promise. And it's definitely not a declaration of undying friendship.

It's a threat.

Hopping to her feet and with her head down as she dodges the incoming gunfire from the Devoted reinforcements, she sprints off in the opposite direction after the lumbering BearCat. I watch in horror as the huge truck slows down with a grinding crunch, blasting up a cloud of red dust.

With a metallic clank and a pneumatic hiss, the armored rear door swings open. Epic reaches down, his marbled hand latching onto Sara's, and he hauls her into the boxy rig.

In my head, Haida's voice says, "*Run!*"

But I'm already sprinting, almost flying, as I bolt away from the Devoted, away from Epic, and now, away from Sara and the big BearCat that go disappearing into the distance.

44

REVELATIONS

Kress drags me by the arm and frisbees me into the Terminus.

Splayed out and spinning, I crash to a stop against Math-olook and Libra, who scramble to disentangle us before clambering up to help me to my feet.

Render and Haida blast into the rig to join us, while their five offspring bank hard and high and soar off toward the mountains.

Rain slaps a palm to an input panel in the cabin, and the thick steel door of the rig grumbles shut and locks with a metallic gasp. Flashes of gunfire from outside light up the small, shielded windows on the side of the truck.

"What the hell was that?" Libra squeals, her hands clamped to my shoulders. "Where's Sara? Why didn't you bring her with you?"

"I tried," I insist, choking on the knot of confusion and anger in my throat. "She wouldn't come."

"Wouldn't...?"

At a loss for words or for an explanation, I settle for just shaking my head. When I do try to talk, I can feel my voice breaking, and I try to sound strong. I was never a big fan of Sara, but she was an Emergent and an Academy student, which made her someone I cared about, whether she was a friend or not.

But then, twin senses of sorrow and failure overwhelm my defenses, and I feel the sting of tears in my throat and behind my eyes.

Staggering, I drop down onto one of the bench seats with Libra and Matholook, unable to stay standing in the surging Terminus, falling into the seats on either side of me.

A fully armed beast of a machine, the Terminus is too fast and too powerful for any of those Devoted soldiers back there to follow on foot or even in their smaller escort jeeps that can't handle the terrain like our top-of-the-line truck. But I wonder how long it would take for them to mobilize their entire army and try to track us down.

After a day of being kidnapped, tortured, tested, and taken on a tour, I take some comfort knowing that at least we're back in good hands for a change.

As reliable as my own heartbeat, Kella and Mayla are up front in the cab. Terk and War, by far the two biggest members of our little Emergents family, are squeezed into the cab's second row of seats. With Mayla at the navigational helm, Kella steers the Terminus at top speed over a sea-sized stretch of land wrinkled with rocks and ridges.

Back here in the cabin, the rest of us throttle against each other and hang onto the grab-bars bolted to the walls around the benches and passenger chairs.

Apparently unaware, immune, or just used to the motion of the Terminus, Kress, Brohn, and Rain sit across from me and my Asylum looking calm and stable despite the bumpy ride.

"We lost Mattea. And now, Sara," I sob. Matholook slips his hand under my ponytail and slides a supportive arm around my shoulders.

"We didn't lose Sara," Kress corrects me. "We never had her."

"I don't—"

"Sara's a Hypnagogic," Brohn explains. He works himself out of his combat jacket and drapes it over his knees. "She has certain abilities she never told you about."

"Because she might not know the extent of them, herself," Rain adds.

"What abilities?" Libra asks in a muted whisper.

"Yeah," Ignacio echoes from where he's planted in one of the rig's middle swivel seats. "What abilities?"

I know why they're asking. Sara has always been a mystery but never more so than when it came to discussing her Emergent abilities.

Kress and Brohn exchange a look, and Brohn nods for her to go ahead and tell us. Kress clears her throat. Twice. "Sara can get people to do what they secretly want to do but know they can't or shouldn't."

"She's a brainwasher?" I ask.

"No. Not exactly. She can't make you do anything you don't *want* to do. Things like brainwashing, blackmail, torture, coercion...those are oppressive actions forced on a person from the outside. Sara's abilities are what we call 'reactive and prescriptive.' She helps you react to your own desires and allows your brain to prescribe a way to satisfy them."

I realize my mouth is hanging open, so I close it. If what Kress is saying is even remotely true—and I have no reason to believe otherwise—the implications are, well, jaw-dropping.

I first met Sara five years ago. And I've been at the Academy with her for the better part of a year. How much of what I've thought, felt, and done since then has been me, and how much of it has been her?

I risk asking my three teachers that exact question. I expect them to laugh it off, shrug their shoulders, or dismiss my stupid inquiry with a casual wave of their hands. They don't do any of those things.

"All of it's been you," Kress says softly.

"Whether it's been the *you* you think you are or the *you* you know you are but try to hide...," Brohn starts to say.

In my head, I will him to stop talking. He doesn't listen.

"She may have allowed certain things to happen, certain... feelings. But she doesn't *create* anything. She's a facilitator, not a manipulator. But that doesn't make the potential she has any less dangerous. We thought maybe we could help her, teach her how to control her abilities." Kress gives him a little elbow nudge to his arm. "But it looks like her abilities have come to control her," he finishes with a heavy sigh.

"And now she's going to help Epic?" Libra asks.

"It looks like it," Brohn nods.

I can't tell which one of us is more horrified or, honestly, less surprised. But now that it's been said out loud, some of the strange things that have been happening over the past few months—the odd way I know we all sometimes felt when Sara spoke in class, the way we couldn't help but agree with her—no matter how wrong, illogical, or flawed her arguments were—even my inexplicable urge to leave the Academy like I did—they all, as of this very second, have a proper and terrifying explanation.

"There's got to be something we can do!" Libra moans.

"What do you suggest?" Ignacio sneers. "Do you want us to turn around and go back?"

Libra glares at him but doesn't answer. What could she possibly say? Going forward means losing Sara. Going back means losing everything else.

"I'm just going to say it," Arlo announces with the gravity of a dying star. "If she's a Hypnagogic like they say, then I for one don't *want* her back."

"It's not that easy," Rain barks. She's five feet tall but packs a verbal wallop strong enough to make Arlo back off and sit up straight. "We're not in the business of choosing who to help and who to turn loose. The abilities you all have make you potential forces for great healing or for great harm. The Academy isn't there to shelter the former at the expense of the latter."

In the stunned silence after Rain's reprimand, Kress inspects her Desert Eagle semi-automatic before clicking it back into its holster on her thigh. "This is what we were most worried about. It's what we most feared."

Brohn tries to nod his agreement, but his head stops, his chin hovering above his chest in defeat. "You know that image of the little guy with horns, cloven hooves, and a forked tail sitting on your shoulder?" he asks into the floor of the Terminus, his eyes down. "The one who tempts you to satisfy your own happiness at the expense of someone else's?"

He looks up when we don't answer. His fists and his teeth clench at the same time. "Well," he says through a grimace, "that's Sara. And, without the Academy and proper training, it could be any one of you someday."

"There was no way you could have known any of this," Kress reminds us. "But privately, it's why we called her 'the Devil's Advocate.'"

"She said we'll meet again," I mumble, half to myself.

"I hope so," Kress says. "There's still a lot we can do for her."

"If we don't manage to track her down," Brohn replies. "There will be some pretty terrible things she can do to us."

Over in his single-seat passenger chair Ignacio swivels around to face the rear of the Terminus. "Um...the Devoted... there's no chance they're following us, is there?"

"No," Kress assures him. "We're safe."

Betrayal. Loss. Failure. Regret. Embarrassment. I feel a lot of things right now. For some reason, *safe* isn't one of them.

We ride along for another several minutes in silence, and I'm just about to take my first normal breath when Kella shouts out, "Holy frack!" from the cab and slams on the brakes, grinding the huge truck to a bumpy, bone-rattling stop.

"What is it?" Brohn calls out as he and Kress launch themselves to their feet, fully prepared to fight any enemy who might try to stand between us and the safety of our hidden mountain Academy.

"You stay here," Brohn barks as he, Kress, and Rain bolt from the cabin into the cab.

We don't listen.

Matholook and my Asylum and I scramble after them and, ducking down, cram into the cab of the Terminus to get a better look out the narrow front window.

"I don't see anything," Matholook says.

I shake my head. "Me, neither."

"Behind us, maybe?" Ignacio says, whipping around to peer back down the length of the cabin. "See? I told you. I had a feeling we weren't out of the woods."

Behind the rig's steering pegs, Kella raises a hand and directs our attention to a lumpy rock in the middle of the road.

"A rock?" Arlo asks.

"It's not a rock," Kella says.

"Then what is it?"

Leaping forward, his huge palms pressed flat to the interior steel panel above the narrow window, it's War who answers. "*Jeff!*"

Turning and knocking through the rest of us and sending us scattering to the side like human bowling pins, War thunders out the cab, through the Terminus door, and is outside on the road before I even have a chance to regain my balance.

When he climbs back into the truck five seconds later, sure

enough, he's got one dusty, slightly dazed looking vulture tucked under his arm.

We all gather around to greet him as he ducks into the Terminus and calls out for Kella that it's okay to keep going.

"He must've sensed you in the rig," Brohn guesses, his nose wrinkled at the sight (or is it the smell?) of the patchy-feathered bird. "He must have tracked us down."

"I don't care how he did it," War says through quivering lips and with happily wet and red-rimmed eyes. "I'm just happy to see this guy again!" He hugs the bird to his bulging chest, and for a second, he looks like a four-hundred-pound five-year-old with his favorite stuffie.

After a few rounds of petting and cooing over the happy reunion, we settle back into our seats in the cabin.

With our enemies behind us and with Render, Haida, and Jeff crouched in a comfortable three-bird roost, we all take the time to tell our stories.

"Start with the leader of the Unsettled," Kress instructs, and I can sense her gearing up to take a spate of mental notes. "He calls himself Angel Fire, right? We haven't been able to get much intel on him," she explains. "Other than we think he must be one cruel and savage son-of-a-bitch."

Libra, Arlo, Ignacio, Matholook, and I exchange a silent, five-person, who-wants-to-go-first look.

And then, despite all the betrayal, loss, failure, regret, and embarrassment, the five of us break into a spontaneous, simultaneous fit of the giggles.

"Let me tell you about Angel Fire and the Unsettled," I pant, one arm pressed to my stomach as I try to catch my breath, "and just how wrong all of us have been."

45

HOME

AFTER MAKING our way through the desert and up some of the old and very steep access roads, we enter one of the three main mine tunnels we use to get the Terminus into and out of the Academy.

The mountain is laced with these old tunnels. Most of them were sealed off a long time ago. The ones that remain, despite Kress and her Conspiracy's best efforts at maintenance and repair, can still be pretty rocky and unstable.

It's a rough ride up the old mountain roads and a tight fit through some parts of the steep, snaking tunnels, but Kella—with her off-the-charts reflexes—steers us through with pinpoint precision.

She's great but not perfect, and every time we hear a dink or ding from the brush of the fortified sides of the Terminus against the curved stone walls, I jump a little and wonder how I'll react if I wind up paralyzed after a horrific crash.

With only the dim cabin lights and the flickering glow from the assorted panels and holo-displays up in the cab, Kress and Brohn and my Asylum sit together in the near-dark and begin to exchange our stories.

I tell Kress and Brohn about everything that happened to us since we first set out on our mission. Chiming in as if on cue, Libra, Ignacio, Arlo, and Matholook fill in the blanks and throw in their own version (often exaggerated, in my opinion) of our experiences with Angel Fire and the Unsettled.

We all sit in a moment of heart-broken silence after Matholook and I recount what happened to Mattea. Kress assures us it'll be okay and that we'll all make sure Mattea didn't die in vain. I find her voice unpleasantly matronly when she tells us about the lessons we've learned and about how we'll be smarter and stronger going forward.

I worship Kress to death, but nothing she says now or in the future is likely to make me feel any less guilty and crushed to my core about what happened to Mattea.

Still, I guess I'm glad she's trying.

In London, I practically lived in a square-mile graveyard. I saw rats and ravens dining on the dead by the thousands.

But Mattea...her death hits me like all of that *times a million*.

(In our history seminar at the Academy, Granden once said a famous dictator pointed out that a single death is a tragedy. A million deaths are a statistic. I don't remember who said it, but, right now, for me anyway, it couldn't be more true.)

As we recall our tour through the Army of the Unsettled, Kress and Brohn ask a few questions. We tell them all about the trial, the challenges, and our ultimately successful appeal. We tell them about the array of vehicles, the shops, the neighborhoods, and the people—kids, adults, and quarantined carriers of the Cyst Plague—that make up the constantly moving city. I have to turn the storytelling over to Libra when I get to the part about Shostakovich and the classical music concert. (If I tell it, I'm going to start crying right here in front of everyone in the belly of the Terminus, and then I'd have to kill myself.)

And, of course, we tell them everything we can remember about Angel Fire, our captor-turned-tour guide.

"And maybe even a friend?" Libra suggests.

"If he's alive," Arlo reminds her.

"He's alive," Matholook assures us. I know he doesn't know Angel Fire's fate any better than we do, but the way he says it—confident and hopeful but not smug or naively optimistic—makes me inclined to believe him.

I know Kress and Brohn are absorbing all this as tactical information for future use, but for us, it's just a bunch of kids telling tall tales of their arse-over-tit adventures in a strange and unexpectedly fascinating world.

Ignacio jumps in to tell about us being trapped high up in the glass-walled cab of the construction crane as the war swept along below.

"Branwynne had a premonition about it," Matholook brags on my behalf.

Balking, I shake my head and tell Kress and Brohn that I didn't have anything of the kind. "It was Haida. I think she's seeing—"

"The future?" Kress asks.

I look up and expect to see her chuckling or making fun of me or something. But she just smiles as Brohn pats the back of her hand.

Brohn, smiling and sparkly-eyed, wags his finger back and forth between me and Matholook. "And this?"

I'm pretty sure the heat from my cheeks could melt the walls of the Terminus. Next to me, Libra giggles, and I elbow her in the side and tell her to shut it.

Matholook, his voice not much more than a mumble, tells Kress and Brohn, "We're friends."

Our two teachers nod knowingly. Maybe *too* knowingly, and

now I'm embarrassed at being so transparent about my feelings for Matholook.

Saving me from any further, flaming-cheeked embarrassment, Arlo leans forward to relate all the details of finding Jeff, winding up exposed on the front lines between the Cult of the Devoted and the Army of the Unsettled, being taken away by Epic, and thinking we were dead. "Until you all showed up," he grins.

"And then we lost Sara," Libra mumbles, her head low.

"And that brings us up to now," I finish. It hurts, but I can accept talking in memorial tones about Mattea. But Sara...she's a totally different story told by a totally different narrator. Who she was and what she may be becoming...it's way beyond my paygrade.

Kress and Brohn compliment us on our work, and I ask Kress what happened during their recon and rescue mission in Nevada's Great Basin National Park.

She demurs, claiming she's not much of a storyteller, herself.

When we press her, though, she gives us the basics. "Terk and Rain set up the infiltration. We encountered resistance."

"What kind?"

"The usual. A couple of not-so-bright guards."

Ignacio makes a scoffing-hacking noise from the back of his throat that makes Arlo laugh. "How come the guards in those Processors are all muscles and guns and no brains?"

"I'm not sure," Brohn tells him. "But it's a good thing. If they had brains to go along with their muscles and guns, we might not be here right now."

Kress slips her hand into Brohn's and leans back in her seat. When he doesn't elaborate on their adventure, she takes over. "After we got past the guards, we rescued four Emergents, including Apex."

Even though we're in the Terminus, grinding along through

the old mine tunnels of the mountain, Libra still puts up her hand like we're in class. "Who is Apex?"

"He's sometimes called 'the Database,'" Kress informs us. "We dropped him off at the Academy after our mission and right before we set out looking for you. You can meet him and the others when we get home."

Home.

How could such a simple word make my heart go wonky and fill my eyes with enough tears to capsize Noah's ark?

As casual as if we were all gathered around an evening campfire, Kress pulls her hair back into a loose ponytail. "Basically, his DNA contains the hybrid digital-binary code Epic is still out there looking for. Most important of all—way more important than what we *did*—is what we *learned*."

"And what was that?" I ask, grateful to hear my mentor willing to share more of what she knows.

"We discovered that what we thought we knew is only a fraction of the truth."

Brohn nods his agreement. "It's like we were asleep and believing a truth that turned out to be nothing but dreams."

We all stare, confused.

Dreams?

Ducking under the ceiling between the cab and the cabin, Terk comes in and gives Kress a status update about one of the truck's mag-boosters and its weapons guidance system. Well, it's not exactly Terk. It's actually the Auditor—the algorithmic techno-consciousness based on Kress's mother living in a black disk on Terk's back and integrated into his Modified parts—who does the talking.

(I'll never get used to hearing her disembodied voice wafting out from around Terk's hulking body.)

Her voice lilting and sweet, the Auditor launches into a bunch of mechanical techno-speak I'm not even close to understanding, but Libra's eyes go wide like this is the most important and interesting thing she's ever heard in her life.

Kress thanks her and issues a laundry list of things they're going to have to do once we get home. And it's a long list.

Ignacio asks if the Terminus is okay. "Are we going to be able to..."

"Make it home?" Brohn finishes for him. "We took a few hits in the National Park, but I think we'll be okay."

Terk grunts a laugh at this. He flicks a thumb toward Kress and Brohn and rolls his eyes before turning his attention to me and my Asylum. "Breaking into a hidden research lab with military-level security, rescuing four imprisoned Emergents, and getting out alive in a heavily damaged rig isn't as easy as *they* make it sound."

"It doesn't sound easy at all," Libra mumbles.

Pushing up one of the sleeves of his white compression top and massaging a nest of raised scars on his forearm, Arlo seems worried. "What did you mean before...," he asks Brohn, "about dreams?"

Brohn blushes and tells him that's more of Kress's area of expertise.

"As Hypnagogics," Kress explains after a gentle eyeroll in Brohn's direction, "Lucid and Reverie have access to and an intimate understanding of dreams. What they know, what they can see and do...it might help us stop Epic. Hopefully before it's too late, and before we run out of time."

"I know what it's like to lose a chunk of your life." Terk pats his Modified parts. "Losing a part of myself, though, is nothing compared to losing time."

"But we're wide awake now," Brohn says. "And I think we're about ready to stand this upside-down world right-side up again."

Kress pats the back of his hand and serves us up a warm

smile. She flicks her eyes over toward the three birds—the black raven, the white raven, and the splotchy Cape Griffon vulture—still perched with enviable serenity on the edge of a metal storage shelf toward the back of the Terminus.

I'd love to sit like that in oblivious comfort. This is one of those times I wish I *were* Haida instead of just connected to her. I'm so happy and relieved that she's alive and well, and I initiate our connection just long enough to tell her so.

It was scary seeing you shot down like that.

~ Not as scary as being shot down like that.

That was a total shambles back there. What did you do to get away?

~ The same thing you'll do someday. I flew.

I must repeat her last word out loud, because Kress asks, "You flew?"

"Oh," I say, snapping back out of my telempathic bond. "Haida was just telling me how she flew to escape the Devoted back there."

Nodding, Kress traces the intricate black swoops, curves, and dots of the bio-tech implants in her forearms with her fingertip. "It's like Walt Whitman said," she grins. 'I will sleep no more but *arise*.'" She tells me she's proud of me. "I'm proud of all of you," she says to Libra, Ignacio, Arlo, and, yes—even Matholook. And now, it's time for you students to go back to school."

"And what about you?" I ask. Kress surveys my Asylum before those steely eyes of hers land on mine. "I guess it's time for us to arise, too."

AT THE RIG'S CONTROLS, Kella drives the Terminus the rest of the way through the mine tunnels and, finally, into the Academy's cavernous vehicle hangar.

She parks the enormous rig on its mag-pad where it sighs to a gentle hover like it's as happy to be home as we are.

My Asylum and I climb down from the Terminus, all of us sagging with the weight of sorrow, loss, defeat, and the satisfaction of escaping from a no-win scenario with our lives.

(Okay, we didn't exactly escape. We were *rescued*. But when you know you're about to die but then wind up safe in a decked-out, twelve-ton military rig with some of the most impressive, powerful people in the world, you tend not to split hairs.)

It's the middle of the night by the time we get back to the Academy. Which is fine with me. If everyone were awake, we'd be mobbed by our fellow students the second we walked into the main hallway.

And I'm in no mood for being interrogated by a bunch of chabbies about our adventures down in the desert. I don't want to talk about Sara. And I definitely don't want to have to explain to anyone else about Mattea.

Kress and the rest of her Conspiracy head to their offices, leaving me and my Asylum to make the trek up to the fifth-floor Dorms.

The halls are dark and quiet, and our dirt-crusted boots make muted, echoing thumps on the glossy floors and all the way up the stairs.

We all need sleep and a sonic shower, but no one seems to have the energy to do anything but slump into the armchairs and one of the deep orange couches in the Lounge.

The Lounge has pinball, pool, ping-pong, and a host of interactive VR-sims we could plug into if we wanted. Right now, though, even the *thought* of play seems far too much like work.

So we sit and try to decompress as we let ourselves collapse into bone-weary slumps.

Before sending us on our way, Kress said there'd be a memorial service tomorrow for Mattea.

It's a strange feeling, losing someone so close to me. We were classmates and friends, two things I spent most of my life without. I didn't expect to miss her this much. After all the thousands of deaths I've seen, I figured I'd be colder to this one. But it hurts in a way I didn't expect.

And now I'm thinking maybe this pain is a good sign. If a single death matters this much to me, then maybe the lives of millions will start mattering even more, and I won't see them as a statistic, and then I won't feel so numb to it all.

The world outside the Academy has been a place of violence and terror for a long time. Thanks to Kress and her Conspiracy, things started getting better. Thanks to the Devoteds' lust for control over the country and Epic's lust for control over *us*, things are about to get worse.

After close to half an hour of sitting in muted, mental and physical burnout, Ignacio slaps his hands to his knees and groans himself to his feet. "I don't know about the rest of you, but I need a shower and some sleep."

Libra yawns and says she agrees.

We start to head to the door leading from the Lounge to our Dorm, but Matholook heads in the opposite direction toward the main door leading to the hall.

"Where do you think you're going?" I call after him.

"Upstairs," he says. "To bed."

"You don't have to sleep up in East Tower anymore, Dummy."

"I don't?"

I take him by the hand and lead him toward our Dorm. "You're one of us now."

"An Emergent?"

"No," I laugh. "Not that. But the Academy is more than just an Emergent bootcamp. And it's more than just a school. It's also an orphanage. A place for kids who have nowhere else to go." I swallow hard before I say what I say next. "And I don't think you can go back to the Devoted any time soon."

"Or ever."

"So it's settled: You'll stay with us."

"And you're sure it'll be okay with Kress and all your teachers?"

"If they thought you were a threat...well, let's just say you and I would be having a *much* different conversation right now." I give him a cheeky smile. "It'd be me talking to your severed head."

His hands cupped around his throat, Matholook pretend-gulps. "I'll be sure to stay on their good side." He takes my hand in his and turns back into the Lounge. "And yours."

Together, we walk into our Dorm where Ignacio is already stripping down and leaving a trail of sweaty, blood-stained clothes in his wake as he heads, buck-naked and unashamed, toward the shower room.

Shaking his head and clucking his tongue, Matholook serves up a low chuckle. "That is one confident guy."

"There are ways to be confident without being a sodding, self-absorbed wanker. Maybe someday, you'll show him how."

We share an airy laugh as Libra and Arlo follow Ignacio into the showers, leaving me and Matholook sitting alone and side by side on my bed.

"I guess you can take your pick," I say, pointing to the two empty beds where Mattea and Sara once slept. "I know it's probably kind of creepy for you—"

Matholook puts up his hand and wags his finger. "I don't believe in ghosts."

"You don't have to believe in something to be respectful of it," I remind him. "Or scared to death of it."

46

MATTEA

IN THE MORNING, we shower and dress like we always do.

We're polished up and in clean clothes for the first time in what feels like years. We've survived a lot, and we're safe in the Academy.

And yet, as my Asylum and I walk single-file downstairs from the Dorms to the Lecture Hall, there's not a smile, a joke, or a happy thought among us.

The halls, stairwells, and landings on the way are somehow colder and more hollow than they've ever been before.

As Head of School and with Granden standing sentinel-like behind her on the stage, Wisp beckons us through the double doors and into the bowl-shaped auditorium with a brisk wave of her hand.

The rest of the Academy—more than thirty other students and our teachers—are already inside with each of the school's Cohorts sitting in their color-coded groups.

The entire student body is here: The Battery of Quails. The Committee of Vultures. The Descent of Woodpeckers. The Exaltation of Larks.

In keeping with the tradition started by Kress and her

Conspiracy, the Academy's Cohorts—my Asylum of Loons, included—are all named after birds.

And yet, weighed down by grief, not one person in this room is anywhere close to flying.

As we go to take our seats, Libra nudges me and tilts her head toward the four new students—all of them looking lost and shellshocked—sitting together off to the side. "That must be Apex," she whispers, aiming a low finger at the dark-haired boy with the sharp cheekbones and the wide-open, glossy eyes. "The one Kress calls, 'Database.'"

"Don't stare," I whisper back. "I'm sure we'll have plenty of chance to get to know the new kids after this."

Sliding into our own row, we take our seats.

In front of us, Wisp stands statue-still on the low stage, her head down, her hands now clasped loosely in front of her. Never one for long speeches, her remarks are curt and clipped.

"This room has often functioned as a place for us to start our day. Today, it's a place of sorrow, regret, and reflection. It's a safe space for us to remember that we are students, teachers, friends, warriors, and—in the sorrow we share today and in the happiness we hope to find again someday—*family*."

Lifting her head, Wisp slips a lock of her short brown hair behind her ear and asks Rain to come up to the stage as she and Granden walk down the three steps to take their seats in the front row with our other teachers.

With nudges from Kress and Brohn, Rain pushes herself to her feet and walks up to the center of the stage. Standing behind the podium, she looks even smaller than usual as she coughs lightly into her fist and beings to speak.

"As Mattea's mentor, I had the honor of working closely with her during these past months as Wisp and your other teachers continued to evolve the Academy and its mission. As most of you know, Mattea had a gift for languages. Due to her brain's hypervariable prefrontal and temporal cortices, radically developed parietal lobes, a marked increase in hippocampal volume, and acute neuroplasticity coupled with a self-correcting motor cortex..." She pauses, closes her eyes, and curls her fingers around the edges of the podium. "Ugh," she chokes through a tight smile. "That sounds so terribly technical, doesn't it?"

Next to me, Matholook takes my hand in his as a chortle of choked-back laughter ripples through the audience of teachers and students.

"We never did really figure it out," Rain chuckles along with us. "They um...they tried in the Processor."

Processor. At the dreaded word, we all clam up.

Libra, Arlo, and Ignacio—along with pretty much every other student in this auditorium—spent *years* in a Processor. And the four new students are only a few days removed from their own captivity.

Clearing her throat, Rain soldiers on. "Mattea lived most of her life as a captive in a Processor in Valencia, Spain." Rain glances down at my Asylum, her dark eyes skimming over Libra, Ignacio, and Arlo. "Along with three of our other fine students in the Asylum cohort. The En-Gene-eers wanted to see what made her brain work the way it did. In the end, her ability as an Emergent was the least important thing about her. And that's something those scientists never figured out. That's because they were asking the wrong questions, pursuing all the wrong goals. In their quest to use her to replicate their techno-genetic formula for creating and recruiting evolutionarily advanced soldiers, they failed to see what made her a truly powerful Emergent: her humanity. Smart. Kind. Empathetic. Loyal. Honest. Hard-working. Mattea didn't need a war to prove her strength. And she didn't need powers to be super."

Rain clears her throat again. Her fingers wring against the edges of the podium a few times. Her eyes—glassy and red-rimmed—raise up to the ceiling before dropping back down to land on all of us. "We played chess sometimes for fun before or after our apprenticeship sessions. But it was Mattea's idea to incorporate our games into her individualized Emergent mentoring lessons. She said chess was really just another language. She said it had its own cadence, grammar, vocabulary, and its own diction and syntax. Honestly, I never saw the game that way. But she did. A lot of you know she and I played from time to time."

There are nods and knowing looks all around. I think everyone in here—students and faculty alike—has participated in at least one of Rain's famous, week-long Chess and War strategy seminars that supplement our primary classes.

"What you may not know..."

Rain trails off, and I look up from my lap where Matholook and I have our fingers intertwined.

"What you may not know," Rain pauses again to work through a snuffling laugh-cry. "What I'm sure you *don't* know, is that she beat me."

A gasp of disbelief cascades through the Lecture Hall.

Rain's Emergent ability gives her acute senses of strategy, logistics, and predictive insight. It's helped her to navigate through some rough spots during her Conspiracy's adventures. It also makes her totally, one-hundred-percent unbeatable as a chess player.

No one beats her. Ever.

"And the reason you didn't know," Rain chokes through a full-on surge of tears, "is that she refused to tell anyone, and she made me promise to do the same. Mattea...our student, our sister, our dear friend...she didn't want to make herself look too good, and...and...and she didn't want to make her stupid teacher look too bad."

Even when I'm not connected with Haida through my telempathic bond, my vision is especially keen. When we're connected, even a little, it ramps up to several times the vision of even the most eagle-eyed Typic. When we're *fully* connected— when everything between us is clicking just right—I take on a superhuman level of sight, with a spectrum of colors, magnetic waves, heat patterns, and air densities available to me.

Right now, Haida's in my head, and she's crying with me.

I can barely see the stage.

47

RELAX

"SAVING the world isn't one big job, Branwynne. It's a lot of little ones. Brohn and I are leaving tonight to complete one of the smaller assignments."

That's the first thing Kress tells me when I step into her office.

"You're not the only one who has homework," she adds with a glinty-eyed smile.

It's been over a month since Mattea's memorial service, and I still can't totally scrub the scent of my own failure out of my mind or off my body.

Fortunately, Matholook has been a source of great comfort, and we spend most of my non-class time together, either in the Lounge or else up on the roof with Render, Haida Gwaii, whichever of their five-bird brood is still hanging around at the time, and, of course, Jeff the vulture, who I think the other birds have adopted into their Conspiracy as an extra-large, lumbering honorary raven.

Matholook still isn't allowed to attend classes, but I think Wisp and the other teachers might be softening on that stance.

(I'm sure it's helped that I've been nagging them pretty much every day about it.)

With some of my focus returning to my training and the rest dedicated to Matholook, I haven't had a chance to get myself in enough trouble to warrant a summons from Kress.

Now, here I am. In her office. *Again.*

I'm barefoot, groggy, and still rubbing sleep from my eyes, and she's talking about saving the world. After all I've been through, accomplished, lost, and survived, only Kress can make me feel like the laziest underachieving git in a git-filled world.

The rest of my Asylum is still asleep upstairs, and I'm barely conscious, myself.

It was Haida Gwaii's voice in my head that roused me awake a few minutes ago in the middle of the night.

For a second, I thought the voice was a dream. Then, I thought (and breathlessly hoped) maybe it was Matholook kneeling next to my bed, whispering me awake. That would make sense. After all, it was him I was dreaming about. But he was still asleep in the bed next to mine, one of his lean, muscular legs bent at the knee and protruding from under his silver blanket.

Likewise, Libra, Arlo, and Ignacio were each immersed in a deep, purring slumber of their own.

After confirming the voice didn't come from any of them, I thought maybe it was just my mind playing tricks on me.

And then I remembered what Kress once told me about how the lines between reality, imagination, fantasy, dreams, and delusions aren't nearly as etched in stone as we've been led to believe.

I blinked hard against the pull of sleep, and the voice rang out inside my head with the crystal clarity of an air-raid siren:

~ *Kress needs you.*

She's tough, I moaned back at the white raven's pleading, edgy wakeup call. *I don't think she needs me at all.*

~ *I don't mean she needs your help. She needs you in her office. Now.*

You know, sometimes I wish you were a normal raven. You make a terrible alarm clock.

~ *I'm just the messenger. Should I tell her you're not coming?*

Only if you want her to charge up here and kill me in my own bed.

~ *We're connected. You're no good to me dead.*

Where are you, anyway?

~ *In Kress's office. I'm saying goodbye to Render.*

At that, I shoved off the last remnants of sleep and sat bolt-upright in bed.

Goodbye? What do you mean? Is he going somewhere? Are you?

~ *Kress will explain.*

And then Haida—her tempered, motherly voice fading into shallow ripples—severed our connection, leaving me to swing my bare feet down to the cold floor, throw my red leather jacket on over my Academy-issued sleepwear, and jog downstairs to Kress's office. I was sure the jackhammer of my heart in my chest was loud enough to wake the school, but I told myself to calm down and stay light on my feet. I managed to make it from the fifth floor Dorms down to her office on the second floor without running into anyone or dropping dead from a heart attack.

Now that I'm sitting here, bleary-eyed, curious, confused, and slightly terrified, Kress won't tell me where she's going, only that she and Brohn need to stop a disaster before it starts.

"And I'm not sure when we'll be back," she adds.

On the window ledge behind her, Haida Gwaii and Render are sitting side by side. Their hackles encircle their necks like spiky shawls, and the feathers on their heads look more like slicked back fur in the light beaming all over the office from an array of holo-projections. Looking like two fidgety chess pieces, the black raven and the white raven take turns looking from me to Kress and then out the window into the darkness, clearly amused by their own reflections in the foggy, frosted glass. They ruffle their feathers a little, flex their talons, and tap their heads and necks together in a gentle display of affection.

"We solved one problem," Kress reminds me as I squirm in the mag-chair across the desk from her.

The room's paneled walls of synth steel and glass reflect the dark hues of the rough, red oak ceiling beams and the floor's overlapping planks of polished white ash. In front of one of the walls, a seven-foot-high holo-projection of the country Kress calls "The Divided States of America" hovers and glints in the air. The map is divided into three vertical sections: a thin white strip on one side and a thin blue strip on the other with a vastly larger red chunk sandwiched in between. I recognize the topography in part of the red middle section as the desert plains where the Unsettled surrendered to the Devoted, where Kress saved us from Epic, and where we lost Mattea forever.

All around the larger map, smaller holo-projections populated with numbers, graphs, shifting charts, and the rotating profiles of a bunch of people I don't recognize glow on hovering rectangular panels of light.

Thanks mostly to Wisp and Kella (and with some more recent help from Libra), the tech in the Academy has gone from Stone Age to state-of-the-art. As nice as that is, it still makes me worry. The Wealthies got to where they are by isolating themselves, hoarding guns, and keeping all the best tech for themselves. Except for the guns—we have a limited supply of those—it's sort of what we're doing, too.

So what's to stop us from turning into them?

The answer, of course, is *literally* sitting in her office chair right in front of me.

Kress lets me take in the distracting flickers and flashes of the colorful schematics for a few seconds before snapping me back to attention.

"I asked you here, Branwynne, because I need you."

"I need you." Three words that rank right up there with "I love you" in terms of pure, heart-swelling, life-changing, soul-surging magnificence.

"Need me?" I ask, willing myself not to blush and doing my best to stop my eyes from drifting around the room again. "Haida didn't tell me what for. Am I in trouble?"

"Yes."

Gulp.

"But not with me."

Whew.

"With everything that happened down there in the desert, what could have stayed a fragile but peaceful balance has been shattered. You might think that was the end. But it's not. It's barely the beginning. So, yes. You're in trouble. And so are the rest of us."

Looking around, I can sense she's not exaggerating. I've been in Kress's office dozens of times—usually to get yelled at for cutting class or for disappearing from the Academy for hours at a time without permission—and it's usually pretty sparse. She doesn't believe in flourishes or fanciness. Most of the time I've been in here, it's been me, Kress, two chairs, and a desk. Now, it looks more like a war room.

Squaring myself up to face Kress doesn't help much with my ability to focus since the spaces above her desk on either side of her are also cluttered with floating images, including more rolling green text, an inventory of weapons and medical supplies, and an array of slowly-rotating, 3D topographical holo-maps in a color palette of vivid reds, greens, yellows, browns, and blues.

Kress taps at one of the floating schematics, which enlarges and then collapses back down as she squeezes her fingers into a loose fist. Pulling her shoulder-length hair back into a ponytail with a synth-leather tie-back, she turns her laser-eyed focus to me.

"As you now know," she says, tucking a few loose strands of hair behind her ears, "the talk about you being valuable to some pretty bad people is real."

I roll my eyes and tell her how much I *love* being the pin in someone else's hand grenade.

"Don't be a twit," she says through a restrained grin. "Listen. We stopped Krug. We're working on bringing some of the country's Survivalists over to our side. We drove the True Blues out of D.C., liberated nearly all of California, freed dozens of Emergents, shut down another Processor, and we've started to expose more and more of the truth about the Eastern Order."

"I know," I agree with a proud smile for my mentor. "It's only a matter of time before you put that lie to rest once and for all."

Kress nods but doesn't seem to share my optimism. "Krug was dug in. He's dangerous even after death."

"How can he be—?"

"He brainwashed a lot of people before we took him down. Weak, insecure, and fearful people still look up to him as their god, their savior from a world full of invented enemies. He's becoming a myth. And to some of the most desperate and depraved, he's becoming a prophet and a martyr. The Wealthies in the arcologies still worship him. And why shouldn't they? According to them, he saved them from all of us. And millions of the poor worship him as their ticket into the world of the Wealthies. Myths are more powerful than people. You can't just throw a myth off a building and watch it go splat on the pavement. We have to keep telling the truth. Whether or not the people we tell it to are willing and able to accept it...Well, let's just say there are a lot of steps between hearing the truth and finally deciding to believe it."

It's cold in Kress's office, so I tug my jacket closed and draw my bare feet up onto the seat of the hovering mag-chair. "Someday you'll have to tell me why so many people fell for the Eastern Order bollocks in the first place and why they refuse to see the truth when it's sitting there slapping them right in the bloody face. I was a little kid, and even I knew *something* was dodgy."

The corner of Kress's lip does a smirky little twitch.

"Okay," I admit with a matching grin. "Maybe I didn't know they were a *total* invention. But I felt *something* was...off about the whole thing."

"Not everyone has your insight." Chuckling, Kress tilts her head backward toward Haida. "Or hers."

"You think Haida is why I've always felt a little...different?"

"I think she's why you've always felt there are more dimensions to the universe than our simple human senses would have us believe."

"Too bad everyone can't have access to her," I mumble.

Kress's muted grin expands. "In my experience, it's one of the hardest things in the world for people to have more faith in what they see than in what they've been brainwashed to believe. I promise to tell you why that is...as soon as I figure it out myself."

I try to laugh at that, but it's not easy. I don't like hearing that there might be things Kress doesn't know or can't do. Maybe it's because I grew up in isolation in the Tower of London, but reading people—figuring out their mental blocks, motives, fears, and desires—has never been my strong suit.

If Kress can't figure it out, what hope do I possibly have?

On top of being cold, I'm restless and uncomfortable in my seat. I'm used to having these intense philosophical conversations up on the Academy's roof during my mentoring sessions, guided by Kress and surrounded by the school's seven ravens.

(My training has been going well. I even asked Kress the other day if I was a Ravenmaster yet. She flicked her hand at me and said I still needed to become a "*Branwynne*-master" first. "And that's coming along nicely," she admitted. "You've made some good strides in the right direction. But don't let the giant leaps come at the expense of all those important little steps in between.")

Now, the focus isn't on me or my training. It's on what the world outside is going to look like when my classmates and I eventually leave the Academy and do what we've been training to do: Expose the corrupt. Defend the weak. Inspire the frightened.

Save the world.

"There are people out there," Kress says, activating a holo-projection off to the side with one hand before turning back to drum her fingers on her desk, "people whose prejudices, fears, and ignorance run deep. They'll do anything—up to and including acting against their own best interests—in order to pursue an agenda of selfishness, hate, and divisiveness."

"This has to do with the Devoted, doesn't it?"

Kress gives me what I *hope* is a smile, but it might be a slightly bitter grimace. She clears her throat and nods. "And Sara. With her in their ranks, the Devoted can bring more people into their Cult while getting everyone else to fight with each other. With Gwernna, they can wage war pretty much forever. Combined, the Cult of the Devoted now have the desire *and* the power to expand well past the point where we can do anything to stop them. After all the planning and jockeying for political position, they're preparing to make their next move."

"What move?"

Kress leans back in her chair and laces her fingers together in her lap. Behind her, Render blinks his coal black eyes and shudders himself alert. Leaving Haida, he hops from his perch at the window and flutters over to land on Kress's shoulder. Outside, it's become sort of normal to see him swoop down from the sky or from a tree or from one of the eaves of the Academy and alight on her shoulder or on her forearm. Sometimes, he'll land at her feet and hop onto one of her boots, nuzzling her leg like a feathery black cat. In the confined space of Kress's office, his small movement over a few feet feels like a nuclear blast of dusky, ruffled feathers.

I'm still not used to it, but Kress doesn't flinch. She reaches into the small leather pouch she keeps on her belt and tosses a marbled, blood-red cube of pulpy meat up to Render, who gobbles it down with a backward head tilt and a quick snap of his powerful beak.

Kraa-ing his delight, he opens and closes his glossy black talons, readjusting himself on Kress's shoulder.

Not to be left out, Haida gurgle-clacks her jealousy and flutters over to land in the middle of Kress's desk where she grumbles and struts through a cluster of hovering holo-projections. The dancing green and gold images bend, distort, and cast a patchwork of wonky shadows on Haida's white feathers. Laughing, Kress tosses her a snack as well.

"It's not just one move," she sighs, reaching over to give Render's hefty beak a delicate stroke with the tip of her finger. "The Devoted are preparing to make *lots* of moves. Simultaneous ones. The kind that could make Krug look harmless by comparison. The communications infrastructure has been down for a long time."

"Wasn't that *because* of Krug?"

"He did everything he could to keep us in the dark. It turns out the Devoted have been working quietly and for several years now, to get the network up and running and completely under their control." A stiffness seeps into Kress's face. Her jaw tightens, and her eyes go narrow and dark. A few strands of hair have fallen out of her ponytail and dangle in loose curls along her cheeks. She doesn't bother to brush them back behind her ear like she usually does. Instead, she locks her eyes onto mine and leans forward just enough so I know I'd better be paying careful attention. "They're doing what they promised to do, Branwynne. They've taken over the Unsettled—the army and all of their vehicles."

Leaning in, I ask, "What about Angel Fire? Is he—?"

"He's alive. The last we heard, anyway."

I'm pretty sure the force of my sigh of relief is nearly enough to blow Kress's hair back.

"But things aren't good. I know you all got close to him pretty fast."

"He's a good bloke. Bit of a nutter."

"His people—what's left of them—are being used by the Devoted. They have them building walls around their Independent Confederation. They call it the NARRA."

"NARRA?"

"The National Autonomous Region of Rights for Americans." Kress makes air-quotes with her fingers. "It's their new nation, their Promised Land. It's the utopia they say history has been leading them to build."

I expect her to roll her eyes at this. She's famously impatient about random acts of stupidity. But she seems beyond deadly serious at the moment.

Maybe even a little scared?

"There are resistance coalitions still forming on the coasts," she continues, pointing at the white and blue strips of the map on the smaller holo-projection to her side. "And we need to help them solidify their positions. Our people are all that's stopping the Devoted from a complete takeover with long term goals of expanding into the ultimate colonial empire."

Haida must sense my tension, because she steps to the edge of Kress's desk before hopping onto my forearm.

Her voice melts into my head but also seeps reassurance throughout my body.

~ Relax.

How can I relax? Kress is sitting here casually talking about the beginning of the end.

~ And you'll need to fight harder and against greater odds than you've ever faced. But that's a problem for tomorrow. Right now, you're safe, and worrying isn't a solution. So relax.

"Don't worry," Kress says, snapping me back into my own head with a reassuring grin. "Only Brohn and I are going this time. We've made the mistake once before of not leaving enough people here to take care of you all. So this time, most of the Conspiracy will stay here at the Academy. They'll keep teaching you and protecting you until it's time to make a full-on move of our own."

Making sure we have enough babysitters—that's what she thinks I'm worried about?

I'm startled when the proximity sensor on the door pings. Behind me, the silver door whooshes open, and Brohn steps into the room.

48

THE END

MY STOMACH DOES A LITTLE FLIP. I don't think I'll ever *not* be nervous in the presence of the Academy's ultimate power couple.

Except for in our combat training classes, the teachers in the Academy rarely walk around armed. But Brohn has his bulky arbalest strapped to his back and a .50 Action Express Desert Eagle with a ten-inch barrel in a holster on his hip. He's in the standard issue Academy battle kit: a blue and white compression top and his black tactical gear, complete with four palm-sized military field knives tucked into pockets across his chest, one on each arm of his armor-plated combat jacket, and one larger knife strapped into a holster slung low on his thigh. Square-jawed, broad-shouldered, powerfully built, and looking like he's two seconds away from leaping from a plane onto a battlefield, he looms in the doorway, an intimidating presence but also a comforting one.

Even though he's a head shorter than Terk and War—who are both pretty gigantic in their own right—he always seems to me like a mountain of a man. With his easy confidence, impossible good looks, and powerful protective instinct, he's actually somehow more approachable than Kress and not nearly as scary.

Of course, I've seen him in action, in class *and* in combat out in the real world. (In those cases, he's completely *un*approachable and *incredibly* scary.)

"Wisp and Granden just got the word from their sources in Denver," he announces, stepping into the room and planting himself in a wide-legged stance next to my chair.

"The Devoted?" Kress asks.

"Yes."

"What about them?" My voice is quaking with an uncontrollable anxiety that feels like it has a mind of its own.

"Justin and Treva have been patient and planning," Brohn says from just behind my shoulder. I turn and glance up to meet his dark, shaded eyes as they lock onto mine. "They're more clever, more ambitious, and far more dangerous than we ever thought. They sided with Krug when he was alive, but that was for their own sake, not for his. With Krug gone, they knew there'd be a power vacuum. They've spent over five years preparing to fill it." Running his hand over his stubbled jaw, he swallows hard, almost like this news has him worried.

But that can't be. What could possibly be bad enough to worry Brohn?

"You told her about the NARRA?" he asks Kress.

"I did."

"The Devoted are really going to try to start their own country?" I ask.

"With their own government," Brohn confirms. "And their own laws and their own rules for what happens to anyone who doesn't quietly cooperate."

"And they're powerful enough to do that?"

"They've got all the weapons, all the vehicles, control over a growing communications network, and the delusional belief that it's their destiny to rule the world. So...yes."

Cradling Render on her forearm, Kress stands, comes around to my side of the desk, and leans back against its edge. Her eyes are sad. "It's starting."

"Starting?"

"The end," she says. "Epic won't stop until he's solved the mystery of the Emergents. And Justin and Treva won't stop until there's no one left to challenge the Devoted."

"They aren't responsible for dividing the country," Brohn cautions. "That happened a long time ago. But they *are* dedicated to making those divisions formal and permanent."

"Our country started out as a colony," Kress reminds me. (Not that I need the reminder. After all, it was *my* country that colonized hers.) "After that," she continues, "it became a collection of independent states. And then, it was a nation. A powerful nation."

Brohn's voice is a low rumble as he adds, "A powerful nation that, as of about an hour ago, doesn't exist."

I half-turn to squint up at him. "Doesn't...?"

"The country's coasts are being established as the East and West Republics. As you know, Granden's people are running things out East. They've got headquarters fully set up in D.C. Wisp's people and the Insubordinates have set up headquarters for the West Republic in San Francisco. We've made progress in Chicago and New York City. If we're lucky, we could even establish a Northern Republic with those two cities as key members."

"Thanks to Epic's intervention," Kress explains, "the Devoted control everything else." She stands and points to the chunky, red portion of the larger holo-map projected out from the wall. "They're creating a government of their own, a provisional alliance with the Wealthies, a slave-class of the Unsettled, and a growing army to ensure their supremacy and to allow for them to expand their reach."

"Nationally, for now," Brohn clarifies. "And ultimately, we think, *globally*."

Still facing me and Brohn, Kress pushes herself up and sits cross-legged on her desk. "We suffered through decades of Krug's corruption and cruelty. We lived through the chaos of the aftermath, and we've had over five years of relative safety here in the Academy. We thought we could tip the scales in the direction of peace and unity. But the Devoted had other ideas. And they're in the process of putting those ideas into very dangerous action."

"And they're killing anyone in their way, aren't they?" I ask.

"They are. And there are a *lot* of people in their way. Their headquarters are in Denver," Kress informs me with a tip of her head toward Brohn. "So that's where Brohn and I need to be."

"You're going to Denver?"

"Tonight."

"Can I—?"

Kress puts up a hand to cut me off. "You'll stay here. If anything happens to us on this mission...Listen, Branwynne. I know you don't like to hear this, but you really are unique. You're our best hope for the future. It's why we're telling you all of this. Someday, you'll finish what we've started. In the meantime, Wisp will continue to train you."

I'm getting ready to object, but her hand goes up again, along with a no-nonsense shake of her head.

"A new era of violence and repression is here," Kress continues while I sulk in my seat, "and sooner than we thought. We weren't kidding ourselves. We knew there'd be push-back against us trying to create a better world."

"It's just that the push-back happened harder and faster than we expected," Brohn admits.

"It's taken us all a long time to recover from Krug. The Devoted are determined to open old wounds and create some new ones, all in the name of securing their position at the top of a new world order."

"And all this is happening now?" I ask through a shudder. "I mean, like, *right now*?"

"As we speak," Kress assures me. "That's why we can't waste any more time."

I know about repressive governments. I lived under one in London. Kress and her Conspiracy lived and almost died under one right here in the Divided States of America. I know what governments like that do and how they work. I've seen them practice policies designed to destroy the very people they claim to care about. I've seen them abandon their own cities, leaving them to rot and implode into pits of starvation, desperation, and violence. As a little girl, I saw survivors break off into their own warring factions and kill each other over food, water, territory, and sometimes, over nothing.

I'm only seventeen, but I've already seen dictatorships, aristocracies, monarchies, oligarchies, and ochlocracies of total mob rule masquerading as democracies. I've seen governments slaughter the innocent, swell with power, bloat with corruption, and spin lie after blatant lie.

And I've even seen those same corrupt governments end.

What I've never seen with my own eyes is the exact moment when one of those corrupt governments *begins*.

END OF *ARMY of the Unsettled*, Book 3 of *The Academy of the Apocalypse* series

49

KRESS BONUS CHAPTER - ARISE

*FROM A*RISE, *the upcoming first book of the Ravenmaster Chronicles...*

* * *

"We have to face facts, Kress," Brohn says, his eyes locked onto mine. "The Devoted won the war."

Sighing, I slump lower into my mag-chair behind my desk. "I know. I know."

"And they did it in record time."

"I know that, too."

Brohn's not wrong. In only five years, the Cult of the Devoted changed from an outlying community of strange and moderately creepy but mostly pleasant people to unchallenged overlords of the entire middle expanse of the country.

Along the way, they ground the unstoppable Army of the Unsettled to a screeching halt.

But they weren't done with them. In fact, slaughtering half of the Unsettled was just the beginning.

The Devoted enslaved the other half and are using them, as Brohn and I speak, to erect a whole system of towering barrier walls around some of the major cities across their vast, inland territory.

Denver, Colorado. Indianapolis, Indiana. Columbus, Ohio. Pittsburgh, Pennsylvania. Philadelphia, Pennsylvania.

And those are just the ones we know about.

The Devoted didn't use force. Instead, they brainwashed the Unsettled into believing this was their lot in life.

And they didn't do it alone. They succeeded thanks to the giant Bendegatefran and his feral half-brother Efnisien. They succeeded thanks to Gwerna, their secret weapon of war with the Emergent power to raise the dead from the field of battle. They succeeded thanks to Epic and his eight Hypnagogic assassins. And, finally, maybe most chilling of all, they plan to continue to succeed with the help of Sara, our former student, whose ability to gaslight people into doing her bidding while thinking they're making the decisions on their own fits right into the playbook of the Cult of the Devoted.

Which is to say that the destruction of the Unsettled and the construction of more exclusionary, cloud-busting arcologies for the privileged behind towering rings of walls, was a team effort.

I'm part of a team, too, of course. Over five years ago, my Conspiracy and I led the effort to take down Krug.

Today, that looks easy by comparison.

At least Krug was just one man. One evil, manipulative, insecure, waste of a man. But still a man. A human mortal, who ended up as a moist splatter on the sidewalk at the bottom of the Old Post Office in Washington, D.C.

The members of the Cult of the Devoted—kind, reasonable, and hospitable on the surface—are a million times worse than Krug ever was.

Across from my desk, Brohn drums his finger on the arms of his mag-chair. "Epic's out there, you know."

"Yeah."

"And he's got eight Hypnaogogics with him."

"So what are you saying?" I grumble. "That we should just quit? Let him find the answers before we do? And then sit back and watch as he sells off more superpowered assassins to the highest bidder?"

Of course, I know that's not what he's saying at all. And I know my getting snarky about it isn't going to solve anything. It's just that it's bad enough knowing the odds are stacked a mile high against us. Being reminded of that fact this late at night... well, that's giving me a minor eye twitch that's two seconds away from devolving into a permanent facial spasm.

"No," Brohn assures me, using that calm baritone of his he knows is so good at blunting my worry and lightening my mood. "I don't think we should quit."

"What, then?"

"I think we need to track down Epic and stop him before it's too late."

"And the Devoted?"

"We need to stop them, too."

"Oh. Is that all?" I do a quick scroll through the Academy's latest weapons inventory currently projected in a holo-field above my desk. It doesn't look good. Our supplies aren't gone, but they're getting seriously depleted. "This all sounds kind of...impossible," I confess, turning my full attention back to Brohn.

"We've faced impossible odds before," he says with a cluck of his tongue.

"Yeah. But this might be pushing our luck."

This time, he offers up a hearty laugh. "We've pushed our luck before, too!"

I lean back in my chair, my fingers laced behind my head. "I thought getting rid of Krug would solve everything."

"Me, too. But we were kids. We know better now. There's no

magic solution, no silver bullet that will miraculously put an end to despots."

"Thinking that there *was* a magic bullet is all that kept me going."

I stand up and walk over to one of the seven-foot-high sets of topographical maps glinting emerald-green in front of the side wall of my dusky office.

Pushing himself up and coming over to stand behind me, Brohn loops his arms around my shoulders. His voice is warm and soft in my ear. "Is that really *all* that kept you going?"

"No," I laugh, spinning around and pushing him away with one hand but drawing him right back toward me with the other. I grip the lapels of his combat jacket in my clenched fists. "I'd be dead without you. Seriously, you've saved my life more times than I can count."

"Eleven."

"What?"

"That's how many times I've saved your life."

"You're insane," I laugh as I give him a playful push to the chest. "And how many times have *I* saved *your* life?"

"Eleven."

"So...we're even?"

"For now, at least."

"What we're about to do," I say, suddenly serious, "it's not like anything we've done before."

"I know."

"We've always fought our way out of messes. Now, we're talking about jumping into the biggest mess of all *on purpose*."

"Then we should do what we've always done with messes."

I nod my understanding. I don't need for him to spell it out. I know exactly what he means. From surviving recruitment to overthrowing Krug to saving Emergents all over the world from the Processors where they'd been imprisoned, we've always done the same thing with the messes left by others: we've cleaned them up.

"Of course, Denver's more of a mess than any we've faced before," Brohn reminds me.

"I know. I know. We'll have the wall to get around."

"Or over."

"Or under."

"Or through."

"And if we manage that—"

"*When* we manage that," Brohn says with a wink.

"There are still the slums. The Survivalists. The Plaguers and the Cysters. Not to mention the arcology they're building. Ugh. It's going to be a fortress."

"Yep."

"A heavily-guarded, armed-to-the-teeth fortress."

"Yep."

"Justin and Treva won't give up easily."

"Neither will we," Brohn assures me before tilting his head back, his eyes on the ceiling. "What about Branwynne?"'

"What about her?"

"Should we take her with us?"

"On a suicide mission like this?" I half-laugh. "I don't even want to take *us* with us."

"All these kids we've got here in the Academy...do you think they'll be all right?"

"If we don't stop the Devoted now, their Cult will get themselves even more entrenched. And then they'll be unstoppable, and there'll be *millions* of good, struggling, desperate kids—and adults, for that matter—who won't be all right ever again."

"Okay," Brohn says, taking my hand in his. "Ready to do the impossible?"

"As long as we're together," I grin up at him, "nothing's impossible."

Hand in hand, we walk out of my office and head downstairs, ready to embark on our mission.

"I know it's just an infiltration," I remind Brohn as we enter the huge vehicle hangar in the sub-basement of the Academy. "But it'll still be just the two of us against a few thousand of the Devoted."

"It doesn't seem fair, does it?"

"No," I laugh. "They don't stand a chance."

* * *

You can read all about Kress and Brohn's adventures in *Arise*, the first installment of the *Ravenmaster Chronicles* available October 25, 2021!

50

A NEW CONSPIRACY SERIES!

For Fans of Kress, **Render, and the original Conspiracy: A new series is soaring your way!**

In a spectacular crossover event of re-emergence inspired by Homer's epic adventure *The Odyssey*, Kress and Brohn leave the

Emergents Academy on a daring mission to confront the leaders of the Cult of the Devoted in their nearly-completed arcology in the center of what's left of Denver, Colorado.

Making their deadly mission even more impossible, Epic— the villainous, marble-skinned techno-geneticist—has turned his Hypnagogic assassins loose on them.

When Brohn mysteriously disappears in the middle of the night, Kress is forced to embark on a perilous quest through a dozen urban districts packed with brainwashers, gunmen, ghosts from the past—and even an entire neighborhood of one-eyed gangsters and their packs of wild dogs—to get him back.

Arise (Coming in October 2021)
Banished (Coming in January 2022)
Crusade (Coming in April 2022)

51

AN EXCITING NEW DYSTOPIAN SERIES: THE CURE CHRONICLES

BEFORE THE BLIGHT, becoming an adult was something teenagers looked forward to.

But now, turning eighteen means certain death.

Unless you prove yourself worthy of the Cure.

On her seventeenth birthday, Ashen Spencer is blindfolded and escorted to the massive, mysterious building known as the Arc to begin her year of training and testing in hopes that she can earn the Cure—a powerful drug given only to those deemed worthy to survive beyond their eighteenth birthday.

Ashen has a chance to rise up from her former life of squalor and be granted a place in society, if the Panel—the mysterious group of powerful men and women in charge of the Arc—deems her year a success.

She's assigned to work for twelve months as a servant for a wealthy family whose son is the most alluring—and confusing—young man she's ever met.

At first, Ashen is thrilled for the opportunity to earn her place in a society she's always dreamed of inhabiting. But as time passes and she begins to learn the truth about the people she admires so much and the home she left behind, she realizes she has a choice:

Be part of the disease...

Or be part of the Cure.

Pre-order the books here, at a special discounted price:

The Cure (Coming in June 2021)
Awaken (Coming in September 2021)
Ascend (Coming in December 2021)

52

ALSO BY K. A. RILEY

IF YOU'RE ENJOYING K. A. Riley's books, please consider leaving a positive review on Amazon or Goodreads to let your fellow book-lovers know about them.

Dystopian Books:

Resistance Trilogy:

Recruitment

Render
Rebellion

Emergents Trilogy:

Survival
Sacrifice
Synthesis

Transcendent Trilogy:

Travelers
Transfigured
Terminus

Academy of the Apocalypse Series:

Emergents Academy
Cult of the Devoted
Army of the Unsettled (July 2021)

The Ravenmaster Chronicles:

Arise (Coming in October 2021)
Banished (Coming in January 2022)
Crusade (Coming in April 2022)

THE CURE CHRONICLES:

The Cure (Coming in June 2021)
Awaken (Coming in September 2021)
Ascend (Coming in December 2021)

ATHENA'S LAW TRILOGY:

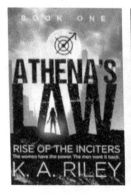 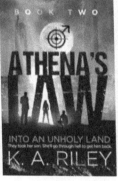 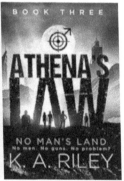

Book One: *Rise of the Inciters*
Book Two: *Into an Unholy Land*
Book Three: *No Man's Land*

Fantasy Books

Seeker's Series:

Seeker's World
Seeker's Quest
Seeker's Fate
Seeker's Promise
Seeker's Hunt
Seeker's Prophecy (Coming in 2021)

To be informed of future releases, and for chances to win free swag, books, and other goodies, please sign up here:

https://karileywrites.org/#subscribe

K.A. Riley's Bookbub Author Page
K.A. Riley on Amazon.com
K.A. Riley on Goodreads.com

CPSIA information can be obtained
at www.ICGtesting.com
Printed in the USA
LVHW030904200222
711562LV00004B/671